A Summer in Europe

Books by Marilyn Brant

ACCORDING TO JANE

FRIDAY MORNINGS AT NINE

A SUMMER IN EUROPE

A Summer in Europe

MARILYN BRANT

KENSINGTON BOOKS

KENSINGTON BOOKS are published by

Kensington Publishing Corp.
119 West 40th Street
New York, NY 10018

ISBN-13: 978-1-61793-427-8
Printed in the United States of America

To My Dad,
who first enchanted me with tales of world travel . . .

To My Husband,
who enthusiastically traveled the world with me . . .

And To My Son,
who now travels with me, so I can see the world anew.

ACKNOWLEDGMENTS

You can hold in your heart a passion for a place that lingers years after you've left it. It takes little more than a flash of film footage, a whiff of a certain delectable scent or a melody that dances through the airwaves and tangos with your memories to bring back the experience full force . . . zipping through you like the exhilarating rush of a speeding train ride, on a warm summer night, with the windows wide open.

Such is my love for Europe.

From holding my mom's hand and gazing out at London Bridge when I was just a little girl to getting engaged to the love of my life on that same bridge over twenty years later, I've traveled at so many significant moments that the experience of embarking on an international journey has melded with my DNA and become part of me. I performed in folk-dance festivals throughout Europe as a college student, backpacked with my fiancé-then-husband through the dust-covered ancient ruins of Italy, Greece and Turkey, touched a glacier on the snow-tipped Alps, strolled along the coastal walkways of the Riviera and explored the vibrant European capital cities from Budapest to Dublin and from Madrid to Oslo. I never tired of the thrill of it.

So, my first thank you is to the people of Europe for your kindness and for helping to make every one of my visits a joyous, memorable adventure.

Thanks, as always, to my wonderful writing chapter, Chicago-North RWA, especially to my critique partners Karen Dale Harris, Laura Moore and Lisa Laing, who each brought tremendous insight to this manuscript. Special thanks to Simone Elkeles for sharing her mah-jongg expertise with me, and to Erika Danou, Sara Daniel, Pamala Knight and Susan McBride for their unflagging moral support. The friendship you've all given me is a treasured gift.

I've also had a team of extraordinary friends—online and off—who make day-to-day life enormously fun. I'm so thankful for Sarah Pressly-James, Joyce Twardock, Karen Karris, Heather Eisenhour, Ann Dingman and Anne Scarano for being my hometown cheerleaders. Love you, ladies—even though you made me sing karaoke once. And hugs of gratitude to my online pals: my 007 Golden Heart Bond Girls, the Girlfriends Book Club, the Austen Authors, my fellow Magical Musings sisters and the generous blogging friends who visit me on Brant Flakes and other sites around the Web. I can't express how much I appreciate you all.

One of the great delights in writing women's fiction has been the opportunity to visit so many fantastic book clubs and have discussions about my novels after their release. This year one book club dear to my heart—The Page Turners—read this novel months in advance and shared their thoughts with me. Huge thanks to Brenda Brown, Gayle Jensen, Jeanne Kircher, Kristi Knull, Julie Leach, Dina Pierce, Michelle Ritchie and Evelyn Webber. Your enthusiasm for this story and your thoughtful feedback was truly helpful. Thanks, too, to Nephele Tempest for your suggestions, and to Barbara Dacloush and Ana Dawson for years of encouragement.

Boundless appreciation to my fabulous editor, John Scognamiglio, and the entire Kensington staff. I feel so fortunate to be working with all of you. Heartfelt thanks to librarians, booksellers and readers everywhere for your interest in my novels and your warm e-mails to me. You're a big part of why I adore my job.

And, of course, my love and gratitude to all my family—most especially my parents, my brother, my husband and my son—who have understood my wanderlust for as long as they've known me and, in many cases, shared it.

If music be the food of love, play on . . . (Twelfth Night)

*

The web of our life is of a mingled yarn,
good and ill together. (All's Well That Ends Well)
—William Shakespeare

* * *

"Life . . . is a public performance on the violin,
in which you must learn the instrument as you go along."

*

"Does it seem reasonable that she should play so wonderfully,
and live so quietly? I suspect that one day she will be wonderful in both . . .
music and life will mingle."

—E. M. Forster (*A Room with a View*)

1

An Unexpected Turn of Events

Tuesday, June 26

The thing no one understood about Gwendolyn Reese was that she was three ages at once: thirty chronologically, forty-five intellectually and fifteen experientially. The people inhabiting her small circle of acquaintances planned to celebrate the first of these maturational milestones with Mylar balloons and devil's food cake. The second, they revered privately, hoping their appreciation would score them a shot at being her partner during the odd game of Trivial Pursuit. But, with the possible exception of her eccentric Aunt Beatrice, they were patently oblivious to the third.

Aunt Beatrice—who clocked in at sixty-seven chronologically, twenty-four intellectually and a whopping one hundred-ten experientially—knew how to have a good time. Even if Beatrice's idea of "a good time" didn't exactly mesh with Gwendolyn's own.

A point Gwen was painfully reminded of when she was awakened—at five a.m.—by the persistent ringing of the telephone and realized that on this, her thirtieth birthday, and in complete disregard of her intentions for a quiet solo dinner and a warm bath to the emotionally soaring melodies of Andrew Lloyd Webber, she'd be spending the evening instead with Beatrice and all thirteen wack-job members of her aunt's S&M club.

The day was off to a disturbingly atypical start.

"Gwennie! Happy birthday!" her aunt chirped on the phone.

Gwen yawned, sat up on her extrafirm mattress, swung her legs over the side and slipped her feet into her sensible beige slippers on the floor. "Thanks, Aunt Bea."

"I know you're an early riser, so I set my alarm special, just to wake up in time to catch you before you left. You're going to your, whatchamacallit, *spinning* class now, right?"

Gwen rubbed her eyes and glanced at the clock—a palindromic 5:05. "Yep. Soon." She didn't have the heart to tell her aunt that she only went to the five-thirty class during the school year when she had a full teaching day ahead. She slept *late* during summer vacation and never, ever got to the gym before six forty-five. Not in June.

"Well, I won't keep you for long then, honey, but it's Tuesday so, of course, the club is getting together tonight. And we have a special birthday celebration planned just for *you*. When can you get here?"

Gwen smothered a sigh. "Um . . ." Her aunt's "club" was something she tried to avoid like mosquitoes at twilight, like filing her taxes any later than March 1, like her eighth-grade math students coughing in her face during flu season. Those *club* people—however sweet, bighearted and well-meaning—were nothing short of crazy, and her aunt always wanted to drag her into their gatherings. All of them were sixty or older, but they acted like irresponsible teenagers half the time and horny college students the rest. Case in point, even though "S&M" technically stood for sudoku and mah-jongg, some of the members liked to imply that they weren't opposed to the *other* meaning.

Retired vet Dr. Louie Strand even had T-shirts made up that said, "I'm into S&M . . . wanna play with me?"

And Mrs. Matilda Riesling, at age eighty-three (and a former Presbyterian Church secretary no less!), apparently thought Dr. Louie's shirts weren't suggestive enough, so she countered with, "The S&M Club: It's even more fun when we're tied."

These were not people Gwen could relate to with ease.

"Gwennie?"

"I, uh, have to meet Richard for lunch downtown. One o'clock sharp, he said. But I could be at your house in the late afternoon or early evening." Maybe if she arrived before five, she'd get to leave by seven.

"Oh, *good*. Come around four-thirty, then. No later than five-fifteen, you hear? We're seniors. We like to eat early."

Gwen agreed.

"And, Gwennie, enjoy your lunch date. You'll tell us all about it tonight, right?"

"Right."

Aunt Beatrice hung up and Gwen was left holding the phone. She stared out the window of her condo into the rising eastern sun of a bright Iowa summer day, the mighty Mississippi River glinting in the distance. June 26. Her thirtieth birthday. She hoped, with a shiver of pure excitement, that she'd have more to celebrate than a new decade by the day's end—provided, of course, she survived until bedtime.

She set about skipping through the paces of her scrupulously well-structured morning. She may have been awakened a tad earlier than anticipated but, on a day as significant as this one, a little extra time to prepare wouldn't be a bad thing, would it?

She performed her series of twelve flexibility stretches, just as she always did, vacation or no. Her one really good friend from the school district, Kathy, her team-teaching partner in the junior-high math department, would always laugh when Gwen would do a few extra stretches during their lunch breaks, and she'd make up goofy animal descriptions of Gwen poses. It made Gwen smile to think about it. Kathy was funny, sweet-tempered . . . and away on a summer-long missionary trip to El Salvador. She wouldn't be calling Gwen up and asking if she were a Squatting Ostrich or a Twisted Ferret today.

She sighed, feeling the twinge of her aloneness spreading like a low, slow ache. She wasn't the type to make hordes of friends, so she missed having another woman to talk to on weekdays. Someone who'd sincerely listen. There was always her aunt, of course, but, well . . . not really. And were it not for Richard, she'd be more than alone this summer. She'd be lonely, too.

She walked into the kitchen and poured one measuring cup of her high-fiber bran flakes into her favorite white ceramic cereal bowl—the one with daisies very cheerfully ringing the circumference. She topped the flakes with two tablespoons of dried California raisins, half of a sliced banana and one level scoop of slivered almonds. She then poured exactly two-thirds of a cup of 1 percent milk over all of it and took her first bite.

Mmm. Wholesomely balanced, delicious and even leisurely. And, because she could indulge in the extra time, she savored her healthy meal to the sounds of Andrew Lloyd Webber's *GOLD: The Definitive Hits Collection.*

She chewed her food with diligence while jumping between tracks. Barbra Streisand's beautiful version of "As If We Never Said Goodbye" stirred her. When she heard the strings, she glanced, as she always did, at the violin hanging on the opposite wall. Her dad's. She could almost imagine him playing that song. Feel the emotion he surely would have brought to it.

She flipped to Sarah Brightman's famous rendition of "The Phantom of the Opera," even humming along since no one else could hear her. But it wasn't until an especially melodious moment in selection #11's "Love Changes Everything" from *Aspects of Love* that she felt the oddest wave of longing rise up and crash into her rib cage. Far more powerful than usual. She didn't know why.

Quite possibly, it was Michael Ball's incredible vocals and haunting musical interpretation.

Or, perhaps, she was still caught in that netherworld of sleepiness and was too easily affected by lyrics that mentioned "trembling" at the sound of someone's name.

Or, maybe, she was just getting old and sentimental.

She inhaled sharply, swiped away an unexpected tear that blurred her vision and gulped the last spoonful of cereal. Maybe, if she had someone to share this music with in the morning, she wouldn't feel the pang of loss that jabbed at her when she wasn't expecting it. Richard might claim he wasn't big into musicals, but that was only because he'd never really gone to any. At least not to any good ones. Hadn't they just watched *Singing in the Rain* on TV? She bit her lip and nodded to herself, remembering. He seemed to enjoy that well enough, so she had reason to be hopeful. Once they were living in the same house together, he would surely understand, wouldn't he?

Then again, Richard prided himself on being very constant in his opinions. Something she generally appreciated about him. She prized this constancy in herself, too.

But, oh, this was the big day!

Gwen snapped off the music, trying to shrug off dancing nerves of indistinct origin. What was with these senseless jitters? This was going to be wonderful! It was the day she'd been waiting for. . . .

She forced herself to take a deep breath and then floated down the hall to get ready. She brushed and flossed, meticulously chose an outfit for her luncheon (white blouse, floral peach and pale pink skirt, brown leather sandals, dangling pearl earrings that had once belonged to her mother—for good luck) and packed her gym bag. She pulled her straight, dark blond hair back into a ponytail and prepared to drive the 8.6 miles to the gym.

The rest of the morning progressed in perfect thirty- to sixty-minute intervals, precisely as planned. She took her class, cleaned herself up, did a few household tasks and even spoke briefly to each of her brothers.

George, six years her junior, called to say, "Happy birthday, Sis," from his computer-programming internship in Atlanta.

And Geoffrey, eight years younger than Gwen, phoned in from his accountancy work-study site in Seattle with the jovial greeting, "So, whoa, three decades! You're an old lady."

"Very funny," she'd said to Geoff, laughing, but she only pretended amusement. As excited as she was about her date with Richard, she'd been dreading this particular birthday for months. *Years*, if she were to be completely honest.

Of course, just hearing her brothers' voices again, while delightful, underscored how alone she'd felt since she'd moved to Dubuque to take this math teaching position. The big city on the

Mississippi may have been less than two hours away from her tiny hometown of Waverly, Iowa, but all of her memories of her parents and her life growing up were back there. Her brothers had moved away now, too, and much farther than she had after their dad died two years ago. They'd expanded their view of the world, and a part of her wished she could shake off her origins just as easily and be more like them.

She shoved away her combination of homesickness and irritation and, finally, when noon came around, she changed into her preselected clothing, put on a touch of makeup and found herself uncharacteristically giddy with anticipation.

This was it!

She sang a few bars of "Love Changes Everything" to herself—aloud!—before she realized it and stopped herself in embarrassment. She was *that* happy. Richard had hinted more than once in the past few weeks that he thought she'd "be pleased" with his gift. Knowing him, she more than suspected she'd love it.

By three this afternoon, four at the latest, she'd no longer be the unattached newish teacher Gwendolyn Anne Reese, the subject of some speculation and slight pity amongst the too-inquisitive junior-high teaching staff at Midland Park School District #76. She'd be the future Mrs. Richard Sidney Banks. And she knew *exactly* what that would be like: warm, caring and secure. Richard was smart, kind, steady, responsible. A man she could understand. She liked knowing what to expect out of people, and liked it even more when they consistently delivered.

"You and Richard seem, um, well matched," her aunt had admitted once, after having polished off half a pitcher of piña coladas. This was as close as Gwen had ever gotten to an enthusiastic endorsement from Beatrice. But, although Gwen had dated casually in college and afterward, Richard was the most serious boyfriend she'd ever had.

"Yes, he's just wonderful, isn't he?" she'd told her aunt, and she meant it earnestly. Gwen had met him after only a few weeks in Dubuque and easily felt more affection toward him than any other guy she'd ever known, aside from family. He was so easy to be with, and so naturally right for her. They seemed to innately understand each other.

And today would be the start of the next stage. A new beginning. Something good. Something that might even make turning thirty worth it.

In her eagerness to get a jump on the afternoon, she headed to The Surfing Cow Supper Club a bit earlier than necessary. It was Richard's restaurant of choice—a high-quality seafood-and-steak place along the river. As she sat in her parked car waiting for him, she breathed deeply and fiddled with her late mother's pearl earrings until she spotted Richard's steel-blue sedan pull into a space by the door, promptly at one p.m. Her heart swelled. Her future husband was fabulously punctual!

She stepped out of her car and waved to try to get his attention. But he didn't see her. He was carrying a small silver gift bag and was focused on getting in the restaurant via the revolving door. This sent a momentary sizzle of delight through her. He looked as excitedly impatient as she felt. And that package was the perfect size for a ring box.

She tried to relax. *Don't rush the moment,* her friend Kathy always said. *Savor it.*

Gwen inhaled again, exhaled and then called out Richard's name. He turned, spotted her and grinned.

She crisscrossed the lot and slid up to him. "Hello, Richard," she murmured, her voice oddly breathy. Was this what it was like to tremble at somebody's name? She thought of the Michael Ball song from that morning. Well, she wasn't shaking, but she *did* feel rather unsettled.

His grin broadened, brightening further his already attractive face. "Happy birthday, Gwendolyn."

"Thank you," she said, pressing her lips to his, feeling the coolness of them despite the scorching summer heat.

He placed a hand on her lower back, a reassuring gesture, as he guided her into the restaurant. "I took the afternoon off, but I'll have to make an appearance at work again later today. We've got a bunch of claims that need to be filed before the weekend."

She nodded, a bit disappointed, of course, that he didn't suggest spending the evening with her, too. Perhaps he'd finish early and surprise her at her aunt's house. Well, no. That was unlikely. Or, maybe, he'd visit her at her condo later in the night. She was, however, used to Richard's industriousness at work. As he did with all tasks, he took his responsibility as an up-and-coming insurance agent at Iowa Insurance Corporation very seriously. Hardworking and ambitious, he even had their company's slogan ("Providing first-rate insurance services to every first-rate Iowan—and, *yes!* That means *YOU!*") printed on a rather large, Day-Glo yellow bumper sticker and pasted across the back of his car. His company devotion was unmissable.

"So, how are you?" she asked when they were seated and had each ordered the Tuesday Surf-n-Turf Special—not Richard's usual meal of baked chicken and mashed potatoes, but a real splurge. Further proof that today was a special day. Gwen smiled, her excitement rising.

"Doing well. Getting things done. But glad to get a little time off to celebrate your big day with you." He raised a glass of the white wine he'd selected to accompany their lunch. She raised her glass in return and they clinked.

She took a sip, appreciating the light, slightly fruity flavor. He'd gotten this brand for her before. A number of times. "Mmm," she murmured. Richard's taste in such things was so competent and experienced, she rarely bothered to wrestle with meal and drink selections anymore. She'd grown accustomed to just ordering whatever he did. And, while her friend Kathy would likely declare she wasn't being adventurous enough, Gwen hadn't been disappointed yet.

Richard smiled affably at her as he chatted about the particulars of his workday. A morning meeting. The latest big claims. Some funny memos from his coworkers. An upcoming conference. After twenty-three months of serious dating, she knew almost as much about the minutiae of his office job as she did about her own school district. It wasn't uninteresting, though. Just kind of . . . unchanging. "And, oh. There's going to be a company Fourth of July picnic next week, so mark your calendar," he told her.

There was an unmistakable sparkle in his eyes as he spoke about this event. Was he thinking of introducing her as his fiancée at the picnic? "Of course," she said, elated.

He beamed at her and chitchatted some more. He remained very much his usual self throughout the meal—indomitably polite to the waitstaff, expressing delight when their platters arrived, enthusiastic about events coming up in the near future—nothing seemed remotely out of the ordinary. This was comforting.

Gwen fidgeted with her fork and studied her plate, heaped with rich foods: a solid cut of Angus steak smothered in a mushroom sauce, shrimp and scallops with melted butter, a few superbly prepared sides. Richard dug in enthusiastically. He looked to be enjoying every bite and fully expected her to do the same. Under normal circumstances, she would have considered it too heavy a meal, perhaps, but she would have appreciated it much more than she did just then. Her stomach was churning strangely, however, and she could barely manage to eat a third of the platter.

"Don't you like it?" he whispered, sounding worried when she told him she was going to ask their waiter for a carryout box. "If it's not cooked well, or if you'd rather have the baked chicken like we usually get, I can order that for you instead."

"No. This is great. Really. I'm just full already, and I know I have to save room for some dinner and birthday cake tonight at Aunt Bea's."

"Ah," he said, not unpleasantly, but Gwen couldn't help but detect the shadow that darkened his face upon hearing her aunt's name. There was a perpetual unease between the two of them and, even though they'd spent several occasions together during the time she and Richard had been a steady couple, an awkwardness that almost approached dislike lingered between them.

It was an odd thing, really. Particularly given both of their compassionate natures. Her aunt, while certainly *quirky*, was a source of everlasting kindness and strength in Gwen's life—the lone mother figure she'd had when her mom (Aunt Beatrice's younger sister) died when Gwen was twelve, and her only living relative in the area. She owed her aunt so much.

And Richard . . .

He'd been there for her when she'd first moved to Dubuque and had felt so alone. He was so calm and gentle with everyone, especially his clients. A remarkably empathetic insurance agent. She'd seen him in action on a few occasions when there had been a car accident or a house fire. He seemed unfazed by disaster. Placid in the face of grief. A guy who could be counted on to be cool under pressure and help out the victims in crisis. How comforting it was to be around a man so reliable and proficient in emergencies!

And, yet, he didn't seem to like her aunt very much, who'd been nothing but—well, her naturally sweet but sort of nutty self with him. Gwen found their silent antagonism endlessly mystifying. But, of course, it would be impolite to mention this to either.

"So, nothing for you from the dessert menu then, Birthday Girl?" Richard asked, clasping her hand on the tabletop and squeezing gently. "Maybe a cup of vanilla ice cream?"

She shook her head. "No, thanks. But this was delicious." She pointed to her entrée, ready to be boxed up, and poked around a little just to make sure nothing special was hidden underneath a fat scallop or a buttery shrimp. Nope. "I'll enjoy the rest later," she told him, a little disappointed that he hadn't thought to be sort of creative with his proposal. Then again, a ring could get really sticky in mushroom sauce.

"Okay. Perhaps just a little more wine instead?"

Once more she saw the sparkle in his clear gray eyes, and she found herself agreeing to another half glass, even though she wasn't sure she could drink it. Her stomach continued to host some kind of gymnastic tournament inside her abdomen. She pressed her palm against the flat of her belly to try to calm the happiness masquerading as anxiety within her. This was a *good* day! She was just moments away from the joy she'd been waiting for—for months.

Plus, she knew she'd have something fun to tell Aunt Bea and those insatiable gossips in the S&M club that night. They were always trolling for details on her love life as if it might be some juicy plotline from *The Bold and the Beautiful*, her aunt's favorite soap opera. Just to appease them in their adoration of the melodramatic, she often spoon-fed them whatever romantic tidbits she could without revealing anything too personal. She knew from her aunt's tone and comment on the phone that they were expecting a fair bit of news tonight, though. It would be a relief to finally get to feed their curiosity by sharing something huge like wedding plans.

Oh, and Aunt Bea! Even if the future groom was Richard, Gwen knew this announcement would be a thrill for her aunt. Bea was in love with the idea of people being in love.

Richard reached down to pull up the silver gift bag he'd carefully set on the floor next to his chair. "I've got a little something for you, Gwen," he told her as he placed the package in her hands. "I hope you'll like it."

"Thank you." With unsteady fingers, she lifted out the loose white tissue paper at the top and laid it on the empty seat next to her. She tapped at the item at the bottom of the bag, wrapped in more tissue still. Hard. Small. Square-shaped. With her heart pounding, she pulled it out and let the paper drop away.

A ring-sized jewelry box. Navy blue. *Oh, here it is!*

She took a very deep breath and lifted the lid of the box. Slowly. Really trying to savor the moment. But her pulse was racing, and she just couldn't wait. She flipped it open and . . . blinked.

Inside, rather than the engagement ring she was expecting, a pair of earrings sat on the velvety cushion. Very nice pearl earrings. But still . . . *earrings*.

Hmm.

"Do you like them?" he asked, his tone anxious.

She exhaled. "Well—yes, of course. They . . . they're lovely, Richard. Thank you."

"You're welcome," he gushed. "I'm so glad you think they're pretty. I saw this pair and immediately thought of you. I think they'll look great on you."

She instinctively reached up to touch the pearl earrings she already had on. Richard saw her do this, and he smiled.

"I know how you like wearing those old ones," he said brightly. "But I figured they were kind of worn-out now, you know. You needed something newer."

She stared at him for a long moment but had no way of responding to this astonishing comment. She'd told him of her sentimental connection to her mother's earrings. She'd even told him that these were the earrings her father had given her mother when Gwen was born. That her mom had always said one day they'd be hers. That she'd give them to Gwen on her sixteenth birthday . . . a birthday her mom hadn't lived to share with her. Could Richard have forgotten this?

She tried hard to see the good intentions behind his gift, but knew it would be impossible to explain all of the ways in which he'd missed the mark. Not without bruising his feelings. But, seriously. Was it possible he really believed such a thing? *No* other pair of earrings could ever hope to replace the ones that had belonged to Mom. These were not "old" or "worn-out," they were treasured and loved. Richard's pair, while quite pretty and very new, lacked the soft luster from wear, the uniqueness of design and the intense sentiment of her originals. How did he not understand that?

Furthermore, while it may have come in a jewelry box, his present wasn't remotely like a proposal, and Gwen was stunned by how much the absence of this pained her. She'd been so sure. Everything about her relationship with him had been so seamless, so predictable.

Until now.

In one last-ditch effort to make certain she hadn't missed an additional gift anywhere, she slid her fingertips along the bottom of the sparkly silver bag as she wrapped up the earrings in the tissue paper again. Nothing else was in there. And nothing else seemed to be in her boyfriend's jacket, either, tucked away from view. Nothing.

She'd thought two years was a very sensible time frame for an engagement. Ideal, in fact. Yet, she must have thought wrong.

She bowed her head and shut her eyes tight. Warring with her hurt and confusion, however, was the acute discomfort that she'd somehow miscalculated something so significant. And her mis-judgment was only accentuated by Richard's behavior. He paid for the meal, helped her collect her things and walked her to her car without a single mention of marriage.

Although she wanted to be understanding, a frustrated part of her also wanted to shake him and cry, "What happened, Richard? You were supposed to propose to me today. *Everyone* expected it— especially *me!*"

But she did not shake him. A new ache constricted her heart, but she kept very quiet, allowing only a few—admittedly in-censed—mental comebacks in the privacy of her mind. For several moments, she merely stood there, struggling to gulp away her dis-appointment, but it lingered in her mouth like the aftertaste of a fruity wine that had soured.

"So, I'll see you in a few days?" he said. "Maybe we can catch a movie this weekend or just . . . hang out." He grinned at her. "Hang out" was his code phrase for making love. An activity that had been very pleasant between them. And always very uncompli-cated.

She nodded mutely. Then, only when she was positive she could speak without her voice quivering, she said, "Yes, and, well, thanks so much for lunch, Richard. And for the earrings. Both were very . . . nice."

She turned to unlock her car door, but he put his hand on her shoulder. "Um, Gwen—" He cleared his throat. "I, uh, want you to know that I've been looking at *other* things, too. Other kinds of jewelry for you. Okay?"

She met his eye and saw the warmth and kindness she'd come to associate with him staring back at her. But there was something else, too. Something she was having a difficult time pinpointing. The flip side of a good quality, perhaps. Not consistency, but rigidity.

"Okay," she murmured.

He inhaled deeply, like this was a speech he'd rehearsed at length, and threaded his fingers through his very dark, very straight hair. "We've been dating for almost two years and, well, I can imagine you might be expecting something more for your birthday than earrings. I was at the jewelry store, you know. I was . . . looking. But a commitment, like marriage, for instance, is a very serious thing. It requires planning and deliberation and lots of consideration. I think an engagement is better suited to a more reflective time of year. Like fall. Or even winter."

She felt her brow furrow as she tried to make sense of this statement. Yes, she'd agree marriage was a very serious matter and it was worthy of much thought and discussion. Why that discussion would have to wait until it was *colder*, however, was beyond her comprehension.

"Okay," she murmured again, but she couldn't help but be tempted to say: *Did you think Halloween would be a more serious time for a proposal? Were you going to ask me to be your very own Bride of Frankenstein? Dress up like a ghoul or some kind of vampire?*

Something inside her chest snapped loose at the thought. She tried, unsuccessfully, to stifle a snicker at the image of straitlaced Richard wearing fake blood and a cape and getting down on one knee, reciting words of love from the more passionate passages of Bram Stoker's *Dracula* or, alternately, a few lines from Mary Shelley's *Frankenstein*, but she was rewarded only with him staring at her as if *she* were the strange one. Maybe she was—or maybe not at all. Truth was, at this point, she no longer knew.

She wished she had someone in her life she could ask to gauge the strangeness level for her. But both of her parents were dead. Her brothers were living thousands of miles away and, besides, they were guys. Aside from Kathy, her teaching colleagues weren't people she considered close enough to share such intimacies with, particularly outside of the school year. And her aunt was, well, not the most conventional person.

So, she just pecked Richard on the cheek and swiftly slid into her car. She needed time to reflect on all of this.

"I'll call you tomorrow," she told him, and with a half wave, he let her go.

What just happened?!

She asked herself this repeatedly. All she'd ever wanted was for the world to make sense. To progress in a way that was rational. With Richard, it should have. But . . . it didn't.

At home again, she reasoned through the events of the afternoon, in minute-by-minute increments, trying to balance Richard's motivations with his behavior, while mechanically cutting up fruit for a healthy appetizer to bring to her aunt's house. But, like two sides of an algebraic equation, there was a variable on one end that remained a mystery:

A (He didn't formally propose to her, but he also didn't NOT propose.) + B (He expressed his intention to become engaged as soon as the seasons changed and the air had sufficiently chilled—an ingredient for "good reflection" she would never have predicted prior to the day's luncheon—but he did not say he desperately wanted to be her husband, or articulate his passion with the assistance of a famed poet's verses, or even profess on his own how much he ardently loved and admired her.) + C (He did not solidify their romantic connection in any way that she'd expected.) = X (Unknown.)

As a result, she felt herself in the odd limbo of being attached to the man by an invisible string. There was a bond, yes. Just not a readily apparent or wholly logical one. And she couldn't help but wonder, in that enclosed cerebral circuit of private introspection that was half mathematical, half literary and entirely academic: How strong was their attachment?

Steadying a tray of fruit kabobs on her hip, Gwen used her key to enter her aunt's house at precisely a quarter to four and stepped into the ruckus that was an S&M club meeting.

"Swear to the sweet Lord child, I'm gonna wrap your head up in an Akan kente cloth, Davis, and twist until your neck snaps!" Zenia hollered, raising her voice with practiced theatrics and standing up to add that extra element of menace.

Zenia Bronson, age sixty-two, was no stranger to emoting. She'd been a local stage actress back in the seventies and was now "A Fiber Artist of the Highest Caliber," or so said the business cards for her shop—Loominous. The current focus of her wrath was

white-haired Davis Whitney because he had the misfortune of
being their mah-jongg dealer or leader or something (they called
him "East" for a reason Gwen didn't understand) in a fierce game
against the formidable Youngs.

Alex and Connie Sue Young were a married couple, ages seventy-
two and sixty-nine, respectively, who'd both honed their math and
gaming skills—and padded their retirement funds—by playing
the riverboat casino circuit. One might say that no one won easily
against either Alex or Connie Sue. One might also say that Zenia
did not accept defeat in any arena without finger-pointing, mild
profanity and an onslaught of creative threats.

"You may have won a measly $126,000 on *Wheel of Fortune* once,
but until you learn how to pick and discard the damn tiles, you're
as worthless as a pair of circular needles on a jack loom," Zenia
spouted, tugging on a couple of her long braids—dyed strands of
jet-black and burgundy, entwined—in a show of agitation and dis-
gust.

Gwen was barely conversant in the rules of mah-jongg, but she
was pretty sure Zenia wasn't happy with her thirteen-tile hand and
wanted to "pick ahead." Davis, a retired calculus teacher, had apparently thwarted Zenia by citing some rule specific to the version
they were playing and dared to call her on cheating for "wanting to
look at her future"—whatever that meant. So, the tall, imposing
woman huffed, puffed and stabbed her silver-and-purple-glittered
index fingernail in the general direction of Davis's heart, but he
just yawned, refusing to budge on the issue. The Youngs ignored
her rant and waved Gwen deeper inside the den.

"Your auntie is in the kitchen," Connie Sue said helpfully. "You
go put that tray down and come back and talk to me, you hear?"

"Sure," Gwen said.

Alex patted his wife's arm affectionately and said to Gwen,
"And we wouldn't be opposed to you bringin' us a coupla Hester's
lemon squares since you're headed that-a way." He shot Zenia a
devilish look. " 'Course, the game'll probably be over soon, and
we'll be able to get up and grab 'em ourselves."

Zenia crossed her arms, sat herself back down and glared at Alex. "You got a winning hand already?"

He examined his rack of tiles and the current year's mah-jongg card that listed every possible winning combination. "Nope," he said with a smirk.

"Then you shut your fool mouth and play."

Connie Sue and Alex laughed, and even Davis broke into a grin. Gwen slid away from the foursome and escaped into the kitchen.

"Gwennie!" her aunt cried when she spotted her. "You got here just in time." Aunt Beatrice, who'd been chatting with Miss Hester Greenwald over vodka-spiked glasses of Fresca (her aunt's favorite drink), broke off her conversation and wrapped her slender but wiry arms around her niece. Despite being a head shorter than Gwen and about forty pounds lighter, Beatrice still managed to crush her with the embrace. It was all Gwen could do to keep breathing and to not drop the fruit kabobs.

"Hi, Aunt Bea," Gwen rasped, sucking in a lungful of air when her aunt let go. "Where would you like me to put these?"

"Oooh, I'll take 'em for you," Hester said, yanking the tray out of Gwen's hands. "What'cha got in here?" Hester, the oldest member of the group at age ninety, a "lifelong bachelorette," as she'd say, and a former schoolteacher "from back in the days of woolly mammoths and *real* liberals," never hesitated to take charge if she felt leadership was needed.

She ripped the foil off the platter and studied the kabobs. "Very . . . colorful, Gwendolyn," Hester pronounced. "And I like the way you worked in all that spatial geometry, too." She gingerly held up a kabob, studying the watermelon spheres and the cantaloupe cubes.

"Ovals, cylinders and trapezoids, oh, my!" Aunt Bea contributed, making note of the green grapes, banana chunks and pineapple wedges as well. "Very thoughtful of you to go to all this trouble, dear, but it's your birthday. We're here to treat *you*."

Gwen was about to protest that she didn't need any special treatment when Hester broke in. "How was your big birthday lunch with that boyfriend of yours?" The old woman leaned forward. "He get'cha anything good?"

Gwen noticed that, even though her aunt was making a show of arranging the kabobs, she was listening. Attentively.

"Yes," Gwen told Hester. "A very nice pair of pearl earrings." She smiled warmly at her and tried to sound very upbeat about it.

Nevertheless, Hester blinked her paper-thin eyelids and took a step back. "What?" The elderly lady snorted. "After all this time together, just some li'l pearl earrings? Not even diamonds? Humph."

Aunt Bea frowned. "No, uh, other jewelry?"

Gwen shook her head and saw her aunt and Hester exchange a pointed glance. Quickly, Gwen added, "But the earrings are *really* lovely," hoping to diffuse her aunt's silent condemnation and defend an absent Richard from Hester's obvious disapproval, too. She'd made the mistake of bringing him to an S&M gathering once, and Richard had hated every second of it. Although he was unfailingly courteous while in her aunt's home, once he was out of it, he let it be known to her that "the chaos, disorder and unnatural degree of impulsivity" of the club members made him uncomfortable. While Gwen often felt the same way about them herself, her discomfort was frequently, although far from entirely, tempered by her understanding that they were well-intentioned. Even when they were being intrusive and embarrassingly immature.

For example, at that very moment, Hester, who'd crossed her arms like a petulant teen, pursed her lips into a credible sneer, hitched her hip to one side and huffed, "Well, we'll show *him*. Don't you worry, dearie. We got you a *good* gift."

Before Gwen could so much as open her mouth to reply, Dr. Louie, wearing one of his S&M T-shirts and an absurdly festooned sombrero, strode into the room with a massive pan in his hands and announced, "Who wants some smoked-barbeque spare ribs?"

Matilda Riesling, trailing him as usual, carrying a ginormous platter and wearing her rival S&M T-shirt and several bright strands of Mardi Gras beads around her neck, said, "Smashed potato pie, people!"

At that, the mah-jongg players in the other room immediately abandoned their tiles and pushed their way into the kitchen to claim sturdy paper plates for sampling the vast array of rich and tasty dishes decorating her aunt's table and countertops. Only Connie Sue and Davis were adventurous enough to try "one of them *healthy* fruit kabobs" and, in Davis's case, it was only because he wanted to show Alex how to construct a model of a water molecule. The melon balls and grapes proved rather helpful.

Zenia, Hester and Aunt Bea were huddled in a corner gossiping about something. Gwen caught them sneaking furtive glances at her a few times while the rest of the S&M crowd grilled Gwen about her summer vacation plans, her luncheon with Richard and, alternately, her favorite sauces or glazes. She didn't have many opinions on the latter. She'd never been one of those *foodie* types like her aunt. She'd halfheartedly put a few items on her plate, but Connie Sue forced a leg of fried chicken on her—"Why, it's my Texan mama's special recipe"—and Matilda was a potato-pie pusher, so Gwen nibbled on those while, at the same time, trying to keep at bay the growing tension headache hovering at her temples.

The group was abuzz with excitement that night since many of them would be leaving on a big trip in just a few days and this was the last time they'd all be together for a number of weeks. Gwen was relieved she'd only have to deal with her aunt and a couple of random club members while the rest were away. Aunt Bea would probably make Gwen watch *The Bold and the Beautiful* with her once or twice a week to make up for Zenia's absence, as the two of them shared a fanatical attachment to the soap, but that was a small price to pay for not being pummeled with personal questions by a flock of nosy seniors.

She looked around and made note of the connections between these old pals. Couples like Connie Sue and Alex, who'd been married for almost five decades, stood out for her. Would that be her and Richard someday?

She chatted with the others, too, some of whom had been

friends for almost as long. Davis slipped away to put on some old music—Frank Sinatra and stuff that'd been popular back in the forties, fifties and sixties—reminding Gwen of her parents.

The S&M club had been together for nearly twenty years, through marriages, divorces, deaths, the birth of grandchildren and even great-grandchildren. Zenia was a relatively new member. Hester was a founding member, who'd met Aunt Bea at some community center social a decade before and reeled her in. Even Gwen's dad, before he'd died two years ago, had been involved periodically with the group, making the trek from Waverly to Dubuque for an occasional gathering or tournament.

"I'm more on the sudoku side," he'd confided in Gwen once. "Don't know how anybody keeps those mah-jongg rules straight."

Gwen smiled at the memory and glanced around her aunt's house, a disconcerting study in a non-updated 1970s decorating style. The colors—a clash of dark greens, old-fashioned creams and burnt oranges—simulated the visual effect of Zenia's green-bean casserole. Gwen had difficulty stomaching both.

However, on the wall was a photograph of Aunt Bea with her kid sister, Madeline, who was Gwen's mother. Gwen couldn't help but stare at the picture of the two young women. It was one she paused to examine every time she visited her aunt. Her mom had been about her age when the photo was snapped.

It was odd to think of that. *She'd only lived to forty. Only ten years more than me.* Gwen tried to turn down the fear this thought created in her, the familiar what-am-I-gonna-do-with-my-life refrain that haunted her whenever she realized that she, too, could just die any day without warning. A brain aneurysm could unexpectedly cut short her time on Earth, just as it did with her mom. This depressed Gwen and made her want to grasp hold of life a tiny bit more. But she'd also vowed when she was young to be more careful about her every choice. She'd play it safe wherever and whenever she possibly could.

She gazed longer at the picture, imagining her mom swaying to the oldies song that was playing and her aunt singing beside her.

Remembering her dad, too, and Bea's husband, Uncle Freddy, who was no longer with them either. Missing them.

She blinked those thoughts away when Connie Sue stepped near her and asked yet another question about Gwen's summer schedule. Nonteachers were always so interested in what teachers did over those long vacations. She answered politely but couldn't help but wonder why, after a day that didn't feel remotely celebratory to her, she was still here, amidst these kindly but rather prying elderly puzzle solvers and game players, eating heavy foods and missing her parents, when all she wanted to do was go home, take a bath and play her CDs.

A chorus of "Happy Birthday" roused her into greater awareness of the rest of the group. Her aunt, who'd managed to light candles on a big, chocolate, sprinkle-covered birthday cake sometime during Gwen's conversation with Connie Sue, came forward in song and, with a couple of balloons in hand, demanded Gwen's attention.

"Thanks, Aunt Bea. Thanks, everyone," Gwen said, when the singing ceased, appreciating their thoughtfulness, although it made her headache reach a painful crescendo.

"Well, make a wish and blow out your candles!" Zenia demanded, her dark eyes twinkling so much Gwen was sure these must be trick lights.

Still, she thought about her wish: to be happy, secure, loved by someone and not so very afraid her life would end before she got to experience this. She took a breath and blew.

Every candle went out. All except one.

"Oooh!" Aunt Bea said. "That's good."

Gwen was about to extinguish this last one but stopped midbreath. "Why? Why's that good? I didn't get them all."

Her aunt laughed and a few of the older women chuckled. "Because, Gwennie, that means there's room for surprises."

Gwen bit her lip and forced a small smile at Bea. She'd had plenty of surprises in her life. She didn't like them or desire more. Of course, she didn't say *that* aloud. She blew out the last glowing candle.

Soon the cake was cut and everyone had gathered around the table to collect their piece and offer their good wishes.

"Take the first bite, honey," Connie Sue urged, and Gwen obliged.

"Mmm. Delicious," Gwen said, not untruthfully, although, like everything her aunt made, there was more butter and sugar in the batter than absolutely necessary. "Thanks."

"Give her the card," Hester said, elbowing Aunt Bea.

Bea looked around. "Who's got it?"

Dr. Louie pulled it out of his back pocket and waved it in the air. "Everybody sign it?"

"Yep," "Yes," "Ah-ha" and "Of course, you numbskull!" followed.

He handed the peach-colored envelope to Gwen and she pulled out the card within. The scripty lettering on the front read "Hippo Birdie Two Ewes" and featured a gray hippopotamus, a cardinal and two fluffy white sheep all in a row. In spite of herself, Gwen laughed.

Then she opened the card.

Inside, there were signatures from everyone in the S&M club and, also, there was a photograph. This photograph wasn't one she felt in any way sentimental about, but it did serve to confuse her. Why give her this? It was a picture of a geographical map of Europe with what looked like red string connecting the major cities in a crooked line from London to Rome. Some new form of "art," perhaps, that Zenia was into?

"Um, thanks," Gwen said. The club members around her were giggling—even the more solemn men, like Davis—which made her a tad apprehensive. She glanced at her aunt, who was positively beaming.

"Gwennie," Aunt Bea began, "we've got a little surprise for you."

Her aunt shot a look at Connie Sue, who raised her eyebrows at Hester and who, in turn, nudged Zenia, who blurted, "Angie's havin' a hip replacement."

"I—I'm sorry to hear that," Gwen replied, slightly taken aback by the non sequitur. Angie had been hobbling around rather a lot in the past several months and her husband, Thomas, at age seventy-five, had insisted on pushing her in a wheelchair, which she hated. The surgery was unfortunate, of course, but hardly surprising. "I hope she'll recover quickly."

"That woman would do anything to get out of a bet!" Zenia ranted, swiping a few beads of sweat off her deep brown forehead with the sleeve of her dazzling green-and-gold tunic and pacing across the room and back. "Said she'd climb to the top of the Eiffel Tower with me." She huffed. "Wimped her way out of it."

Gwen squinted at her and nodded slowly. Perhaps the combination of all of the carbs in the potatoes, the cake and the lemon bars were getting to the older lady. Zenia had to watch her blood sugar. "That's too bad," Gwen said, wondering if she should offer the woman a glass of water or, maybe, a comfortable chair in which to sit down.

"What Zenia means, dear," her aunt interrupted, "is that Angie and Thomas aren't going to be taking the trip with the group."

The trip. The trip. Some madcap bus tour through Europe, complete with a stop at a sudoku festival in Brussels. Gwen pursed her lips to keep from sighing. She'd heard rather enough about "The Trip" in the months prior and altogether too much that night. She'd been so relieved when her aunt claimed lack of interest in the month-long jaunt. . . . She didn't want to have to worry about Bea frolicking around like an adolescent through the streets of Paris or getting lost in the Alps or hooking up with some Italian octogenarian or anything.

Then it hit her.

The careful explanation. The photograph of that map. The freaky focus on how surprises were "a good thing."

The first wave of alarm started like a slow tsunami and rose to dangerous heights before the realization drenched her in dread. She stared at Aunt Beatrice, praying she'd somehow completely misunderstood.

"So, I bought their tickets and transferred them to our names," her aunt said brightly. "We're going on the trip instead."

"Surprise!" the S&M club members cried in gleeful harmony.

Gwen's heart paused, as if not sure whether it should keep beating. The anxiety at the prospect of undertaking such a journey with this nearly insane crew tangoed with the allure of her first foreign adventure. *I could see a world I've only read about. . . .*

"Oh, my God," she murmured to herself, but no one, not even her aunt, heard her.

"And we leave in two days," Hester said with a hearty cackle. "So you'd better start packing!"

2

From Home to Rome in Search of
Adventure and Authentic Gelato

Thursday–Friday, June 28–29

Normal people, Gwen thought, would have had nothing exceptional to say about a typical transatlantic flight and would have spent their hours in the air discussing just about anything *other than* the actual plane ride. Yet, between Dr. Louie, Matilda and Davis—her seatmates in economy class, row 22, center—no mathematical point of interest was either too small for analysis or too insignificant for general commentary.

"Oooh! Did you hear that?" Matilda pronounced, in the midst of an energetic game of canasta with Dr. Louie. "The captain says we've dipped to 30,000 feet. A little more than four-fifths of our cruising altitude during his last announcement."

"And can you feel the deceleration?" Dr. Louie remarked, discarding a three and drawing a more favorable ten and queen.

"A reduction of at least twenty-five percent from our previous speed of approximately 500 miles per hour," Davis replied, glancing up at them from the puzzle he was working on in a level-six Sudoku Master Challenge workbook. As one of only a few S&M members who qualified for the competition in Belgium, he had to be ready.

Gwen, accustomed to far more quiet time than she was getting that day, was starting to feel as though she may have made a terrible mistake in coming—European adventure or no. She gazed across the compact seats to look out of the windows. The point of their numerical scrutiny was that they'd be landing in Rome in less than an hour. For the past two hours, she'd been forced to overhear the three of them debating the Boeing 747's position, location, elevation and speed with stunning absorption.

Aunt Bea, who was sitting just across the aisle from her, was snoring softly in the seat next to Connie Sue. Alex was next to his wife, wide-awake and staring out the window.

Gwen took a deep breath, closed her eyes and pretended to listen to her iPod, which needed recharging because it had run out of juice somewhere over the Atlantic. While the music had been playing, she'd been all right—she'd felt much as she had at home, in her kitchen, listening to her soundtracks and preparing for her day. Without the songs, though, she felt immediately just how far away from Iowa she really was. And from Richard.

Richard, who, when she'd called him to tell him about her aunt's gift, had said, "*Four* weeks in Europe? What on Earth are you going to do there for *that* long?"

"It's technically five weeks," she'd replied, having had a chance to study the itinerary at some length. "And we're going to visit famous sites. Bunches of them." She'd been reading up. A lot. She already knew a fair bit of European history and welcomed the chance to learn more, but she couldn't help but fear this book knowledge wouldn't be enough to fully understand the experience. She'd only left her home state a handful of times in her life. The S&M members were world travelers compared to her. What would the people she encountered in Europe think of her when they realized just how very noncosmopolitan she was? She probably shouldn't venture an opinion aloud—on anything—for the first week at least.

There was a pause on the line. "But what about the Fourth of July? You won't be able to come to the picnic."

"I'm afraid not, Richard." She didn't say, although it was implied, that they wouldn't get to "hang out" that weekend, either.

Perhaps, if they'd actually been engaged, she would've had the nerve to turn down her aunt's offer, but Gwen didn't have the ready excuse of needing to spend the summer making wedding plans. (And *that* was Richard's own fault.) She couldn't bear to see Aunt Bea's joyful expression turn to disappointment without some really good reason. "You'll be so busy over the next month, you'll hardly have a chance to miss me," she told him, hoping this wasn't true, but suspecting it might be.

He cleared his throat. "Of course I'll miss you, Gwendolyn."

"Well, I'm glad we got those passports now," she said, thinking he'd be pleased to hear this. He'd had a conference scheduled last summer in Ottawa, and he'd asked her to drive up there with him. She'd been really excited to go, and they'd both gotten passports. But when the conference dates were changed, he'd canceled the trip, and they'd ended up not going anywhere together. Not even to Canada.

"Yeah. Yours will come in handy now," he replied, his voice almost tart.

Was he envious? Perhaps he was really sad to see her leave.

"Hey," she'd said. "I have an idea! Don't you have a few days of vacation left this summer? Why don't you join us for a little while?" Buoyed by this rare burst of spontaneity, Gwen held her breath, awaiting his reply.

Richard kept her waiting for at least twelve seconds. She'd counted. "I'll think about it," he said finally. "But it would have to be somewhere English-speaking."

And, so, they'd left it that, *maybe*, he'd join the group for their final days in London, since that was where the tour concluded. The possibility of this reunion with him, and the romantic closeness it might inspire, was what had kept her going for the past forty-eight hours. She mentally gripped her daydream of that moment, clung to it like a lifeline.

A sudden jolt caused by an air pocket—"Clear-air turbulence," Matilda informed them, evidently figuring they ought to know the technical term—jerked Aunt Beatrice awake.

"Good morning, Gwennie," her aunt said with a yawn.

"More like 'Good afternoon,' " Davis inserted, after a peek at his wristwatch. "We're on Italian time now."

Aunt Bea chuckled. "So we are." She yawned again, stretching her bony arms far enough to knock both Connie Sue and Alex in the head, had they not shifted away just in time. "I'm looking forward to finally seeing the others."

Gwen squinted at her. "The *others?*" she asked, already worried that being on a plane with such an offbeat cast of characters might be resemblance enough to a plotline from *Lost*. She didn't need there to be "Others," too.

"Oh, yes," her aunt answered breezily. "Our friends from our English sister city are flying down from the U.K. today. We've only met online so far. Tournaments. Facebook. You know."

Gwen didn't know. Or, more accurately, she only vaguely remembered. "Dubuque, Iowa, has a sister city?" she asked slowly. "In England?"

"It does for our club!" her aunt exclaimed.

"They're really into S&M there," Dr. Louie said with his booming baritone. The flight attendant walking up the aisle swiveled around and shot him an odd look. Most of the passengers in rows 23, 24 and 25 abruptly stopped talking. Half of row 21 craned their necks to glance back at him. Gwen slunk down in her seat.

"Hey, where do these people live?" some random guy, sitting two rows behind them, asked with a laugh.

"Surrey, dear," Aunt Bea called to him.

"Like the carriage," Connie Sue piped up.

"Or the show tune," Matilda supplied helpfully.

Dr. Louie, who was seated between Matilda and Gwen, tossed down his playing cards and all but leaped up to wave at the guy who'd asked the question. With a frighteningly delighted look on his face, he burst into song, much like some teen in *Glee* or *High School Musical*, only not. "Hens and mice and sheep better scurry-yy, when I take my friends in my surrey-yy—"

Aunt Bea laughed, but Matilda interrupted him. "Oh, stop it,

Louie! There were no *sheep* in that song. There were chicks and ducks and geese, I think, and maybe a cow somewhere, but I know—"

"Then join me!" Dr. Louie enthused, half lifting a startled Matilda out of her seat and getting her to lead the midsection of the plane in the first verse and chorus of "The Surrey with the Fringe on Top."

It was like a *Twilight Zone* version of a musical come to life. Gwen was sure the ghosts of both Rodgers *and* Hammerstein were spinning in their graves and, quite possibly, planning for Flight 435's crash landing and consequent fiery destruction just off the coast of Corsica. Good thing Richard wasn't along. He'd be horrified by the spectacle.

But was the flight attendant doing anything to curtail this display? *No.* She was laughing. And when Louie and Matilda went on to butcher the song "Oklahoma!" next, the woman in uniform actually joined in the singing, as did at least sixty percent of the passengers in the economy-class section. Dr. Louie had snatched Davis's pen away from him and was using it as a conductor's wand. On top of that, instead of the wind sweepin' *down the plain* the wind was sweepin' *cross the plane,* with Dr. Louie pretending to blow a gust of air across the aisles from the windows on one side to the windows on the other.

Gwen's self-consciousness rose to unparalleled heights. Although she knew every verse of every song they sang, she didn't have the nerve to exhibit herself that way. *Didn't this prove they were nuts?!* She'd never be someone who'd get coerced into impromptu karaoke-like singing in public, no matter how much these wacky seniors tried to cajole her into joining them.

And, furthermore, this trip that she'd expected to be a semiserious learning experience was turning out to be far less like a European documentary than a continuously looping sitcom. Their flight, already an eternity, seemed to drag on even longer.

Aunt Bea paused long enough in her warbling to say to Gwen, "Isn't this fun? And we're not even in Rome yet!"

* * *

After disembarking, they were greeted at the international arrivals terminal of Rome's Leonardo da Vinci Airport by a short,
older gentleman wearing a plaid cap and chunky glasses. The
portly, bespectacled man spoke in brief sentences with a thick Italian accent and introduced himself to the group as "Guido."

"*He's* the hot tour guide Cynthia was going on and on about?"
Zenia hissed at Connie Sue.

Connie Sue shook her frosted blond head. "Can't be."

Gwen's aunt, standing near her friends at the back fringes of the
crowd, shrugged and said, "Anything's possible, but he doesn't
look at all like Cynthia described him."

"Or like his Twitter profile photo," added Zenia, unable to disguise her resentment.

In Gwen's opinion, Guido did not look like the kind of person
who would embrace social networking of any kind. He looked like
the beefy security guard at her bank—one whose conversational
exchanges were limited to intense nonverbal glances that said,
"Step away from the vault" and "I'll use this Taser if I have to."
She cleared her throat. "Um, who's Cynthia?"

"She's one of the Brits, dear," Aunt Bea explained. "Cynthia
Adams. She's in her early forties but still single. She likes to travel.
Hopes to find 'The One' someday."

Zenia rolled her eyes. "Stupid goal." But then, Zenia, Gwen
knew, had been happily divorced for thirty-one out of her sixty-
two years. She didn't have much use or patience for the male segment of the species. Not that she was above a one- or two-night
stand every now and again.

"She took a tour through Spain and Portugal with this company
before, honey," Connie Sue told Gwen. "She was the one who rec-
ommended it to us."

"What a mistake." Zenia dropped her carry-on bag on the noisy
tile floor, sighed heavily and crossed her arms. "She's a dolt if she
thinks that man is in any way fling-worthy."

Gwen was imagining Cynthia as a forty-something Bridget
Jones, flaky and a little chubby, perhaps, until her aunt said, "She's

not a dolt. She's a tenured mathematics professor at the University of London."

Huh, Gwen thought. Not so Bridget-Jones-like, then.

Hester strode up to them, indignant and as fast as her spindly ninety-year-old legs could carry her. "Cynthia promised us our guide would be a really foxy dude." She shot Guido an accusatory glance. "He's not tall *or* Austrian!"

Gwen studied Guido from a distance of a few yards. He was speaking in short but commanding bursts of Italian to a couple of members of the airport staff. Something about baggage claims, Gwen gathered.

"Seems there's been a little-bitty change," Connie Sue murmured.

"I'll text Sally and Peter," Zenia informed them, pulling out her special, just for Europe, pay-as-you-go cell phone and punching a few buttons with rapid-fire thumb action. "Maybe they'll know what's going on here."

Gwen was almost afraid to ask, but she said, "Who are Sally and Peter? More Brits?" She had no idea how she'd be able to keep all of these new people straight without an attendance list and a seating chart. Invaluable tools in a classroom of eighth graders but, perhaps, even more necessary here.

"Yep," Aunt Bea said. "The Bentleys. They finally saved up enough for their honeymoon trip."

"That's so nice," Gwen said, relieved there would be at least a couple of people closer to her age on the tour. Her aunt's elderly friends, while certainly *lively*, weren't exactly the kind of company she was looking for—even when they weren't crooning their way through musical numbers in public places. "How long have they been married?"

"Forty years," her aunt said.

"Oh."

Aunt Bea looked at her with an expression that could only be described as compassionate. She reached out her thin fingers to grasp Gwen's arm. "Don't worry, Gwennie. I'm sure there will be someone you'll find interesting on the trip. If not on the tour, then in the cities we visit. Grand European vacations are made for adventure. Romantic and otherwise."

"Romantic?" Gwen blurted. "But I'm with Richard."

Her aunt shrugged. "Of course you are, dear, but you never know. Life's full of surprises, possibilities and changes—both pleasant and unpleasant—but that's better than the alternative, right? Got to stay flexible, keep yourself open to experience."

"Yep," Zenia said, pulling her gaze away from the rotund Guido for a moment. "Plus, if someone's really good, they'll hold their own against the competition. Just like Ridge beating out his half brother Thorne for Brooke's affection in *The Bold and the Beautiful* a few seasons ago."

"And if they don't," added Connie Sue, "it's a surefire better thing to know about it sooner rather than later."

"Here, here," chimed Hester.

Gwen forced a smile at them, despite their usual—and mostly benign—meddling. She wasn't oblivious to their game, even though she was becoming increasingly annoyed by it. She understood they were trying to broaden her experiences and give her a chance to see men besides Richard and view the world beyond the borders of Iowa. She could appreciate that. Really. But it was scary to be so far away. Exciting, yes, but also overwhelming. She'd watched *The Wizard of Oz* with her mom when she was a little girl. She knew there was no place like home.

Eventually, they emerged from the entropic chaos of the airport and found themselves deposited, along with their luggage, in the heart of the city of Rome. The Hotel Adriatica was located on the famous and expensive Via Veneto, not far from the Spanish Steps and the Piazza Barberini. As Guido wrestled their bags off the bus, they were met in the hotel lobby by a lean-muscled, six-foot-something, very well-dressed blond gentleman who went by the name "Hans-Josef."

"Oooh," Hester hooted. Leaning in toward Aunt Beatrice and Gwen, she whispered, "Finally, the Austrian."

Zenia, who'd been unable to reach the Brits via text, grinned in relief. "So, I won't strangle Cynthia after all."

Hans-Josef informed them that he'd worked for the tour company for eleven years, spoke "five languages fluently and three adequately" (English was, ostensibly, one of the fluent ones), was a native of Salzburg and would be their guide through Italy, Switzerland, Austria, Hungary, Germany, France, Belgium and England. He assured them they'd "take a big bite out of Europe" and do everything from visiting famous museums like the Louvre to climbing the Swiss Alps to going for a dip in the balmy Mediterranean Sea.

"I think I'll just have to take a big bite outta him," Zenia said, smacking her lips as their guide spoke.

Connie Sue whistled softly behind Gwen, Aunt Bea and Zenia. "I can't wait to see that darlin' man in swim trunks. Or out of them." She sighed. "How many days until we get to the French Riviera?"

Her husband gave a faux offended huff. "I'm standing right here, sweetheart."

Connie Sue snorted. "Oh, relax, Alex, he's half your age." She turned away from him and tapped Zenia on the shoulder. "Is sixty-nine too old to be a MILF?"

Zenia smirked. "Lordy, I'd say sixty-nine is great for a lot of things."

Aunt Bea erupted with laughter, loud enough that Hans-Josef stopped talking and blinked his blue eyes at them. "Everything here is good, *ja?*"

"*Ja,*" Aunt Bea said, barely unable to contain her chuckles.

"Oh, *ja,*" Connie Sue and Zenia chorused.

Gwen couldn't help but feel awkward around them. These women, decades older than she was, were so comfortable with themselves and their sexuality. Even though she had a hard time imagining her widowed aunt in bed with anyone—nor did she want to!—she knew Beatrice and Uncle Freddy had a healthy sex life before he died. It seemed her aunt had always been blunt, though. Never speaking in hushed euphemisms like she and Richard did. Would Gwen eventually outgrow her embarrassment, too? Once she hit forty? Sixty?

As she considered this, Hans-Josef continued making his intro-
ductory speech in precise Germanic-toned English. Guido, who, it
turned out, was their bus driver for the duration of the tour up
until the ferry crossing to England, dragged in the last few suit-
cases and turned them over to the hotel bellhops.

"I am pleased to say that most of our group has arrived." Hans-
Josef consulted his clipboard and made a few tick marks on one
side. "There will be a few late arrivals this weekend, but we are in
great shape." He said "vill" instead of "will" and "ve" instead of
"we," but Gwen was pretty impressed by his command of the language. She'd taken a couple of semesters of German in high school
and succeeded only in being able to ask, "Where is the post office?" and "How long is the train ride from Munich to Vienna?"
and, topping the charts on usefulness, "May I have the *Wienerschnitzel*, please?"

"So, you will change your clothing, *ja?* Freshen up and relax
for"—he checked his watch—"one hour and twelve minutes. Dinner will be at seven-thirty."

Dr. Louie prodded Davis about something, and Matilda began
to ask about room keys, but Hans-Josef snapped his fingers.
Everyone in the group stopped moving and talking. "Don't be
late!" He paused, then broke into a smile that infused his well-
chiseled face with light. Even Gwen had to admit that he *was*
quite attractive. "I will get the keys now. Oh, also. For anyone
not"—he paused as if searching for just the right phrase—"suffering from jet lag, you are most cordially invited for a first view of
Rome at night. We go after dinner."

By the time Gwen and Aunt Bea had collected their keys,
trudged up to their room, unpacked and changed out of their
travel clothes, it was time for that meal. A few members of their
group were already seated when they walked into the hotel restaurant but, before Gwen could sit next to someone familiar, her aunt
cried, "Sally!" and rushed up to a woman Gwen had never seen.

"Is it really Beatrice?" the sixty-something woman said in a soft
British accent. She embraced Aunt Bea. "Your photo on Facebook
is an excellent likeness."

"Yours, too." Her aunt radiated delight at Sally. "And where is Peter?"

"He'll be along shortly. It's shameful the way he preens before any formal dining experience." She shook her head in mock exasperation. "Worse than any sixteen-year-old girl, I'm afraid."

Aunt Bea introduced Gwen to Sally Bentley and, eventually, to Sally's husband, Peter, as well. "The honeymooners," her aunt called them, and Bea insisted on dining at the same table with the two of them. Thus, Gwen was subjected to the usual getting-to-know-you questions, which she always disliked because, in explaining her life to others, she could never escape how ordinary and boring she sounded:

Yes, she was thirty, and a schoolteacher.

Yes, she liked kids.

No, she wasn't married, however, she *did* have a serious boyfriend.

No, she'd never been to Europe before. (Or, really, anywhere at all.)

And, yes, her first impressions of Italy were definitely positive, but, no, she hadn't seen more of Rome yet than what they'd passed on the drive from the airport to the hotel, etc.

How very dull they must think her, even though she smiled at them and tried to be friendly.

"Well, that will surely change soon," Sally said with a kindly grin. "You shall get to start exploring Rome tonight. With us."

And Peter, upon learning that Gwen taught eighth-grade math, began regaling them with "jokes" related to her subject area. The man had an astonishingly comprehensive memory of juvenile math teasers and puns. And he didn't hesitate to divulge each and every one of them—before they'd even made it through their appetizers to get to their entrées.

". . . but this one is my absolute favorite," he said, after enough previous one-liners to exhaust even a grade-schooler.

It was all she could do not to plead, *Oh, please stop talking. Silence is preferable to inane chatter. . . .*

But Aunt Bea said gamely, "Tell us."

"Right then." He rubbed his mostly bald head and chortled in anticipation. "Who was the roundest knight at the table and why?"

Gwen managed a faint "I don't know."

Aunt Bea squinted and appeared to give the question some serious thought before twisting her lips and saying, "Lancelot, maybe? But I can't figure out why."

"Stumped, are you?" Peter asked. "It's Sir Cumference, of course. Because he ate a lot of pi!"

Aunt Bea laughed in delight. "Oh, that's funny!"

"Peter's always been a fan of King Arthur," Sally explained, grinning back at Aunt Bea and patting her husband's arm with obvious pride.

Gwen bobbed her head politely at them, but she could tell it was going to be a long night.

During their main course, she glanced around at the other tables and noticed a number of new faces—Brits who had filtered in and found S&M pals from "across the puddle" to chat with over dinner. Aunt Bea helpfully pointed out Cynthia Adams, the woman the ladies had mentioned earlier. She most assuredly did *not* look like a math professor, at least not Gwen's idea of one. Maybe, Gwen thought, her first impression of the woman as a forty-something, slightly svelter Bridget Jones was closer to the truth, at least in appearances. She was dressed to entice and seemed decidedly intent on using this to her advantage. As was another English woman sitting by her—Louisa Garrity—who Sally informed her was "a young fifty-four" and married to a rather inattentive husband. Louisa and Cynthia were reportedly "the very best of friends."

"How nice for them," Gwen murmured, striving for a tone of perfect neutrality, but she didn't like the chilly vibe they gave off. Not at all. They were like British Popsicles. The "Britsicles," she dubbed them privately.

Finally, there was a father-son duo. The dad, Kamesh Balaraj, had been an immigrant to England from his native India a quarter of a century ago, and his son Ani, age fifteen, had been born in Guildford, Surrey. Sudoku masters, both of them, they'd qualified for Brussels along with a few others in the British group. According to Peter, they were on some Englishmen's version of a guy bonding trip.

Gwen nodded. They seemed okay, although it concerned her that the person in the room closest to her age was a teenage boy. Well, no. There was also Hans-Josef, she admitted, whom she spotted being pulled into the orbit of the Britsicles. Their tour guide stood next to Louisa and Cynthia's table and listened to them with well-bred Austrian courtesy and stellar levels of refined respectfulness. Even from a distance, Gwen could tell the ladies were batting their eyelashes at him flirtatiously and pretending to hang on his every word. Or maybe that last part wasn't pretense. They seemed determined to get him to sit down but had not, thus far, succeeded.

Before they'd even managed to get to their piece of tiramisu for dessert, Gwen felt the heaviness of the meal affecting her stomach and the claustrophobic conversation affecting her brain. She excused herself without fanfare or explanation and slipped outside to the balcony overlooking Via Veneto to get some air.

The bustling street was much like the meal, a bit too rich for her tastes, but the activity below at least injected her with a much-needed bolt of energy. Although exhaustion had her eyelids drooping and the new sensation of jet lag made her stance feel slightly imbalanced, she appreciated the reviving effects of the charged atmosphere.

She gazed at the passersby, squinting slightly at the sinking summer sun and then back at the people. She caught sight of a young couple zipping by on a Vespa. They were laughing as the motor scooter zoomed down the street. Not wearing helmets, however, she noticed. And the contrast between the stride of a businessman in an expensive suit, leather briefcase in hand, and an old, old woman in a thin print dress, dragging a wheeled shopping cart behind her—the eggplant, zucchini and leeks bouncing inside the little metal cage—was profound. Both extremes existed in kinship on these Roman streets.

Gwen couldn't help but twist the information she'd gleaned

from textbooks, guidebooks and the Internet on the history of Europe and try to imagine the past in play here. Only, in her mind's eye, the power of that mental image (gladiators roaming the street, men and women clad in togas and sandals) was heightened by her other senses: the sound of feet clicking briskly or clomping stodgily along the Via Veneto. The warmth of the summer evening air. The faint scent of pasta sauce wafting up from the hotel kitchen. The smooth feel of the black, wrought-iron railing, cool to the touch beneath her fingertips.

She felt a curious rush of exhilaration, but it was tempered with a tremor of her usual anxiety. History was about life that had come and gone. Any gladiator she might've enjoyed imagining was, of course, dead. And Rome had so much history. All of Europe did. It was, in a way, like a parallel universe, where the thread of this history connected the past and present with stunning vividness. So many humans had once trodden this sun-kissed land, and even this balcony where she was standing. Most were long ago buried and, in many cases, forgotten. How many years would pass before she, too, would be a wispy, unremembered woman in the shifting winds of time?

She swiveled around, away from the balcony's ledge, and almost plowed into her aunt.

"Gwennie, are you all right?"

She tried to nod but wasn't able to manage it. "I—I'm not feeling well," she blurted, not at all exaggerating.

"Do you need to lie down?" her aunt asked, worry etching lines of concern into her already creased forehead.

"Yes," Gwen said without hesitation. "I want to go to bed."

Aunt Bea's eyebrows pulled even closer together. "I'll walk you up to the room and stay with you."

But as they took a few steps in the direction of the exit, Gwen remembered. "Isn't everyone going into Rome now?"

"Yes, but I can visit the piazzas tomorrow, dear. Let's get you upstairs."

Gwen forced herself to stop hyperventilating. *I'm okay, I'm okay,* she repeated like a mantra until she almost believed it. When they reached their room, she splashed some cold water on her face and urged her aunt to go out. "Please, Aunt Bea," she said. "It's just the jet lag. I've never flown out of the country before, so I'm not used to it. You go have fun on the town with your friends."

Her aunt gazed longingly at the window, but said, "I shouldn't go anywhere if you're—"

"I'm fine," Gwen said. *I'm okay, I'm okay!* And, though it took a full ten minutes of insisting, she finally got Beatrice out the door. Then she collapsed into bed, too exhausted even for fear to trespass on her dreams.

The next morning, Gwen awoke with a resolute, refreshed air and a dogged determination to put yesterday's lengthy travel day behind her. She fully intended to get up, get dressed and get a jump on the Friday sightseeing. Rome must be explored, and today was the day to do it.

She slipped out of bed and, being mindful of not wanting to wake Aunt Beatrice, she did her flexibility stretches in careful silence. She then tiptoed to the small desk in the corner and pulled out one of the stationery pages provided, running her fingertip across the lettering at the top that said Hotel Adriatica in flowing gold script. Uncapping a nearby pen, she studiously compared the names of the most famous places in the city with the planned sites on the tour for that day. Breakfast was scheduled to begin in an hour, but then Hans-Josef and Guido were going to drive them on an orientation bus tour to take snapshots of:

The Colosseum
Circus Maximus
Roman Forum
Pantheon
St. Peter's Basilica

This would be followed by a guided expedition through the Vatican and the Sistine Chapel around noon.

Gwen wrote these down on the paper and further consulted the itinerary. There was a break at this point for a late lunch and, if desired, a return to the hotel. For those hardier souls, the bus would drop them off at Piazza Navona and they could wander around independently from there until dinnertime. Gwen referred to her *Viva, Roma!* guidebook and made note of any other classical Roman landmarks or well-known sites. She then added:

Trevi Fountain
Spanish Steps
Piazza Barberini
Tiber River
Borghese Gallery

There was more she could include, of course, but this looked fairly comprehensive. She studied the paper, regarding the places written on it much like she did the tasks on her classroom checklist at the start and end of every school year. These sites were objectives to attack and then cross off with a sense of satisfaction. She would see each one, get through it in a timely manner and then move on to the next. By the day's end, she would have tackled Rome thoroughly and efficiently. She'd finally know something of Europe!

She was in the process of drawing empty boxes next to each site, so she'd have the perfect place to put her check marks, when she heard a rustling sound behind her. She turned and saw her aunt. "Good morning, Aunt B—"

"Oh, my dear. What in the name of the Holy Roman Empire are you doing?" Beatrice asked her, staring at Gwen's sheet with an expression of astonishment.

Gwen smiled and held up her carefully printed list. "Just writing down the sites I know we'll want to see." She pointed to the tour itinerary. "Tomorrow there's that big excursion to Pompeii and the optional trip to the isle of Capri. We need to get this Rome stuff taken care of *today*."

Her aunt, still very much in sleep mode, rubbed her forehead and shot Gwen a perplexed look. "Taken care of, huh?" She sighed. "Today is just an introduction to Rome, so you'll know a little of what the city holds in store. It's just the beginning. . . ." Her eyes focused on Gwen's sheet of paper again. "Reading your list has exhausted me, Gwennie. I may have to go back to bed."

Gwen laughed, thinking this was a joke. Aunt Bea, however, wasn't kidding. She shuffled to her bed, climbed in and promptly fell asleep for another forty minutes, making it to breakfast with only enough time to grab a Nutella-slathered bread roll and an espresso en route to the tour bus. Gwen didn't consider this a particularly healthful morning meal (rather unlike her own muesli with milk) but, as her aunt sat beside her in the bus's big cushy seat and sent her several concerned glances in between sips of strong coffee, Gwen had sense enough not to say so aloud.

With her list folded and tucked into her front pocket, Gwen faced off with Rome for the duration of the morning. She dutifully trailed after Hans-Josef as he pointed out the architectural highlights of the Colosseum, helped them to visualize the area that was once the Circus Maximus (it was pretty much just a lot of empty space now), talked them through the remains of the Forum and Pantheon as Guido slowed the bus so they could take pictures. Finally, they arrived at St. Peter's and headed toward the Vatican Museums and the Sistine Chapel, where they'd had a special group reservation, thank goodness, and were able to avoid the hideous tourist lines.

Much of the time, though, Gwen felt unequal to appreciating these sites. While she knew a fair number of academic facts about each and could recite a few more, if pressed, thanks to her guidebook ("Construction of the present St. Peter's Basilica, over the site of the old Constantinian basilica, began on April 18, 1506 and was completed on November 18, 1626 . . ."), and while she certainly had no trouble imagining the ancient Romans marching around in the crumbling ruins, she still found herself a bit disappointed in her own lack of connection with Rome. Blamed herself, of course—not the city—for not being more blown away by it.

She stood in the jet stream of tourists flowing through the Sistine Chapel, all of them *oohing* and *ahhing*, praising it in about fifty different languages. She stared up at the famous painted ceiling where Michelangelo's Adam—who was noticeably naked—was touching index fingers with God and, apparently, being given "Life." She exhaled, trying to hide her mystification. What on Earth were people *feeling* (that she was *missing*) when they saw this? She wanted to like it and, certainly, it was a highly decorated ceiling with many pretty and even evocative scenes, yet they didn't strike her as any more inspiring than a well-painted mural by a group of art students. What was it about classical art that *spoke* to people?

As for the building itself, it was kind of dark, even a bit dank. Gwen swiveled around in disorientation when she heard some guy with a heavy Texan accent say, "Don't'cha think his place coulda used some larger windows, Marge?" A few nearby tourists gasped but, though she never would've admitted a thought like that aloud for fear of sounding uncultured, she had to agree with the Texan.

She sighed. Well, anyway, now she'd seen it and, if ever Richard or one of her colleagues brought up the subject in conversation, she could speak somewhat knowledgeably about it. She pulled out her list and checked "Sistine Chapel" off of it just as soon as she got enough light to see the paper clearly.

Aunt Bea, who'd been one of the *oohers* and *ahhers*, caught her in the act. Her aunt crossed her arms and gave Gwen a displeased groan. "Put that silly thing away, Gwennie. You're missing everything good."

Gwen tried to disagree with her. She'd seen *every* site so far. She'd paid attention to every single stone arch or broken pillar their guide had pointed out to them, even when she didn't understand his avid enthusiasm for it. Intellectually, she accepted the importance of these sites as being historical treasures. Emotionally, though, she felt a bit cool toward them still. They left her with a feeling similar to that of caressing cold marble. A beautiful statue—like the *Pietà* in St. Peter's—was something one appreciated from a distance, but visitors didn't touch it, and it would chill their hands if they did.

Guido dropped them off at the Piazza Navona, where Hans-

Josef instructed those of them staying downtown on good luncheon spots. The rest of the people returned with Hans-Josef, via Guido-driven bus, to the hotel.

The honeymooners—Sally and Peter—who'd been trailing Gwen and Bea all morning, were, thankfully, tired and went back. So did Hester, Connie Sue and Alex. The Britsicles—Louisa and Cynthia—disappeared into a boutique. Dr. Louie and Davis went shopping as well. Zenia, Matilda and the British-Indian father-and-son team trooped off as a foursome to see an art gallery.

"The Borghese has the best collection of Bernini sculptures anywhere," Zenia had insisted to Bea and Gwen when the group was about to disperse. "A few great paintings, too. They've got a Titian, a Raphael, a Rubens. Come with us, you two! You shouldn't miss it."

Gwen would've done it. She could've crossed the Borghese Gallery off her list right then and there. But her aunt said no. She said there was somewhere else she wanted to take Gwen next.

So, after a late and very quick pasta lunch at a little café, Aunt Bea hired a taxi to take them to a place that wasn't a major site at all—at least not one Gwen had heard about—Santa Maria in Cosmedin.

"Uh, what's the historical background of this . . . church?" Gwen asked, stepping out of the taxi and feverishly flipping through her *Viva, Roma!* guidebook for more information. But her aunt didn't need reference material to answer. Bea had this site committed to memory.

"*La Bocca della Verità* is here," her aunt told her. "The Mouth of Truth. It's well-known in certain circles. Some think of it as a marble representation of the god of the Tiber River. Others consider it more of a lie-detecting oracle. Your uncle and I came to Rome many years ago and visited it then." She laughed as if recalling some inside joke. "There's a famous scene in the film *Roman Holiday* where Gregory Peck and Audrey Hepburn stop here, too."

Gwen followed her aunt into a very small enclosure and, to their left, was a large, round, facelike orb with a thick crack running from the upper-right side to the right eye and lots of lines around the facial features, giving off the impression that it was a very old man. The oraclelike thing was attached to the wall, and a handful of Asian tourists were taking pictures of it. A few of them posed by it, sticking their fingers into its open mouth and giggling.

Odd. Gwen turned to her aunt. "Why are they doing that?"

Aunt Bea whispered, "Legend has it that if you place your fingers into the Mouth of Truth but have been untruthful, it will bite off your hand."

Gwen squinted at the marble orb. Bizarre belief. Then again, ancient people thought the world was flat and there were dragons lying in wait at the edges of the ocean, too. Aunt Bea would, of course, like some strange sculpture like this. Gwen shrugged and pulled out her camera. "Okay, Aunt Bea. I know you're truthful. Why don't I take your picture by the Mouth thingy?"

Her aunt shot her a wicked grin. "Of course, my dear. After you."

Gwen swallowed and walked up to it, patting the face with the tips of her fingers. The marble was shaded and cool, and the whole piece was larger than she'd thought. She slipped about half of her hand into the mouth but, for some reason, didn't want to put it in any farther. She knew her hesitation was completely irrational. There was no magic or anything here. She could *see* how solid the wall was behind the *Bocca*. Nothing was there to bite off her hand.

Aunt Bea was fiddling with her camera and making more comments about Uncle Freddy. "He just thought the whole idea of it was so funny. He mugged for pictures, just like Gregory Peck did, and made everyone around us laugh." She sighed. "Well, maybe you'll come here with your husband someday and he'll do the same thing."

"With Richard?" she blurted before she could stop herself. It was hard to imagine Richard even visiting Rome, let alone putting his fingers into the mouth of some pagan oracle. There had to be a ton of germs in that mouth, what with all the hands touching it. Richard wasn't big on germs.

"Do you think he'll be your future husband?" Aunt Bea asked, holding up the camera finally. "Do you love him?"

Gwen froze, thinking about it. She respected Richard very much, appreciated his levelheadedness and his constancy and his security. Those were traits that she knew inspired love, so she must, indeed, love him. It was just . . . well, a little hard to be *absolutely positive* about it since she hadn't experienced the sensation with anybody else. But she felt so close to Richard, closer than to any other man she'd ever met. She *wanted* to marry him. She'd *expected* them to marry. They shared so many values and goals that she knew they'd be good partners in life. To Gwen, this qualified as a very mature kind of love—not some lustful adolescent thing or a soap-opera-like relationship drama.

"I think so," she said, but she pulled her fingers a little farther away from the back of the marble mouth.

"I know he didn't give you a ring, but did he propose? Informally?" her aunt asked, clicking a few pictures while Gwen pursed her lips into a half smile for the benefit of the camera. "You'd tell me if he did, right?"

Gwen pulled her hand out of the mouth altogether and stepped away from the orb. "Of course I'd tell you, Aunt Bea. And . . . no. No, he hasn't proposed. Not really."

Her aunt eyed her curiously and posed for a couple of pictures herself by the *Bocca*. "What do you mean by 'Not really,' dear?"

"Well, fall is a more serious and reflective time to talk about marriage than summer is," she heard herself say aloud. A part of her couldn't believe she was parroting Richard's words, but she had to say something. She had to give her aunt an immediate explanation, and that was the only one she could come up with at present.

Her aunt laughed. "That's nonsensical!" She laughed some more, stroked the side of the *Bocca* lovingly and then kissed its cheek. "For a smart girl, Gwennie, you say the silliest things sometimes."

Gwen refrained from commenting on anything for a while after that.

Finally, they strolled slowly through the most ancient part of Rome until they reached the Trevi Fountain. When they got there,

Aunt Bea dug into her small handbag and pulled out three different coins—a ten euro cent, a twenty euro cent and a fifty euro cent—all golden in color. She pressed these into Gwen's hand. They looked and felt peculiar to her. Very foreign. While inspecting them up close, she was overcome by a wave of homesickness. It was the littlest of things that made her realize just how far away from the familiar she really was.

"You need to make three wishes," her aunt commanded. "Face away from the fountain, use your right hand and toss each coin over your left shoulder. Two of the wishes can be whatever you want. The third wish should be to return to Rome."

"But why?" Gwen asked, genuinely surprised. "I'll have seen every major site in the city after today."

Beatrice responded by rolling her eyes in exasperation. "Just *do* it."

"Okay, okay. I will. . . ."

She held the three euros in her palm and, as her aunt commanded, faced away from the fountain. Pedestrians were milling about the piazza, everywhere, it seemed. Many were doing the very same thing, and the swarm of people—the noise of their laughter and chattering—kept Gwen from being able to concentrate on thinking up her wishes.

She spotted a few people from their tour group, hanging at the periphery of the piazza. Those two inseparable British women babbling at a couple of men, probably Italians. One of them—a tall, sort of sandy-haired guy—wore an amused expression as he scanned the touristy crowd. Just as Gwen was preparing to make her first wish, his gaze met hers, and he held it.

She blinked him away, or tried to. He had an unusually intense stare, which both intrigued and puzzled her. But she blindly tossed the first coin, the one worth the most, into the Trevi Fountain with this silent wish: *I want to know for sure if I'm in love.* Then, with the middle coin, she made her second wish: *I want to stop being afraid of life.* And, finally, with the coin of the lowest denomination, and only because she didn't want to break the rules, she sent into the water her last wish: *I want to return to Rome someday.*

"All right. I did it," she told her aunt, who'd tossed a set of coins into the fountain herself and was waiting for Gwen to finish.

"Good," Bea replied. "I hope every one of them comes true. Now, let's celebrate! There's a dessert you just have to try."

"All right," she murmured, noticing the gaze of the tall, sandy-haired man still trained on her as she followed her aunt's footsteps in a beeline toward a gelato stand.

The only thing Gwen knew for sure was that the distinctly uncomfortable sensation she suddenly felt low in her abdomen was *not* caused by hunger and certainly not by some great desire for Italian ice cream, no matter how flavorful Bea professed it to be. She suspected she could eat a whole tub of the creamy stuff and not extinguish this troubling feeling. But, like the stirrings of any new awareness that might signal change, she wasn't yet prepared to dig deep enough to identify its origins.

That night at dinner, they got to sit next to Connie Sue and Alex, who were discussing their tour guide. It was hardly sparkling conversation but, after her long day of sightseeing, she appreciated a low-key meal with people she didn't have to explain herself to all evening long. From across the room she could see the honeymooning Bentleys having a pleasant chat with Zenia, Davis and the father-son pair. She was pretty sure sudoku was one of the topics of discussion. Davis had his workbook on hand, and the boy had an electronic version of sudoku he was demonstrating to the adults at the table.

Alex said to Gwen, Aunt Bea and his wife, "I really like our guide, but his name is funny. Even if he is Austrian, imagine getting stuck with some old emperor's name."

Connie Sue shook her head. "No, honey. You're thinking of Franz Joseph, not Hans-Josef. I don't think our tour guide is a Hapsburg."

Alex shrugged. "Anything's possible."

"Well, maybe you can ask him tonight," Connie Sue proposed. "At that tarantella show we're going to."

"Oh," Aunt Bea said. "I think Guido is leading that excursion.

Hester told me it's Hans-Josef's night off. She said she wasn't going anywhere if he wasn't leading. Said she'd dance the tarantella only in her dreams."

Connie Sue looked disappointed. "Aw."

"Still can't wait to go out anyway, though," her aunt continued. "Maybe we'll run into the Pope. Not at the show, of course, but somewhere else."

"Eating gelato, maybe?" Connie Sue suggested.

"He has to go out for ice cream sometime, right?" Bea said hopefully. "Everybody—even the Pope—loves ice cream." No one dared to disagree with her.

Gwen found her aunt's sudden interest in the Pope odd, given that neither of them was Catholic. But, then again, they *were* in Rome, and she wanted Aunt Bea to have fun looking at (and for) whatever pleased her. She, however, was going to pluck a card from Hester's deck and spend tonight going to bed early again. She'd expected her aunt to be relieved to get a little break from her, but Aunt Bea just looked deflated by the news when Gwen told them she'd be staying in.

"Are you *sure?*" Aunt Bea asked.

She nodded. She'd originally planned to go to see it—where there was dancing, there would be music—but she'd gotten so much sun that day and was just too tired to keep her eyes open for much longer. "We saw lots and lots of great stuff today," Gwen said, refraining from mentioning that she'd secretly checked off every single item on her list. In her estimation, Rome had been completed. "But, much as I'd love to see this show also, I just don't have the energy for another activity tonight."

"Of course, maybe you just want to stay in with Hans-Josef, too," Connie Sue suggested, grinning. "He'd be quite a catch, that boy."

Alex laughed. "And he's been watchin' you, Gwen."

"What?" Gwen said. This was news.

Aunt Bea swiveled around in her chair, nearly knocking over the bottle of sparkling water and sending the bowl of olives teetering. She looked jubilant to the point of elation. "*Really?*" She didn't stop scanning the dining room until her gaze landed on Hans-Josef, who was, indeed, looking at their table. Specifically at Gwen. Of course, with four sets of eyes staring at him, he abruptly glanced away.

Her aunt beamed waves of delirious joy at her. "Yes, dear. You should stay in. Get some rest." She turned to Connie Sue. "What's his room number?"

Gwen endured their teasing and pointless speculation about her possible "evening with the emperor" until they finally left on their special night excursion. Hans-Josef was on hand in the lobby, helping the tour members onto the bus with Guido at the helm and fielding any last-minute questions.

After the final person going on the tour had been ushered to the bus, Hans-Josef surveyed the lobby and caught her eye. "Are you not going to the tarantella?" he asked politely.

"I don't think I could handle an evening out right now," she admitted. She couldn't help but notice he looked fatigued, too. It was obvious he needed a quiet night off—perhaps even more than she did. She smiled warmly at him, deciding to chat for a few moments just to appease her aunt, who'd be pleased to know tomorrow morning that her niece at least talked to the handsome tour guide, even if she didn't end up going to his room. *Ha! Imagine.*

"I cannot handle an evening out either," Hans-Josef agreed. He took several deep breaths and seemed to be studying her, perhaps trying to decide whether or not she'd welcome further conversation.

She returned the light scrutiny. He was, after all, rather nice to look at. Mid-thirties. Very toned and trim physique. Impeccably groomed and dressed. Empirically speaking, he was a considerably attractive man.

She felt a sudden pang of guilt on Richard's behalf for thinking these thoughts. Then again, Hans-Josef reminded her of Richard in a number of ways. As with Richard, she was comforted by Hans-Josef's precision and the sense of security he seemed to effortlessly emit. Richard, too, was a reasonably attractive, well-dressed man. But, above all, it was the air of competence that united these

two men in Gwen's opinion. Her tour guide, she realized with a
start, was a German-speaking version of her almost-fiancé.

Gwen was about to excuse herself to go up to her room when
the Britsicles appeared, all decked out in fancy eveningwear—
clothing not suitable for a mere tarantella show. Clearly, they were
headed somewhere ritzier. They were met at the door by the men
they'd been talking to at the Trevi Fountain earlier that day. One
of the two men—that taller, sandy-haired one—sent her another of
his uncomfortably inquisitive glances before *winking at her* and
striding away with the other three. It disrupted her train of
thought and messed with her senses to such a degree that she
completely missed Hans-Josef's question.

"Pardon?" she asked him.

"Well, I said I am going into the bar for a drink. You will join
me, *ja?*"

And Gwen, in sudden need of a distraction, and justifying her
decision by knowing she'd be able to tell her aunt that she actually
had a drink with the hot tour guide, heard herself say, "*Ja*. I mean,
yes, Hans-Josef. Yes, I will."

3

A Clash of Philosophies

Saturday, June 30

She awoke to the chirping of baby wrens and the lingering effects of what felt like a hangover. This much she remembered: She'd only had two of her own drinks ("Bellinis," Hans-Josef had called them when he ordered them for her) and just a few sips of one of his, not sure *what* was in that one, but her tolerance for alcohol was pretty low, and she hadn't eaten all that much at dinner.

At some point in her conversation with Hans-Josef, she felt so weary she almost had to rest her head on the counter, much like schoolkids sleeping at their desks. But that wasn't what actually drove her out of the hotel bar, away from the tour guide and into the safety of her bed . . . alone.

No.

It was when, in the midst of one of his monologues about his Austrian homeland—something about how he really missed his beloved pet hamster, Rolf, while he was away from Salzburg and giving tours (the rodent in question was currently safe and in the keeping of his sister)—that she heard a melody on the radio in the bar. It was a classical piece, featuring a violin, and it reminded her so much of the music her father used to play when she was little that, for a few precious moments, she tuned out Hans-Josef and just listened.

She thought of the way her father's playing had moved her, even as a child. She remembered the way her mom used to curl up on the sofa and invite Gwen to cuddle up next to her as Gwen's dad practiced, so they could listen together. He was not a professional musician, but he'd been a passionate and dedicated amateur and would sometimes be asked to play at dance recitals and weddings by people in the community. He loved doing that. And he'd loved teaching Gwen to play, too . . . for a few years, at least. Until her mom died. Then the house slowly grew quiet.

When she finally refocused her attention on her tour guide and realized that, indeed, he had not even noticed her lapse in awareness—had not even sensed that her mind had gone on a tour without him—she took a final sip of her drink, felt the heady swirl of the alcohol in her mouth then down her throat and stood unsteadily to leave.

"You are tired?" Hans-Josef asked, surprised.

"I am," she said simply. And because he was like Richard, because she knew precisely what to expect out of him, even after so short an acquaintance, she let him perform his gentlemanly deed of walking her to the stairs and shaking her hand good night.

"You will go on the trip to Pompeii tomorrow?" he asked.

"I'm planning on it," she said, stepping away from him as she spoke, breaking apart the easy connection she felt to him, much like pulling a magnet off of a refrigerator. She couldn't help but come to the dawning realization that the slight attraction she felt was not toward the man himself but to the effortless familiarity of being with that man.

"I will look forward to seeing you then." Hans-Josef bobbed his head slightly and allowed her to go upstairs by herself and collapse, nearly comatose, into bed.

But she was awake now.

For the first time in at least five years, Gwen skipped her morning stretches without good reason. She slid out of bed and got dressed, glancing around the room for Aunt Bea. She didn't see her aunt, but a note had been left for her, taped to the bathroom mirror with a Band-Aid:

Off to breakfast! Heard you were in the BAR having
FUN last night!! Don't be late for the bus or you'll
disappoint our tour guide—ha!

xo,

B.

Oh, no.

By the time she got down to the breakfast room, her aunt had already left—probably off gossiping about her somewhere in the hotel before the morning's excursion to Pompeii. She didn't see Hans-Joseph there either, but she knew where she *would* see him. Checking her watch (7:23 already), she downed half a glass of juice and a small pastry—no time for oatmeal—and grabbed a banana to go. Just twenty-four hours of being with her aunt in Rome, and Gwen was starting to turn into her. A disconcerting trend.

She hopped onto the bus and spied her aunt waving to her, just moments before Guido was due to depart for the two-hour ride.

"Good morning, Gwen," Hans-Josef said from the first seat, his welcome cordial if somewhat reserved. He eyed her with careful courtesy.

"Good morning," she murmured back. Then she nodded at Guido, sitting in the driver's seat and . . . Was he smiling at her?

Yes, he was. His grin broadened and he said a hearty, *"Buongiorno."*

"I, um, *buongiorno*," she managed. Now she *knew* her aunt had been gossiping about her. She hastened to her seat.

The bus had barely pulled away from the hotel when Aunt Bea began her inquisition in hushed, excited tones. "Hester said she saw you in the bar with Hans-Josef last night! Good girl!" She all but rubbed her hands together in glee. "What did you two do?"

Gwen didn't remember seeing Hester last night, but being a part of this tour was much like living in a small town. Eyes were always watching. "We just had a couple of drinks and talked a little, that's all," she told her aunt. But when Gwen glanced around the bus and spotted Hester, the old woman gave her two thumbs up and a huge smile.

"What did you talk about?"

"Oh, just stuff about his life as a tour guide. He told me about his pet, er, Rolf. We were there for less than an hour, so . . ." Gwen let this thought trail off, hoping her aunt would drop the subject. But that wasn't Aunt Bea's way.

Beatrice lowered her voice and said, "So, you went somewhere else then? Did he walk you up to the room after that? Kiss you good night?"

Gwen sighed. "No. Neither. I just came upstairs by myself and went to bed."

"Oh." Disappointment etched a frown on Aunt Bea's face. "Well, never mind. There's always tonight. Or tomorrow."

Aunt Bea was clearly incapable of remembering Gwen's attachment to Richard, but Gwen remembered it. She was, in fact, surprised and moderately concerned that she hadn't heard from him. She'd sent him an e-mail from the Hotel Adriatica's lobby the afternoon they'd arrived, just to let him know they'd gotten to Rome safely. Though she'd checked several times since then, he still hadn't e-mailed her back.

Before Gwen could protest or remind her aunt for the umpteenth time that she had a boyfriend already, Davis decided to join their conversation. He leaned forward from his seat behind them. Sudoku workbook and pen in hand and eyes glittering with unusually good humor, he said, "Stop trying to fight it, Gwen. Don't you know that you'll *have* to fall in love with someone on this trip? It's what young people are supposed to do. With drama like that going on, it makes us old folks feel like we're watching good cable. Don't wreck it."

Dr. Louie, who was Davis's seatmate for the bus ride, laughed into his fist. "Yeah," he boomed. The man was seemingly unable to whisper. "Doesn't matter if you're dating someone else back home. All bets are off here. A long trip like this is a different reality."

"Another world," Davis added with a nod.

"A parallel universe," Louie said.

Gwen swiveled around in her seat to talk to them both. "A parallel universe?" she asked softly.

"Exactly," Davis said. "We're the same players but in a different play. And when the set changes, so do the plotlines."

Matilda, who'd been eavesdropping without apology from across the aisle, bent forward until her neck was almost at Gwen's shoulder. "You need to have at least one fling in this play," she insisted. "Get all angsty about it, mess up your relationships—at least temporarily—and feel your heart breaking so badly you'll think you're dying. That's the unwritten script, Gwen." She smiled merrily. "Follow along."

"Yeah!" Davis said, getting into it and raising his pen in emphasis. "You're young, so go wild. Dance until dawn. Disobey your relatives. Live free!"

Aunt Bea reached over the seat and slapped him on the chest with a formidable thwack. "What do you mean she should 'disobey' her relatives, Davis? That's just nonsense talking now. You shush." Her aunt paused, glancing between Davis, Dr. Louie and Matilda. "All of you are right about the rest, though."

Gwen suppressed a powerful desire to roll her eyes. In her opinion—not that they'd listen—they were *all* talking nonsense. But there was little she could do to either comment or get away from them at the moment. She also squirmed under the steady gaze of Hans-Josef, who, being that he was only four rows ahead of them and trying to give the group a previsit lecture on Pompeii, could not have helped overhearing and certainly seeing some of her aunt's and her aunt's friends' antics on the bus. These S&M people were like schoolchildren on a field trip.

Upon arrival at the famous tourist spot, Hans-Josef purchased their tickets and introduced them to their on-site guide, a thin woman named Maria-something-or-other, who was going to spend a couple of hours walking them through the city of Pompeii, starting with the "Street of Abundance." He waited until Maria had control of the group and had done her little intro spiel on how there had once been 15,000 people living there. How it was a commercial center with villas, shops, inns, a marketplace, baths, taverns, even theaters. That they would soon see the amphitheater, which predated the Colosseum by one hundred years. And that the artwork, paintings and frescoes, excavated in the eighteenth century, had sent the Europe of the time into a neoclassical whirlwind intent on copying the style and artistic opulence of Pompeii. Only then did Hans-Josef slip to the back of the group, content to let this expert take the reins for a while.

At the earliest opportunity, somewhere near the Temple of Jupiter, Juno or, maybe, Minerva, he pulled Gwen aside and asked, "Are you feeling well this morning?"

"Yes," she said. Then, figuring she'd better deal with this head on, she added, "I'm sorry for departing so abruptly last night. A wave of . . . exhaustion caught up with me. Thanks again for the conversation and the drinks, though."

He squinted at her. "That is all right," he said, sounding cautious. "Perhaps we try it again another time, hmm?"

She nodded. "Sure. Perhaps."

They walked along in affable silence, and Gwen reflected that it was an odd blessing, really, that this should be so easy. She could use a friend in Europe, particularly one who was used to knowing more about the history and culture here than anyone around him (so he would be less likely to be horrified by any gaffes she'd make). And he, too, must be craving companionship from people his own age to overlook the relative oddities of her behavior.

"So, what's it like being a professional tour guide?" she asked him, glancing first at his very straight profile and, then, at her feet. The dust from the well-trodden path coated her new, white and oh-so-American sneakers with a thin film of rusty, ancient earth. "You are certainly well suited to it. Very organized and efficient."

Next to her, his posture straightened even more than usual and his chest puffed out a bit. Again, a nonverbal reminder of Richard. She smiled, thinking of her boyfriend and the way he took such pride in his work.

"*Danke.* Thank you," Hans-Josef said. "It is a career that keeps me busy. I am gone from home for several weeks at a time, yet I see many fine places in Europe like this—" He swept his hand across the expanse of open space, mostly empty save for a collection of column rubble and some buildings their lady guide said had once been the Pompeiians' forum and public marketplace. The heart of their city.

Gwen noted a few ragtag "fountains," some kind of bakery area and a bunch of tiles dotting the ground that they were told had once been stones to reflect the moonlight in the town square so the citizens of Pompeii could see where they were walking at night. She supposed Hans-Josef meant his words to be complimentary, but, to her, it only underscored how lonely he must be if visits to barren ruins like this—however impressive from a purely historical standpoint—were the highlights of his workweek.

"What is it about a place like Pompeii that makes you enjoy visiting it again and again?" she asked him, truly mystified but wanting desperately to understand.

He paused and pursed his lips. "I think you will see for yourself in a moment. We are nearing the site where they keep the plaster casts."

Sure enough, their guide Maria led them toward a shedlike area with windows all around. An enclosure called the "Garden of the Fugitives." It took no special leap of imagination to visualize the past here. It presented itself to them in the form of human-shaped plaster casts—hollow outlines of the dead in a fragile graveyard— accessible to anyone willing to look at them.

"It is interesting, *ja?*" Hans-Josef said. "You can see the figures of the people as they were on the day when Vesuvius erupted. They are frozen in time for us."

Gwen nodded. These people had been killed in the summer of 79AD by the volcano's poisonous gas, and then covered in twelve feet of ash. When the site was more thoroughly excavated in the 1860s, plaster had been injected into the spaces left by the long-disintegrated bodies to get the shapes of the humans who'd inhabited the area two millennia ago. She looked closer at a couple of the figures—a man on his elbow, having lost the battle to get back up again, a woman curled in a ball, eleven others who had fallen.

The wrathful volcanic lava trapped these unlucky individuals forevermore in its negative space, preserving only the vaguest lines of facial expression, but Gwen could recognize a look of terror when she saw one. If her own expression were to be set on infinite pause for future centuries to gawk at, she wouldn't want it to be like that. She wouldn't want her very last look at the world to be one of such fear. Such horrified shock.

"The Italians have a saying," Hans-Josef told her. " *'The nearness of death exalts life.'* " He nodded at her as if reading her phobia and hoping to erase it.

Didn't work.

Gwen said, "Oh," and glanced up at Mount Vesuvius, towering above them just six miles north. The nearness of death, indeed! She then studied the people on the tour with her. There stood Zenia, who was laughing with Davis over something, her face a beam of delight. Davis, by contrast, had only a sly smile playing about the edges of his mouth, a more reserved grin. The honeymooners appeared interested in the lady guide's discourse when not distracted or confused. Gwen noticed that Sally seemed intent on finding something in her purse and had pressed her husband into service by getting him to hold its contents—item by item—while she sifted through her belongings.

Aunt Bea caught Gwen's eye and took in that she was standing near Hans-Josef. Nothing short of mischievousness danced across her face. To Bea's left, Hester was huffing in exhaustion, her expression a study in determination laced with the pain of fatigue. Gwen remembered with an unpleasant start that the dear lady was ninety, after all. Not only old, but also a multiple of ten. Gwen *hated* those. Too many people she'd loved had died on an exact decade: Her mom at forty, her dad at sixty, Aunt Bea's husband, Uncle Freddy, at fifty . . . and she was thirty this year. She knew she wouldn't sleep soundly until she'd made it to thirty-one.

"So, you see?" Hans-Josef said, breaking into her thoughts. "It is like these ancient Pompeiians are alive again for us."

"That's true," Gwen said, but she refrained from adding the follow-up to this thought. That the people alive and well on the

tour were just a moment away from death, too. That the only difference between the plaster-figure woman and Hester or Aunt Bea
or Gwen herself was the air in their lungs and the fact that their facial expressions could still change.

Connie Sue passed by Gwen and paused with her to examine
the people—the human fossils, really—through the windows of
the enclosure. She then turned her gentle gaze on Gwen and whispered, "It's sad, isn't it, honey? There's that saying, most people—
or maybe it's just most women—live lives of quiet desperation.
Here, all of their regrets are etched on their faces."

Gwen met her eye, bobbed her head in agreement and exhaled
. . . because she *could*. Because she wasn't yet petrified in ash.

After the morning tour, there was a split. Whoever was tired and
wanted to go back to the hotel would be sent back via train from
Naples. Hans-Josef, in a hired van, would transport them to the
train station and have a large cab at the ready to meet them at the
station in Rome, returning them to the hotel by early afternoon.
Also, at the Naples station, he would be picking up the passengers
who'd slept in late or who'd spent the morning meandering
through the streets of Rome but who now wanted to join the afternoon jaunt to the Isle of Capri. So, he would be gone for a couple
of hours taking care of this exchange.

Heat and fatigue claimed quite a few of the early birds: Hester,
the honeymooners Sally and Peter, even Connie Sue and Alex.
But Aunt Bea professed herself to be as energized as ever, and
Gwen had heard of the island but knew little about it. Well, nothing about it, actually, besides what she'd read in the tour company's brochure. The accompanying photo had succeeded in
piquing her curiosity, though, and she felt a surprising burst of for-
titude as the moment to depart for the latter half of the day's excursion approached. She felt, most oddly, as if something momentous
was on the verge of happening.

It did not, however, appear to be happening with any immediacy.

In fact, the bus ride with Guido to the Amalfi Coast, while providing breathtaking views, was still somewhat tiring, even with
Gwen knowing she'd get a few hours respite from being under the

watchful gaze of Hans-Josef and, thus, no teasing or suggestive remarks from her aunt. Gwen was under the mistaken impression
that she could finally sink into her seat and relax. She pulled out
her iPod and found the songs on her Andrew Lloyd Webber
playlist, but she'd only made it halfway through the title track
from *Starlight Express* before Aunt Bea nudged her.

"Look at the scenery, Gwennie! It's beautiful, isn't it?"

Gwen removed one earbud and nodded. "Yes. Lovely." She put
the tiny headphone back in her ear and continued listening, her
eyes drifting shut at the soothing, familiar melody . . . until her
aunt nudged her again.

"This day is just gorgeous! And Italy is zipping by us outside.
Don't you want to *see* it, my dear? Don't you want to *interact* with it?"

Gwen regretfully set down her iPod, removing both earbuds
this time and clicking off the music in an attempt to give her aunt
the attention she needed. It wasn't that Aunt Bea wanted Gwen
to interact with Italy inasmuch as she wanted Gwen to interact
with *her*.

"I have been seeing it and it's gorgeous," she told her aunt
truthfully. "I spent the morning looking at everything, and now
we're headed on a lovely drive to Sorrento. It's all been very pretty
from the bus window. Very interesting." Although she refrained
from explaining that she still felt detached from Europe somehow.
Even with the fascinating history lessons. Even with everything
she'd read or heard about it through the years. She couldn't quite . . .
connect.

"Yes! The world is *out there*, you know! You need to keep your
eyes open. Get to know the people. Embrace the wonder of Europe," Bea insisted, unable to disguise the mild reprimand in her
voice. But then, Bea was an extrovert. It did little good to tell her
that the world was *in here*, too. That it was also in Gwen's private
and deliciously solitary communion with her favorite music. That
the swell of the orchestral strings calmed her soul and gave her a
shot of rejuvenation. Enough to keep her going through the
energy-draining *interactions* she was having with all of those people
out there.

Only when, in spite of herself, Aunt Bea finally dozed off for the last ten minutes of their drive did Gwen get a bit of that needed recovery time. A couple of songs from *Evita* were just enough to help her transition to the next phase of their travel journey.

A hydrofoil to Capri awaited them on the coast—a little vessel they shared with a handful of others from a different tour. It would be a while still before Hans-Josef made it to the island, but Guido was going with them and he'd said watercrafts—either hydrofoils or ferries—departed every half hour or so. He also said it would only take them about twenty minutes to traverse the Gulf of Naples from the town of Sorrento, on the exquisite Italian coast-line, to the gorgeous island City of Capri, where they'd get to pass the afternoon and early evening. Gwen was eager to be on the water.

Upon docking, Aunt Beatrice, Zenia and Matilda professed un-bearable starvation and, as this was their late lunch stop, Gwen was talked into going out to eat first and exploring the island second.

"You should slow down. Savor your meal," Matilda instructed, reminding Gwen of her friend Kathy's frequent advice. Matilda demonstrated by expertly swirling her spaghetti marinara and spearing a fat portabello mushroom with the tip of her fork. She placed them both into her mouth and chewed, a wave of rapture washing over her face.

Gwen raised her eyebrows and studied her rigatoni. It wasn't swirlable but, just so she wouldn't get any further lectures from Bea or her aunt's friends, she tried to make a showing of euphoria when it came to eating her lunch.

The little café was situated nicely on an outdoor patio with a view of the island's main port, Marina Grande, on one side and the floral-covered hills on the other. The display of colors was awe-inspiring—vivid reds, brilliant pinks, royal purples, lush greens, deep blues. These tropical flowers ("Bougainvillea," Matilda said, correcting her when she commented on them) were everywhere, adding an air of festivity to their luncheon.

Much as Gwen considered it a pleasant pastime to sit and look at the sea and landscape, she found herself anxious to actually walk in it. *Interact* with it, as her aunt would say. So when Bea, Zenia and Matilda wanted to linger over coffee and discuss their favorite prime numbers, a topic that arose periodically in the S&M club, Gwen elected to wander off on her own on the pretense of trying to get a picture of the famed Blue Grotto.

"Just be careful you don't slip," Aunt Bea instructed. "There are lots of stairs. Probably more than three hundred thirteen." Her favorite prime was 313.

Zenia consulted her watch. "And don't forget, Hans-Josef is meeting us in the little harbor area here"—she waved her hand in the general direction of the small square near the water, populated by cafés and shops—"in four hours, or approximately two hundred and forty-one minutes," she added, showing off, since 241 was prime, too. "If you miss the boat back, you'll have to stay on the island all night."

Matilda rolled her eyes. "She would not. She'd just take a later hydrofoil to Sorrento—I believe there's one at about 6:07," she said, raising a victorious eyebrow at her clever insertion of *her* favorite prime. "But she'd miss the bus ride back to Rome and would have to get to the hotel another way. Probably by train." She paused. "That could be interesting, though."

"Do you think maybe one of those handsome Italian men on those cute motor scooters could zip her back to Rome?" Aunt Bea speculated. "I've always wanted to ride on one of those things. A strapping young Roman with a full head of black hair, tanned olive skin and a rippling set of abs that I'd hold on to as he steered us through—"

"Okay, then!" Gwen interrupted, having had quite enough of her aunt's romantic fantasy. "I won't be late, and I'll see you ladies later." She backed away from their café table with a wave and a smile. "Enjoy your coffee."

She heard them chuckling behind her as she skirted away but, for a few hours at least, she was independent and free.

In the past few days, Gwen had been exposed to more famous sites than she could count, although, being a child of a mathematically inclined family, she *tried* to count them. That afternoon, however, proved to be a different experience for her. Although she'd put the Blue Grotto on her checklist for the day, she couldn't find anything else that approached that level of touristy fascination on the Isle of Capri. A motorboat tour beginning in Marina Grande took her on a short visit to the smaller harbor, Marina Piccola, and then into the Blue Grotto, where tourists practically had to lie on the bottom of the boat in order to be rowed into the little cave.

It was interesting. She snapped a picture or two—it really *did* look blue in there—and she could see why the locals avoided it for so many years before finally investing in its tourist potential. Apparently, legend had it that the little grotto was inhabited by witches and monsters. Gwen didn't see any of those. She did, however, spot the Britsicles near the landing back in the main harbor. Hmm. Hans-Josef must have arrived on the island with the others from the tour.

She wandered around Marina Grande for a few minutes alone and came upon a funicular—a tramlike thing—that took visitors up to the village of Capri. She was told there was a chairlift that could cart passengers up even farther, to the very top of the island, where she could visit the Belvedere of Tragara, a panoramic promenade lined with expensive villas.

She shrugged at that news. She was curious about the promenade, not about the villas. Not the expensive newer villas or the ruins of the Imperial Roman ones, which were also considered an attraction on the island. Capri may have been a resort since the time of the Roman Republic (a helpful historical tidbit gleaned from Guido on the boat ride over), but it was the scenery not the houses that intrigued her.

And, possibly, it was that very thing—the overwhelming amount of nature on Capri, not merely a collection of old disintegrated stone buildings—that finally succeeded in fully capturing her curiosity and raising her wonderment to the nth degree. Had the island always been this picturesque? This vibrant, leafy and bright? She'd lived her entire life in Iowa, taking a few short trips here or there, but certainly not traveling anywhere a Midwesterner would consider exotic. She'd never even gone to Florida for spring break or to Mexico for a girlfriend's bachelorette party or to Jamaica for any reason whatsoever. She'd never seen anything like this island paradise, aside from photos or TV shows, and truly felt herself to be a stranger in a strange—but stunningly beautiful— land.

She rode the funicular up to the village and window-shopped for a while, trying to decide if the promenade was worth a visit, when she spotted a young girl giggling on a path nearby. Capri had staircases crisscrossing the island from top to bottom—the hardiest walkers didn't need a tram or a chairlift—and Gwen knew instinctively, from the girl's familiarity with the path, that this child was a resident not a tourist. She was about eleven, maybe twelve years old. Dark hair, curling at the tips, flowed behind her as she skipped down the stairs. A man, probably her father, and holding a paper sack filled with something, trailed behind her.

Gwen edged closer to the walkway so she could see what the child was doing. She watched as the girl's strong, tanned legs carried her down the stairs with the speed of a baby gazelle. The child was racing the wind, laughing as she descended. Flinging her arms out to the sides and, then, above her head, and catching a few crimson bougainvillea petals with her grasping fingers.

An embodiment of youth. And joy. And life.

Gwen wanted to be a part of it, too.

By the time she'd reached the path, the girl and her father were gone, but Gwen looked down the staircase and took a few tester hops in descent. Her sneakers may have been dust covered after wandering around Rome and Pompeii, but they were still new and cushiony. She sprang down the next set of steps, the air filling her lungs as she swallowed a whoop of delight at the dizzying rush of wind on her face and the roller-coaster flip of her belly. It was a carnival ride, only it was under her power to set the speed of the drop.

She paused and glanced from left to right on the path, breathing hard, although not from fatigue; after all, she did a forty-five-minute spin class every weekday. She could see no one in any direction and she hoped the reverse was also true. In some ways she felt like a girl on the school playground who'd just discovered a fantastical piece of equipment, brand-new to the children. A vertical merry-go-round-like thing, where the riders spun wildly and, then, straightened into a line and plummeted down an open slide.

Gwen spun once in place—she remembered doing things like this as a kid!—and then plunged down the stairs again in a giddy, light-headed flight to the level below. The flowers blurred by in a swirl of dazzling pastels as she whisked past them. She might be hovering at the dangerous age of thirty, but when she did this sprint against the air currents and the tropical breeze, she felt young. *Alive!* A thrilling feeling she hadn't remembered experiencing since she was as little as that dark-haired girl.

She wiped a few beads of sweat off her forehead and took a moment to feel the sun warming her cheeks, her heart beating and sending blood pumping through her limbs, her lungs breathing in the floral-scented air, her feet solidly on the paved staircase. Then she laughed to herself and flew down another set of steps, as if the wind might really catch her this time.

She couldn't say how long she did this. A half hour? An hour? She felt only a fleeting dance of time, rippling across the dimensions of space and making her lose track of it. So strange for her! She resisted the familiar urge to check her watch and, instead, bounded down another flight, laughter bubbling from her lips.

Finally, her spellbinding game was broken by a swift movement, caught in her peripheral vision. A flash of color that didn't originate from the island's natural flora. It was yellow. Gwen turned to look at it. The yellow was a sleeve that turned out to be attached to the bright soccer jersey the young British-Indian boy, Ani, was wearing. The teen was waving to her from a café patio several yards away, grinning. She grinned back at him and lifted a hand in a corresponding wave but, before she could let herself reveal the full extent of her joy in this gorgeous day, her gaze caught another couple of faces—Ani's father and Hans-Josef, the latter of whom was eyeing her rather confusedly. The two of them were standing beside a table, chatting with each other, and Gwen felt, uncomfortably, that she'd been under surveillance by the trio. She smiled tightly and turned to slip away—more serenely in departure than in arrival—but it appeared she'd overlooked yet another grouping.

The Britsicles, forever joined at the hip, it seemed, were sitting at a café table with those *same two men* again! That sandy-haired one who'd winked at her and the other guy, a little shorter in stature and with darker hair. Jeez, were they everywhere?

Gwen was increasingly certain that the two ladies had picked up these guys by the Trevi Fountain the other day. The women had awakened Gwen briefly with their inconsiderate door slamming and their laughter at three a.m. when they returned from their evening out in Rome, as their room was adjacent to Gwen and Bea's and hotel walls were thin.

At the moment, however, the women clearly took in Gwen's now-tangled hair and her body, glowing from perspiration and the thrill of sailing down the stairs, and they visibly winced at her unsightliness. Gwen involuntarily reached up to smooth her hair, but still the women gawked at her as one might stare at an unsuspecting cockroach prancing around in one's kitchen. Their desire to squash her with a handy shoe was palpable.

Gwen slowly let the oxygen drain from her lungs. She felt child*ish*, suddenly, not child*like*. Spied upon by people who were judging her and finding her lacking. That was what happened when she tried to just let go and live. People looked down on her and criticized—silently, if not aloud. And worst of all, when a person was living freely, when she thought the world was beautiful and wonderful and awe-inspiring, bad stuff happened to wreck it, covering the happiness in a blanket of gray ash, like an angry Vesuvius. And if that person wasn't prepared, if she didn't run away long before the destruction hit, if she made the mistake of keeping her heart open . . . then she'd be left in shock. Gasping for air.

Out of the corner of her eye, she saw Hans-Josef motioning for her to come join them, but she pretended not to notice this. The two women at the table regarded her with irritation and proprietary glances at their tour guide, while the two men she didn't know (who *were* these Italians?) had swiveled around in their seats and were observing her with surprised interest. Kamesh, the

British-Indian father, appeared merely impatient to regain Hans-Josef's attention. Only the teenage boy seemed capable of both sharing her moment and, yet, not interfering with it. So, she smiled directly at Ani once more, and then waved blindly at the group, before continuing her descent to a level beyond their sight.

She spent the remaining time before departure wandering alone through the lower paths near the harbor, not allowing herself to be tempted again by those magnificent island staircases. Instead, she meandered in and out of a bunch of shops and even purchased a small pastry at a little food stand as a treat.

Although the sun was just as bright as before, the sky and the water just as sapphire blue, the flowers even more vibrant than one of Zenia's African-woven tunics, Gwen couldn't recapture the giddiness she'd felt when she'd raced down the steps. The world she'd shrugged off her shoulders for that precious hour had settled back on her again.

Finally, it was time to meet the others at the dock and board the hydrofoil back to Sorrento, en route to Rome. Gwen sighed when she saw the two men from the café still walking beside Cynthia and Louisa. She knew it was unrealistic, but she couldn't help but wish the four of them could have accidentally missed the return trip with the group and wound their way back to Rome by some other method. They were all making her feel so uncomfortable. And the men, while somewhat less tanned than many of their fellow Italians, certainly had a confident and competent air about them. Surely, they could figure out some alternate mode of transportation, maybe stopping off at a nightclub on their way back, falling asleep on the couch of one of their buddies' apartments, making the women miss tomorrow morning's bus ride to Florence. Well, okay, Gwen knew she wouldn't get *that* lucky, but she could hope, right?

However, all thought of getting out of a hydrofoil ride with the unbreakable foursome was put to rest when Hans-Josef shepherded the group onto the watercraft and addressed them all.

"Welcome" (or, rather, "Velcome"), he said, "to the final members of our tour. We have three people who just arrived from England yesterday, and some of you Americans have not yet been in-troduced to them. Here is Colin Pickering—" He pointed to a hunched-over old man who couldn't have been younger than eighty-something. Gwen hadn't noticed him before, but the man, apparently befriending Matilda, had been in the midst of chatting with her when their tour guide began speaking. Colin smiled somewhat vacantly at the group and snapped a few photos of Hans-Josef and the receding island before returning his attention to Matilda.

"Hello, Colin!" a few of the tour members chorused.

"And, also, we have a pair of brothers," Hans-Josef continued. "Ralph and Henry Edwards."

At this point, several of the tour members—mostly British but a few Americans, too—shouted, "Emerson! Thoreau! Here, here!" Others laughed, and the two men each bowed their heads like ac-tors at a play's finale. None of these reactions made sense to Gwen, although with a wave of embarrassment and more than a little un-easiness, she realized those two men were not, in fact, Roman playboys that the Britsicles had picked up on the town yesterday.

She leaned toward her aunt. "Are those guys British members of your club? Why's everyone calling them those names?" She'd been trying to whisper, but the noise of the vessel on the choppy Gulf water made complete discretion impossible. One of the men, the one with the sandier hair and the more pronounced expression of amusement on his face (some might call it smirking), overheard her.

He raised an eyebrow, stepped near her and said, " '*In the pres-ence of nature, a wild delight runs through the man, in spite of real sor-rows.*' "

Gwen blinked at him.

"The immortal words of Ralph Waldo Emerson," the man ex-plained with a distinct English accent and a knowing wink of one golden hazel eye. "My namesake." He patted his chest with his palm and then reached out with it to shake her hand. "I'm Ralph Waldo Edwards, but my friends all call me Emerson."

"Gwendolyn Reese," she murmured, her fingers shaking

slightly at the firmness of his grip. The intensity of his gaze wasn't calming either. "Gwen."

He hitched a thumb in the direction of the darker-haired man. "Gwen, this is my elder brother, Henry David Edwards, also known as Thoreau."

Thoreau extended his palm as well, his handshake gentler than his younger brother's and not nearly as disquieting. "Our mum has always been keen on philosophy," he explained. "Pleasure to meet you, Gwen," he added, his tone lacking some of the animation of Emerson's, but she appreciated the more peaceful sensation of his presence.

"And you as well," she said.

Cynthia, evidently concluding that these introductions had taken long enough, fiddled with her digital camera for a moment before summoning the Edwards brothers with two of her fingers and the sharp word, "Gentlemen." Then, in an attempt to temper the directness of her command, she laughed in that fake show of delight people put on when they want to appear good humored. She motioned for them to view the screen on her camera. "At our club's last dinner in Surrey," she said, purposely excluding not only Gwen but all of the Americans present. She laughed again. "Isn't this one funny?"

The brothers looked at it and laughed.

Gwen imagined someone must've been doing a Highland jig on a barstool or something equally outrageous—while dressed in a kilt or, possibly, wearing nothing at all—to warrant Cynthia's level of gaiety. And her dear friend Louisa looked on over Thoreau's shoulder, getting much closer to him than absolutely necessary.

Gwen shot a look at her aunt. Beatrice's face registered only surprise and enjoyment in the scene, as if relishing a rather juicy soap-opera episode. This was not the disapproval Gwen had expected. (Wasn't Louisa *married?*) No. Her aunt wouldn't be overly concerned about such conventions. Not when there was fun to be had, sunshine to bask in and romantic entanglements to observe. What had Davis said? Something about this being like good cable for the people in their club?

Yeah. It was like Gwen had walked onto the set of *The Bold and the Beautiful: Italian-Style* this summer. And, try as she might, it didn't look as though she'd get out of watching an extended episode, live and in person. She hoped she could keep a nice, safe distance from the cast—and that no one would try to drag her into playing a role, too.

Because the return trip to the hotel would take them over two hours, their group stopped for dinner in scenic Sorrento, and Gwen finally got a taste of Southern Italian nightlife in the form of a hopping *ristorante* and bar.

"Yoo-hoo! Bread basket. Send it this way," Zenia commanded, flagging down Matilda, who was sitting at the opposite end of the long, picnic-bench-style table that seated their current crew of fifteen.

"Stop waving your impatient little arms," Matilda shot back but, nevertheless, passed the basket to Ani, who handed it to Davis, who sent it along to a few other people until it finally reached its eager recipient.

Gwen was positioned somewhat unfortunately between Kamesh on her left (nice man but engrossed in an hour-long conversation on chess strategies with Davis, Guido and his son Ani) and Louisa on her right (less nice and, also, alternately focused only on the dark-haired Edwards brother, Thoreau, who sat to her right, and on Hans-Josef, who was next to Thoreau at the head of the table). This left Gwen with few conversational outlets. It did, however, provide her with ample opportunity to observe Cynthia, seated directly across from Gwen, in full flirtation mode with Emerson, who was wedged between Cynthia and Zenia—the latter of whom had perched herself at Hans-Josef's right elbow and was shooting questions at the Austrian about upcoming activities during the tour.

"I wanna get my hands on some of that Yorkshire wool, you know the kind I mean? That premium raw fleece. Some natural. Some spun and dyed. Are we gonna have time to get in some decent shopping when we get to England?" Zenia pointed her butter

knife at their leader which, though she was only pausing in between buttering her roll, appeared rather threatening to the poor
tour guide.

"I will see what can be arranged," Hans-Josef said quickly, leaning back from the offending weapon.

Gwen smothered a grin and looked away, only to have her gaze
collide with Emerson's. He, too, was grinning. But at *her*. She immediately glanced in the other direction, down the table toward
where her aunt was sitting across from Matilda. But, while Gwen
knew she would have been welcome to immerse herself in their
conversation, whatever it might have been, she was seated too far
away to believably join in.

Cynthia, who'd quite literally perfected the art of giving Gwen
the cold shoulder, had angled her body so her sleeveless right arm
was facing Gwen but the rest of her was pivoted toward Emerson.
She was chattering at him like a yapping magpie about something
(wanting to buy leather boots in Florence, perhaps?), and he was
nodding slowly while eating and, with increasing frequency, scanning the table for a more interesting topic. Gwen didn't blame
him, but she wished he'd stop looking at her.

The waiter had just refilled his wineglass, and Emerson was
tracing the stem with his fingertip as Cynthia moved on to her
shopping wants and needs in Venice.

". . . and when we get there, the first thing I intend to do after
the obligatory gondola ride is purchase some more Murano glass
jewelry," Cynthia said, sounding so world-weary and sophisticated
that Gwen felt like a country bumpkin sitting across from her. "I
already have a millefiori bracelet and a necklace from my last visit.
This time, I shall get earrings."

Automatically, Gwen reached up and checked the earrings she
loved best—the pearl ones her mom had once worn—making sure
they were still secure. Even though she was far less attached to the
pair Richard had given her on her birthday and wouldn't have worried quite so often about losing one of those in Europe, she'd left
his gift at home. Her mom's earrings were a touchstone for her.
She couldn't give them up for over a month.

Her motion, however quick, did not escape Emerson's notice. He lifted a curious eyebrow at Gwen as Cynthia blathered on. Then, in a move so swift and unexpected, he pushed himself to standing, interrupting Cynthia midsentence, and he raised his wineglass to the group. Even Kamesh stopped talking about castling in chess long enough to listen.

"I say, my fellow travelers—" he began in a mesmerizing and semistagey voice. "We are living under the reign of Bacchus on this land. The god wrapped in grapes, warmed by the sweet kiss of the Italian sun and fermented into a drink suitable for deities. We will no doubt commence our own festival of pleasure with a taste of this tangy nectar." He raised his glass higher. "And under the guidance of our fearless leader"—he nodded respectfully at Hans-Josef, who nodded back with some bemusement—"we will prepare ourselves for the diversions and the delights of an adventure." He smiled, visibly pleased by the effect of his speech on his listeners. Then, concluding with a rhyming couplet, which sounded to be of his own creation, he said:

"Celebrate, friends! Let wine flow through our veins,
Until no sting of memory remains."

Thoreau leaned back somewhat dangerously in his chair and laughed aloud. "You're so full of rubbish, baby brother. Sit down."

Emerson, clearly accustomed to friendly antagonism from his elder sibling, did nothing of the sort. Instead, he again addressed the group. "Ignore this wretched beast, good people of Surrey and Dubuque! Raise your glasses with me and toast the start of our grand tour."

"Here, here!" Dr. Louie roared from the other end of the table.

Zenia clapped and raised her wineglass enthusiastically.

Hans-Josef squinted at Emerson, plainly unsure as to what to make of this pronouncement.

And Thoreau himself leaped up this time, his own wineglass in his hand and a counterproposal on his lips.

"I will drink to the good people of Surrey and Dubuque," he said, with a theatrical tone to match that of his brother's. "I will drink to our helpful guide and to the start of our merry journey. I will not, however, heap praise upon your idol Bacchus, for he stirs up only trouble, little brother, and you well know it."

Emerson grinned wickedly at him and seemed intent on needling him further. "Agh. Another of your boring theories, Thoreau. You know not of what you speak. You serve only to dampen the fun of the rest of us journeyers."

"It is *you* who knows not of what you speak," Thoreau shot back with mocking melodrama. "Have you already forgotten your history? Your geography? Do not play the fool when you are well aware that we stand in the shadow of the mighty Mount Vesuvius. It is long believed that God punished poor Pompeii by burying it because of the sins of its Bacchanalian worshippers—like you." He chuckled and pointed an accusatory finger at his brother as the rest of the group laughed with him. "The drinking. The erotically charged lifestyle. The scandalous art. You all know what I'm talking about."

Ah, yes, they did.

Everyone at the table mimicked gasping in shock (though they could scarcely restrain their delight) at the mere mention of the eroticism in Pompeii. Thoreau was, of course, referring to The House of the Vettii, home of the two wealthy Vettius brothers, which featured a lush garden courtyard with columns, astonishing frescoes of naked cupids and a particularly evocative painting of Priapus—the famed ancient god of sex and fertility—who was poised in the entranceway, and for all of eternity, weighing his enormous phallus on a scale. Even though the Edwards brothers hadn't gone on the morning's excursion to Pompeii, it was clear they'd been there before and seen every suggestive piece of art on display.

While on the tour, Gwen had glanced away out of awkwardness at the erotic images a few times, surprised that a place so desolate in many ways could contain this startling artwork. But she nevertheless remembered the paintings vividly and blushed at the recollection.

"Well, then," Thoreau said to the group with a barely repressed smirk, "you all see the wisdom in listening to me over my misguided sibling."

Emerson took the taunting in stride and parried with a retort that, in no uncertain terms, called into question his big brother's virility. Thus, the games were set in motion.

It soon became obvious to Gwen that while the theater may not have been either of their full-time professions (what did these men *do* anyway?), the Edwards brothers had a natural knack for performing and grew animated at the prospect of debating differing points of view for the entertainment and enlightenment of their peers. She found herself spellbound by the spirited argument between these "philosophers."

Much as she appreciated the older members of the tour, these two men injected something intense, youthful and disquietingly sensual into their structured little trip. They made the nucleus of the tour group more unstable somehow, but infinitely more energetic and interesting. It was like introducing a couple of new electrons into an atom's orbit and forever changing the nature of the element. She could feel Hans-Josef's command of the group slipping away as fast as golden sands inside an antique hourglass. His precise explanations of European history would not be forgotten, of course, but they would be reduced by this new powerful duality of leadership, one in which he was no longer one of the leaders.

When the waiters returned to clear their plates and serve coffee, the brothers made a show of shaking hands across the table and, at last, sitting down. Their audience clapped, cheered and raised their hot espressos in tribute. Emerson and Thoreau soon shifted from their theatrics into a more inclusive discussion of mah-jongg and the art of *smooshing* tiles. Anyone who wanted to could take part in their open debate. Gwen had nothing whatsoever to contribute to this exchange, but she enjoyed watching. Listening. Breathing in the conversation like a fresh and unexpectedly invigorating scent. Like the sweetness of a distinctive new wine.

And Emerson, though he didn't speak a word to her personally at the *ristorante*, looked over his shoulder at her when they were preparing to leave and winked at her again.

The beat of her pulse seemed to amplify in her brain and body, but she forced herself not to look away. To smile in response. And to accept it as the gift it was.

Sure, there would still be talk of historical dates, soap operas and strategy games, but having witnessed Emerson and his brother take the stage together, the promise of Europe's magic became spectacularly alive for Gwen. With it, came a rush of passion that had been stirred on Capri but had been in danger of returning to stillness again. And it would have, had she encountered only crumbling buildings, staid conversation and the silent weight of dead history on the mainland.

Instead, that slight awakening had been strummed to greater rousing, making everything in the air around her vibrate like a vigorously plucked string. She could almost hear the notes of her heightened senses humming.

And she had these two men to thank for that.

The bus ride back to the Hotel Adriatica for their last night in Rome was uneventful but, for Gwen, something essential had changed. She felt x-rayed by Emerson and Thoreau—scanned by both of them as they passed her in the hotel lobby—and prodded with questions by Aunt Bea, who, just as soon as they got to the room, wanted to know what she thought of the Edwards brothers. But Gwen refused to assume that anything she saw meant more than it probably did. At least not to anyone but her.

She only knew that, in the parallel universe of the tour world, and heading as they were into their next day's adventure to Florence, there was a quivering excitement within her that she couldn't control. She didn't know how to tune it to the right pitch so it would ring clear and harmonious and not be jarring to her. But she did know these two brothers were playing a song she'd never heard before that night, and she wanted to hear it again, all the way through.

4

The Birthplace of the Renaissance

Sunday, July 1

Late the next morning, after brunch and, for those who wished to attend, Sunday morning mass (it was *Rome,* after all), they checked out of their hotel and embarked on a three-hour bus ride up to Florence.

Gwen had been sitting with her aunt for the first half of the drive, but Aunt Bea and Matilda launched into a discussion about Sicilian-style cooking when they all got off for a fifteen-minute rest stop. As they returned to the bus, the two older women chose to sit side by side a few seats ahead to continue their conversation for the last leg of the journey and, consequently, Gwen found herself alone, the window to her right her only companion.

A splinter of restlessness jabbed her, making her tap her feet against the unyielding floor. She stared out at the Italian country-side whizzing by and knew they were getting closer to entering the famous Tuscany region. She wasn't sure what, precisely, would distinguish Florence and its surrounding hills and vineyards from any other area in Italy, but she knew this was the home of the Renaissance. In a strange way, it felt like a literal "rebirth" to her, too. True to her promise from the night before in Sorrento, she was finally ready to jump into this trip with both feet. To open herself up to every emotion. To try to embrace the spirit of the adventure.

She exhaled. The moving wheels of the bus beat out a rhythm on the paved roadway. *Staccato-swish-swoosh. Staccato-swish-swoosh.* She felt it in her feet like the pulse of high-decibel bass on a dance floor.

As she unzipped her bag to pull out her iPod, a tall body slipped into the seat beside her. She glanced sharply to her left to identify the intruder. Thoreau.

"Hello," the elder of the two Edwards brothers said. "If I'm disturbing you, I'm happy to move back there." He pointed indistinctly in the direction of some seats a few rows behind them. "But I was bored with my brother's conversation and hoped you might not mind if I joined you for a time."

Gwen swiveled in place until she could look behind her. She spotted Emerson, who was not alone but sitting, instead, with Louisa. Cynthia was in an empty seat just ahead of the other two, which was where Thoreau must have been the moment before. The woman didn't look pleased by his defection. "No, of course not," Gwen said quickly.

"Good!" He smiled at her. "So, what brings you to Europe? A love of sudoku and mah-jongg?"

Gwen swallowed and tried to compose her thoughts. The man didn't waste time admiring the scenery. He seemed to want to dive right into conversation with her. "Not exactly. The trip was a, um, present. From my aunt." She nodded toward where Bea and Matilda were sitting. "It was very kind of her, don't you think?"

Thoreau squinted at her as if looking deep into her soul. "Absolutely." Then, lowering his voice, he added, "But it would have been even kinder had it not been a big surprise, correct? If you would have had more time to get used to the idea."

She shot him a wary glance. How did he know that? "How—" she began.

"Did I know that?" he finished for her.

"Yes."

He grinned. "Perhaps I'm a psychic."

She shook her head. "You're not." Gwen didn't happen to know *anyone* who was a psychic, so it wasn't as though she could deny

Thoreau's claim with any certainty, but she considered that good manners and basic propriety would keep someone who might be a *real* psychic from announcing such a thing in public.

"Fine, you're right," he conceded. "I'm a clinical psychologist."

"Now *that* I believe," Gwen said, finding herself relaxing in his presence in spite of herself. The senior Edwards brother had a very low, soothing voice, which could be dramatic, but, unlike the overly animated tones of his younger sibling, didn't seem to make the tiny hairs on her arms stand up or set her spinal cord tingling. She appreciated this.

"So, are you glad you came regardless? Even though this was not a trip you were expecting to take?"

"I am," she admitted. And then, surprising herself with her own honesty, she told him that, for a few days, she'd found it more overwhelming than fun. "But I'm starting to get into it now."

He just nodded. "People always expect vacations to be easy. That the enjoyment will just happen, with no work involved. I suppose there are places in the world that are fully relaxing. Places that meet the expectation for simple, mindless entertainment. Sitting on a beach somewhere, perhaps, where cocktails are delivered to your lounge chair on the sand, as you soak up the sunlight. That can be pleasant. But a cultural experience, like visiting the great cities of Europe for the first time, is not like that." He picked at the cuticles around his thumbnail for a moment then bit at them. "It's not meant to be, so don't be too hard on yourself. The first time Emerson and I were in Italy, we took naps every afternoon like tots. We were exhausted."

"How old were you then? On that first trip?" she asked, thinking they may have been teens, perhaps, or in their early twenties.

Thoreau laughed. "I admit, we were ten and five—"

"Argh!" Gwen exclaimed.

He held his hand up as if in self-defense. "But my point is that this wasn't like a trip to Grammy's cottage in Chester. We weren't sitting out in the backyard, playing with her baby chicks, taking breaks for teacakes and lemonade. We were hiking through

Roman ruins and wandering around on the rim of Mount Vesuvius. Behind the safety line, I assure you," he explained after glancing at her face and what must have appeared to him to be her horrified expression. "Our parents were very good about giving us a full European adventure, but we always knew we weren't to expect a *relaxing* vacation. Learning experiences are supposed to challenge you."

Well, she certainly felt challenged by Europe, so she must be learning something. "So, why did you come again? That trip you took as children wasn't the last time you were in Italy, was it?"

"No," he said. "Emerson and I have visited the continent several times together, twice with our parents, twice just the two of us and a number of times individually. But every visit is new. I always get something inspiring and revitalizing out of it. And I needed a fresh perspective this summer."

Gwen felt very bold in doing so, but she had to ask, "Why?"

He eyed her curiously and then bobbed his head, as if suddenly deciding to trust her with a big secret. "There's someone . . . back home. And she and I are . . . well, at a crossroads, you might say. I had a month's holiday coming to me, so I took it. I'm using it to step away. To test her. And me." He shrugged. "It's not as though we didn't talk about our issues. We're both psychologists. Practically all we did was talk." He paused and half smiled. "Well, we did a few other things, too. But it wasn't more talking we needed. It was time to think and consider. At least *I* thought so."

"But she disagreed with you," Gwen realized with a start. "She wanted you to stay, right?"

Thoreau sighed. "Yes, yes, she disagreed. Very vocally, I might add. But I still do not believe I'm wrong." He brushed invisible dust off of his black slacks. "I've worked on my issues. She's worked on her issues. But there's still more work to do, you understand? And psychologists—we're especially dreadful. I suspect some eighty-five percent of us go into this field just so we can avoid paying for decades of personal therapy." He pointed his index finger at Gwen. "Just so you know, I may have had a number of horribly self-destructive past relationships and some latent paternal power-struggle problems, but that doesn't mean I'm remotely like a commitmentphobe."

She blinked at him. "Okay."

"Furthermore, I was married once, which was more than Amanda ever was, so . . . there's that."

"Your girlfriend's name is Amanda?" Gwen guessed.

He exhaled. "Yes. And on top of it all she has to have some prissy, girly name. Really, the woman drives me crazy in every single way. Even the way she puts away her clothes is irritating. She likes those little scented sachets with the satin and the lace. And, you know, I find them when I pull my shirts and pants out of the drawer. My boxers smelling like bloody Pomegranate Passion." He paused and appeared to be thinking back on what he'd just said. Replaying it. "Would you consider that an inappropriate disclosure?"

Gwen tried to shake her head but didn't quite manage it. "Well, um . . ."

"Yes, yes, I'm working on that. So sorry. Anyway, that's precisely the reason I'm here on this trip. For perspective."

"And your brother?" she asked. "What's his reason? Is he escaping some very girly person in England, too?"

"Oh, no. The bugger was just bored with London in summer. Too many tourists, he claimed, and not enough new theater."

"He's an actor then," she said, as a statement not a question. She *knew* it!

Thoreau laughed and shot a glance over his shoulder at his brother, who paused in his conversation with the two British women, raised his eyebrows at Gwen and Thoreau and studied their faces with visible suspicion.

"No. Not at all. At least not in the way you mean," Thoreau said, still looking with amusement at his brother.

Emerson narrowed his hazel eyes dangerously.

"What then does he do . . . uh, normally?" Gwen whispered, turning in her seat and glancing uneasily between the two Edwards brothers.

"He would say it wasn't only what he *did* but what he *didn't* do. Not merely where he *was* but, also, where he *wasn't*. That's a boff for you. A bloody theoretical physicist. Always spouting that genius relativity rubbish and talking in circles. Pain in the bum, if you ask me."

She leaned a little closer to Thoreau and pivoted slightly so Emerson, whose gaze was trained on them like a teacher surveying the naughty kids in detention, couldn't read her lips. "He's a physicist? For real?"

"Indeed. A true boffin. What you Americans might call a geek or nerd." Thoreau moved a couple of inches nearer to her and added, "He's a lecturer and a fellow at Queen Mary, part of the Uni of London, and he has three months holiday now, but my salary is higher." He flashed a triumphant look at her. "Emerson and Cynthia are colleagues at the college, which is how we ended up being part of the sudoku and mah-jongg group in Surrey. She talked him into joining, and he talked me into joining, just to try to get even with me." He grinned and raised his voice slightly. "I used to whoop him in chess when we were lads, and he's never forgiven me for it."

Emerson scowled at his brother.

"He was a piss-poor player back then," Thoreau said, lowering his voice but enunciating carefully. Perhaps so his lips would be easy to read.

Gwen had no doubt whatsoever that Emerson knew exactly what his brother was talking about, whether or not he could hear each word clearly. The younger of the two Edwards had crossed his arms and leaned back in his seat with the lethal expression of a viper biding his time before a strike.

Thoreau's grin broadened. He whispered in Gwen's ear, cupping his palm so as to shield his mouth from Emerson's view, "I think, perhaps, we've worried him enough. We ought to sit face forward again."

She nodded and turned back around in her seat.

Thoreau did the same, laughing openly. "I never tire of provoking him," he said. "Sibling rivalry. One of the cornerstones upon which both social hierarchies and economic systems have been built." He looked pleased with himself. "Also, it's even more fun than board games."

Gwen hadn't experienced much of that herself. Her brothers had more than a touch of sibling rivalry between them, but they'd both protectively kept her out of their battles. She recognized it as an attempt at kindness on their part and, perhaps, that they viewed her more as a mother figure than a true sister—she'd certainly taken on that role after their mom died—but she couldn't help but feel excluded, too. Marginal to their good-natured name-calling and semi-abusive floor wrestling. Even now, at twenty-two and twenty-four, Geoffrey and George still loved to play practical jokes on each other on the rare occasions when they were both in the same place at the same time. She suspected, however, that despite the show of antagonism they liked to display, they were actually much closer to each other than she was to either of them. In any case, she'd always envied their relationship.

"I don't think he's just going to forget about your comments, though," she said. "He didn't look especially forgiving."

Thoreau smiled warmly at her. "Naturally. But Emerson's grown too accustomed to having his way. At work. With Mum. Out on the town with the ladies. It's not good for him. He's in need of a good challenge every now and again to keep him stretching. Like playing a strategy game with a master player. A man needs to reach." He thought for a second and said, " '*In the long run, men hit only what they aim at. Therefore, they had better aim at something high.*' " He nudged her gently with his elbow. "Henry David Thoreau. My namesake."

Gwen found herself giggling like a little kid who'd just understood a grown-up joke for the first time. "You two are quite a pair."

"We like to think so," Thoreau said.

When they arrived in Florence that early afternoon, they checked into their new hotel, the four-star Loggia Lucida, just off one of the city's main streets, Lungarno degli Acciaiuoli. Hans-Josef instructed them to have lunch at one of the nearby *trattorias* but to be back in the lobby no later than a quarter to five. They all had reserved tickets to get in to see the famous Michelangelo sculpture *David*, which closed to visitors at 6:50. The bus would collect them at the hotel and take them to and from the Accademia Gallery so they wouldn't miss this Florentine treasure.

Gwen, having spent enough time sitting on the drive up, planned to have just a quick bite to eat or maybe grab a sandwich to go. She longed to explore some of the city, and their hotel was just footsteps away from the beautiful old bridge, the Ponte Vecchio, which crossed the Arno River.

Her flight out of the hotel lobby, however, was intercepted by Emerson.

"So, Gwen," he said, striding up to her and crossing his arms. "What were you and my devil-spawn of a brother talking about so conspiratorially on the bus, hmm?"

She smiled, remembering how pleased Thoreau had been in having something to provoke his younger sibling about and, out of a sense of loyalty to that budding friendship, she refused to divulge what they'd discussed. Emerson was decidedly displeased by this.

"Truly? You intend to be *that* way about it?" He regarded her with mock censure. "Fine. I can clearly see you're someone I'll have to keep a fixed eye on then. I'm afraid I'll be monitoring you more closely. Can't let Thoreau—or you, it seems—get away with this." He sighed heavily and took a step forward.

Gwen raised her eyebrows at him, but she didn't budge. Perhaps because she'd been relaxed, refreshed and oddly recharged, both by being in a new city and by her conversation with his brother, she couldn't help herself from picking up on Emerson's playfulness and responding in kind. Wanting to poke at him, just a tiny bit, the way Thoreau had earlier. "Why, what a surprisingly adolescent reaction, Dr. Edwards."

He rolled his eyes with such blatant childishness she almost laughed aloud. "Oh, he *told* you about that, did he?" Emerson said, half groaning through the sentence. "*He's* a doctor, too, you know, and if I may say so, a little too attached to the title. That show-off needs therapy for his prideful behavior, his oversharing and his obnoxious tendency toward exhibitionism."

At this, she did burst out laughing. Her typical self-consciousness was overthrown by the remarkable absurdity of this statement. "*His* exhibitionism? These are the words of the man who stood up in the middle of a crowded restaurant and proclaimed, 'We are living under the reign of Bacchus,' and then you nattered or prattled—or whatever you Brits say—about how we should all drink to excess and look at more erotic art. Wait, now. Exactly *who* is the exhibitionist here?"

He blinked at her. "That's not at all what I said last night." He paused, considered. "Well, yes, I *did* say that—and how charming of you to have remembered." He winked at her. "But I never natter. Or prattle."

It was her turn to roll her eyes. "You were speaking merely to hear the sound of your own voice. I doubt you meant half of what you said."

A laugh erupted from his lips. " '*My words fly up, my thoughts remain below: Words without thoughts never to heaven go,*' " he quoted. "*Hamlet.*"

"I'm familiar with the play. And I suspect—" she said, further emboldened by his obvious delight in the conversation and the fact that, thanks to her mother's love of English literature and her overflowing home library growing up, at least on the subject of Shakespeare she wasn't a complete neophyte. "I suspect your words at dinner were just as disingenuous as the King's in Act III. But you *were* funny," she conceded. "And Thoreau's retorts were equally amusing."

"Oh, they were not! Mine were far superior." He studied her. "Yes, I was certainly right to question you. You're too easily influenced by my clinically insane brother." He shook his head with faux sorrowfulness. "I see there's only one thing to be done."

"And that is?"

"Keep you away from him. You can no longer be his seatmate on the bus." He wagged his index finger for further emphasis. "And you must be my partner for the museums here in Florence. I'm not giving you a choice. Say yes. Now."

He looked adolescent. So very age thirteen. Not much older than her eighth-grade students in demeanor and, yet, there was no question he was a man, not a boy. It was so humorous to her to see this dichotomy that she couldn't help but keep chuckling.

"That's a yes, is it not? Say it, Gwen." Then he softened, "At least for today, all right?" Another pause. "Please?"

How could she refuse an invitation given so earnestly? She nodded.

He grinned and marched over to Hans-Josef, who was still in the hotel lobby. Emerson politely requested their Accademia tickets. "We shan't be taking the bus," he told the tour guide and Gwen at the same time. "But we shall meet you all there at five."

Hans-Josef shot her a puzzled look, as if waiting for her to protest. But when she didn't, the tour guide just shrugged and said, "As you wish." He handed a couple of paper squares to Emerson and added, "Be mindful of pickpockets."

"We will," Emerson assured him.

They left the hotel with Hans-Josef squinting after them, Zenia, who'd overhead the exchange, nodding at Gwen in approval and even Davis giving her a surreptitious thumbs-up. She had no doubt her aunt would be told of her afternoon plans at once, and with no small amount of merriment.

The Florentine sun accosted them as they strolled down Lungarno degli Acciaiuoli toward the Ponte Vecchio. The Arno River glistened with dappled light as they approached the old bridge. Gwen had been reading up on it. It was built in 1345 by someone named Taddeo Gaddi to replace an earlier version of the bridge, and it used to house butchers until a sixteenth-century Medici, Cosimo I, aka the "Grand Duke of Tuscany," evicted them because he didn't like the smell of raw meat. Instead, he brought in the silversmiths and goldsmiths, and they've occupied the bridge with their trades ever since.

"It's lovely," she murmured, pausing for a moment to admire

the structure, an imposing yet undeniably lovely collection of arched wooden segments spanning the river. The shops from end to end were dotted with colors but, like an Impressionist painting, these were blurred from a distance.

"It's also rather chaotic when you walk onto it," Emerson said. "We shall weave our way across it once and back, so you might get a decent sense of the bazaarlike atmosphere. Then, perhaps, we'll take away something quick at a *mercato*, a food market, and work our way up to the Accademia, yes?"

"Sounds good," she said, allowing him to lead her toward the entrance of the bridge. "Thank you."

As he nodded his "you're welcome," she couldn't help but feel grateful to him for the oddity of this experience. Typically, after having spent so many hours with S&M club members, she would have expected less adventurousness out of herself. More of an intense desire to be alone and to relish the revitalizing power of silence. Yet, Emerson had presented her with a couple of immediate and intriguing bonuses for not lapsing into her old habit of solitude.

First, she'd foolishly neglected to give any thought to safety when she'd bolted toward the hotel exit but, of course, Florence wasn't a city she knew well. Until Hans-Josef had mentioned the pickpockets, she hadn't considered the possibility that she might inadvertently walk away from a safe touristy zone and into a more dangerous neighborhood. She'd read in a book once that there were actually *gypsies* in Florence.

Second, after having conversed with his brother for over an hour on the bus, Ralph Waldo "Emerson" Edwards was even more fascinating to her than he'd been the night before at the Sorrento *ristorante*. And that was saying something. She would have a chance to study him up close for a few hours and, perhaps, discover what it was about him that brought out her curiosity. Much like a square of unknown integers in a game of sudoku, there was an enigmatic quality Emerson possessed that, were it to be identified, it would be similar to figuring out the central mystery number out of a set of nine. It wouldn't take more than an additional hint or two before the entire puzzle could be unlocked. So being with him, Gwen told herself, was almost more mathematical than personal. Something even Richard might understand, were she pressed to explain her interest in the Brit.

But then again, Richard wouldn't be asking any questions because Richard wasn't here. He hadn't even sent her a single e-mail yet!

She exhaled and forced away the irritation, focusing instead on the scenic jumble of man-made items and natural beauty that flashed before her as they walked onto the Ponte Vecchio. There were jewelry shops everywhere, golden charms and necklaces shimmering in the slanting afternoon light. A kaleidoscope of bright colors—scarves, clothing, throw pillows, even a few carnival masks—plus a flash of postcards whirling around on a revolving display.

Gwen found herself taking steps to purposefully engage her senses. Smelling the hot, sun-scorched pavement, which strangely evoked a memory of popcorn, until she realized the scent was coming from one of the nearby vendors. A warm meal of some kind—buttery!—and a not-so-subtle reminder of the lunch she'd skipped. She felt the wondrous and strange pang of *wanting* . . . that rumble of hunger that craved both food and something else as well.

"Mmm," she heard herself murmur.

Despite the noise of the passersby, Emerson heard her and responded. He swiveled in place, glancing over his shoulder at her with a half smile. "Smells heavenly, yes?"

She nodded and tried to pull her mind away from the puzzle of him, again using her senses as bait. The jingle of silver bangles and the tinkling of wind chimes harmonized with the laughing lilt of the Italian language swirling around her. She heard the splash of a stone being thrown into the languorous waves of the Arno and a child's high-pitched giggle. The rustle and patter of fellow tourists, punctuating their walk with an unpredictable syncopation, added an undercurrent of rhythm to the soft hiss of rushing water and the whisper of silk scarves dancing on their secured metal hooks.

"Something catch your fancy?" Emerson asked. "If you want to go into any of the shops, we can. There are some beautiful gold chains for sale. Charm bracelets. Earrings, too." He paused. "Although you seem to like best those pearl ones you have on. You're always wearing them," he observed. "They're lovely."

She reached up to touch them. "Thanks. They're . . . special."

He bobbed his head. "Yes. So, perhaps, a golden, er, roach broach instead?" he suggested, pointing toward a shop that had an unappealing solid-gold cockroach pin in the display window.

She winced.

"Perhaps not, then," he concluded, laughing.

She smiled and studied a few other pieces of jewelry in the window's case. "Oh, there's that Mouth thingy from Rome," she said, before she could stop herself.

But Emerson didn't seem to notice that she'd said something sort of foolish. He leaned forward and surveyed the case. "Certainly. You mean the Mouth of Truth. Yes. *La Bocca della Verità* in pendant form. It's well crafted. Would you like to take a closer look?"

"Oh, I don't know. I probably shouldn't spend money on silly things. And that was . . . such an odd site. My aunt made me put my hand in its mouth," she confided. "Did you and your brother go there, too?"

"We did." He shot a speculative glance at her and hooked his thumb in the direction of the vendor's door. "Come. At least look at the necklace. It's not as though you're required to buy it if you don't like it."

She assented and, just a few minutes later, found herself holding the delicate gold chain and the penny-sized Mouth of Truth pendant in her palm.

"You wear it, yes?" the vendor said hopefully. "I put around your neck." He motioned clasping the golden chain. "And you try.

If you like, you buy. If no"—he shrugged—"then *pfft*. You forget it. Okay?"

"Um," Gwen said.

"Just agree with him," Emerson whispered.

"Yes, sure. Okay," she said, allowing the vendor, an older Italian gentleman who reminded her somewhat of their bus driver, Guido, to slip on the pendant.

It didn't weigh much, really. Every part of the necklace was pure gold, but the chain was very fine and the Mouth thingy, though exquisitely detailed to look like that marble oracle in Rome, was incredibly thin. She found herself rubbing it like a talisman for several moments before she realized that both the vendor and Emerson were grinning at her.

"You do like!" enthused the vendor.

"Well, yes, it's very pretty," she said, reaching to unclasp it. "But I probably should wait to make any purch—"

"Gwen, just a moment," Emerson said. "Before you take it off. You do realize wearing the *Bocca* makes you rather like a human truth teller, right? Not only must you be honest or face the consequences, but everyone else must be honest with you."

She rolled her eyes. "You know that's not true." She reached for the clasp again.

Emerson covered her left hand—the one nearest to him—with his warm fingers, stilling them. Setting even her pulse on pause and stealing her breath.

"It may well be." He moved a couple of steps forward. "And wouldn't that be bloody brilliant? I know I'd love it. That kind of truthfulness."

She blinked at him and, suddenly, he released her hand and stepped back.

"You do like!" the vendor gushed again, interrupting the oddly charged moment between Emerson and her.

And Gwen, to her own surprise, caught herself nodding in agreement with the older Italian. "I do," she added unnecessarily. The man had already pulled out his calculator to compute the cost for her in U.S. dollars versus euros.

After some quick haggling between Emerson and the man, during which Gwen ignored the bargaining and, instead, imagined a universe of required candor, her tour mate whispered that the agreed-upon price was fair. "If you really *do* wish to get it," Emerson told her. "Otherwise, you still are free to walk away, but I believe it will be a great keepsake from this trip. And, you know, I'm holding out hope that it will really have trustworthy and honest oraclelike qualities."

She chuckled briefly as she paid the vendor, who shook her hands with such zeal he got the blood flowing through her shocked fingers again. But the rest of her still felt enchanted by Emerson's presence, and more than slightly unstable. Being around him was like what she'd always envisioned it would be like to be under a spell or in some kind of trance. She still considered herself fully conscious, but she also found herself acting in ways that were not—at least not for her—typical.

Kind of like sleepwalking, she mused, *where everything you're doing is part of a dream. It feels real and you really ARE moving. Just not for the reasons you think.*

As they headed back across the bridge to the street where they'd started, Emerson nudged her and said, "You'll be wearing the necklace for the rest of the day, correct?"

She ran the pad of her thumb over the face of the golden *Bocca.* The feel of it made her emboldened with a kind of courage. "Yes. So?"

"So, you are now bound by the Roman deities and, indeed, by all the gods of Italy to speak the truth." He caught her eye and with a smirk added, "You *have* to tell me what you and my brother were talking about on the bus this morning—or else." He mimed getting a hand chopped off.

She burst with laughter at this, an overly free, nearly giddy eruption that sounded more like her teaching partner Kathy's laugh than her own. "Nice try, wise guy," she told him, in much the same amused-but-firm tone she'd use with a classroom of squirrely eighth graders.

He shrugged. "Well, I had to give it my very best effort, didn't

I?" He pointed down the Via Por Santa Maria, a cross street of Lungarno degli Acciaiuoli. "I'm famished. How about we get some food now?"

"Lead the way," she said.

And he did.

Under his guidance, they strode with unerring precision through the twisty walkways of downtown Florence, reaching San Lorenzo's vast market, next to the church of the same name, and stopping by the well-known Mercato Centrale for prosciutto and provolone sandwiches, Italian lemon-lime sodas and a paper sack filled with small, sweet oranges.

They sat on a bench at the edge of the market and began devouring their late lunch, watching the passersby with curiosity and, on occasion, even commenting on the bustling, colorful scene before them. The day remained bright. Mother Nature and Italian Commerce mingled cheerfully in the square.

Gwen hadn't really taken the time to do this in Rome, as she'd been so focused on seeing the hot tourist spots. But her out-in-nature experience in Capri gave her a taste for more than mere guidebook interactions and an appreciation for the sights and sounds of a local's Italy. A reaction, she had to admit, she hadn't really had until she'd raced down those stairs. Perhaps her aunt had been right at the start of the trip. Maybe she'd been "missing everything good" after all.

Well, not anymore.

After they finished eating, they meandered back and forth, weaving through a flock of leather stalls, packed souvenir carts and potential pickpockets. (Emerson steered her away from a handful of very tactile children that, he later explained, were trained thieves.) Vendors hawked their wares, wanting to sell Gwen everything from a smartly crafted leather purse to a Swiss Army knife to a portrait of herself in watercolor.

She said, "No, thank you" to each of them—she already had a golden Mouth of Truth hanging around her neck after all—and if she wanted to buy additional souvenirs, she'd get them later when she could be sure that they would be meaningful to her.

She sighed, thinking of Richard, though. She had no idea what to bring back for him from Italy. Not that he deserved any special gifts at the moment. She remained puzzled by his lack of communication and, if truth be told (which it must be . . . she was wearing the necklace), she was also tremendously hurt that he hadn't responded.

As they walked nearer to the Cathedral of Santa Maria del Fiore, with its famous Duomo—the enormous cupola that defined the Florentine skyline—and reached the Piazza della Signoria, there were still more leather goods to be found, including belts, sandals, wallets. This time she studied them with a bit more care and with Richard in mind.

Emerson, it turned out, was rather tempted by these manly items himself.

"What do you think of this?" he asked her, trying on a finely tooled brown leather belt with a gold-plated buckle that was shaped to resemble the mouth and tongue of a cobra.

"Uh . . ." she began, surprised to see him lifting his shirt so he could slip the belt around his waist. He had a very fit waist, she noticed. And just the lightest dusting of hair on his lower abdominals. Not that she stared at it for long. He pulled the shirt down again so very quickly, but—

"Gwen?"

"Right. The belt," she mumbled. "Were you, by chance, born in the Year of the Snake?"

He shook his head. "Year of the Tiger. Or so say the place mats at my favorite Chinese takeaway spot in London."

"Oh. Well, you're definitely making a . . . slithering statement with that one."

His hips were kind of lean, too. And the way he draped the belt around them was . . . huh. She tried not to dwell on this, but the phrase "undeniably sexy" flashed through her mind more than once. More than twice, if she were to be honest. (Again, a requirement of the necklace.)

"Hmm. Perhaps not, then." He put it back and, for a moment,

she was relieved. But a minute later he reached for another brown belt, this one featuring a leopard or some kind of mountain cat.

"Yes! That one," she said, before he could even put it on. Close enough to a tiger for her! "I think that one will look great. Really. Just get it."

He squinted at her. "Let's not run astray, darling. I appreciate how you've embraced Florentine shopping so very enthusiastically, but I need to make sure this fits my body."

The way he drew attention to his body gave her an unwelcome shiver. She was altogether too aware of it already. Uncomfortably so. To distract herself, she averted her glance and looked, instead, at her watch—4:36. Oh, jeez. They had less than twenty-five minutes to hike up to the Accademia Gallery to meet their group for the tour.

"We're cutting it close on time, Emerson," she said, projecting a sense of urgency as she spoke, "if we're going to get to the *David* by five."

"Oh, right." He slid the new belt through the loops of his khaki slacks and fastened it. "Take a look-see. Yes?"

"Absolutely!" she said with a zealousness that was almost feverish. She barely allowed her gaze to rest on any part of his lower body. "It's perfect. And . . . and it even matches what you're wearing. So, buy it and let's go! It's Michelangelo time."

He stared at her. "Remind me never to give you an entire soda again. You're overactive from all the sugar, I think." Nevertheless, he paid for his purchase and they made quick work of hoofing it to the gallery.

Hans-Josef and their tour group were already at the entrance, just waiting for the exact time of their reservation to be let into the building. As she and Emerson approached them, Gwen could hardly escape the raised eyebrows of interest from many of the tour members (particularly Aunt Bea), the squint of shared disapproval from Cynthia, Louisa and even their tour guide and, finally, the twist of amusement on Thoreau's lips.

Emerson, either for reasons of fairness and a desire not to budge in line or because he wished to avoid his brother—Gwen wasn't sure which—marched them to the very end of the line and, after a brief wave at Thoreau and the Britsicles, literally turned his back on them and continued his conversation with Gwen.

"So, what did you think of Michelangelo's other sculptures? The *Pietà* and the *Moses* in Rome?" he asked.

"Mmm. Nice," she murmured while, inwardly, she groaned. Half the planet seemed to be caught up in a love affair with Michelangelo Buonarroti. She knew she'd have to see his famous *David*, of course—it was an expectation in Florence—and she'd been feigning delight at the prospect for days. Certainly she was curious, but it wasn't as though she was a big art fan. If she couldn't get excited by either the *Pietà* or the Sistine Chapel, that *proved* there was a major artistic disconnect somewhere within her, right?

Emerson cocked his sandy head to one side and said, "*Nice?*" He opened his mouth to say something else, but the clock struck five and, so, they were all ushered into the Accademia.

The gallery was smaller than Gwen had expected. There was a section for paintings off to one side and there were some other sculptures lying about, but just about everyone's attention was drawn to the tribune at the far end of a long hallway.

Was it really the *David?*

Yep. There it was.

An unmistakable figure carved out of marble. Lean and . . . *beautiful*. Gwen caught her breath. Now this . . . *this* was different. She tried to understand what, specifically, made her have a reaction to the statue. Perhaps the enormity of it? The remarkable condition it was in? The intriguing look on David's marble face, which made him seem so very real? That body of his—so muscular, sinewy, fit?

Or maybe it was that Emerson kept nudging her, spoon-feeding her new facts about the sculpture and sending her pulse scurrying on a wild footrace whenever he touched her. Maybe it was natural to react strongly to art of any kind when the piece in question reminded the viewer of someone in real life.

She was standing in a small gallery between two tall and powerful men. One made of flesh, blood and bone, the other made of marble. One clothed in cotton and khaki, the other naked. Yet, they both had a simultaneous pull on her. Their natural charisma forced a divide in her attention. She compared them. Contrasted. Found there was more of an overlap than not. Both possessed blatant magnetism, although only one of them was fully unaware of the depth of his charm.

"He started it in 1501," Emerson jabbered, "and finished it in 1504, when he was only twenty-nine. Remarkable work, is it not?"

"Yeah."

"And, as you probably already know, Michelangelo believed the images of his sculptures already existed in the slab of stone. His job was merely to free it. To chip away at the superfluous material until the image emerged," he said.

"Uh-huh."

"He was fond of the concept of *disegno*, too," Emerson continued, chattering blithely, "which involves some tricky witchcraft and the lighting of small rodents on fire."

Gwen began to nod, but his words struck an odd chord. "What?"

He laughed. "Just checking to see if you were listening. With all those American 'yeah's' and 'uh-huh's,' I couldn't be sure."

"Sorry, I'm just—just new to this," she admitted, feeling the warm blush of embarrassment sweep up her neck. "I don't know what that Italian word meant. The one you just said."

"*Disegno*," he repeated. "And don't feel bad about your lack of familiarity. It is hardly common knowledge. It's Italian for fine-art drawing, but it refers to more than just literally sketching something. It is what elevates visual arts like sculpture, painting or architecture from a simple craft to a truly fine art, making the art equivalent to literature or music."

"How so?"

"Well, it was initially a Florentine thing. Artists like Leonardo da Vinci, Botticelli and Michelangelo embraced the concept. Take a look at the incredible attention Michelangelo paid to David's muscles, especially in his limbs and his neck." He pointed at the imposing statue, his palms sweeping the air as if sliding along the marble.

Gwen nodded. "It's very realistic," she agreed. Although David wasn't exactly, how should she put it? Well-endowed . . . Particularly for a man who had such large hands and feet. She did not mention this to Emerson.

"Yes. It's highly realistic because Michelangelo was a *disegno* follower," he said. "Artists like him felt it was the key intellectual element in art. That the use of careful drawings was the cornerstone of a good painting or sculpture. This contrasts to the Venetian School and their preference for *colore*."

She squinted at him. "I don't know that term, either."

"No worries," he said. "One of the reasons I love coming to Italy is because, with every trip, I learn just a little more. Titian, for instance, whose work we'll see at the Uffizi and in Venice, has these bloody gorgeous reds. Breathtaking colors and so natural. He, Rubens and others followed the *colore* philosophy and directly applied color to a canvas without drawing the picture first. I love that, too, but to sixteenth- and seventeenth-century Italians that was considered merely a painting technique, rather than a well-thought-out artistic creation. *Colore* is much more spontaneous, of course, but it's also dependent upon the model being right there in front of the artist."

She eyed Emerson curiously. Sure, he'd visited Italy a number of times but still . . . how did he know all of this? He was a *physicist*. Why did he care so much about artistic techniques? "Do you draw or paint?" she asked him.

He shook his head. "Not me. My mum. She's always really enjoyed it—both the studio-art skills and the philosophic component. She gravitates much more toward *disegno*. She prefers it herself because she's very much a planner and thinker, and the preliminary sketches *disegno* followers use are so studied and complete, the artist is able to work without models at all. As a result, they can be more imaginative in their creations." He grinned at her. "Even though she's not an artistic genius like Michelangelo was, Mum plans out her projects just as carefully, incorporating her skill in having learned to draw from life, but also being able to design much more intellectually and inventively on the canvas. Renaissance-era Italians considered this the highest form of art."

Gwen grinned back at him, even though a sadness she couldn't name filled her heart. Her mother had enjoyed artistic things, too. Not to the same extent as Emerson and Thoreau's mom, but Gwen would have loved to have been able to tell her mom about these different art styles. To share what she'd learned on this trip with her.

She sighed. "Thanks for explaining all of that to me," she told Emerson.

He shrugged. "I suspect I really was nattering on this time and boring you. But it was either painting philosophies or talking about David's tiny willy. I made a choice."

She laughed aloud then quickly covered her mouth with her hand when a few tourists shot her strange looks. Her blush returned full force, making not just her neck but her entire head feel very hot.

"Don't tell me you didn't notice," Emerson continued. "That poor, poor man. Good thing the gent had such great aim with a rock or, really, he would've been shamed in every way."

"Shh!" she said. "That's terrible of you."

Emerson ignored her. "In a competition, Priapus would win every round against David," he said, referring to the god of sex and fertility that they'd seen painted in Pompeii. "And I'd be willing to challenge them both in a—"

"Is my brother boasting again?" Thoreau broke in, having managed to disentangle himself from Cynthia and Louisa for a few moments. He rolled his eyes at Gwen and smirked at Emerson. "Really, if Mum could hear the way you go on in public." He shoved his brother out of the way and took a step toward Gwen. "So, what do you think of the *David*—his expression in particular? We've been having a bit of a debate with the curator over there." He pointed to the middle-aged Italian man in the process of being accosted by the Britsicles and their slew of questions. "Do you think Michelangelo depicted David in the moment just before his battle with Goliath or in the moment just after?"

"You cannot budge in here and make such a nuisance of yourself, Thor—" Emerson began.

"Would you hush up for two minutes and let her answer a simple question?" Thoreau replied calmly. "Gwen?"

She studied the famous marble face, noting the pensiveness of David's expression. He didn't take this battle lightly. He was serious and determined, qualities she could appreciate in somebody challenged to tackle something (or someone) much larger and more fierce than himself. He was holding the rock, so she supposed it could be that he'd picked it up again after having thrown it . . . or that he hadn't yet released it. In either instance, she felt for him and the magnitude of his task. In recognizing the extent of her own empathy, she couldn't help but realize what a masterpiece Michelangelo had created. She was feeling sorry for a man carved out of marble!

She glanced at Thoreau. "I don't know for sure. I think good arguments could be made for either view, but . . ."

"But?" Thoreau prompted.

"But, to me, he still seems really tense. As though he's made the decision but hasn't yet acted."

Thoreau pumped his fist. "Yes!" He motioned between him and his brother. "We were always taught that the sculpture represents 'the moment between conscious choice and conscious action' for David." He bobbed his head toward the curator. "The lackwit over there keeps telling us it's after the fact. I don't believe it." He bowed slightly. "Thank you, Gwen, for your fresh perspective." Then, to Emerson, "Try not to brag too much and annoy her." Over his shoulder he added, "And you don't stand a chance against Priapus."

"Bugger off," Emerson called cheerfully after his brother.

Thoreau got in the last word or, rather, the last gesture with a very rude hand signal.

The group spent another forty-five minutes or so viewing many of the other pieces. At one point, her aunt cornered her while she was alone and looking at the *Slaves* sculpture. Aunt Bea whispered, "I like seeing you having such a good time, Gwennie. You should do more of this. Stay out late with Emerson. Have fun tonight."

Gwen tried to remind her aunt that she wasn't really a late-night person and, besides, she'd spent several hours with the man already. If she stayed out late with him people might start talking.

To this, Bea replied, "Eh, so what? They'll talk whether you go out or not. Don't come back before ten." And she zipped away.

With this familial edict in mind, Gwen didn't object as she might have when Emerson suggested they skip the return trip to the hotel and go, instead, on a stroll down the Via del Corso. There was a *trattoria* he wanted to check out ("Thoreau raved about it, and if it meets his standards, it's sure to be good. He's dreadfully choosy. . . ."), and he was looking forward to a return to his favorite *gelateria*, too.

"You will love this place," Emerson assured her. "It has the finest Italian ice cream in the country. And they're closed tomorrow, so we'd best get there tonight."

They eschewed the bus yet again, had a quick dinner at the little eatery Emerson's brother had liked (it *was* good) and found themselves at an ice cream shop in downtown Florence called *Festival del Gelato*.

Gwen had tasted several scoops of gelato since arriving in Italy, and she'd had to admit it was a particularly delicious treat, but there shouldn't have been anything too different about the cone she had this time. It was one of their double scoops, which sat next to one another on their specialty cones—*fragola* (strawberry) on one side and *cioccolato all'arancia* (chocolate-orange) on the other—but the portions were generous and the company was captivating. Maybe that was why the flavor seemed even stronger, the texture even creamier, the sweet coolness even more refreshing. The burst of taste sensation when she licked the *fragola* was so powerfully fruity, Gwen was convinced it almost *had* to be healthy!

And sitting across the small circular table from her, Emerson nipped at his cone and swirled his tongue in the flavors he chose—

stracciatella (chocolate chip) and *malaga* (rum raisin)—mesmerizing Gwen with the attention he paid to the ice cream and the pure pleasure on his face as he consumed it.

The oddest thought crossed her mind as she watched him: This was how making love should be. A rapturous feast. A whirl of delight. That a lover's facial expression should reveal at least as much enjoyment in kissing her as Emerson's did in eating his ice cream.

And, of course, this reminded her yet again of Richard. She paused, trying to remember how he'd looked at her when they were in bed together. It was usually pretty dark—Richard preferred it that way—but, even so, she was having difficulty recalling a time when he had treated any part of her with the reverence Emerson brought to his gelato. This was troubling.

"A euro for your thoughts?" Emerson asked. "You seem a light-year away, Gwen. Don't you like your flavors?"

She slowly let out a breath she hadn't realized she'd been holding. Perhaps the time had finally come to tell him a little more about herself. About her relationship. "I—um, I was just thinking about my boyfriend at home. Richard. I don't think he's ever tasted gelato." She studied the Englishman's reaction to this disclosure.

As he seemed to do with most things, he took the new information in stride. "Well, what's not to like? You should tell your Richard to fly on over to Florence and give it a try. There's another popular *gelateria* in the city, Vivoli's, which is known the world over, although"—he pointed to the shop's ice-cream counter—"this place is my favorite. Most definitely." He then returned to lavishing affection on his cone.

She mustered her courage and asked, "So, is there someone special for *you* back in England? A woman you, um, love?"

"Yes," he said without hesitation.

Though Gwen had no reason whatsoever to feel the plummeting disappointment that followed these words, she was, nonetheless, surprised by her sudden resentment. She bit her lip and was about to press for further details on this mystery lady when Emerson swiped a paper napkin across his mouth, grinned at her and said, "My mum."

"What?" she said. Then it registered. "Oh! Your mother. Well, yes, of course you love *her*." Gwen laughed, her emotions yo-yoing from uneasy to strangely hopeful. "But what I meant was—"

"I know what you meant." Emerson sucked the *malaga* side of his cone until it formed a perfect creamy peak. "I was just fooling with you." He hesitated for several moments then added, "I date. A few women, actually. But there isn't one that's particularly serious now. There usually isn't. I'm not like Thoreau."

She squinted at him. The two men may have been unalike in subtle ways—a handful of personality quirks, a few physical traits—but she found more similarities between them than differences. "In what sense?"

"Despite his first messy divorce and consequent death spiral into self-destructive thought patterns, my brother still believes in getting married, settling down with one woman, having kidlets and, eventually, playing endless games of chess with his grandchildren." Emerson shrugged. "I don't."

Gwen shook her head, not sure she processed his comment fully. "You don't *ever* want to get married? Not even if you meet the right person someday? The One?"

He snorted. "There's no such thing. There are many Ones . . . plural, not singular. You think you can identify happiness in one person, but when you try to tie it down, it slips away. Like with electrons in quantum mechanics. You can't know precisely where they are, and by trying to pinpoint their location exactly, you lose them. The scientist has a much better sense of where their properties and locations are in space if he *doesn't* attempt to force the electron into a tiny box and tell it to stay there. If he honors and encourages the natural freedom."

She tried to wrap her mind around this theory, a difficult concept for somebody who'd spent the past two decades of her life hungering for attachment. "So, you're saying happiness in a relationship is impossible unless both parties are essentially free radicals. That women are unknowable entities to you if a formal bond with them is required, and that trying to create the bond itself causes the problem. Did I get that right?"

He met her eye and nodded—a determined, almost sad motion. "Yes, Gwen. That's correct."

She felt the drip of gelato on her knuckles—she'd been neglecting her cone—and quickly wiped some *fragola* away. "I'm not sure," she said, "that we could be more different in our opinions." She licked the edges of her cone thoughtfully. "When it comes to relationships, we may not, in fact, even be the same species."

"Perhaps not." Emerson laughed and cocked his head to one side, as if assessing her carefully. "But you don't think that's going to stop us from shagging, do you?"

5

Lying to Emerson and Aunt Bea and Cynthia and Thoreau

Monday–Friday, July 2–6

For a full five seconds, Gwen was left speechless by Emerson's remark. So much so that it took the dripping of more gelato on her fingers to get her to close her gaping mouth and break eye contact with him.

Oh, he tried to play off the comment as a joke, claiming his usual flippancy, but it was too late. The idea had already infiltrated her brain and forced a shift in her perception of him. *Shagging meant sleeping together!* That he'd even made a comment like that meant his attentions to her weren't similar to those of Hans-Josef or even Thoreau—a kind of hoped-for friendship. No. Even if Emerson wasn't serious about it and had no intention of following through with any plans of seduction, he had imagined her in bed with him. And he hadn't hesitated to openly share that idea with her—however teasingly.

To his laughing brush-off response of "Oh, relax, Gwen. I'm just teasing you," she'd immediately shot back, "Of course you are. I'm practically an engaged woman," and she'd had the satisfaction of seeing him look surprised and hold his palms up in a "hands off" pose before changing the subject to that of good vineyards in the Tuscany region. A subject he could speak of with some authority, it turned out (he claimed to have tried many local wines), and a topic she knew nothing about, of course.

But, although she might've been an unsophisticated, uncultured schoolteacher from the American Midwest, she wasn't *that* naïve. This British man, no matter how charismatic he might be, meant serious trouble. And, as soon as possible, she insisted upon returning to the hotel.

She could not, however, rid herself of him.

Their tour group spent the next two days immersed in Florentine splendors and, for almost all of these visits, Emerson was at her side, sticking to her with the rebounding tenacity of rubber cement.

Monday, the major museums in the city were closed, so there would be no vast Uffizi to lose herself in, much as she would have loved the anonymity.

Hans-Josef said, "We go there tomorrow" (or, rather, "Ve go . . ."), "but today we go to places that are open to us. Starting with the Duomo."

The Cathedral of Santa Maria del Fiore was the famous church attached to the incredible cupola that defined the eternal Florentine skyline, and San Giovanni's Baptistery next to it, with the glinting fifteenth-century gilded bronze doors, captured bits of sunshine and sent them into the piazza. If Lorenzo Ghiberti could see his gleaming "Gates of Paradise" today, Gwen suspected he'd be very proud.

Guido dropped them off at the tourist-filled square where caricature artists were already lined up in hopes of snagging new customers. Crowds strolled in and around the vendors, but Gwen's attention was fixed on the buildings themselves, particularly on that impressive dome, raised by Brunelleschi in the early 1400s. It was so large, so imposing, so . . . high.

"To climb to the top of the Duomo, it will take you four hundred sixty-three steps," Hans-Josef informed them. "I will lead a group up, if anyone would like to go."

Thoreau nudged his brother. "Shall we race?"

Emerson snickered and sent him a steely-eyed competitive look in return. "You're on, brother." Then he turned to Gwen. "Will you join us?" He paused. Quirked his lips. "As I recall, you're *fond* of stairs."

She blushed, remembering him watching her in Capri. "I might," she replied. And, ha! She'd beat him, too.

He grinned.

"Either of you ladies up to the challenge?" Thoreau said to their two British women friends. Louisa opted out on account of wearing strappy sandals, but Cynthia was definitely game.

"Of course," the woman said, already tightening the laces on her light pink sneakers and laughing girlishly.

To Gwen, Cynthia seemed a formidable athletic opponent— trim with well-shaped calf muscles—but, however youthful she looked, she was forty-four to Gwen's thirty. Gwen didn't think it would be much of a competition. Why she even felt she had to compete with this unpleasant person perplexed her, though. In a strange way, she felt her honor was at stake or, at least, her reputation with Emerson. But, again, why she even cared about his opinion was a mystery.

With a peculiar and unexpected bolt of realization, it occurred to her that she had spent much of her life preoccupied by the perceptions of others and that—for once—she shouldn't care about *anyone's* opinion. Not Emerson's, Cynthia's, Thoreau's, Louisa's, Hans-Josef's, her aunt's or that of anybody else on this tour. Nor should she be worrying about Richard's thoughts or her teaching colleagues' or her brothers' or some other person, present or not present in Florence at the moment. She should climb the stairs if she wanted to or, just as freely, say no if she didn't. Period.

Emboldened by this insight, Gwen marched up to the entrance to the Duomo, waited until Hans-Josef procured the tickets and prepared to race to the top as fast as the other tourists and the site's rules of safety allowed.

Considering this was a pretty athletic undertaking, Gwen was surprised by how many of the older people seemed up to the challenge. Dr. Louie and Matilda were in line to walk up, as were the honeymooners, Sally and Peter. Zenia was raring to go, not letting Hans-Josef out of her sight.

Aunt Bea, however, begged off the idea and told her niece she'd be spending the time wandering around the piazza instead with that elderly British man, Colin, who took pictures constantly and annoyingly.

Emerson wedged behind her, though, with Thoreau and Cynthia trailing him. Kamesh and Ani joined in as well, and the climb to the top began.

Hans-Josef talked about the interior frescoes as they started their ascent. "They were designed by Giorgio Vasari, but most of them were painted by a student of his named Federico Zuccari." He paused suddenly on the walk up and Zenia very nearly ran into him. "Zuccari was not considered to be as talented as Vasari, but he was, at least, innovative with color."

"Enough talking," Emerson murmured in her ear. "Let's just *go*."

Gwen shot a look at him over her shoulder. "That would be rude," she whispered. Much as she would have loved to race around their tour guide and zip to the top, Hans-Josef would consider it a personal slight, and it would be disruptive to the other people trying to listen to what he was saying. "Besides, you *like* to hear about art, don't you? You certainly like to talk about it. At length."

Emerson frowned. "No call to get snippy." He looked longingly up the stairs and, then, met her gaze. "Perhaps you're right, but I'm not a patient man. Not in anything." A specific message seemed to underscore his words.

Gwen looked away. Even given the little she knew about him, she considered this statement a rather unnecessary one. Emerson had been eyeing her with continued interest that morning and, though she had been doing her best to discourage it, she had no experience with a man like him. They were poles apart. He was so extroverted, sophisticated and clever to the point of frightening. He'd said their differences shouldn't keep them from having sex—just last night!—which was an *incredibly* forward thing to say to a woman he barely knew. She could only imagine what little tolerance he must have for everyday social niceties.

Eventually, they reached the top, with Zenia surprising them all by being the one to move ahead of Hans-Josef on the final stretch and get there first. She may not have been a small woman, but she could move when she was so inspired. "Getting ready for the Eiffel Tower," she informed Hans-Josef triumphantly. "You gonna be leadin' us up that, too, right?"

"She'll probably force him to the top at knitting-needle point," Cynthia remarked snidely to the Edwards brothers, but Gwen overheard her and hoped Zenia had not. Gwen's dislike of the British woman intensified.

To get away from her, Gwen bolted up the last flight of stairs, but Emerson was on her heels. "Nice strong level of cardiovascular fitness you have there," he said, not remotely winded or bothering to disguise that he was studying her legs.

She suddenly felt very self-conscious in her knee-length shorts. "Thanks," she murmured, but she didn't return the compliment, even though she could have with honesty. Emerson looked very *healthy*.

Instead, she pivoted toward the view and scanned the panoramic vista below. It was pretty and brilliantly clear, but not tempting enough to entice her to stay longer in Emerson and Cynthia's orbit. So, the moment Emerson had his back turned, she slipped away to the exit and skipped down to the ground level again, tapping each descending stair like the patter of raindrops on a roof. It wasn't much by way of defiance, but it felt good to take a stand, however small.

He looked at her inquiringly when he got back on the bus, but he didn't comment. She thought, maybe, he was finally getting the hint to keep his distance.

Next up were quick stops at Piazza della Repubblica and then Palazzo Vecchio, where the outdoor replica of the *David* was located, before they headed to see the Santa Croce.

"It's a bit like an Italian Westminster," Thoreau commented as they walked in the church. "The best artworks are the Giotto frescoes over there." He pointed ahead. "Some of them were shown in the film *A Room with a View*. The one Merchant and Ivory did. Familiar with it?"

She shook her head. She'd read the E. M. Forster novel the film was based on years ago, but her recollection of the plot was vague and she'd never gotten around to seeing the movie. However, if this place had been one of the settings, she was pretty sure she wouldn't have liked it. To her, the church looked overly Gothic on the inside. So gloomy and imposing. And it seemed unusually depressing to her with its dim cloisters, dark graves and wall monuments to the dead.

Hans-Josef took them first to see where the bones of Michelangelo were laid to rest. The renowned artist had died of a fever in Rome at age eighty-nine, but the Florentines snuck his body back here, despite the Pope's wish to bury him in Rome. Dante Alighieri, the poet who wrote *The Divine Comedy*, was also given a memorial, as was Niccolò Machiavelli, sixteenth-century Florentine statesman and author of *The Prince*. As a group, they saw the floor tomb of Baptistery-door sculptor Lorenzo Ghiberti, a famous altarpiece by Giorgio Vasari and a nineteenth-century piece honoring the remains of Gioachino Rossini, composer of *The Barber of Seville* and *The William Tell Overture*.

Then, as if that weren't enough of a focus on death, they also were taken to visit the grave of the legendary Galileo Galilei, who'd lived from 1564 to 1642 and who'd figured out everything from the law of bodies falling at the same rate regardless of weight to the discovery that the Earth revolved around the sun. Although Italians still brought fresh flowers to his grave, Gwen didn't think any tribute could be more solemn than Emerson's, who paid his respects to the scientist in several long and uncharacteristically somber moments of utter silence.

For a few minutes, he seemed so serious that, to Gwen, he almost appeared to be another man. He wasn't mocking, winking or dramatizing anything. Hardly the Emerson she'd come to know over these past several days. And when he looked in her direction next, it was with a demeanor so subdued and free of his typical smirking that she literally took two steps back. He'd pierced her with the sadness of his gaze, and then looked through her and away.

She thought about that look often for the rest of that day and throughout the next, especially since Emerson seemed at last to respect the hands-off signals she'd been sending him and did, indeed, give her some space. The moment he followed directions, of course, was the very moment she found herself missing his company and conversation—not that she intended to admit that to him or to her meddling aunt.

"Gwennie, I like seeing you with these energetic young people. Don't feel you need to hang around me all the time. Go off and be with them." She pointed toward the unbreakable foursome.

"Who could be more energetic than you?" Gwen replied, smiling. "And, besides, I love spending time with you." This skirted the edges of truthfulness, yes, but far less so since they'd been in Europe together. Gwen was finding new things to appreciate about Aunt Bea every day. The dynamic between them had changed in this parallel universe, and since no one—not even her aunt or the Dubuque S&M members—could challenge her as much as Emerson, Gwen appreciated her aunt's company all the more.

Aunt Bea squinted at her in disbelief but elected to say nothing. Internally, Gwen sighed, her relief tinged with just a few speckles of guilt, and she tagged along with her aunt and her aunt's friends for the rest of the day.

Tuesday proved to be a packed cornucopia of touristic delights, beginning with reservations to the Uffizi and seeing Botticelli's *Birth of Venus* and *Primavera*, along with an early da Vinci, a Michelangelo panel painting and a string of work by artists she could only jot down in a notebook. Her eyes were soon swimming with them: Titian (just like Emerson promised), Giotto, Vasari, Raphael, Canaletto, even a couple of pieces by the Spaniard Goya and a Flemish section featuring Rubens and Van Dyck.

Caravaggio, the baroque master of a painting style called "chiaroscuro," that forced extreme contrasts by the use of harsh light and deep shadows, even had his version of *Bacchus* on display, but that wasn't the only one they saw.

A few hours later at the Museo Nazionale del Bargello, Florence's premier sculpture museum, Emerson, his smile matching the mischievousness of Donatello's *Cupid,* zipped past the famous sculpture to archly point out Michelangelo's version of *Bacchus* to his brother and their friends. Gwen was beginning to get the idea that between the triumvirate of Caravaggio, Michelangelo and the Vettius brothers, Emerson himself would soon be channeling the spirit of the partying god and would, undoubtedly, become a living replica of him. This particular sculpture, carved by Michelangelo when he was only twenty-two, was clearly inspired by the classical works the young master studied in Rome, but it was also imbued with the Renaissance artist's sense of realism. The god of wine and revelry was portrayed as a young man, holding his cup unsteadily and reeling back on his knees as if literally tipsy.

"He's drunk," Emerson said to her, his tone amused, indulgent. Then, more softly, "Having fun is part of the human experience, you see? For centuries, people celebrated it." He nodded again at the sculpture, beautifully crafted in Italian marble. "They honored good food, good drink and each other. It's not a bad thing to want to enjoy the light as well as the shadows. The sweetness as well as the bitterness." He swallowed. "It's part of being alive."

Then he strode away, and she was left wondering if it was his *intent* to disturb her equilibrium or if he, in fact, thought he was being helpful while creating these unsettling feelings inside her. All she knew was that, since coming to Europe and meeting him, she felt less like herself than ever. He'd thrown her off balance and it would take a serious readjustment to right the scale. No one person should have so powerful an effect on another.

Their busy day wound down with a visit to the famous Medici palace (the Palazzo Pitti), the Boboli Gardens and, finally, concluded with a bus ride to Piazzale Michelangelo for a panoramic view of the city at sunset.

Hans-Josef said, "This is one of the most popular squares in Florence, and it offers the best view of the city." He waved his palm at Fiesole's green hills in the distance and pointed to the most notable landmarks as they watched the sinking sun bathe the ancient city in glittering light.

He nodded at the famous cupola that dominated the city's skyline, reminding Gwen of their visit to Brunelleschi's dome just the day before. Hans-Josef told them that Brunelleschi had died in 1446, knowing he'd created an awe-inspiring masterpiece of both art and engineering, one that was still much admired in their present generation. And that Giorgio Vasari, who wrote *The Lives of the Artists*, said that Florentine artists and architects excelled because they were hungry. That their fierce competition for commissions against each other kept them hungry.

" '*Competition*,' " Hans-Josef said, quoting Vasari, " '*is one of the nourishments that maintain them.*' "

"Yes. Competition is a good thing," Emerson murmured to his brother, his tone one of mocking.

"Particularly when you know you're stronger than your opponent," Thoreau shot back.

Although their tour guide and most of the trip members didn't hear them, Gwen was close enough to listen to every word the Edwards brothers said to each other and to watch their reactions closely. They were good-natured men, yes. They loved one another, also true. But their sense of competition was very real. And, in an odd way, she understood she could easily be made a pawn in their game. Whose side did she really want to play on? Both? Neither? Would it be better to wait to see what they did next or to take a position of offense?

She also eyed Louisa, whose glance was fixed on something in the distance, and Cynthia, who was staring back at Gwen with the oddest expression of speculation.

Gwen looked away.

But, as the sunset lingered, splashing the buildings with golden waves, she came to the utterly logical conclusion that, if she were to err greatly, it would most likely be on Emerson's side. She couldn't go too far wrong with her friendship toward Thoreau. It lacked almost every worrisome element. Besides, men and women could become friends at any time and stay friends—so long as one person didn't try to transform the friendship into a romance. Thoreau was too hung up on that Amanda person in England to try anything inappropriate. This certainly could not be said of his brother.

She took a step toward Thoreau, but Louisa, who appeared to have finally emerged from her hypnotic state, turned to him and asked a question. And Cynthia, who'd spotted Gwen moving in their direction, wasted not a single second in hooking her arm through Emerson's and literally jerking him away toward some other corner of the piazza.

Gwen blinked after them, her posture oddly off balance since she'd been ready to spring into action just the moment before. She let herself down easily. Let herself relax back to the ground again. Told herself it was better this way. And tried to recover by turning her attention once and for all to the scenic vista that was spread buffet-style before her.

Like a spray of summer showers, the last ray of sunshine sprinkled Florence with droplets of liquid gold, then dried quickly and evaporated into the night air. With the coming of the evening there was the new brightness of houselights and street lamps. This was not a city that would dwell in darkness for long, although, like one of Caravaggio's chiaroscuro paintings, there were distinct areas of deep shade. Secrets hidden in the shadows.

"We go out now for gelato," Hans-Josef announced, clapping his hands, breaking the spell and herding them all onto the bus. Gwen recognized the name of the place right away since Emerson had already mentioned it.

At Vivoli's, "perhaps the world's most famous *gelateria* and one that has been in existence since the 1930s," or so Hans-Josef informed them, Gwen bought herself and her aunt double scoops of ice cream and, privately, she judged the merits of this cone against the one she'd had at Festival del Gelato. (She selected the same flavors for proper comparison purposes.) While Vivoli's *cioccolato all'arancia* and *fragola* were very tasty, she noted slight differences as well. There had been larger candied orange chunks in Festival del Gelato's version of the *cioccolato all'arancia* and there were simply more strawberry bits in Vivoli's *fragola*.

But, though she appreciated the taste sensation of both versions well enough, she had to admit she'd enjoyed her former gelato experience more. Most likely not at all on account of the ice cream, but only because she'd been at Festival del Gelato with Emerson. Just the two of them. Alone.

She watched him laughing about something with Ani and his father, the three of them standing in the ordering line. The boy looked up at Emerson, obvious admiration in his young brown eyes, and a respect that Gwen knew was hard to elicit from a teen.

All day Gwen had spent trying to escape the allure of the man. But that night, sitting across the room from him, she realized this wouldn't be possible while they were still together on the tour. Despite her wishes to the contrary, it was undeniable how much more fun she'd had when in his company. And it wasn't only his conversation she craved. His energy was what moved him to be fascinating, in her opinion, even without words spoken.

She frowned and studied her cone.

Aunt Bea, Matilda and Dr. Louie were debating the strengths and weaknesses of their chosen flavors.

"This *caffè* gelato is like coffee-lite," Matilda complained. "I was hoping for a stronger hit of caffeine."

"It isn't supposed to taste like your morning espresso," Dr. Louie said around a mouthful of *amarena*. He paused, licked and grinned. "Oooh. Got a big cherry this time."

Aunt Bea thoughtfully tasted each of her two new flavors: *lampone* and *fico* (raspberry and fig), a combination that had Gwen a bit baffled, but it was what her aunt had wanted. "I really like the tartness of the *lampone*," Bea said, "but it's the sweet creaminess of the fico that would make me order this one again."

Quite a tribute in her aunt's book. Bea hadn't ordered the same two gelato flavors (or was it more correct to use the plural—*gelati* flavors?) since they'd set foot in Italy.

For a few minutes more Gwen mimicked their dialogue, commenting on the taste and texture of her gelato, listening to Aunt Bea and her friends rave about Tuscany's foodie splendors and tolerating their ribbing about her being a potential object of interest for Hans-Josef, Emerson *and* Thoreau.

At first she tried to laugh it off, but they wouldn't allow for an easy denial, even though Gwen knew the truth of the matter and it was as simple as a Venn diagram: Circle One contained the single women on the tour. Circle Two contained the women within the general age bracket of the three thirty- or forty-something men. With Louisa being married (not that she acted like it), Zenia being decidedly single (but over sixty), the only women in the intersecting segment of those two circles were Gwen and Cynthia. Three available men. Two available women. And one group of pesky seniors determined to get a pair or two of them together. Not that it would work.

Additionally, she was starting to feel an uncomfortable sensation that, at first, she'd thought was indigestion—but, instead, it was her ire rising. There *had* to be more to this trip for her than just letting herself get scripted into some relationship drama for the amusement of her aunt and her club pals. Was this what being on a tour reduced life to? A hyperfocus on relationships? What about *big-picture* things—art, history, culture, the meaning of life? Why did male-female attraction intrude upon these loftier ideals and supplant higher intellectual interests with the pursuit of base desires?

Gwen had promised herself she'd embrace the travel adventure and, yet, here she was stepping away from it again. Hiding in plain sight behind the wackiness of a bunch of elderly gamesters. She'd gotten close to being in the whirl of excitement when she was alone with Emerson, but had shied away again the minute he'd propositioned her.

She touched her Mouth of Truth pendant. Could she be honest with herself? Maybe the problem was that she'd let Emerson control their interactions and lead their conversations. Maybe what she needed to do was be bold enough to take the reins away from him and direct their discussions and their activities to *her* liking and comfort level. Heaven knew, with *him*, there were bound to be surprises enough, even if she was as assertive as possible.

She saw Hans-Josef strolling toward them, and Matilda nudged Gwen's side in delight. It was enough to bring Gwen to her feet at last and get her to finally make a decision, however small, that supported the handling of her own destiny.

"Excuse me," she said. "I need to ask the Brits over there a couple of questions."

Dr. Louie's eyes twinkled as he nodded at her, Matilda grinned and Aunt Bea emitted a little squeal of encouragement.

Gwen slipped away before they could actually form embarrassing sentences and verbalize them, taking daring strides toward the circular table where Emerson, Thoreau, Louisa and Cynthia were seated. There was one empty chair available—between the two women. Her breath caught in her throat when she reached it.

But then Thoreau said, "Hello, there. Wish to join us?"

Louisa (although not Cynthia) shuffled her chair over a bit to make room.

And Emerson, whose cocky gaze ping-ponged between Gwen's face and her ice-cream cone, raised a dark blond eyebrow. "Tell me those are not the same two flavors you got last time? The chocolate-orange and the strawberry? Hmm. Not too adventurous of you," he chided.

She slid into the seat, aware of Cynthia's resentful glance to her right, Louisa's mystified one to her left and Thoreau's general amusement in front of her.

"They are the same flavors," she admitted to Emerson, "but I won't make that mistake again. I was just testing a theory this time."

"I like theories. And your conclusion?" he asked.

"It's the company not the cone," she shot back, watching as he analyzed her remark in an attempt to determine whether it was a compliment or an insult.

He opened his mouth, no doubt on the verge of asking her directly, but Gwen was prepared to seize the conversation as she'd intended. This *was* a competition, after all, even if there would be no romantic intrigues between her and *any* of the men. The boys could play their games in whichever openly abusive manner they wanted, but it was high time Gwen came to understand the psychology of her opponent.

She took a breath, swiveled to face Cynthia and smiled. "So, tell me about yourself. How did you get to know everyone here?"

The next morning at breakfast, by the coffee bar, Thoreau murmured, "Delightful chess match, Gwen. Well played."

Gwen blinked at him. "What are you talking about? I haven't played anyone in chess."

He raised both brows at that. "To me, it looked like white pawn to e4 in a covered attack against the black queen at d5, threatening her into backing away from the center squares so you could cleverly capture the black knight at f5." He crossed his arms and regarded her smugly. "Thank you for letting me assist last night, if only as a poor white bishop on g2."

She pretended innocence at his insinuation. "I don't really know how to play the game."

He laughed. "Bollocks. I'm impressed. If you're not formally trained, then you're an intuitive player and far better than you think. Not sure my brother stands a chance against you in a live chess match—although I doubt he knows it yet."

She shook her head. Sure, she'd used a *strategy* of sorts, but it wasn't quite as calculated as Thoreau seemed to suggest. "I just asked a few questions. I was trying to be . . . conversational."

"You asked Cynthia enough questions to make her think she was the cover story in the next issue of *People*. And it was a very clever opening move because she liked the attention. Quite a lot. Your interest caught her off guard and it distracted her from noticing she'd lost her controlling position in the center of the board."

He glanced around the room. The Britsicles were chatting in a far corner. Louisa glanced over at them and raised her hand in a wave. Cynthia looked, too, and actually smiled at Gwen.

He lowered his voice further. "Plus, you may have even made a couple of new friends." He grinned. "Let me know if you ever want to learn the board-game version, Gwen. It would be great fun to teach you. A few more moves like that and you'll find yourself at the backline becoming a new white queen." With a parting nod and a cup of Italian espresso he was gone.

She knew enough about chess to understand what he'd meant about the pieces and the positions, but his analogy had her worrying her bottom lip, not at all certain if she should be flattered or insulted that he considered her such a crafty pawn, even if it were just for the duration of one game. She couldn't help but feel the powerlessness of her position. Interesting, too, that he tagged himself as a bishop—an adviser of sorts on her team—and Emerson as a dashing knight on the *other* team that'd gotten cornered between her and Cynthia (the overly attentive yet easily sidetracked queen). Thoreau hadn't bothered to give Louisa a position. Perhaps he considered her irrelevant in the chess match.

But if Gwen thought she'd finished with all game-playing exercises for the day, she was mistaken.

It was the Fourth of July and, at long last, she received her first e-mail from Richard that morning:

> *Dear Gwendolyn,*
> *Sorry I wasn't able to respond sooner. My home computer got a virus, so I haven't been using it. And at work the server was down this week, and I couldn't access my e-mail until it was fixed. Glad to hear you're having fun in Italy, though. I'll be thinking of you when I'm at the picnic.*
>
> *Richard*

Just "Richard." Not "Love, Richard," "Fondly, Richard," "Yours, Richard" or even his most formal "Sincerely, Richard." He pretty clearly was still upset with her for leaving.

And then, of course, there was the mention of the company picnic. She could have been spending the day in ninety-degree Iowan humidity, eating charred hotdogs, drinking sugary lemonade, picking at a scoop of heavy, mayonnaise-covered potato salad and, maybe, if she was lucky, getting a cherry snow cone for dessert . . . or she could be walking onto an air-conditioned tour bus headed to the Italian Lake District via the Leaning Tower of Pisa, with wine, pasta and gelato waiting for her.

Even with the matchmaking antics of the elderly tour members, the mystifying behavior of her British companions and her own feeble attempts at social stratagems, it didn't seem much of a contest, did it?

Upon arriving in Pisa, Davis, Dr. Louie, Kamesh and Ani immediately began debating the Leaning Tower's degree of tilt from the ninety-degree perpendicular.

"It looks to be about a five-degree angle," Dr. Louie guesstimated.

Davis whipped out his pocket protractor—yes, he actually had one!—and held it up so he could gauge the correct angle from a distance.

"We learned in school that it was a little less than four degrees," Ani said.

"Used to be five and a half back in the seventies," his father contributed. "But they did all those renovations in the nineties to stabilize it, and they straightened it by eighteen inches."

"*Ja,*" Hans-Josef said, overhearing them. "It now leans three point nine meters to the southwest from where it would be if it were perfectly vertical, and it stands about fifty-six meters high. Who wants to go up to the top?"

Emerson shot her a mischievous glance and mouthed, "More stairs."

There were 294 steps on one side and 296 on the other, to be precise. She smiled back at him but waved him off. She didn't feel like racing against anyone that day, not even herself. Instead, she hung around the grassy square, strolling past Pisa's Cathedral and the Baptistery, drinking in the site of the famous landmark and the sunshine.

And she observed.

She watched and, yes, eavesdropped on two married couples

this time—Connie Sue and Alex, Sally and Peter—as they sat on a shady bench on the edges of the square and discussed the date the tower was built, who was in political and religious power at the time, what the history surrounding the construction and reconstruction was like and so on. Aside from their professed delight in finally seeing such wonders in person, there was also a constant search for meaning within the numbers and patterns that made Gwen pause.

"It took 177 years to build in 3 stages and work was first begun in 1173 . . . all 1's, 3's and 7's!" Sally exclaimed.

"And the same pope, Alexander III, that led the Church when they were breaking ground on the Leaning Tower *also* laid the foundation stone for Notre Dame in Paris," Alex added enthusiastically.

On one level, Gwen found it funny—this incessant DaVinci Coding of Europe—but it also made her wonder what the point was of all the analysis. Like a game of sudoku, wasn't the puzzle merely an intellectual exercise? Even if a pattern could be found based on the scant clues given, it wasn't as though it was the cornerstone to anything important . . . to any profound truth . . . was it? To Gwen, it all felt like conjecture without hope of an answer key.

She listened to them a bit longer. The honeymooners were a jovial but disorganized pair. Sally professed that she'd wanted to take this trip for so long, but was overwhelmed by it, too.

"There's so much to remember. Medications. Glasses. Dietary restrictions," Sally confided to her friends. "Peter and I wouldn't have had to deal with all of this if we'd been able to go on our honeymoon forty years ago when we were young and full of vigor."

"Ah, love," Peter said, cupping his wife's hand in his. "You know I'm as vigorous as ever when it comes to you."

Connie Sue squealed like an excited teen and pretended to fan herself. "Why, Sally, honey, I do believe you've got a romantic one on your hands."

"It's gonna be a hot time in the old *loggia* tonight," Alex predicted.

The foursome laughed and broke open a package of big vanilla Rondo biscuits and a bottle of sparkling water to share.

In overhearing their discussion, Gwen was reminded of how she'd been taking youth for granted. Not just in Europe, but over the past several years. She worked hard to stay healthy, yes, and from a medical standpoint, her persistent fear of death was groundless (though accidents *did* happen). She reminded herself to take time to appreciate that she didn't need any prescription drugs or have to impose any physical or dietary limitations on anything she did. At least not yet.

She sent a silent prayer of thanks to the heavens and was about to walk on when that British man, Colin, all but leaped in her path. Well, inasmuch as an eighty-one-year-old man could leap.

"If y-you p-please, stay th-there," he stuttered, holding up his camera. "It's l-l-lovely like that." He motioned behind her and, when she glanced over her shoulder, she saw the Leaning Tower positioned just off to her left with only the grassy park and a cluster of colorful tourists separating them.

"You want me to be in your picture?" Gwen asked.

He nodded and clicked a few shots with unsteady hands.

Gwen was confused. "But why don't I take one of you, instead?" She stepped toward him, but the man winced and pulled the camera close to his chest.

"No, no . . ." he mumbled.

"I'll be very careful with your camera," she said, thinking this must be his concern. "I just thought you'd want to have a picture of *you* with the Leaning Tower."

Colin looked up at her, the clouds in his eyes clearing a little. "Maybe that would be a good thing, but—but—I don't know right now."

Something was definitely off with this guy. He didn't seem dangerous, but he sure was behaving strangely.

Gwen took a step back. "Well, okay. If you change your mind then I'll—"

"There you are!" Aunt Bea said, coming up unexpectedly from a side walkway.

"You were looking for me?" Gwen asked her, surprised since she'd told her aunt not more than a half hour ago that she'd intended to wander around independently.

"No, dear. For Colin." Bea strode over to him, stood close and smiled warmly. "Are you feeling well?" she whispered.

He looked unsure.

Aunt Bea murmured a few things to him Gwen couldn't hear, then turned to her and said, "Gwennie, I'd like to introduce you to my friend Colin Pickering." Then, to the older man, "Colin, this is my niece, Gwendolyn Reese."

He laughed and carefully held out his hand to shake Gwen's. "That rhymes."

Aunt Bea patted him on the shoulder like she might a young child. "It does."

Gwen shook Colin's hand but glanced at her aunt in curiosity. What was going on here? They'd already been introduced twice before. She could understand, perhaps, why he might forget the first time. But the second as well? What was wrong with her that she was so unmemorable?

Her aunt managed to convince the man to let Gwen take their picture together in front of the Leaning Tower. "You ought to be in a few shots yourself, Colin," Bea said lightly, her wiry arms pulling him tight beside her.

He gave a rueful chuckle. "I'm not at all sure I want to remember myself."

Nevertheless, he let Gwen snap a couple of quick photos. Then, he and her aunt wandered off together as Gwen watched and, perhaps, began to understand.

She was reminded of a conversation she'd had with Aunt Bea about her late uncle Freddy during those dark months after Gwen's father died. Bea had said she was sad to have lost her husband, but that their memories lasted forever. "I'll always have those youthful adventures to remember when I'm old and gray."

Gwen had looked at her aunt and smiled. To her young mind, Aunt Bea had been old and gray for over a decade, but she'd always seemed so capable. For Bea, there seemed to be nothing uncertain about the power of love and the lifelong allure of fond memories. She had a storehouse of both. But what if the ability to remember began to deteriorate? What if a person could no longer draw upon that power?

Gwen gazed across the grassy expanse of lawn, suddenly aware of how fervently everyone around her was trying to *live:*

Sally and Peter with their long-awaited honeymoon.

Colin with his incessant picture taking, whatever its meaning for him.

A bunch of tour members with their attempt to experience Europe through better math equations.

Her aunt with her reliving the kind of adventure she'd once had with her husband.

Gwen caught sight of the British-Indian father/son duo—Kamesh trying to ease his son through this coming-of-age experience on his way toward manhood. But it was also interesting, Gwen noticed, watching the alacrity with which Ani helped his father adjust their digital flip camera. The way the youngest among them was far from useless, even if he was inexperienced.

Everyone had value. Perhaps she, too, was capable of doing more than she'd done. Perhaps she, too, could share her skills, test her limits and take a leap into the unknown. Challenge herself more than she had thus far. Her resolve was only underscored by the next conversation she eavesdropped into—this time between Zenia and Hester.

"Look at the way it's stacked," Zenia said, pointing at the Leaning Tower. "Like an eight-layer wedding cake."

"The plastic bride and groom would fall right off and crack their heads with a cake like that," Hester observed. "I wonder how many of them skinny columns there are goin' 'round the tower."

"Don't know." Zenia studied the structure silently for a moment. "But that pattern they form with the arches would be real pretty in a knit vest or scarf." She pulled a pen and a piece of creased paper out of her fanny pack and began sketching a few design elements.

Hester admired Zenia's artistry, but then returned to staring at the tower. "I bet'cha there could be some exciting chase scene up there," she told her younger friend. "It'd be perfect for a thriller. Like a J. D. Robb novel." She elbowed Zenia and then stabbed the air in the direction of the famous building. "Just think about it. All those floors with bad guys running up the stairs, out on the balconies, around in a circle. They'd get to the top and have a battle to the death." She snapped her fingers. "It could be a wedding party. On the Leaning Tower wedding cake! And someone would fall off and crack their foolish little head open. . . ."

She began ticking off characters with her fingers. "There'd be the killer bride, the clueless groom, the cheatin' best man, the sweet maid of honor, the interfering mother of the groom, the thievin' father of the bride, a ring bearer and a couple of sneaky flower girls. It could be called *Problem Proposal in Pisa*. Or, maybe, *Nasty Nuptials*." She shook her head. "No, that's not right. I'll think of a better title later."

Zenia snorted. "Plot sounds too farfetched to me. But you write J. D. Robb an' you tell her you got her one damn good story idea. Maybe she'll write it for you."

But Hester had a different idea. "No," she said with a happy cackle. "My muse is tellin' me to write it myself. I'm only ninety. I figure I got me at least another few years. Can't take longer than one or two to write a book, can it?"

Zenia glanced between the Leaning Tower and the old woman. "Not for a smart cookie like you." She dug into her fanny pack again, pulling out another crumpled piece of paper and a second pen. "Why don't you jot down a few of your ideas? Don't want you to forget 'em."

Hester snatched the paper and pen, gave Zenia a quick arm squeeze in thanks and began scribbling. Gwen could only admire them both and their drive to be creative no matter what their age. She ought to try to be just a little more like them.

"Perhaps it's true that the only thing worth writing about is, after all, the human heart, when it's in conflict with itself," a voice behind her murmured.

Gwen felt the oddest tremor in her chest at the sound. She

swiveled around to find Emerson standing there, arms crossed. She didn't immediately recognize the literary reference and she said so.

"Faulkner," he replied, eyeing her coolly. "He said something like that once."

She nodded. "Oh, okay. So, what? No more Ralph Waldo? No more Shakespeare?"

"I'm versatile," he said, his lips remaining in a straight line, but his hazel irises glinting more than a bit in golden amusement. "Why? Do you not like the sentiment?"

She swallowed. What was she going to do with him? Why was he always laughing at her? Asking her questions?

"Why—Why do you keep poking at me like that?" she blurted. "Why do you even care what I think? We're nothing alike. My opinion shouldn't matter to you."

"I'm a scientist." He shrugged, as if this were all the explanation needed.

She blinked at him. "And?"

His lips twitched. "*And* I believe that to really know something, you need to both observe it and disturb it. At different times, of course."

"So, wait. You're saying I'm an object you've been . . . studying . . . and disturbing? Like some kind of experiment?" She was surprised how incensed she was by this. It was different, of course, when she observed people. She just *watched*. He, apparently, had been watching and also plotting out schemes to annoy her as a way of gathering empirical data. She *knew* he'd been trying to mess with her. *Men*.

"Not an object. A woman," he corrected. "Only, the Heisenberg uncertainty principle is in effect, so I've been screwing it up."

She squinted at him. What was he talking about? *The Heisenberg uncertainty principle?* "What?"

"In quantum mechanics," Emerson explained in an infuriatingly patient tone, "certain pairs of physical properties—like momentum and position—can't both be known with complete accuracy. The more precisely we know one property, the less precisely we can know the other." He held out his palms as if they were a scale, lifting one side and then the opposing side. "The measurement of a particle's momentum, for example, necessarily disturbs its position. And vice versa. So, according to Heisenberg, it's impossible to simultaneously determine these qualities in an electron, at least not with any degree of certainty."

"And this relates to me . . . how?"

"To really know the nature of something you need to do more than just observe it. You need to interact with it, too. Test it. See how it responds to different elements, stimuli, challenges. However, interacting with the subject irrevocably disturbs it. It's no longer in its native state, so, you can't be certain that you've measured correctly." He crossed his arms and regarded her with surprising seriousness. "This is true for getting to know new people, as well. As it is in physics, so it is in life."

Gwen sighed, battling exasperation and the unsettling understanding that Emerson likened their burgeoning friendship (was that what it was?) to the relationship between a scientist and a confusing electron. There was very little that struck her as romantic or admiring about this comparison.

"So . . . so your question to me at Festival del Gelato—that was a *test* of yours? Because, before, you said it was a *joke*."

"Most jokes are tests," he shot back. Then he grinned. "But only a coward would use that as an excuse in this case. And I'm not a coward, Gwen." He met her gaze and held it. "I meant what I said to you."

She didn't know how to respond to him. He possessed the ability to challenge her without asking her a single thing, let alone when he openly propositioned her. She felt perspiration dampening her palms but was saved from having to mumble something inane by the interruption of Hester and Zenia.

"How about *With This Ring I Thee Kill?*" Hester suggested to the other lady as the two strolled past them.

Zenia said, "I kinda like that one."

"Or *Something Borrowed, Something Bludgeoning* . . ."

Emerson snickered as soon as they were out of earshot. "See,

Gwen? There could be worse fates than getting stuck on a five-week trip through Europe with a collection of mathematical misfits. You could be a character in Hester's upcoming debut novel, *Here Comes the Assassin Bride*."

In spite of herself, she laughed. Well, yes. If marriage meant murder, it was best avoided. But, somehow, she was sure Richard didn't intend to say his wedding vows and then push her off the top of a tall building. He might, however, continue to give her the cold shoulder for another month. Or two.

It occurred to her—standing in the Italian sunshine, the figure of the Leaning Tower casting a peculiar shadow on the lush lawn—that Richard, thousands of miles away at his little company picnic, had no right to hold a grudge and try to spoil her fun, albeit via e-mail. And that the man hovering beside her—for all his faults and excessive verbosity—might annoy her mightily, but he wasn't one to be petty or rancorous. He was not, as he so boldly stated, a coward.

Not in the least.

They spent the next two days basking in the splendor that was the Italian Lake District. Aunt Bea and Matilda roped Gwen into joining them for pedalo boat rides on Lake Como. Gwen and her fellow tour members had leisurely meals overlooking the sparkling water. They enjoyed strolling in the warm sun, watching it set behind the colorfully dappled northern Italian hills. And they marveled at how being in the midst of this scenery was like walking into a Howard Behrens painting.

On Friday morning, Gwen found herself on the hotel terrace, enjoying the peacefulness and beauty of the region, when she spotted Hester tiptoeing past her.

She waved to the older woman and was about to say, "Good morning," but Hester put her index finger to her lips with one hand and motioned for Gwen to join her with the other.

"Where are we going?" Gwen whispered.

Hester's eyes glittered. "To get a treat." And she led Gwen around to a side entrance, near the hotel kitchen, where a plump

forty-something lady cook and their bus driver, Guido, were awaiting them.

"Just-ah in time!" the lady cook said, pulling out a piping hot
pan of freshly baked bread twists.

The aroma was overwhelmingly delicious, like strolling into a
bakery and actually being wrapped up in a warm bread roll. Despite not being a foodie like Hester or Aunt Bea, Gwen wasn't immune to the scrumptiousness of the scent.

"You try it with olive oil, yes?" Guido suggested, smacking his
lips. "You will like. I know."

As the lady cook was sliding the steaming twists onto small
paper plates for each of them, the side door swung open and
Thoreau slipped through it. "I heard a rumor—" he began.

The lady cook laughed and handed him a plate with a bread
twist.

Thoreau kissed her on the cheek—both sides—in return.

Hester, Guido and the lady cook began chatting about something while nibbling on their hot bread. Thoreau brushed both his
twist and Gwen's with a strip of golden oil and pointed toward the
door. "Shall we take a stroll?" he asked her.

She nodded. And, after thanking the generous cook, they
stepped out onto the walkway near the hotel and began meandering on the floral path alongside the lake.

Gwen blew on her twist and took a small bite. "Ohh . . . mmm."

"Heaven, isn't it?" Thoreau said.

"Is it me, or does *everything* taste better in Italy?"

He laughed. "It's not just you. But every country has its specialty. We claim some outstanding curries in London, and you've
never had shepherd's pie until you've tasted my mum's."

"Iowa has . . . great corn on the cob. That's mostly what the
state is known for, at least as far as food. *Field of Dreams* was filmed
there, and the book *The Bridges of Madison County* was set there,
too."

"Haven't read it," Thoreau admitted. "Emerson may have. The
man reads everything. I'll have to ask him if he owns a copy."

"Speaking of books, did you hear that Hester is writing a

novel?" she said. "She was telling Zenia about it yesterday. It's so wonderful of her to be undertaking something ambitious like that at age ninety."

"Well, she has a lot to offer the world." He took a big bite of his twist but, after swallowing, he said, " *'How vain it is to sit down to write if you have not stood up to live.'* " He looked pleased with this latest quote. "Henry David Thoreau."

Gwen rolled her eyes. "You and your brother."

He grinned. "We're a troublesome pair, aren't we? Have we been bothering you too much? I know Emerson has a tendency to be a pest, but you don't mind us really, do you?"

She didn't immediately answer. Then, "It's not that I mind. It's just that I'm not sure I fit with either you or Emerson. I'm not even sure I fit anywhere on this tour," she admitted. "Certainly not with your crowd. Your lady friends are very . . . protective of their time with you."

He smiled at her gently. "Louisa is in a cold, loveless marriage, Gwen. I can empathize with that as I have less than fond memories of my ex-wife. So, in Louisa's case, I realize she needs a little hand-holding and, sometimes, she can be a bit clingy and cliquish. But she's rather nice when you get to know her. Cynthia, however—" He shook his head. "She's what you Americans would call 'a piece of work.' She's not someone who's easy to encapsulate. If she likes a person, she can be very kind and giving. If she doesn't, she can be . . . oh, how to best describe it?" He paused and thought. "Kind of a bitch."

Laughter Gwen couldn't control bubbled out of her. "Thoreau."

"Well, it's true," he said, laughing as well. "In some ways she's just a hurt little girl—wanting love or, barring that, wanting revenge. She was incandescent with rage when her father left her mother—not as a kid, but four years ago when she was just forty. To her it was the most grievous smack of disloyalty a person could give to another. And she's most certainly a firm believer in loyalty. She seems to be warming to you. A little."

Interesting, Gwen thought. But she still wasn't going to be a big Cynthia fan.

Thoreau told her a few details more about the ladies but, though Gwen appreciated getting some insight into these two women and was now less inclined to use the term "Britsicles" as a nickname, she couldn't deny it was Thoreau's brother she really wanted to hear about. They kept circling around him conversationally. She wasn't sure whether Thoreau had picked up on her interest in discussing Emerson and wanted to deflect her away from that, or if he simply didn't realize her degree of fascination with the man.

She thought back on their dinner after the Capri visit, when she'd had her first really good look at the brothers. While Thoreau had been polite, he hadn't been nearly as attentive as Emerson had been. The latter seemed to notice everything about her, although he hadn't tried to engage her in conversation. He must have been studying her even then, no doubt as one of his scientific experiments. She wondered what his impressions had been of her that night in the Sorrento *ristorante*. Had he liked how she looked? Had he picked up on all of her nervous habits? Had he tried to figure out what they meant?

As always, she reached up to feel her right earring, touching it as she did several times per day and remembering her mother. But when she did the same with her left one, her fingers grasped only a naked earlobe. She stopped, midstep, on the circuitous lake path, feeling for the earring more carefully and, when she couldn't locate it, combing through her hair with her fingers in hopes of finding it caught there.

"Oh, no . . ." she breathed.

Thoreau, who'd stopped walking when she had stopped, said, "Did you lose something? An earring?"

She nodded, on the verge of panicking. *Her mom's earring.* "Oh, no," she said again, trying to keep her voice from shaking, but her heart pounded like timpani and her vision blurred at the thought of having lost it.

"What does it look like?" Thoreau asked.

She motioned for him to look at the other earring, still in place, then she bit her lip to prevent her cry from coming out and

searched frantically on the walkway around her and a few steps behind. *Find it! She had to find it!*

"Be still for a moment," he commanded, sweeping her hair off
her left shoulder with one hand and picking at something near her
neck. "Here." He detached an object and held it up to her. "It was
caught in your jumper."

She let out a huge breath she'd been holding. "Oh, thank you.
Thank you so much. I—I was so scared—" She paused to inhale
and exhale several times and say a mental thanks to her friend
Kathy, who'd gone shopping with her in the spring and insisted
she buy this light knit summer sweater (a "jumper," apparently, in
British-speak), with holes perfect in size on which to hook an earring.

Thoreau was staring strangely at her. "You *were* scared. Why was
that? Why are these earrings so special to you?"

"I, um—they were my mom's," she sputtered, still trying to
slow her racing heart. "She gave them to me or, rather, she would
have, if she'd lived until I was Sweet Sixteen,". . . *and ready for
love*, Gwen added to herself. That was what her mom had always
said. She tried to explain to Thoreau that having them on was a little bit like having a piece of her mom always with her. That it reminded her of her parents and their love for one another. Of course
she didn't tell him that wearing them was like a talisman of hope
that she would one day find the same devoted love. She refastened
the fishhook wire, getting the earring back on again, and checking
both sides several times to make sure they were secure.

"I have a few items of my father's that I feel that way about,"
Thoreau said kindly. "They're irreplaceable to me, but they don't
bring him back. Some days I'm tempted to put every single sentimental piece in a box and just stuff them in the attic because, at
times, the memories are more sad than happy, and they keep me
from moving on. Especially when I start comparing my father's life
and happiness in love with my own disaster."

"Do you really think of your situation as such a 'disaster'?" she
asked him. "I know you've been having some challenging times

with your girlfriend, but it's not like you're avoiding making a commitment to her, right? You just needed time away to reflect."

He grinned. "You make me sound like a remarkably sensible man. I suspect Amanda would paint a very different portrait of me, however."

They headed back to find the hotel guests fully awake and roaming around the scenic property. Colin Pickering was out in the back garden photographing floral clusters. Gwen learned from Thoreau that her hunch about the older gentleman was correct.

"He's suffering from the early stages of Alzheimer's. He's been on a quest for the past several months to take hundreds of photos to remember the things he loved best in his life." He sighed, regarding the man with compassion. "Colin had traveled a great deal when he was a younger man, and this trip features many of his favorite sites."

As they neared the entrance, she was about to ask Thoreau a few more questions about Colin and his life, but she heard something that made her pause . . . and listen. A piano. The sound coming from the hotel lobby.

"Someone's playing," she said. She listened some more. It was a classical piece. Beethoven, maybe. Not performed by a virtuoso—it wasn't flawless—but it was more than merely competent. "Whoever that is, they're quite good."

Thoreau paused to listen, smiling at first, then scowling. "He's such a bloody show-off," Thoreau mumbled.

Gwen shot him a sharp look. There was only one person he could mean. "That's your *brother?* He can play piano, too?"

Thoreau rolled his eyes like the irritated elder sibling he was. He ushered her into the lobby and approached Emerson, who was playing a sonata with feeling in one corner of the room. A few hotel patrons hung around the edges of the lobby listening, and Gwen's heart fluttered at the sound of his passion for the instrument. Ralph Waldo "Emerson" Edwards: a guy of many talents, numerous skills and surprising depth. A modern-day Renaissance man.

Her companion was not nearly so impressed, however. "He's always carrying on about the connection between physics and music. Blah, blah, blah . . . more of his theories," Thoreau said loudly, unable to disguise his mockery.

The music stopped.

"Not theories, brother, but scientific and mathematical principles." Emerson wiggled his fingers at Thoreau then placed them on the keys again. "He just hates that I'm a better musician than he is. You should hear him on saxophone." He grimaced. "Sounds like an animal's execution the way he plays."

"What?!" Thoreau said, indignant. "Oh, bugger off." Then, whispering in Gwen's ear, he added, "He's right, I'm dreadful, but I'd never admit that to him. Passive-aggressive and denial privileges of being the eldest."

She laughed and Emerson shot them a semivenomous look. "What's the bastard saying now?"

"Don't tell him," Thoreau warned as he strode away, grinning.

"I'll kick your bum later," Emerson called after him.

"Like hell," his brother called back. And, then, he was out of earshot.

Gwen walked over to Emerson as the small crowd of hotel visitors that had been listening to him dispersed. "Sorry to scare away your audience," she said. "You play wonderfully."

He shrugged. "It's no big trick. The oscillations of each note are absolutely mathematical. If you know the starting tone, you can figure out the remaining notes easily with relative pitch. And harmonics are a simple equation of—"

"I know," she murmured. "I know the relationships are very logical, very reasonable and, yet—"

"Thank you!" He plunked a white key for emphasis. "Thoreau is full of rubbish. It's nice to talk to someone, finally, who understands."

"You didn't let me finish," she said. "The relationships may be mathematical, but music is more than math."

"We give it meaning, perhaps. Ascribe meaning onto it. But I think the meaning is innate. A function of the math itself. And our response to the beauty of those mathematical relationships when

we listen is hardwired into our DNA. Call it math, call it music—
it's the same," he replied.

She considered this but knew she'd need more time to lay out a
convincing argument or even be sure of her own position. Did she
agree? Disagree? She briefly debated her options and figured she
needed more proof. That aside, her most disturbing questions
were these: Why had she never had such a discussion with another
person before? More specifically, why didn't she have conversations like this with Richard?

Before she could even open her mouth to explain her inability
to immediately comment, Emerson met her gaze. His eyes were so
illumined by the intensity he felt on the subject, it rendered her
speechless. His facial expression mirrored physically what she felt
privately about music. She wasn't alone in her passion.

With a sweep of his palm, he ran his fingertips up the keyboard,
offering it to her. "You wish to play?"

"Oh, no . . . I can't. I don't know how to play piano."

A look of astonishment flitted across his face. "You're too interested in music not to play *something*. Don't tell me you only play
your iPod, Gwen. What's your instrument?"

He asked this as if it weren't a question packed with sentiment
or tinged with her personal fears. She swallowed. "It used to be violin. But—But it's been a long, long time."

"Hmm. It's a nice choice, though. And string theory is much
easier to demonstrate with a violin than with a piano."

This amused her, of course. "Yes, that's what I always say, too."

He swiveled on the bench, his whole body toward her. "No
need to use that sarcastic tone. The concept isn't as tricky as
everyone seems to think." He grinned and mimed finger-picking a
violin. "When you pluck a violin string, it will vibrate more wildly
if it's plucked vigorously than if it's plucked gently, right?"

"Right."

"That's precisely what one would expect. And so it is in our
great universe," he explained. "Just as the strings on an instrument respond to different vibrational patterns, causing different
notes at varying decibels, the tiny superstrings that make up our

cosmos, when strummed in particular ways, create different masses or force charges. String theory shows us that everything from the Big Bang's primordial fireball to the movement of sub-atomic quarks operate under one master equation. That the princi-ples governing all aspects of the universe—from the massive to the minute—are the same."

"As it is with the galaxies, so it is with the violin," she said, in-toxicated by this correlation, although still not quite understand-ing what it had to do with his earlier hypothesis.

"Yes," he replied, turning back to the piano and playing a quick run on it ending with a flourish in the form of a minor trill. "As it is with this keyboard, so it is with planetary orbits and the tiniest of particles."

"And you say this is true of *all* things, Emerson? What of poetry . . . or chess?"

"You'd best speak to my brother if you want to talk of chess," he said dryly, playing one last run before standing up and facing her fully. "But poetry, I know a bit about. Remember your Shake-speare," he said. "Think of *The Merchant of Venice*, that scene when Shylock's daughter had just eloped with Lorenzo. The new couple is sitting in the moonlight when the musicians enter. You know the section? She tells Lorenzo that the sweetness of the music never makes her merry, and he responds—"

"By saying the sadness she feels is because her spirit is so atten-tive to the music," Gwen finished for him. She *knew* this passage.

"Exactly. Her spirit is calling out to the celestial powers in re-sponse. The notes pierce her soul. It was a long-held Elizabethan assumption that the musical harmony of the planets, stars and moons was a manifestation of the universal order—the order God created when He made heaven and earth. In other words, the music of the spheres. In the play, Lorenzo reminds his new wife that music has the power to affect even the wild beasts and to calm even the most rambunctious of them. That if a man has no music in him, he is not someone to be trusted. Nothing good in nature is immune to its power."

"I see . . . I think," she said, pausing.

There was much in this discussion that unnerved her, not the least of which was that Emerson was a man who elicited chaos within her and, yet, he proposed a worldview of perfect order, rationality and interconnectedness. It was the diametric opposite of her feelings toward Richard. With her boyfriend back home, the world *should* have made sense, but she found it didn't quite. With Emerson, it definitely shouldn't have, but—oddly—it sort of seemed to.

She tried to summarize what she *thought* she understood about his premise. "So, you're saying it's a given that the arts reflect human emotion and our response to their influence is profound. Not only because the arts are intrinsically meaningful, but because we're physiologically compelled to find good rhymes, clear harmonies, well-proportioned drawings or sculptures, et cetera, to be aesthetically pleasing. That this pleasure is a powerful scientific truth, so strong that it connects us to the universe itself. . . ."

"Yes," he said, nodding. "Keep going."

She took a deep breath. "The pull of music, literature or painting on us is like the plucking of a string. Literally, in the case of music. Sometimes gently, sometimes vigorously, but it always causes a reaction. Our innate response brings us in synchronized harmony with the elements in nature—from the smallest atomic particle to the largest heavenly body. We're connected through these vibrations to nature and to each other. So, really, *everything's* connected."

Emerson looked at her anew—approvingly, inquisitively and only partially like she was an interesting "experiment" he was studying. "Why, Gwendolyn Reese," he murmured. "I do believe you're rather brilliant."

She smiled at him, shyly at first, then wholeheartedly. Not really believing she could ever match him intellectually, in spite of her own analytical gifts, and still puzzling through his presumption that math and music were one and the same. But she appreciated that in this area, at least, she could hold her own. A passion for music created its own special understanding. One that gave her a key to further unlocking the other disciplines.

Reprising their conversation in Pisa, she feigned a shrug and added, "Well, of course, Emerson. As it is in physics, so it is in life."

He chuckled. "That's what I always say."

6

All the World's a Stage

Saturday–Friday, July 7–13

The next several days passed like one of those dialogue-free montages Gwen always found so delightful yet unrealistic in the movies, where the passage of time speeds by and lively music swells to fill the cinema as the onscreen characters are seen joyously partaking in a myriad of activities:

Strolling along the sunny boardwalk in Nice and taking a quick dip in the cool waters of the French Riviera.

Taste-testing pastries at a sidewalk café in Lyon at a stop en route to Geneva, Switzerland.

Riding by train to the Alpine hideaway of Zermatt—the Matterhorn rising in the distance—and hiking up to see and touch an actual glacier.

She'd been a bit confounded by the tour's itinerary at first, but had been too busy getting ready when they were back in the States to question it. Once she was actually meandering along France's southern coastline, however, admiring their lovely view of the Mediterranean, she had to ask about this.

"So, we've left Italy to go to France and Switzerland, but then we'll be *returning* to Italy later. . . ." she said to her aunt one afternoon in Nice. "Isn't that inefficient?"

Bea only laughed. "You don't get to check Italy off your list,

Gwen. Not just yet, anyway." She reminded Gwen of the proximity of the French Riviera to the Italian Riviera. "It would be *more* inefficient to crisscross the country twice, especially with Venice being so far to the east and much nearer Hungary," Bea explained, "which is where we're headed after Venice."

Gwen couldn't deny the practicality of this and she eventually conceded that, yes—geographically—they'd made a logical move. But she wasn't able to abandon her extensive list of sites (or her desire to check them off) until she'd realized, during one particularly mountainous trek up to see the glacier, that she'd lost her sheet of paper for Switzerland. And she further realized she didn't really need it.

Checklist or no, she was seeing *plenty* in Europe.

Every once in a while, she would step outside of herself and examine these experiences. It was phenomenal, really, when she took time to think about what she was doing. How different it all was from her "real" life back in Iowa. But, in the parallel world of the tour, such marvels had become a daily reality. She'd come to accept them as normal, if not quite ordinary, and had managed to slip into the life of a tourist, who rose to greet each summer day with the certainty that her high sensory expectations would be met during Hans-Josef's various excursions.

And though she was still often wowed by the wondrous sites she'd seen and the privilege of being gifted such a summer adventure, she suspected she wouldn't fully assimilate all that she had encountered in Europe until many months after she'd returned home. Sometime, perhaps in midwinter when she was sipping a cup of peppermint tea during her prep period, she'd remember what it felt like to run her fingers over one small corner of that glacier in Zermatt, and she would feel the full thrill and comprehension of that experience.

But on this bright Wednesday, as the bus ambled its way to a rest stop in Verona, Italy—having left the Alps behind for a time as they headed toward the mysterious city of Venice—Gwen knew she'd only been collecting memories from these excursions, much like Colin Pickering had been collecting photos. She would have to sort through them all later to select her favorites and to find the ones that were the most meaningful to her.

"We will stop here for two hours to stretch and have lunch," Hans-Josef informed them. "Then, on to *Venezia*."

Gwen found herself lured by Aunt Bea, Matilda and Dr. Louie into grabbing a hot calzone to go and visiting the supposed balcony of "Juliet." (Which was not, of course, *real* because Juliet was a *character* in a play. Not that the native Veroneans wanted to be reminded of such a thing.) Sally and Peter tagged along, carrying water bottles and a couple of Italian chocolate bars for extra sustenance.

Since Gwen had spent a number of excursions in the company of the younger people, she didn't want to keep abandoning her aunt—regardless of Bea's encouragement to do so—and she had been making an effort to divide her time equitably between the two groups.

Nevertheless, she kept an eye on the Brits, and she spotted Emerson, Thoreau, Cynthia and Louisa having lunch together at an outdoor café downtown, near the city's imposing amphitheater. She was pleased to watch as Connie Sue, Alex and Davis were welcomed to their table. A nice intermingling of American and English S&M members . . . of young and young at heart.

"What do you see when you look at Sally's water bottle?" Peter asked her, jarring her from her thoughts as was his habit.

"Er . . . um—" she began, not knowing what, precisely, he was getting at. The object he was referring to looked very much like, well, a water bottle.

"It's that question about how you see life," Sally hinted.

"Oh," Gwen said, understanding. "In that case, I guess I see it as half full," she replied, wanting to be perceived as an optimist, even if that wasn't strictly true.

"I say half full, too," boomed Dr. Louie.

"Me, too," piped Matilda.

"Without a doubt," added Aunt Bea.

Sally chuckled, and Gwen sensed that a math joke was imminent.

"It's all in your perspective," Peter said, stating the obvious. "The optimist says the glass is half full. The pessimist says it's half empty. And the engineer says it's a container twice as large as it needs to be."

"Ha!" burst Dr. Louie.

Aunt Bea said, "Ah, that's clever, Peter. And so true."

Gwen fidgeted with the silk scarf she was wearing loosely around her neck and had to reluctantly agree with Peter's assessment. It *was* all in one's perspective. Certainly, if Emerson were to take a look at any glass, he would describe it like a highly intelligent physicist. Or an extroverted musician. Or, maybe, a somewhat deranged and overly dramatic poet. She smiled to herself. He was all of these, in her opinion. No one category could define or contain him.

As they approached "Juliet's balcony" (a tourist trap, to be sure, but at least it was a free one), Gwen studied the tan-brick building, the enclosed boxlike balcony above them—similarly tan and covered with arched design, the large rectangular doorway leading to it, the ornate window beside it and the two arched windows just below. She didn't spot any signs to label it as such, but people in the know were snapping pictures.

Gwen could, with very little imagining, picture the scene where the star-crossed Romeo and Juliet first declared their mutual adoration.

Dr. Louie—simply because he was being himself—gazed up at the smallish balcony and pronounced in singsongy tones, " *'But, soft! What light through yonder window breaaaaaaks? It is the east, and Juliet is the sunnnnn!'* "

Gwen glanced over at him with mild amusement and spied Matilda trying to blink away a stare of enraptured awareness. While Gwen had always suspected Matilda harbored feelings for the retired vet, she hadn't understood until that moment that it was more than some cute, old-lady crush. Gwen watched her more closely as she was watching him, and the truth was clear.

Matilda loved him. Truly *loved* him. Loved every crazy, loud, unbelievably exuberant thing the man did. There was a full-length feature film behind that single affectionate gaze. But, though he appeared to greatly enjoy their friendship, Gwen couldn't detect reciprocal romantic feelings from him. He seemed oblivious to Matilda's deeper admiration. Was it because he didn't feel similarly? Because a relationship with an "older" woman wasn't something he'd want? She was, after all, eighty-three to his seventy-five.

No. Gwen decided it wasn't a question of age. Matilda was physically spry and mentally sharp. Yet, inside that perfectionistic persona of hers beat the heart of a woman still very capable of falling in love. Perhaps the only difference between Matilda and Dr. Louie in that regard was that—in spite of love's challenges—Matilda was willing to risk romance again, and Dr. Louie was either unwilling to do so or unable to open his eyes to the possibility of love standing there.

Is it ever too late for us? Gwen wondered. *Are we ever too old to open our hearts?*

She was still mulling over her observations by the balcony when they wandered back toward the bus. The tour-group members gathered together in friendly cluster, awaiting the word to board again.

Emerson glided up alongside her. "So, you visited the famously fictional balcony?" he asked. When she acknowledged the truth of it with a nod, he said archly, "Deny thy logic and refuse thy sense, Juliet. Or, if thou wilt not, be but sworn to partake in a time-wasting tragedy."

"O, Romeo, Romeo," she mocked. "Why did thou not become an actor? I feel thou hast missed thy calling."

He laughed. " *'She speaks: O, speak again, bright angel!'* "

"You and your quoting," she said, smiling. "I can't keep up with you or your brother. I am—a bit out of my depth with the two of you." There, she'd said it. Let him think of her what he may. She wouldn't feign sophistication. She couldn't pretend to be the Renaissance woman to equal him. But, if he hadn't figured that out by now, he was hardly as clever as she'd been giving him credit for.

He shook his head. "Gwen, I think you keep up very well indeed." Then, softer, "I am, I realize, a somewhat challenging per-

sonality. I can be, I know, very forward and kind of a know-it-all."
He paused, letting these understatements sink in. "But there are
things about you. Things you do that I admire, too. Your way of
being is different from mine, but it's . . . it's—"

"We are leaving," Hans-Josef commanded, sending a stern look
in Gwen and Emerson's direction, even though they were hardly
the last to get on the bus. When had their tour guide directed them
to start boarding?

"It's, uh . . ." Emerson said, seemingly distracted by the other
tour members grazing past them, talking.

"It's *what?*" Gwen whispered to him.

He waited until Thoreau breezed by, eyeing them with one
brow raised, to say, "It's lovely. You have a gentler way of being in
the world, and there's more to you than that sweet and smooth surface. Something deeper and a bit darker underneath. But the more
I get to know you, the more I like you." He exhaled and nudged
her toward the bus. "Shall we get onboard?"

Most of the seats toward the front were taken, so they meandered to the back. Rows behind Aunt Bea, who was sitting with
Colin. Rows behind Cynthia and Louisa, who were sitting together. Even rows behind Thoreau, who was sitting alone. Emerson led her to the very last row and let her sit by the window.

Aside from a few pleasantries directed at a couple of fellow travelers near them, he was unusually quiet for much of the drive to
Venice. But, even in his silence, she remained acutely aware of his
presence. She felt . . . oh, how did she feel? It was an odd emotion,
actually. The simultaneous danger of him and, yet, the glorious-
ness of what she recognized as a heady infatuation. She found she
couldn't lose herself in the pretty Italian scenery no matter how intently she tried because, with him seated so near to her—even un-
speaking—he had a way of displacing the air beside her and
forcing her to acknowledge every shift in its currents. On a molec-
ular level, he was absolutely disturbing her, but it wasn't an upset-
ting sensation, per se. Just one so palpable as to be impossible to
ignore or deny.

She was reminded of Pythagoras in his bath, finally discovering the key to displacement when he stepped into the filled tub and an equivalent volume of water sloshed out. He'd cried, "Eureka!" as the solution he'd been seeking finally became apparent to him. Gwen felt she could just as easily shout the same.

Thinking back on the day Emerson had played piano at their Lake Como hotel, she'd appreciated his scientific explanations, his attempt at forming his personal "Theory of Everything," but she'd needed more reflection time herself to know her own mind on the subject.

She'd gotten that time. She'd let a handful of experiences and observations collide around outside of her, and within her.

There was Shakespeare's Juliet. A girl on a balcony, giddy with anticipation, professing her adoration for a teen boy by saying, " '*This bud of love, by summer's ripening breath, May prove a beauteous flower when next we meet.*' "

There was Matilda, professing a much more mature love with a mere glance.

There was Andrew Lloyd Webber's song "All I Ask of You" from *The Phantom of the Opera*, where the heroine pleads with her romantic young lover to help her live in the light, away from the Phantom's haunting darkness.

There was Gwen's father, playing his violin in her memory. Surprising her and her mom with a series of fun staccato notes after several minutes of flowing classical melody.

There was Emerson, playing piano as he spouted off his explanation of string theory. Trying to convince her that the universe vibrates the same way as her dad's violin strings . . . as Webber's harmonies . . . as Shakespeare's poetry . . . as Matilda's beating heart . . . and as the air currents between a man and a woman who were strangers not two weeks before.

What if it all really *was* connected?! What if Emerson was right? Oh, boy. She couldn't help but believe he might be onto something.

Not that she could prove anything, even if locked in a physics lab and forced to work out some long theorem. But it worked for her, intuitively as well as logically. It reminded her of that saying,

"Only connect . . . only connect the prose and the passion, and both will be exalted. . . ." If Emerson and the philosophic scientists of his ilk were right, if humans needed only to connect their words with the ardency of their love, would both be made glorious? Would inspiration and illumination be theirs? Would death itself feel less finite if the power of such connection in life were realized?

The world seemed, suddenly and simultaneously, more expansive and wondrous, yet, more intimate and explicable, as she sat beside Emerson—breathless—and watched the scenery whiz by. Faded gray pavement cutting through the lush green hills. A hot-air balloon in the distance dashing a crimson streak across the cerulean sky. Nerve-tingling excitement hiding beneath the placid cloak of pale skin . . . her own. The unexpected fire of infatuation dancing in step with the temperance of the mundane.

A study in contrasts and contradictions—the grandiosity of the world outside meeting the complexities of the world within.

She pulled off her scarf and folded it on her lap, letting herself enjoy the softness of the silk against her fingertips. She slipped one hand beneath it. Feeling it, nearly weightless, but not quite. Appreciating the subtlety of the distinction.

Emerson watched her do this, still in silence, but he must have sensed a shift in her. A response to his unarticulated question.

He touched the folded silky edges first, then slid his fingers beneath the fabric to meet her hand. He coaxed open her palm and laced his fingers with hers, holding her hand so gently but firmly that she could feel her blood pulsing hard in her wrist at the point where her thin flesh met the air between their hands. It was not, however, empty space. That shared current radiated between them.

She feared so many things. Too many to want to count them. Some she would not even want to try to justify.

But his touch?

Surprisingly, this was not one of them. It was a physical manifestation of their twelve days of acquaintanceship. Their holding hands succeeded in making visible what Gwen already felt: That on a number of levels, she and Emerson were bound together. That, just as their fingers interlocked, so were their fates connected.

From that second onward, Gwen didn't try anymore to pretend she didn't care about Emerson. She *did* care. She just told herself it was a temporary thing. A function of the trip's magic. She clung tightly to Davis and Dr. Louie's notion that travel created a kind of parallel world and her usual behaviors, while not having disappeared, were currently dormant. She would have known this might happen if she'd taken a foreign tour before. She wouldn't have been quite so blindsided by it then. Next time, she told herself, she would expect personal upheaval. Anticipate it.

As it was, she'd only managed to do her flexibility exercises about five times on the trip so far—she was tired in the morning!—and she found herself eating all sorts of unusual things during the day that she would've considered unhealthy at home. Still, she had to admit that these lapses in routine had not caused any ill effects (at least not yet), and she hesitantly but definitely embraced the fact that, as long as she didn't compromise her principles, everything else was reversible. No real harm would be done in the end.

Of course, that was before they sailed into Venice.

Transport into the famous city was more challenging than for most. They couldn't just drive the big tour bus into the historic center of a town that had rivers in place of streets. So, the bus traversed the Ponte della Libertà ("Freedom Bridge") causeway, then parked safely near the rail station, loading everyone and their luggage onto a large water-bus, called a *vaporetto*, to glide them toward their hotel on the Venetian Lagoon.

Gwen and Emerson were sitting next to each other as the *vaporetto* sped through the water, en route to San Marco's Square. The late-afternoon sun played a game of hopscotch on the small, multicolored homes and apartments lining the Grand Canal. The combination of the buildings, bridges and red-and-white striped poles jutting out of the water created an interesting visual effect. So very vertical, Gwen thought, but ostensibly impermanent. To her, it looked as though the paint was sliding off its structures and seeping into the water. Behind her, she could hear the feverish clicking of Colin's camera, as he attempted to capture a view too elusive for mere film.

But, even as she was thinking this, Gwen's breath caught in her throat as the water-bus rounded a bend in the canal and San Marco's materialized like a fantastical mirage before her eyes. This wasn't what she'd expected! Not because it didn't look exactly like the photographs she'd seen in guidebooks in the past or on TV . . . but because it *did*.

It was a medieval civilization coming alive. With no cars to dispel the illusion, the canals with their gondolas and gondoliers, the people meandering across the square—far enough away to be blurred and indistinct, the laundered fabric flapping from high windows and the flight and swarm of resident pigeons, all joined together to portray a scene that could have been from any generation in the past five hundred years. She may well have stepped into one of Canaletto's paintings, like those she'd seen in Florence at the Uffizi Gallery, depicting the Venice of the 1700s. A two-dimensional, meticulously illustrated tableau cast in oils that had suddenly been brought to life.

To Gwen, it felt as though she had *really* entered a parallel universe. That she had, perhaps, gone back in time. The past and the present were connected here with a fervency that surpassed even her experiences in Rome and Pompeii. How many people had strolled in a lazy diagonal across the tiles of San Marco's? How many people had seen the rise of Venetian canals, flooding the sloped pavement of the square, and watched it recede again? How many people had lived and died in this city built on more than one hundred islands? A place where its residents were so close to the sea that they almost slid into the water, too, much like the weathered paint from the buildings, bridges and poles . . .

"What do you think of it?" Emerson whispered. "People usually either love Venice or hate it. It's not a city that inspires tepid emotions."

Gwen laughed. "No, it's not." She paused, trying to form words that could express what she saw . . . heard . . . felt . . . upon finding herself in the middle of this extraordinary place. But she couldn't pull those just-right words out of the wind or the water, so she just murmured, "It's breathtaking, Emerson."

He smiled at her. "Delighted you think so. Tomorrow we'll have to explore it together."

As part of the tour group, their itinerary included a nice dinner in the hotel restaurant that night and a planned outing on the Venetian Lagoon. Some kind of gondola-ride thing. Gwen had been, admittedly, lost in her own thoughts as she and Aunt Bea freshened up after dinner for their evening excursion. In her mind, always anxious to move on to the next major event, the night had sped by and it was morning already. She'd been making a mental list of questions she wanted to ask Emerson when they were alone and, thus, paid scant attention to her aunt's chattering until Bea made a comment that pierced through her inattention.

". . . of course, everything's trickier when you're juggling multiple men. I like them younger sometimes. Dated a few before I met your uncle Freddy. One boyfriend was five years younger. Thirty years old when I was thirty-five. But then, no one probably told you about that whole situation."

Gwen shook her head. She'd heard a number of wild stories about Aunt Bea and her various boyfriends, but all of those were from Bea's widow years, told with gusto by Hester or Zenia. Gwen's mother died before she could reveal many tales from their childhood and her father wasn't one to be talking about dating unless positively forced.

Aunt Bea's eyes danced at the opportunity to enlighten her, however.

"Before I met Freddy, I'd been going steady with this younger guy for a couple of months. He was nice but, by the time I met him, I was pretty sure I'd always be a single girl. Your mom was nine years younger than me, but even she'd had more serious relationships than I'd had. Anyway, one day in early spring, I'm at the gardening store looking at hanging flower baskets. They were all full of blossoms, but none was exactly the color combination I was looking for and all were a little too expensive for me. This guy comes walking by carrying a bag of weed killer or something for his lawn. I can tell he's older than me by a handful of years and not as handsome as my young boyfriend, but I smile at him anyway. He scowls in return and points to the hanging baskets. 'They're ugly,' he tells me. 'You want nice flowers? Grow 'em yourself.' And he stalks off." Bea laughed, her thin body shaking from the motion. "I thought he was wacko and was glad he'd left. But five minutes later he comes stompin' back. 'Got these for you,' he tells me, and he hands me a couple of plain white flowerpots filled with rich black soil and a baggie of specialty hydrangea seeds. 'You grow these first and then put 'em in a hanging basket later if you want.' He doesn't crack a smile the whole time, but he looks at me as though he really can see me. As though I'm someone he already knows."

She stopped, apparently lost in the colorful twists of times recollected.

"So, your boyfriend didn't know you very well, but this stranger seemed to understand you better, right?" Gwen asked, feeling slightly unsettled at the notion of not really feeling *known* by one's boyfriend. She and Richard might have differing viewpoints on a few topics, but she felt certain they were on the same page most of the time. Really, until recently, until she'd met Emerson, she'd never had cause to even doubt her connection to Richard.

"That's right, yes, but I didn't like it. The young boyfriend was a good fit with my family. This guy at the garden shop? I knew he would set your grandmother on edge if she ever laid eyes on him. There was just something really intense and irritated in his expression. I was drawn to him, but I didn't want to be. I wanted to like the nice, polite boyfriend. I walked away from Freddy and that garden shop as fast as I could."

"What happened next?" Gwen asked, surprised but certain there had to be more to the story since Aunt Bea had ended up marrying the man.

"I kept running into him—it was a small town. Happened when I was alone the first few times, then once when I was with your mother and even a time or two when I was out with my boyfriend. I remember this one night when my boyfriend and I went to see a movie and Freddy was there with a buddy he knew from his days in the service. We were all talking in the lobby and it was just so . . . awkward." Bea shivered as if some of the social discomfort still lingered. "He gravely shook my boyfriend's hand then asked me if the hydrangeas had bloomed. I had to admit that, yes, they had. That he was right. That I liked mine better than those store-bought ones. And, though he was hardly prone to huge displays of emotion in those early days, he smiled at me that night in a way that nuked my nerve endings. Standing there, my insides quivered like a frightened bird. I remember that my boyfriend glanced over at me oddly but didn't say anything right then, which was good 'cause I couldn't speak a word after that smile. But later my boyfriend remarked, 'I didn't know you grew flowers.' Now it was my turn to stare at him because I'd actually *shown* him the plants. I knew I'd mentioned them to him at least twice when he was at our house. Your mom was even with me outside with him when I pointed out the first few green sprouts." She raised her eyebrows significantly. "He just wasn't paying attention to me."

"Did you talk to him about it?"

Aunt Bea shook her head. "Not that night, but I talked to your mom about it. She made excuses for him. Said he was a real good guy and maybe I was just overreacting. I didn't try to argue with her. What she said was reasonable, but it still didn't sit right in my gut. And the next time my boyfriend came over to the house, I realized why."

Gwen's curiosity was definitely piqued. "Why?"

"Because he wasn't the only one who'd been inattentive. When I really watched him and saw the way he acted around your mother, I realized he'd been looking at her and thinking about her the way I'd been looking at Freddy and thinking about him. We were both smitten by other people—people we didn't want to let ourselves fall in love with. He and I didn't want to admit this to each other or even to ourselves. It was a pretty honkin' huge realization for me."

Gwen blinked at her. She had most assuredly *not* heard this story. "Wait, Aunt Bea. You're saying your boyfriend fell in love with my mom? Did he ever go out with her?"

A funny smile crossed her aunt's lips. "Why, yes, to both questions. He and I had a little chat. I told him I'd met someone else and wanted to see where that relationship might go. And I encouraged him to feel free to date any other girl he might want to go out with. At first he looked surprised, then relieved and then he said, '*Anyone?*' I realized he knew that I knew who he was thinking of, so I said, 'Yep. And my sister's still single.' He laughed. The next week he asked her out. Freddy and I got together and eloped about six months later. About a year after that, my old boyfriend and your mom . . ." Bea paused, her eyes twinkling.

Gwen's breath caught in her throat, suddenly understanding. "Got married?" Her aunt nodded. "*You dated my dad?*" Gwen squeaked.

"Just for a few months, dear," Aunt Bea said. "It wasn't ever serious. Steve was always more Madeline's type than mine. Sometimes siblings can share things. Books. Music. Clothing. Sometimes not. This was one of those 'not' cases."

"Erm, yeah," she murmured. This was not a story that had come up at any family Thanksgivings! She wondered why, after all of these years, her aunt decided to reveal this to her now.

"Your dad was a very good man, Gwennie. He just wasn't the right one for me. Freddy on the other hand—" She laughed. "He was a challenge, but a worthy one." She pointed out the window at the closest canal. "He and I came to Venice together once and took a gondola ride by ourselves. Made out like teenagers in the back of a car park." She smacked her lips. "Don't know who I'd do that with tonight, though. Maybe we'll get a real cute gondolier, eh?"

"Aunt Bea! Now you're starting to sound like Zenia."

"Well, a woman can hope. What about you, dear? You got some man in mind to make out with?"

"Of course not," Gwen lied, gulping away any thoughts of kissing a man like Emerson. "And certainly not in public." She shook her head vigorously for emphasis. Perhaps too vigorously because her aunt shot her a very amused look.

Bea rummaged through her bag for a light sweater and regarded her niece with continued amusement. "I think our actor friends would say, 'The lady doth protest too much.' " But before Gwen could attempt to defend herself, her aunt all but pushed her out the door. "We don't want to be late for this excursion. It's gonna be a fun one."

As Hans-Josef had promised them earlier in the day, a trio of gondolas awaited their group, along with three gondoliers of varying ages. All had donned those black gondolier hats, the brown poles for steering and the distinctive navy-and-white striped shirts that marked these men as official tour guides of the Venetian waterways.

Matilda, Dr. Louie, Connie Sue, Alex, Kamesh and Ani piled into the first gondola, manned by a twenty-something Italian with enormous biceps, dark eyes and a lopsided grin. Aunt Bea, Colin, Sally, Peter and Davis trailed Zenia onto the last gondola, with a thirty-something Tom-Welling-as-Clark-Kent lookalike at the helm—square jawed with a twinkling blue-eyed gaze—but with flowing brown hair. And Hans-Josef shepherded Gwen onto the middle gondola, along with Louisa, Cynthia, Emerson, Thoreau and Hester, their forty-something gondolier very stout but experienced-looking and capable.

"*Buona notte*, Antonio," Hans-Josef said in greeting to their man, clearly a friend of his from tour groups past.

The gondolier smiled in acknowledgment, returned the greeting and snagged their tour guide's attention long enough for Cynthia to take control of the seating arrangements. Deftly sliding behind Gwen, the British woman steered her to a comfortable seat in the gondola that could accommodate one other person, but when Emerson moved forward to join her there, Cynthia very sweetly but firmly stepped between him and Hester and directed the older woman to the spot instead. She put Louisa between Thoreau and the seat nearest to where Hans-Josef was standing, and propelled Emerson to a cozy seat next to herself on the opposite side of the gondola.

"Oh, my! This is going to be deliciously romantic, don't you think?" Cynthia chirped as Hans-Josef finished his conversation with the gondolier and looked pleased that everybody in his boat seemed ready to set sail.

It was all Gwen could do to keep from glaring at Cynthia. While the woman hadn't been venomous in her maneuverings, she certainly wasn't stepping graciously out of the game. Thoreau shot her an arch glance over his shoulder and whispered, "The chess match continues, my American friend. Are you going to be a pawn or a queen?"

And Emerson, who was sitting across the watercraft from Gwen and Hester, facing them, looked momentarily perplexed at Cynthia's antics, but he didn't seem especially angered by them. Of course, he probably felt there was nothing to get too ruffled about anyway. All Gwen and Emerson had done was talk like the casual acquaintances they were, flirt a little and, in a peculiar moment of connection, hold hands once. While this was most unusual for *her*, he probably behaved like that with lots of women. Hardly a reason for *him* to be upset or even mildly inconvenienced, she thought.

"Nice and snug in here," Hester commented. "Bet'cha it'd be easy to stab someone in one of these contraptions. Or at least hold 'em at knifepoint."

Gwen reluctantly agreed that might be true, but she wasn't prepared to help the elderly woman come up with strategies to murder her hapless characters. Wedged between Hester's angular body and the padded side of the gondola, she forced herself to listen politely as their gondolier Antonio regaled them with historical tidbits about the *Venezia* of old. She studied Cynthia as she scooted unnecessarily close to Emerson on their bench. And she gazed out at the other two gondolas, wondering if other people were experiencing any of the socio-relationship dramas she'd been dealing with on the trip.

Was Matilda thinking more about her fondness for Dr. Louie than about the ride through the Venetian Lagoon?

Was Aunt Bea missing Uncle Freddy that night and wishing she could relive their kiss on the canal?

Was Hans-Josef wondering about his pet Rolf or wishing he'd had more friends on tour? Maybe a girlfriend upon whom he could shower his affection?

It seemed a shame to waste such a romantic atmosphere on simply a boat ride.

The gondoliers took turns singing songs in Italian, offering up harmonies to support each other. When it was Antonio's turn to take the vocal lead, Gwen found herself falling under his musical spell. Not that she understood the words to his song—she didn't. But she understood the longing in the melody laced with the lyrical verses.

As they sailed under the famous Rialto Bridge, lit up at night along with the rest of the city, the bridge's crisp white paint appeared to be a classic cream in the soft light. Gwen found herself glancing again at Bea, a look of rapturous delight on her aunt's face at the twinkling bulbs that illuminated the antiquated buildings and set the water sparkling. She tried to imagine her dad dating the young Beatrice while secretly loving the even younger Madeline. It was a piece of her parents' history she'd never known, and it brought a certain weight to her dad's friendship with Aunt Bea, even after both her mom and Bea's husband died. They had been more than just in-laws. Even more than just friends . . . if only for a short time. Her dad had once said that he'd been introduced to her mom by Aunt Bea, but he'd never hinted at any further significance, and Gwen hadn't thought to ask if there'd been one. Was his hesitance to divulge that history because he'd wanted to keep the primacy of his relationship to Bea to himself? Because he worried the knowledge might reflect poorly on her aunt, her mom or himself in some way? Gwen thought of all of those S&M gatherings her dad had driven to in the years before his heart attack. Might Aunt Bea or her father ever been interested in rekindling that first relationship?

No. Gwen suspected not. Her dad showed not so much as a flicker of interest in ever dating again after her mom died. Not even in unguarded moments. The problem with having something special—some really deep and true romantic connection—was that it made every other relationship pale by comparison. She knew this intuitively, having spent years poring over the attachments of literary lovers like Shakespeare's Benedick and Beatrice, Austen's Darcy and Elizabeth, Brontë's Rochester and Jane. Once you knew how powerful something could be, you didn't want to settle for something lesser.

Gwen knew this was true of other things, too. She'd always enjoyed her CD player until she got her first iPod. She'd liked the creaminess and mild flavor of ice cream well enough until she tasted her first gelato cone. And she'd thought her physical attraction to Richard was perfectly adequate until she met Emerson and began questioning it. . . . Just the awareness that there might be *a real difference* changed everything.

She breathed in, letting the warm Venetian air fill her lungs. How bad would it truly be to explore her relationship with Emerson in the context of this trip? She shot him a look. Across the gondola, his gaze met hers and locked. He smiled at her, seemingly oblivious to Cynthia's chattering for a moment. Time was put on pause, as if their shared glance happened in the space between the seconds. Gwen returned his smile but swiftly looked away in an attempt to quiet the fluttering deep in her abdomen. *Bad*, she murmured to herself, in answer to her own question.

She wasn't allowed to wallow in this realization for long, however. In the first gondola, a startling burst of sound drifted across the short expanse of water and crashed like a discordant wave against Gwen's eardrum.

Dr. Louie.

With his gondola mates held captive and the receptive indulgence of his young gondolier, the retired vet had launched into the enthusiastic opening verse of "That's Amore." Matilda (*of course*), Alex and Connie Sue gleefully joined in, and the madness spread from one boat to the others like a rampant case of the Black Plague in the city's dark history. All three gondoliers were rowing in time and, soon, almost everyone was singing along. The only holdouts were Ani, who didn't know the lyrics because he listened only to Indo-Euro rap and alternative punk, and Gwen, who couldn't bring herself to be so exhibitionistic.

"Let's do it as a round!" Dr. Louie suggested. "We'll start in this gondola with 'When the moon . . .' You guys"—he pointed to Gwen's gondola—"you begin singing when we get to 'pizza pie.' And everyone over there." He motioned toward Aunt Bea's gondola. "You all join in on 'amore.' Got it?"

Naturally, the Edwards brothers could sing, Gwen noticed. They could do just about anything, it seemed, and had strong musical voices on top of all their other gifts. Not remarkable enough to star in a West End production, perhaps, but their tone and range were nothing to be embarrassed by, either.

In spite of herself, Gwen found she was swaying a bit. Well, Hester kept rocking into her, forcing her to move whether she wanted to or not, but she actually kind of hummed along with the melody. She was pretty sure no one but, maybe, the older woman beside her could hear her, since she always worked hard to keep her vocal contributions virtually inaudible. Still, Gwen *tried* to come out of her shell. After all, how many times would she be on a gondola in Venice?

Even Cynthia had joined in. Gwen studied her. Sitting next to Emerson—singing shrilly and vaguely out of pitch—Cynthia looked *happy*. More contented than smug. Gwen got the sense that the other woman craved love and companionship so much that she'd put aside any possible ineptitude in the attempt to get it. And while it seemed, to Gwen, to be obvious that the Brit had thrown herself at Emerson that night, Gwen couldn't discount the powerful aphrodisiac of courage. Cynthia was going after what she wanted in a way Gwen had not. A man who had guts, like Emerson, couldn't help but admire that.

He caught her staring at them, grinned and motioned for her to open her mouth and sing. She shook her head. His brother then nudged her foot with his and said, in between verses, "You must know the words to this." She shrugged and hummed just a little harder. Before the end of the song, both of the Edwards men had rolled their eyes at her in exasperation, making her certain that her persistent self-consciousness was, indeed, a character flaw. Not that she could do anything about that. Not really.

Back at the hotel, she was startled when Emerson broke away from his gang to come up to her, though, and whisper in her ear, "Don't make any plans for tomorrow morning, all right?" He leaned in toward her. "I'm coming to knock you up at eight."

She pulled back and stared at him, unable to mask her astonishment. "You're going to do *what?*"

He tilted his head as if perplexed, balled up his fist and moved it as if he were pounding against something. Gwen knew she didn't get around much, but this looked to be a very sexually suggestive gesture indeed. "Knock. You. Up," he said slowly.

That he was saying this in a normal tone of voice floored her. She covered her open mouth with her palm and shook her head vigorously. She removed her hand. "I can't believe you just said that. Stop it."

He laughed out loud. "Oh, Gwen, you're such an American. I'm just playing with you. I know your country's idioms. It's time you learned a few of ours. 'Knock you up' is a common English expression. It means, literally, to knock on your door. In order to wake you up." He laughed at her some more and lowered his voice a tad. "It does not mean to impregnate you. Although"—he paused and shot a wicked grin at her—"I'm like James Bond. I never say never."

She felt her face flush hot as he swiveled on his heel and headed back to the other Brits, who were looking on with amusement (Thoreau), irritation (Cynthia) and confusion (Louisa). Gwen raced out of the lobby as fast as she could.

The next day, true to his word, Emerson came knocking on her door just after eight a.m. To his credit, he only smirked a little bit when he was picking her up. Aunt Bea, on the other hand, was not nearly so circumspect.

"Have fun, kids!" her aunt called with an unnecessary zing of energy. "And just so you know, I'll be out of the room for most of the morning, just in case you get tired and want to . . . um, take a break here before the afternoon tour."

Gwen glared in horror at her aunt, but Emerson just laughed good-naturedly and said, "Many thanks for the offer, Beatrice. We shall keep that in mind."

"Where did you want to go?" Gwen asked as soon as they were outside and she had recovered her voice. "To San Marco's Square?"

"I have a few sites planned, starting with the Rialto," he told her. "I know we saw it last night, but it's different during the day. Plus, we couldn't stop the gondola to get out and shop yesterday."

"True. Is the shopping as interesting here as it was in Florence?" she asked.

"I'll let you decide for yourself." He scanned the twisty path they were on, bustling with tourists, until he spotted something several yards away. "But first, gelato." He picked up the pace.

She glanced at her watch and had to skip a few times to catch up with him. "It's not even eight-thirty, Emerson. No one eats ice cream this early in the day. Not even the natives."

He shot a look at her over his shoulder. "Willing to wager a bet?"

As it turned out, no, she didn't want to make a bet. Not with him. And certainly not after seeing a line of people waiting at the gelato stand. While the couple in front of them ordered their cones in fluent Italian, Emerson raised one eyebrow at her and nodded wordlessly.

"Fine," she murmured. "So what if you're right?"

He grinned. "You'll find I am often right."

She didn't waste her breath bothering to contradict him, but he remained a distinctly different breed of man than any she'd encountered before: cocky, but strangely good hearted; juvenile, but undeniably intelligent; a fan of the arts, but unquestionably masculine. Even after two weeks in his company, she still had little idea what to make of him—except that she felt persistently out of his league.

They took their cones and meandered in what Gwen thought

was an aimless promenade, but Emerson, apparently, knew his way around Venice—no easy-to-master skill given the serpentine walkways, the flowing canals at every turn and the countless unmarked little bridges. Suddenly, they turned a corner and there was the Rialto Bridge, about twenty yards ahead of them, flashing brilliant white in the scorching sun and already packed with a swarm of visitors.

"Oh!" she exclaimed. "We got here fast."

"Yes, well, I knew a shortcut." He stopped to study the view. "Pretty, is it not?" Before she even managed to form an answer, he elbowed her and said, "Oh, look at that."

He pointed to the window of the shop nearest them on the sidewalk, and she peeked at the object of his interest. It was a chess piece—the knight from an elaborate set—displayed as a centerpiece behind the glass. "It's lovely," she said, leaning closer and noticing the rest of the chess set resting atop a polished board on a decorative table behind the ornate horse and rider.

"Bloody gòrgeous," he whispered. "Handcrafted, too. Made of pewter. Painted with real eighteen-karat gold and sterling silver. Hmm."

"How do you know that?"

He motioned toward a little placard near the piece. "It says."

She glanced at it and almost rolled her eyes. Yes, it said it all right. In Italian. "Is there *anything* you don't know how to do?"

He paused. Scrunched up his handsome forehead in thought. Squinted into the distance. "No." Then he laughed heartily. "Of course, Gwen. There are scores of things I don't know or cannot do. It's because I didn't know something, but I worked up the nerve to ask somebody or to give it a go anyway, that I learned. You need to stop being so afraid of looking foolish."

Or sounding foolish, she thought, remembering the impromptu singing in the gondolas the night before.

"I'm going to slip in here for a moment. If they sell individual pieces, I want to pick one up for my brother. He celebrates a birthday next month. What do you think he'd like best? A knight? A king? A rook?"

She recalled that one morning Thoreau explained the *moves* he'd thought she made in her ever-so-polite battle against Cynthia. "A bishop," she told Emerson. "I think he'd like that piece."

He shot her an inquisitive glance. "Interesting choice. I always prefer the boldness of the knight myself, but Thoreau does use his bishops in surprising ways sometimes. Sneaks up on a gent." He finished his last bite of gelato and tossed out the napkin. "Huh. I'll be back momentarily."

While he was inside making his purchases, she saw a few paper flyers posted for some event coming up called the *"Festa del Redentore,"* and she asked Emerson about it when he emerged from the shop.

"It's a big celebration that dates back to the late 1500s," he explained. "Always held on the third weekend in July. A feast day of thanks for the end of the plague that'd killed thousands, including the famous painter Titian, whose work I admire. There are fireworks, decorated boats in the Grand Canal and a long procession to the Church of the Most Holy Redeemer." He shrugged. "It's charming. Too bad we'll be all the way up in Paris then."

Oh, she hadn't thought of that. Paris! Just a week away. This trip was zipping by, almost too fast for her to assimilate it. She needed more time for reflection. Time to process everything she was seeing, hearing, feeling. But this was the thing about the tour that made it so very odd for her. That caused that parallel-universe sensation. Because she *didn't* get a break from the constant activity and new sites, she was as overstimulated as a toddler during the first week of preschool. And if it wasn't Hans-Josef introducing her to some new place or new cultural item, it was Emerson.

They dashed up the stairs on their side of the Rialto and began inspecting the vendors crammed onto the bridge. Much like their bazaarlike experience on the Ponte Vecchio in Florence, there were simply too many objects to focus on at once—a cacophony of colors, if she could hear them rather than see them. Nevertheless, she tried to direct her attention to one single thing at a time and found herself drawn to a particular piece.

"Is that a *Phantom of the Opera* mask?" she asked, pointing to-

ward a collection of Venetian masks hanging askew on a jaunty
display pole. She walked over to it and picked it up. It reminded
her of a mask she'd caught a brief glimpse of back in Florence and,
of course, the most famous costume relic from her favorite musical.

"Looks quite a bit like it, but that's a very traditional style," he
commented. "This one is a popular shape and it seems to cover a
little more of the face than the one the Phantom wears in the play.
But it's been a long while since I've seen the production. Why? Do
you wish to purchase it? Take it home, hang it on your wall and
pretend you're Christine?"

She laughed, far too embarrassed to admit how close to the
truth he was, but she didn't answer him of course. Instead, she fingered the black laces that were meant to tie the mask in place and
ran her thumb across its white lacquered cheek. She noticed several masks in front of her that were similar. In peering at a competing mask vendor a few spaces down, she saw even more of them,
along with others that were painted to look like suns, moons,
leaves, jesters. The one she was holding felt very commonplace all
of a sudden.

She slid it back on the hook. "Are there any mask shops anywhere nearby? Ones that might have a larger selection or, perhaps,
some truly original designs?"

His eyebrows rose and the corners of his lips curled into a mocking grin. "My, haven't you become quite the avid shopper? And so
discriminating as well."

She shot him an annoyed look.

"Gwen, this is *Venice*. There are masks and mask shops *everywhere*." He paused and scanned the buildings along the canal. "I'll
take you to my favorite."

She followed him through a series of more twisty walkways and
bridges, quickly losing all sense of direction herself, until they
reached a little hole-in-the-wall place with a brightly painted
wooden sign above the entrance. Upon it, in heavily slanted calligr-
raphy, were the words *Il Carnevale*.

"The Carnival," Emerson translated unnecessarily. "Pronounced
'eel car-nee-vall-ay' in Italian. There's a huge Mardi Gras celebra-

tion every year in the city. It's crammed with people. About a hundred thousand tourists show up. And it lasts for a couple of weeks. Never had the daring to try to come down here then, though." He waved her through the door and into the shop. "Come. Take a look around."

Gwen entered what appeared at first glance to be some kind of artisan's workshop rather than the store she was expecting. She realized quickly that was precisely what this place was: a workshop. This wasn't merely a spot to exhibit masks—although there was an entire wall filled with them and a window display, too. No. This was where they were created.

Emerson, chattering at her as always, was attempting to explain the different types of masks that were made there. There were the oval *moretta* masks with black velvet and veils, the very simple *volto* masks and the *bauta* masks, which were the kind historically linked to Venice ever since the Middle Ages. Many of these masks covered the entire face with just eye slots, no mouth, and lots of gilding, while others concealed only the upper part of the face from the forehead to the nose, but allowed the wearer to talk, eat or drink as desired.

"They're useful for a number of purposes," he said, picking up a striking, one-of-a-kind catlike mask and holding it up to his face so that he resembled a somewhat deranged lion. "Especially illicit romantic encounters."

She shook her head at his choice of *bauta* and pointed to this harlequinesque character mask that she'd seen depicted in a number of places around the city. "This seems to be a popular design. What is it?"

Emerson set down his leonine selection. "You mean *who* is it, don't you?" Emerson said, a split second before an older lady, who had to be one of the artists, walked in.

She saw Gwen pointing and said, "That is Arlecchino. Do you know the opera?"

Gwen shook her head.

"It is a one-act opera. German," the Venetian woman said in heavily accented English. "But the roles—the characters—they

come from the Italian *commedia dell'arte*. It's a funny story. A—"
She paused, searching for the exact word. "A parody, yes?"

Emerson nodded at her. "Yes. The main character, Arlecchino,
has little faith in marriage and fidelity. He's married to Colombina,
but he wants to be with the tailor's wife, the lovely Annunziata. It's
rather like a comedy of errors and a game of masks and disguises
but, instead of everyone ending up with their spouses, the players
get switched around. Arlecchino is united with Annunziata as his
lover. Colombina gets a different guy for herself—"

"Leandro," the Italian woman interjected with a grin. "And
Dottore and Abbate become lovers, too. But the poor tailor, Matteo . . ." She sighed.

"Matteo, who is Annunziata's husband, ends up alone," Emerson explained. "And in the finale, as all the new couples form a
procession onto the stage, Arlecchino removes his mask at last and
addresses the audience. He explains the new arrangement of the
couples."

"And he says they will last 'until something new happens,' "
added the woman. "So there is no promise of fidelity at the end,
even among the new lovers."

"Huh," Gwen managed. It figured Emerson would like a play
like that. "I'm sure it's hilarious," she said wryly. "You probably
just have to be there to appreciate it."

Emerson's grin broadened and the Italian artist lady smiled gently. "You are just recently married?" she asked.

"What? No!" Gwen cried. "We . . . um, we're—"

"Friends," Emerson supplied. He cleared his throat. His grin
remained unchanged.

"Ah, friends. *Amici. Si . . . forse.* You will tell me if you need my
help, yes?"

"*Molto grazie,*" Emerson replied with a nod. When the woman
had busied herself in the corner of the room, he pointed at the
rows of unusual masks. "Well? Any you wish to take home with
you?"

She ran the pad of her thumb over the gold Mouth of Truth that she'd been wearing around her neck since Florence and said, "I tend to spend quite a bit of money when I'm with you, don't I?"

"Perhaps. But you're purchasing quality items."

She agreed, even though she suspected Richard would consider just about everything she'd bought on the tour so far an extravagance. She picked up a mask that was perched on a stick. No ribbons to tie. The wearer had to hold it up to her face. The design was a beautiful combination of celestial bodies. Suns, moons, stars and comets were all represented. And the colors! Rich shades of navy, teal and purple accented with silver and gold. It was like peering into the Milky Way.

"This one is gorgeous, but I don't want to get it now," she said decisively. "I'd have to carry it all through the Doge's Palace this afternoon. Maybe I'll come back tonight or tomorrow before we leave Venice."

"As you like," he said with a shrug. He took a closer look at the mask and laughed.

"What?"

"It's just . . . you know what? Never mind. You won't enjoy it." He bit back a smirk and took a few steps toward the door. "Let's go."

"No," she said, feeling a bolt of stubbornness rooting her feet to the floor. "I want to know."

"Fine, but no mocking me later." He inhaled deeply and squinted into the distance. " *'Nun glüht mein Stern! Die Welt ist offen!'* " he recited enthusiastically. " *'Die Erde ist jung! Die Liebe is frei! Ihr Halekins!'* "

"Let me guess," she said, unable to hide her sarcasm. "String theory in German?"

"I said no mocking. And, no. It's from the opera *Arlecchino.* Loosely translated it means, 'Now shines my star! The world is open! The Earth is young! Love is free! You Harlequins!'"

She squinted at him. "How many languages do you speak?"

"Just one. The language of love," he said, as overly dramatic as he'd been at that *ristorante* in Sorrento.

She groaned. "Oh, please. Save the acting for when you're putting on another show with your brother."

He feigned a stab to the heart. "I am struck."

"No, you are insane," she shot back. It was impossible to take *anything* that man said about emotion seriously. She glanced at her watch and carefully hung up the celestial mask she liked. "We have less than an hour before we need to meet the tour, so we probably should get something to eat now."

He gave a long-suffering sigh. "So be it. I know where to go for that as well." He tossed her a playful look. "You would be quite lost without me. Admit it."

"I'd get by," she said, the bolt of stubbornness strengthening.

He shrugged. "It's possible. But you would scarcely see as much and you would have far less fun."

She refused to admit this was 200 percent true.

They stopped for lunch at a little café with a daily special that included linguini in a choice of meat sauce or a white sauce with something called *calamaretto*. A kind of cheese, maybe? There were samples of them behind the counter, and they both looked tasty. She wasn't sure which one to order, so Emerson said, "You're not allergic to seafood, are you?"

She shook her head. Before she could ask where on Earth he saw seafood, he said, "Good. We'll get one of each and share."

When the plates came they were heaped with pasta. Gwen stared at them both, trying to figure out a way to split the meal into two so they could share without noodles spilling over onto the table. She was just about to ask their server for a couple of additional plates when Emerson stuck his fork right into the center of his pasta mountain—the one in front of him had the meat sauce—and swirled.

But, instead of devouring this forkful, he lifted it to her lips and said, "I would like you to take the first bite." And when she didn't immediately open her mouth because she was staring at him in *shock*, he added, "Really, Gwen. Taste it. You should savor it, like a fine Tuscan wine."

So she opened for him . . . and let him feed her.

She chewed slowly, dutifully at first, but then she pulled her eyes away from him and let herself actually relish the combination of flavors, textures and scents. "Mmm," she murmured as she swallowed.

"Good. Now take a sip of this to clear the palate." He poured her a glass of sparkling water with a hint of lemon. She followed directions, curious to see what he'd do next. He reached across the table, swirled his fork in the white-sauce linguini and brought this to her lips, too. "All right. Time for the second act."

She let him feed her that forkful of pasta as well. She chewed. Savored. Swallowed. And thought about how very, very . . . intimate it was to share a meal like this with someone. Especially with someone like Emerson.

It was, in fact, a novelty. Not so much the meal, though it was very well prepared, but the *being fed* aspect. By a man. Richard might order fine food on occasion, but he had never—not in the entirety of their two years together—*ever* fed her so much as a morsel of anything from his plate.

Emerson was watching her, tilting his head. Clearly, he was musing over something, too, but she wasn't sure what. "Which do you like best?" he asked, still not having taken a bite of either type of linguini himself. His careful attention to her reactions was unsettling, but in a heightened-awareness sense rather than in an awkward one.

"I—I'm not sure," she mumbled, trying to blink away this new odd vibe between them. She needed to take some immediate action, so she plunged her fork into the pasta closest to her and swirled it just the way he had done. Then, when she was sure there would be no dripping sauces, she reached across the table and presented it to him in the same manner that he'd given it to her. "Your turn," she said, trying to sound bold. "Taste this."

He opened his mouth—his expression serious, sincere—and took it from her.

Gwen learned something new, swiftly and powerfully: If being fed by a man created the sensation of intimacy, feeding him in return exponentially increased that emotion. Not only was Emerson crossing all of her borders, invading her personal space and treating her with unprecedented familiarity, but he was letting her traipse into his private world, too. And there was something almost intoxicating in that gesture.

She fed him from the second plate as well. "Which is *your* favorite?" she asked, after he'd had a chance to swallow.

He wrinkled his forehead as he stared between the two heaping dishes. "I'm not certain either. Probably means we need to try both of them again, yes?"

He didn't smirk when he said this. He looked at her with the earnestness of a teen boy waiting for permission to make the next move. To put his arm around her, perhaps.

She nodded and, in response, he fed her a forkful of each type of pasta all over again. Then she did the same for him. And they repeated this—feeding one another and watching as the other one savored each bite—for so many times that Gwen lost count. She didn't even freak out (too much) when he finally confessed what *calamaretto* meant.

"I'm eating *small squid?*" she said.

He replied with his usual nonchalance, "Naturally. Venetians live off the sea."

But there was nothing nonchalant about any of this to her. In Gwen's opinion, this dining experience was the single most erotic thing she'd ever done without physically touching—or being touched by—someone.

When they finally got up to leave, he took her hand in his, out in public this time, and held it gently as they reentered the Venetian crowds.

"Right. Let's get you back in time to meet the ghosts of Doges past," he said.

She laughed and glanced around them. Not that she had any intention of admitting this to Emerson, but she was utterly lost—as if in a cornfield maze intended for Halloween revelers. He, however, knew just how to get them back to Piazza San Marco, not letting go of her hand until they reached the bustling square. They made it with only eight minutes to spare for the afternoon tour of the Doge's Palace, the viewing of the famous Titian painting *Assumption of the Virgin*, the infamous Bridge of Sighs and a dozen other sites on Hans-Josef's carefully planned agenda. As much as Gwen tried to focus on the history, though, and on the stunning artwork and architecture around them, she found everything blurring together after a time, like the oil paints on a novice's first attempt at Impressionism.

He fed her linguini. Her mind and body still hadn't quite assimilated this romantic, intentional, affectionate act. This sarcastic, dramatic, incredibly bright man . . . was also tender. She tried to swallow away her feelings of attraction toward him, but she could still taste the sauce on her lips from their meal, and her fingers still tingled from when he'd held her hand.

He also didn't believe in long-term commitments, she reminded herself, if only to keep from slipping into some kind of adolescent reverie. Plus, he lived in another country.

But he liked her. She knew that for sure.

That was something.

For their final day in Venice (a Friday the thirteenth, no less, but Gwen had never been superstitious that way), they were instructed to pack up their bags right after breakfast. They could keep their luggage in the hotel baggage area, but they needed to check out of their rooms because the tour group was going on a morning glassblowing excursion to Venice's sister island, Murano.

She was sitting next to Aunt Bea on the *vaporetto* as they pulled up to the workshop and could see the glassblowers sheltered inside as they approached. It was strangely picturesque. Much like her first impression of Venice on the day they arrived, Gwen had no problem sensing an immediate connection to the history of the region.

The sound of happy chitchatting in the water-bus, combined with the swish of the waves and the call of the seagulls, made for a lyrical entrance, but not necessarily a twenty-first-century one. In staring at the working glassblower and his assistants framed in the open doorway, Gwen could almost make her vision of them shift and blur in her mind, much the way kids stared at those optical-illusion cards until the images swirled and blended and emerged from their flat 2-D form into watercolory 3-D, right before their eyes. For a brief moment, with the musical tones of her surroundings and the distorted view she created, Gwen felt again as though she'd been given a motion-picture-like window into the past.

When they disembarked, she had a chance to witness the act of glassblowing itself—a perilous occupation if ever she'd seen one—but she couldn't help but admire both their craft and their courage.

Zenia, who responded to any performance in the artistic realm with the enthusiasm of a five-year-old in the Magic Kingdom, watched with rapt attention the process of creating just one, thin, red vase, rimmed with gold. "I can't weave the red glass into any of my projects," Gwen overheard her whispering to Hester. "Too dangerous. But I can replicate that color. And I can add some gold ribbon to mimic the visual effect."

"Bet that'd look beautiful," Hester said appreciatively.

A half hour later, after they'd had a chance to inspect the gift shop and purchase Murano glass of their own (Cynthia was in raptures over the jewelry), Gwen found herself near Hester and Zenia again, this time on their way back to the *vaporetto*. On the dock, looking out at the canal, Gwen tried to see the collection of islands the way the people of the past must have viewed them. She spotted some gondoliers in the far distance and smiled. Her fantasy Venetians were mental mannequins, stand-ins for the humans who'd once sailed these waters. And being here, walking where they had once walked, seeing what they had once seen, made her feel as though they were a part of her. Their daring in conquering this amphibious land allowed her to stand here today. Even though they died decades or centuries ago . . . in her experience, trailing their footsteps, they lived on.

"I know what I want the sequel of my Pisa book to be called," Hester informed Zenia, who was clutching a carefully wrapped replica of the red-and-gold vase she saw the glassblower make. *"Death in Venice."*

"Wasn't there already a novel called that?" Zenia asked.

"Yeah," Hester said, stepping into the *vaporetto*. "But it's high time there was another."

Gwen smothered a smile at this, and Aunt Bea, who couldn't help but overhear, too, as they all boarded the water-bus, shot her a cheerful grin.

"Live every moment of your life, Gwennie," Bea said, nodding in Hester's direction. "The years zip by faster than any of us think." She threw her head back and laughed at the rays of sun warming her pale skin. "You should dance. Sing. Buy extravagant things every now and again. Make time for love and good food. And take a nap when it all gets to be too much."

With that, her aunt took her own advice and slept the whole way back to the hotel.

"We have just one hour and forty-three minutes before we must leave Venice," Hans-Josef reminded them upon their return. "We depart for Budapest at two o'clock sharp. So, have lunch or a snack. Buy any last souvenirs. See San Marco's Square one more time, but be back here by two. You all understand this, *ja?*"

"*Ja!*" everyone chorused dutifully in response.

The mask shop. Gwen had almost forgotten about the celestial mask she'd liked so much. Somehow, it seemed more important to her than ever to go back for it.

She pulled Emerson aside to ask him directions. "I remember it was called *Il Carnevale*, but I was hoping you might draw me a map."

"No." He crossed his arms and waited.

"No, that's not what the shop is called, or no, you won't draw the map?"

"The latter. When will you learn that I like to spend time with you, hmm?" he chided. "Besides, we don't have hours available. It would take me longer to draw the map than it would to just take you there myself. I don't want to be the one responsible for getting you lost in Venice. Come with me." And before she could blink he was already three yards ahead of her.

It took a solid thirty minutes of walking—she hadn't realized just how far they'd meandered the day before—to get back to that little place, but that wasn't what increased her pulse or made her feel breathless.

"It's gone," she whispered, scanning the wall frantically for any trace of the mask she'd held yesterday. "Oh, no."

Emerson squinted at the wall display and then, apparently not seeing it there either, he began to inspect the various pieces on the tables and near the window in search of it. He shot her a regretful glance. "Maybe if we ask the man over there?"

It was a different person working in the back this time. A guy. Someone not as friendly or as welcoming as the lady artisan from yesterday. But, nevertheless, Emerson approached him and described the mask Gwen was looking for.

The man scowled and kind of shook his head. Gwen's heart clenched. It was her own fault. She shouldn't have waited to buy it. Some things should be snapped up the moment they're seen. Or, like a saying her father was fond of, "Good things come to those who wait, but not to those who wait too late." She sighed, disappointment seeping deep inside her. She took a step toward the door.

"Gwen, wait," Emerson said. He pointed in the direction of the now-empty chair. Where had the man gone?

The Italian emerged from the backroom a moment later . . . holding her mask!

"Oh, thank you!" she cried. It was as lovely as she remembered, perhaps even more so because she thought she'd lost the chance to have it. The sun, moon, stars and comet sparkled on the face of the mask like the night sky on a cloudless night.

The guy shrugged, gave it to Gwen and said something in brusque Italian to Emerson, who chuckled lightly. Then the man returned to ignoring them.

"He said that the lady who was here yesterday is the owner of the shop. And she'd set aside the mask for you." Emerson smiled at Gwen. "I guess she overheard our conversation."

Relief and delight collided within her. How grateful she was to that woman for her thoughtfulness and, perhaps, for her romanticism—however unfounded. "That's so kind." She lifted the mask by its handle and held it up to her face. "How does it look?"

"Excellent," he said with enthusiasm. "Now I need one."

They looked around the shop like giddy children for a minute until another Phantom-like mask caught her eye. It was similar in the simplicity of the design to the ones they'd seen on the Rialto Bridge, but it was clear that the craftsmanship of this mask was superior. And there were little distinctive touches that gave it an unusual elegance.

He saw her staring at it, so he picked it up. "You do realize we have the option to go to see *The Phantom of the Opera* when we get to London, right?"

Oh, yes, she knew.

"Aunt Bea told me." She watched as he fastened the mask to his head.

If anything had tipped Gwen over the edge as far as going on this trip, it was that. But she was afraid to so much as think about seeing the musical live for fear she'd jinx the experience. She didn't want to be as acutely disappointed as she knew she would be if they ended up going to see another theatrical production instead.

"Should I tell you to sing for me, my Angel of Music?" he asked, looking very much like the Phantom, indeed, in spite of wearing a T-shirt and khakis instead of a black cloak.

She held her mask firmly to her face. "I do not sing in public, Emerson. Not ever."

"Well, what's stopping you? Your voice can't be that bad."

How to explain? It wasn't really about her voice being *bad*. It was more about being vulnerable. About showing her love of the music to the world. That love wasn't for public consumption or display. It was . . . personal.

Before she could even try to stop him, he began humming the first few ominous bars from the musical's title track. Now he looked and *sounded* like the Phantom. "Come. Hum the notes with me at least," he said.

She was behind a mask and there was no one in the shop, save for an Italian man, who was determinedly ignoring them, and Emerson, who was her friend. She managed a few notes, which were oddly amplified by the acoustics of singing directly into lacquered papier-mâché.

"Very good," Phantom Emerson said. He hummed some more and made her join him in that, too. Just when she was starting to get into it a little and lose a touch of her self-consciousness, though, he paused.

"What?" she asked. He was staring through his mask and hers, deep into her eyes. "Did I hit a wrong note?"

He shook his head. "*Tu sei una stella . . . la mia stella,*" he murmured. "You are a star . . . my star." He took a couple of steps closer to her, never breaking eye contact, and slowly unfastened his mask.

She lowered hers and watched as he removed his and placed it gently on the table next to them. Then he slid her mask out of her hands and set it beside his.

In her mind, the air around them still vibrated with their music. The humming of those notes harmonized with their environment, and every object in the shop pulsed silently along with them.

Even with their façades on the table, the song seemed to continue.

He took another step forward, and then another, until there was nothing between them but the abrasiveness of fabric. With his right hand, he brushed a few strands of her hair behind her ear and didn't let his fingers come to a stop until they rested at the base of her neck. Then he hummed, soft and low—a soloist this time. His lips were still quivering with the notes when he brought his mouth to hers and coaxed it open. She heard herself gasp.

A kiss with Emerson . . . What could she say about it?

A poet would try to use flowery phrases to describe it—and would never succeed in capturing the warmth and strength and passion of it.

A mathematician might be able to quantify how long it lasted, but that would be all.

A physicist, with some state-of-the-art equipment, perhaps, would be capable (at most) of determining the force their bodies exerted upon each other.

But in that moment, Gwen was herself a musician. Notes danced in the air between them. And the only words she could think of were snippets of lyrics from a different Andrew Lloyd Webber song—one of her favorites—"Love Changes Everything." To her, kissing Emerson meant that nothing in the world would ever be the same.

And then the memories of her life outside of her private musical finally caught up with her. They had to get back to the tour. Her aunt would worry. And there was always Richard. . . .

She pulled away from Emerson, breathless for yet a new reason. "I like this," she blurted. She swallowed, licked her lips and swallowed again. "I do. But I can't do this now. I think you know why."

He'd pressed his lips together when she'd stepped away, but he, too, licked the corners of his mouth quickly and swallowed. "Your boyfriend."

She nodded.

"All right," he said. "But for the record"—he pulled out his wallet and removed several large bills, thrusting them at the Italian man—"that was a bloody fantastic kiss."

"I know," she murmured, too low, perhaps, for him to hear her. She watched as he picked up both of their masks. Then he steered her out the door, not letting her stop for even twenty seconds to reimburse him for her part of the purchase.

"Later, Gwen," he said with an exasperated sigh. "We're going to be late to meet the group as it is. And if I'm not moving—quickly—I'm going to want to finish what we started."

As it turned out, they made it to the hotel lobby with seven minutes and thirty-five seconds to spare. (Yes, they walked *that* fast.) Emerson disappeared from her view the moment they crossed the threshold, so she no longer had him to talk to, and she was afraid of being interrogated by matchmaking seniors if she stopped to chat with any of them. Instead, she waved with faux cheerfulness at her aunt and her aunt's friends and briskly strode over to one of the express computer stations near the front desk. It had been two days since she'd checked her e-mail.

She glared forcefully at the screen, trying to block out any distractions as she Googled her e-mail provider and punched in her password. Problem was, the distractions were more internal than external. She couldn't focus them away.

There were two pages of messages awaiting her, most of them spam. She took pleasure in deleting them. But one—*one*—was from Richard and, of course, she needed to read that:

> *Hello, Gwendolyn,*
> *I've been thinking about you. And us.*
> *Just wanted you to know that I booked my plane ticket*
> *today. I got a good deal on a flight. So, don't have too*
> *much fun without me (ha, ha!) and I'll see you in London*
> *in two weeks.*
>
> *Fondly,*
>
> *Richard*

7

A Prelude to the Music of the Night

Saturday–Sunday, July 14–15

Gwen could scarcely imagine a place more foreign-sounding than Budapest. Not that it looked vastly different from some of the other splendid European sites they'd visited already, she decided, as they crossed the famous Széchenyi Chain Bridge, which traversed the Danube River and divided the antiquated cities of Buda and Pest. But Hungary was *really* far from Iowa.

Davis helpfully provided the exact distance from their hometown. "Four thousand nine hundred seventeen miles," he told her. Not only was this *not* a prime number (as Matilda was quick to point out) but, for Gwen, as far as the outlandish and unfamiliar, the Hungarian capital city was on par with Cairo, Montevideo and Kuala Lumpur. Exotic locales she'd only heard referenced in history books or on *World News* reports.

Their bus tour that afternoon had included stops at Heroes' Square ("A World Heritage site," Hans-Josef informed them), St. Stephen's Basilica and the Millennium Underground Railroad, along with majestic views of Buda Castle and the Hungarian Royal Palace. They'd been guaranteed a visit to some iconic shopping boulevard ("We go to Andrássy Avenue next," Hans-Josef promised), but Gwen doubted there would be anything to tempt her in any store. She'd already gotten a few very unique items, and every time she thought of her purchases in Europe, she naturally thought of Emerson.

Of course, this was only a partial truth. Every time she *thought*—period—she thought of Emerson. His words. His touch. His kiss in Venice. And his cautious glances at her ever since.

Gwen had never before been so eager to short-circuit her mental processes, but she was a woman who knew she lived too much in her mind. It was unimaginable for her to lose herself in sensory experience and forget about anyone. Certainly not Emerson.

And not Richard either.

She stepped carefully off the bus and glanced in either direction. Shops and more shops. This was going to be an exhausting hour of trying to contain her memories.

Connie Sue nudged her. "Alex, Sally, Peter and I are going to sit down for a glass of lemonade at one of the cafés. Would you like to join us, sweetie?"

Gwen smiled at her. She'd spotted her aunt zipping down the block with Colin and Hester, while Kamesh and Ani headed in a different direction with the Edwards brothers. Louisa and Cynthia were already through the doors of an upscale Bohemian boutique known for their crystal vases, and the rest of the tour members seemed otherwise occupied as well.

"Thank you," Gwen said, grateful for the gesture. "But I think it'll do me some good to stretch my legs for a little while. There's still the operetta tonight."

The older woman laughed. Hans-Josef had already warned them that their evening's musical excursion would last several hours. "Just be careful, okay?" she said to Gwen before taking her husband's arm and crossing the street.

Gwen watched Alex and Connie Sue meet up with the honeymooners on the other side of the grand avenue, appreciating the decades of loyalty and devotion the married pairs shared. To agree to spend a lifetime with someone, an individual had to take a leap of faith. They could gather personal information, analyze the potential spouse's behavior, logically predict—based on observations over the course of their dating history—how the other person would *most likely* act in a given situation, but there was no way they could know for sure. Not about the other person. Maybe not even about themselves.

Take Richard, for example.

She wouldn't have guessed that his *fondly* would return so quickly to his e-mails. That he would've been thinking about their relationship quite so much. That he would've actually *booked a flight*. What an effort he'd been making, especially for someone so resistant to all things he deemed *foreign*.

She stared without really seeing into the window of some luxury watch shop. Richard would be standing next to her in London. *In two weeks*. He and Emerson would meet. In person. What on Earth would *that* introduction be like? She tried to wrap her mind around the future moment and project it accurately onto the screen of her imagination, but it felt too much like a battle between matter and antimatter. They were such different men that they were likely to negate each other on contact.

"Knackered already?" a male voice a few feet behind her asked. She recognized it immediately.

"Hi, Thoreau." She smiled. "I thought you were with your brother and Kamesh and his son."

"I was. They're obnoxiously dwelling on some model train down there." He pointed vaguely toward a block of shops. "I saw you still standing here, though, and had a question for you."

"Oh." She thought back. *Knackered* was British-speak for tired. "I guess I am a little . . . knackered, yes."

He grinned. "I *did* ask that, yes, but that wasn't the question I had in mind." He nudged her in the direction of the store Emerson was in. "Shall we walk around here for a bit?"

She agreed and then asked, "So, what was your question then?"

Thoreau cleared his throat. "What, uh, exactly, are you doing to my brother?"

She blinked. "What am *I* doing to him? I'm not doing—"

"He's rather set on edge, Gwen." He raised a dark eyebrow. "He's been in a fight-picking mood for a week, and I've heard him mention your name more frequently than any other person's on this trip. At first I thought it was just the obvious draws about you that had him interested, but after Venice . . ."

Gwen held her breath. He'd let that thought trail off, but she suspected Emerson may have told his brother about their kiss, which made her cringe. She wasn't sure what to say or how to defend herself. Emerson had been the one making all of the moves, hadn't he?

She squinted at Thoreau, remembering something else he'd just said that struck her as odd. "What do you mean by the *obvious* draws about me?"

"Ah." Thoreau held up one hand and started ticking items off with his outstretched fingers. "Well, you're an American, for one thing. Emerson is fascinated by your country's music, movies and pop culture, and he's visited the States almost as many times as he's visited Italy. I know he's been to New York, Boston, Chicago, Houston, Phoenix, Washington, D.C., Seattle, L.A." He shrugged and touched another finger. "You're smart but not smart-alecky. He likes that and wants to impress you." Then another. "You're pretty. Enough said." He gave a slightly embarrassed laugh then tapped another digit. "You're quiet. Emerson is absolutely intrigued by introverts. He has no idea how their minds work and likes to study them." Then, finally, "You've been playing a tad hard to get. He really likes that game—usually." He grinned at her. "I'm not saying any of these is a problem, just that there seems to be more to it all of a sudden."

"Why? Does he usually kiss and tell?" she asked.

Both of Thoreau's eyebrows shot up this time and the look he gave her was both surprised and speculative. "Do you mean that literally? He kissed you?" When she didn't immediately answer he laughed. "Oh, now I see."

"Now you see what?" she said, unable to hide the sharpness in her voice. So, Emerson *didn't* tell his brother? Perhaps she didn't understand his behavior as well as she wanted to believe.

"I see that he fears losing." He laughed again. "And possibly, for once, he fears it for precisely the correct reason."

Gwen didn't know what to make of this, only that Thoreau

seemed awfully smug about it. She got the uncomfortable sense that she'd unwittingly given away a very important piece of information and that this would have some consequences in whatever war was being waged between the brothers. A battle that had started years ago and was still very much in progress.

Her discomfort only intensified when Emerson, Kamesh and Ani came out of the shop and spotted them half a block away. It was an odd moment. Live gypsy music floated down to them from a side street, setting the soundtrack for their meeting. Even from a distance, the look Emerson sent her made her nerves vibrate like the voice of the gypsy singer. Like the rhythm of his acoustic guitar. Music was a pulse here. As prevalent on street corners as it was in concert halls. A part of the Hungarian way of life. However foreign Budapest might seem to Gwen, this element resonated with her. She could tell it resonated with Emerson, too. As the father-son pair waved to them, then headed in the other direction, Emerson moved in time to the song as he approached.

Thoreau spoke first. "Had enough of playing with toys already, brother?"

"It was a fascinating train system," Emerson said with sniff. "Your loss." He eyed his brother with wary interest for a split second before returning his attention to Gwen. "No boutiques for you this afternoon?"

She shook her head. "I'm not really big into shopping."

The twist of amusement on Emerson's lips was hard to ignore. He was about to say something else, but his brother jumped in.

"You should join us," Thoreau said to her. "We're making a pilgrimage to Vajdahunyad Castle in the City Park. We're going to ditch the bus ride back to the hotel and wander around down there instead."

Emerson shot him an odd look. "Yes, you *should* come," he agreed. "We already told Hans-Josef we were adding in this excursion." He glanced at his watch. "We're all leaving in about ten minutes and we'll be back to the hotel with time to have a sandwich and change before the operetta tonight. What do you say?"

She'd heard about this castle. It was fake. Or, rather, it was a replica (parts of it, anyway) of a castle by the same name in Transylvania, Romania, which had imprisoned the infamous "Vlad the Impaler." She shivered. "I don't kn—"

"Oh, come with us," Thoreau said. "You'll like it."

Again, Emerson looked at him probingly before turning to Gwen and seconding the offer. "There'll be others with us, too, so you don't have to worry about being . . . er . . . the only lady present. It's a . . . group outing."

Momentarily, she wondered why Emerson, of all people, was selecting his words so carefully. Why he felt he had to clarify this point. Did he think she'd be afraid to be alone with the two of them? Or did he have some other reason for warning her?

She considered her options: pretend to shop by herself on Andrássy Avenue then go back to the hotel to take a nap before the concert . . . or slip away from the tour with the Edwards duo and visit an unusual site in Budapest. Her friend Kathy back home would be thrilled to hear that Gwen leaned toward being adventurous.

However, she'd no sooner said, "Sure, thank you," when she realized why Emerson had been hedging on the invitation.

"There you gentlemen are!" Cynthia called, emerging with Louisa from the Bohemian crystal store, several packages between them. "Let us drop these off at the bus—I'm sure Guido can stash them for us—and we'll be ready to go."

Gwen pursed her lips. Of course *they* were coming.

Thoreau pointedly avoided her gaze, but Emerson sent her an apologetic look. The question she asked herself, as she silently studied Emerson's face, was whether he had been trying to protect her from the discomfort of being around the Britsicles or if, instead, he had been trying to safeguard his time alone with them. Furthermore, she wondered why Thoreau had been pushing to have her join their excursion, despite knowing for a fact how awkward she felt in the company of those two women. Regardless, she knew she couldn't cancel now and felt even more like a lowly pawn in someone else's game.

After the flurry of a few minutes—entrusting purchases to the bus driver and informing their skeptical tour guide that they'd be back at the hotel and ready to go to the operetta on time—they took off as a fivesome, down Andrássy Avenue, toward the enormity that was the City Park.

As they strode along the boulevard devoted to the worship of material luxury, Cynthia chattered mindnumbingly, describing the handbags she'd seen as if they were the Hungarian crown jewels.

Emerson contributed a few price comparisons between men's colorful silk ties and the best-crafted belts.

Louisa moaned softly every dozen steps and complained about a bothersome strap on her leather sandals.

Even Thoreau observed that the sterling silver versus platinum cufflinks he'd seen in one shop window were hard to distinguish from each other without closer inspection.

In what appeared to be a never-ending discussion on clothing accessories, Gwen—in her simple T-shirt, knee-length shorts and sneakers—felt like a fifth wheel, and a badly dressed one at that.

She pretended to glance at a store display, slowing her pace so the two couples could shoot ahead of her. Oddly, it was Thoreau who noticed first.

He nudged Louisa forward so she could join the line leaders, Cynthia and Emerson, while he slipped back to wait for Gwen.

"What's with this dallying?" he asked lightly, as if he already knew. "Aren't you anxious to get to the fake vampire castle?"

She allowed a small grin. "Who wouldn't be?"

He rolled his eyes as they fell into step together, several yards behind the other three.

"So, you're deep in thought," he said. "What big mystery of the universe are you trying to unravel?"

A gust of wind caressed her face and she closed her eyes for a second, breathing in the still-humid city air. She had a number of mysteries she could ask about: What war was being played out between the Edwards brothers? Why had Thoreau insisted on including her while Emerson hedged? Who were these men, really, and what were her feelings for them . . . and vice versa?

But she didn't ask any of these. Instead, she decided to turn the tables. "What's been happening with you and Amanda lately? Have you called her? Texted or e-mailed?"

He blinked a few times in surprise, but he didn't look shocked by her redirection. "She's . . . all right. I guess. I think."

Gwen raised her eyebrows at him. "You don't *know?*"

"I know what she *tells* me. I'm not sure if it's the truth." He paused. "Look, I don't really know how *I* am either. When I think about her, I miss her. I feel the absence that makes the heart grow fonder, rather than an out-of-sight, out-of-mind reaction. But I don't know if my brain is playing a trick on me. I'm not sure if I'm remembering our real relationship clearly or merely my wishes for how I wanted it to be."

She could understand this. A part of her was questioning her memories of Richard, too. Had she been remembering him unfairly while on the trip? Either unkindly or *too* kindly?

"What about when you see other, um, women? Like"—she made an almost imperceptible pointing motion with her index finger—"Cynthia," she whispered, even though she was far enough ahead not to overhear. "Is she someone you find yourself attracted to?"

"Bitchiness and all?" he murmured.

She nodded.

He squinted at the trio walking and talking half a block ahead of them now. "She's not unattractive," he admitted. "Nice legs and, when she's in a mellow mood, a rather pretty smile. But no. Not seriously."

"Because of the age difference?"

He shook his head. "Four years is insignificant. No, it's more because of the 'familiarity breeds contempt' cliché when it comes to her—or, at least, exhaustion. She drains me because I can tell she doesn't know what *type* of man she wants. She simply wants one."

Gwen shot him a puzzled looked. "How do you know that she doesn't know—"

Thoreau cut her off. "Because she's made advances at a number of us. Emerson. Hans-Josef. Even me. And that's on this trip alone. I've observed her trying to hook up with a dozen different blokes back in England. I don't know the personalities of all of those men, but speaking of the three of us here, we couldn't be more different underneath the skin. To behave as if she wants all of us is, actually, to want none of us. She's not being properly discriminating." He shrugged. "She sees men who are tall, well-educated, reasonably cultured, and she springs into action, completely missing important things like my brother's dark side, our tour guide's bizarre attachment to his pet rodent, my catastrophic relationship history. She's not interested in a flesh-and-blood man. She's after an illusion."

Gwen swallowed at his words and at the undisguised bitterness behind them. She wouldn't admit this aloud, of course, but she felt a sudden spark of empathy for Cynthia. In Gwen's case, there were only two men she'd been concerning herself with—Emerson and Richard—but they were different enough to have her questioning whether *she* knew what she wanted in a man. She comforted herself with the certainty that she at least hadn't been oblivious to Emerson's darker side. She'd caught him in serious moods and conflicted moments. She knew he wasn't always the fun-loving extrovert he appeared to be.

Not that she was prepared to discuss *that* with his brother, either.

There was, however, a part of Thoreau's confession that required greater candidness from her than she typically felt comfortable sharing. She touched her Mouth of Truth pendant, took a deep breath and prepared to be honest. "I'm not sure of the accuracy of my memories either. For my boyfriend," she whispered. "He's going to be here soon, at the end of the trip, and I—I'm a little afraid of what it'll be like when we see each other again. We've been together for two years and have never been apart for more than a couple of days. But now—"

"Now your eyes are open to the wider world," he finished for her, nodding. "It happens. It's rather like being a teenager, is it not? How we all think we know everything at fifteen or sixteen, but then we eventually leave home for work or university and, suddenly, we realize how many experiences are left untapped."

She bit her bottom lip and bobbed her head. Much as she didn't want to admit this, even to herself, Aunt Bea may have been right. Gwen probably *did* need to see more of the world, more of life, before making any big decisions.

To her, this realization trickled down her spine like midnight sweat. Like the terror she might've felt in the hour before taking a final exam in math—one where she'd thought she'd been well prepared because she'd studied everything in her algebra notebook—only to find out that the test included geometry, trigonometry and calculus, too. And she hadn't even gotten notes for those yet.

It was a good student's nightmare.

Real perspiration beaded up on the back of her neck, which she quickly swiped away. Thoreau, however, seemed not to notice that.

Instead, he grinned at her, as if finally connecting a couple of puzzle pieces. He threw his arm around her shoulders and pulled her close. She stiffened slightly in surprise.

"Wouldn't it be simpler," he said in a low voice, "if we could just get together? You and I? We're friends. We can talk to each other without all of that relationship angst," he reasoned. "No Amanda and her issues. No—what's your boyfriend's name?"

"Richard," she said, laughing and allowing him to lean into her a bit more.

"No Richard and whatever his annoying traits are. No people making unwelcome romantic advances at us." He nodded comically in the direction of the threesome ahead, and Gwen laughed again. Thoreau was funny, although she wasn't sure she'd necessarily term Emerson's kiss as *unwelcome,* just unanticipated.

"We could actually enjoy our sightseeing without all of those aggravating undercurrents on the trip or worries about people waiting to bawl us out back at home," he added, devilishly bringing his face closer to hers as if to rub cheeks. "Wouldn't it be nice if—"

He stopped talking. He stopped walking, too, and so abruptly that Gwen was inadvertently yanked backward. "Uh-oh."

She followed Thoreau's gaze and immediately encountered a lethal glare from Emerson, directed like a burning solar flare at his brother. The trio had paused to look in a shop window, but Emerson wasn't yakking it up with Cynthia and Louisa anymore. He was standing in the middle of the sidewalk, arms crossed tightly, looking very, very irritated.

Thoreau made a show of removing his arm. "Now we've displeased him," he said, far too delightedly, and Gwen was again reminded of the sibling chess rivalry currently in progress.

"Nice," Emerson hissed, not quite under his breath to Thoreau when they reached him. Then he turned his attention to her, his harsh stare softening, but his eyes still troubled. "Hello, there," he said.

"Hello." Gwen smiled carefully at him, the pull of her attraction to him warring with her desire to be a principled person, one who honored her commitments to other people. But she was having a harder and harder time determining right from wrong when she was around him. And she didn't know what to say or do when in his company.

Cynthia appeared to be not nearly so conflicted. "Pay attention, Emerson," she demanded, stepping away from the shop window and playfully slapping him on the chest. "Louisa keeps insisting that the necklace in the corner is tanzanite." She pointed toward the display they were ogling. "I think it's tourmaline. Could you just take a peek—" She paused and glanced at Gwen and Thoreau. "You two, as well. I would like to know what this is."

Clearly, the discussion of accessories had not yet ceased.

Gwen glanced at the necklace but wasn't certain what it was. To her, the gemstone looked like a cross between sapphire and aquamarine in color. Emerson hazarded a guess that it was tanzanite, but he didn't look very closely. Thoreau studied it far more carefully and took Cynthia's side. "It's tourmaline," he proclaimed. "Of the Brazilian indicolite variety. Beautifully cut."

"Well, thank heavens we know the truth now," Emerson murmured dryly. His brother shot him a cool, triumphant look, but the two other women appeared oblivious to their antagonism.

The rest of the walk to the park went quickly, all five of them clustered together like an imbalanced molecule—Thoreau ahead with Cynthia and Louisa, Emerson with Gwen just behind. But their pilgrimage to Vajdahunyad Castle was stymied by an unusually early closing time for visitors that day. It housed the city's agricultural museum, and there was a private event scheduled. So their excursion morphed into a full tour of the City Park instead.

"At least we can look at the building from the outside," Louisa said, taking several steps back from it. "That section over there is quite sinister." She indicated the façade that, according to Thoreau, most resembled the castle in Transylvania.

Gwen studied its gothic architecture and, as the sun hid momentarily behind the clouds, she could almost see Dracula escaping from the imposing building and into the darkening night, black cape flying behind him. Too bad Richard hadn't joined them on the trip sooner. He could have had the perfect setting for his "serious" Halloweenesque proposal.

The mental image of Richard with a vampire cloak and fake teeth offering her an engagement ring never ceased to amuse her. She laughed aloud and Emerson, still by her side, said, "What's so humorous?"

She shook her head. "Just a memory that never happened."

He eyed her with surprise. "A very poetic way of phrasing it. I was hoping you'd say it was a highly explicit sexual fantasy involving neck biting."

She laughed again, but didn't reply. She'd let him think what he wanted.

He was still staring curiously at her. "Fine, don't tell me. But I like the sound of your laugh. It's charming."

"Um, thanks," she managed, but she could feel herself blushing at his words and his attention. She tried to remember if there had been anything Richard had ever said to her that had made her blush. She couldn't, but it had been a long time since their early days of dating. And, besides, Richard wasn't an outrageous flirt like Emerson. He never set out to make her feel self-conscious and unnerved.

Before Emerson could make any new embarrassing comments, Thoreau pointed out a statue of a man with a pen in the nearby courtyard.

"It's famous in Budapest," he said. "It's called *Anonymus*, and it's, apparently, the anonymous notary of one of the kings. Probably King Béla III, who wrote the first history books on Hungarians, mostly based on legends." He pointed at the pen held in an eternal grip by the man in bronze. "One local superstition is that you'll have good luck if you rub the pen." He raised his eyebrow, walked over to it and caressed the pen tip with his fingers.

Cynthia and Louisa immediately followed suit. Gwen, feeling the pinches of peer pressure and, also, not willing to turn down any good luck she might get, dutifully stroked the pen, too.

Emerson, of course, had to be contrary.

He shrugged at his brother, crossed his arms, sighed heavily and acted no better than a petulant kindergartner. "I'm lucky already," he said with an arch glance.

Thoreau strode by him, murmuring loud enough for only Gwen and Emerson to hear, "Ah, but not as lucky as you want to be."

Gwen noticed a decided shift in the air after that. The atmosphere between the men felt charged with a more competitive edge than usual. The brothers—typically assertive and frequently oppositional in regards to their interactions with each other—had become silent but uncompromising. It was like being the knotted rope in the center of a tug-of-war match. Both sides trying to wordlessly draw the knot closer, but neither man fully succeeding in wrestling the advantage from his opponent.

And then, of course, there was the problem with the map. A problem the Edwards brothers claimed didn't exist.

The five of them had meandered around the City Park for, perhaps, a half hour, and then for a half hour more into the neighborhoods at the outskirts of it. Caught up as she was in their explorations, and distracted by the nonverbal jousting of the brothers, Gwen had lost track of their precise location and had simply trusted the others to know how to return to familiar roads. She was not the only one holding this false assumption.

"Where is our hotel from here?" Louisa asked, an innocent enough question to Gwen's ear.

But Thoreau sent her a momentarily offended glare, and Emerson, who'd been entrusted to snag a city map from Guido's stash on the bus before they parted from the tour group, waved the folded paper in the air at her like a fan. "No worries. It's not far." Without so much as a glance at the map, he pointed down one of the nearby streets. "We can start walking toward it."

His brother, however, seemed to want to autocorrect Emerson's directions, like a GPS device dead set on "recalculating" at every turn. After yet another half hour had gone by, Gwen couldn't help but notice that they'd been traveling in an odd stair-step pattern, first in one direction and then in the other. She recognized a few buildings she knew they'd passed, and she realized, with a bolt of shock, that the guys didn't actually *care* about the direction they were headed. In studying them silently for a few turns, as they chattered at the three women (although they exchanged not a word with each other), it dawned on her that their interest was in testing whose leadership was more persuasive. In determining who could more often steer the women down one street or other simply by the magnetic pull of his personality.

Fascinating? Yes.

Conducive to getting them back to the hotel on time? No.

She shot each brother a warning glance before pointing at her watch and saying, "We only have an hour left before the bus leaves to the show. Perhaps we need to check the map now. Just to make sure we're going in the right direction. I'm pretty sure our hotel is *by the river*."

Emerson laughed off her suggestion without comment. Thoreau pretended not to hear her and led Louisa around another corner . . . onto a street that Gwen *knew* would take them back toward the City Park and away from the Danube.

Cynthia shared a concerned look with her as the certainty of their whereabouts—or lack thereof—became as evident to the British woman as it was to Gwen.

"Gentleman, Gwen had a clever idea about checking the map. Or, if you'd rather, we do know the name of our hotel," Cynthia said reasonably. "Shall we just hire a cab and ask the driver to take us—"

"No," both men said together, cutting her off.

She blinked in surprise and eyed Gwen again as if to say, *What the hell?*

Gwen rolled her eyes and Cynthia actually smiled and mouthed, "Men . . ." Then, to the guys, she said, "Well, Hans-Josef would know how to get us back the fastest way." She pulled out her mobile phone threateningly. "I'll ring him and—"

"Not necessary, Cyn," Thoreau said, his voice, perhaps, a touch too sharp.

And Emerson swiveled around and bit his lip before shrugging and pulling out the paper map in resignation.

Gwen stifled a snicker. She had to hand it to Cynthia. Effective tactic. She nodded approvingly at the other woman, who nodded back and motioned for Louisa to come join the two of them.

"The Edwardian games are afoot," Cynthia murmured to Gwen and Louisa as Emerson studied the map several yards away and Thoreau, standing as far away from him as possible, studied the bark of some roadside tree.

"Do they get like this often?" Gwen asked.

"Only when they've spent too much time in one another's company," she whispered with a soft laugh. "Christmas is usually the most dreadful. They try to score points off each other during the entire Yuletide season and will play with anything, or anyone, in their path. They bat everyone around like a cricket ball."

This time Gwen looked at Cynthia more seriously and realized Thoreau had been dead wrong in his assessment of her. Cynthia saw him. And Emerson. And probably Hans-Josef, too. She saw them all very clearly . . . but, for some reason, she just liked them anyway. Liked each man despite his faults. And in spite of—or, maybe, because of—his differences from the others. Liked them without bitterness, even when they were using her. Or dismissing her.

"They're rather intense," Louisa agreed, as the three women watched Thoreau reach the limit of his patience.

He pushed away from the tree he'd been faux inspecting, strode over to his brother and snatched the map out of Emerson's hands.

"Bloody bastard, don't just grab—" Emerson began.

"This is in fucking *Hungarian*," Thoreau said with incredulity, pointing at the paper. "Why the hell didn't you—oh, here's a bright thought—get a map in a language you can read? You know enough of them."

Emerson said something distinctly unflattering about his brother, first in German, then in Italian and, finally, in French.

"What? Saving the Arabic and Russian insults for later?" Thoreau muttered.

Emerson replied with a string of obscenities in a language Gwen couldn't identify. Then he crumpled up the map, lobbed it at his brother and took several purposeful steps away from the path he'd been heading. "I know where we are and precisely how to return us to the hotel," he insisted, a point which Gwen *almost* believed. At least, she believed *he* believed it.

Men from around the globe were united by one common conviction: They'd rather be put to death by fire than ask anyone else for directions. Or even read a stupid map.

Which was why she was in no way surprised when Thoreau, instead of uncrinkling the map and piecing together their location based on the few landmarks they could identify in Hungarian, tossed the paper out, surveyed the streets and the position of the sun critically and then grudgingly agreed that Emerson was, at last, heading in the right direction.

By the time they reached their hotel, some of the brothers' steam had dissipated, but the bus was just pulling away from the front drive. It had to be clear to everyone in their tour group that the five of them were nowhere near ready to go to an operetta. All of them were still wearing their street clothes and a few perceptive tour members likely guessed they hadn't even eaten their dinner yet. Hans-Josef was understandably ticked.

He had Guido stop the bus and open the door. Dressed in a stylish navy suit that complemented his eyes and offset his fair hair, he descended the steps quickly. "You are very late," Hans-Josef said, arms crossed, enunciating every word with precision laced with annoyance. "I left your tickets with the concierge, but we must go now. Join us . . . or not."

Emerson was the first to step forward and offer an apology. "It was my mistake. We'll change and arrange to go to the concert hall as soon as humanly possible."

Thoreau cleared his throat. "Thank you for waiting as long as you did. We appreciate it. We will do our best not to be disruptive when we come in."

Their tour guide was slightly mollified. He shrugged, reentered the bus and nodded seriously at them once as the tour group pulled away. Gwen caught sight of Aunt Bea's jubilant expression through one of the windows. Gwen waved to her elated relative and tried very hard not to sigh at the obvious enthusiasm.

They agreed to meet back in the lobby in a half hour—time enough only to wash up quickly, change into something semiformal and eat a snack to tide them over until after the performance.

"We'll treat you ladies to a nice meal when the operetta ends," Thoreau told them before they dashed off to their rooms. And Emerson demonstrated his wholehearted agreement by not arguing with his sibling for once.

When they reconvened, it was as a changed and oddly bonded group. Cynthia, looking stunning in a black, low-cut, sequined cocktail dress with a gauzy matching shawl, leaned over to Gwen, who was wearing a simple but classic tea-length ivory silk, and said, "You look lovely." And Louisa, dressed boldly in a dazzling red gown, nodded approvingly at the other two women as the guys approached them.

Thoreau was, without question, attractive. He was a classically tall, dark and handsome man. Strong bone structure. Eye-catching physique. Warm smile, when not scowling at his kid brother. Intelligent expression in his eyes.

But, to Gwen, Emerson was a different kind of attractive. He had many of the same physical features as Thoreau, save for the shade of his hair color and a few additional inches in stature, but her internal response to the totality of Emerson created an altogether distinct chemical reaction. Like when a scientist mixed two clear, liquid compounds in a beaker and ended up with something that immediately turned a shocking violet. Had he mixed either of those clear liquids with something else, they would have remained unchanged or, at most, the clear one would have taken on the hue of the other compound, had it been tinted. But get the right two chemicals together and—

"Ready to go, ladies?" Emerson asked them, but he was looking directly at her.

She, Cynthia and Louisa said they were set.

"Good," Thoreau said. "We rang the desk from our room. They should have our taxi waiting."

They made it to Vigadó Concert Hall—a "place of merriment," according to the cabbie's translation—in record time. They missed only the opening song or two and, during the applause, they were discreetly ushered to their seats.

Gwen found herself positioned between Thoreau and Emerson, directly in the middle of the fivesome. Cynthia was to Emerson's right and Louisa sat to Thoreau's left. Hans-Josef and most of the tour members were in the row just ahead of them. Their guide glanced back at them and smiled briefly. It lit up his face, but there was something more to it. A delight in his expression that was new. Gwen didn't understand why at first. Then she looked more closely at the program.

"*Operettenkonzerte,*" it read. "*Die schönsten Melodien aus Lustige Witwe, Zigeunerbaron, Zirkusprinzessin . . .*"

Ah, German. The orchestra was from Budapest, but the songs, Emerson explained, were going to be performed in Hans-Josef's native tongue. Gwen gathered that, after weeks of Italian, Hungarian and altogether too much English, their tour guide was craving a little bit of home.

Their highlighted selections featured music from four composers—two Hungarians, Lehár and Kálmán; and two Austrians, Strauss and Stolz—but Gwen didn't understand a word from any of the solos or duets in the program.

She did, however, appreciate the energy and spiritedness of the performers, and she truly liked the setting. The hall was warmly lit and the concert stage relatively small but tastefully decorated with long-necked vases and pastel floral arrangements. An intimate place for a show compared to some of the great auditoriums of Europe, but it was this very quality that made the performance so unique. So personal. The strings were like a lively row of perfectly in-sync seamstresses, each flick of their bows like the pulling of yarn through fabric as they wove through the melody. She watched them, mesmerized.

Yet, even these musical delights were not enough to completely block out the interpersonal drama she was—quite literally—in the middle of when it came to Emerson and Thoreau. Their movements were an exercise in subtleties and nearly imperceptible gestures. If she happened to whisper a comment to one brother or even lean more toward one of them, the other would invariably counter with a word or a motion intended to bring her closer to him instead. She was the knot in the center of their tug-of-war rope again but, thankfully, smart enough to know it wouldn't have mattered who was sitting in her seat. *Anyone* in her position would have gotten this unenviable role. Even Cynthia shot her a sympathetic glance a time or two during the concert.

On the other hand, she tried to get what benefit she could from the situation. Both Edwards men were more than happy to translate bits of the performance to her. Turned out that Thoreau had spent one college year abroad in Vienna studying psychology ("Freud's city, you understand," he explained), so his German was stellar and, actually, even better than Emerson's, whose reason for picking up that particular language stemmed from his innate unwillingness to let his elder brother best him in anything. Apparently, decades of sibling rivalry made both brothers better linguists.

"And better musicians," Emerson added, when she confronted him on this point.

Thoreau overhearing, of course, chimed in, "And better drivers," to which his kid brother sent him a steely glare. Gwen gathered there was a family story involving cars that she hadn't yet heard.

"Better public speakers," Emerson lobbed at him.

"Better athletes," Thoreau countered. "And, naturally, better chess players."

Emerson snickered and took a deep breath. "Better lovers," he shot back, raising his voice just enough that a couple of older women in the row behind them gasped.

"Okay, guys. Enough," Gwen said firmly. And for the rest of the concert neither of them spoke again. Not to each other, and not even to her.

When the show was over, Hans-Josef couldn't contain his jubilation. He kept turning to everyone around him, shaking their hands and exclaiming, "Oh, *wunderbar!* It was good, *ja?* To hear songs from *Das Glücksmädel* and *Die Fledermaus* . . ."

What could Gwen say to that but *"Ja."*

Aunt Bea overheard her and slapped her knee, laughing silently.

They slowly filtered out of the hall, Guido already waiting with the bus to return the group members to the hotel for the night. The Edwards boys, however, had promised the three women a meal and had no intention of letting Gwen, Louisa or Cynthia escape the commitment. But the decision of where to go next was just another opportunity for a brotherly battle.

"Pardon us a moment," Emerson said grimly as he nudged his brother to one corner of the lobby to discuss their options, leaving Cynthia, Louisa and Gwen to exchange looks and talk amongst themselves for a few minutes. The glow of the performance faded somewhat as the concert hall emptied—at least for Gwen—but Louisa smiled, her gaze distant and wistful.

"I remember having a night out like this in Budapest once before," Louisa confided to them. "It was utterly delightful."

"With Ian?" Cynthia asked, her tone one of surprise.

Louisa nodded. "Hard to believe, I know," she told Cynthia. Then, to Gwen, she added, "My husband. We'd come here once in our second or third year of marriage. It was just for one of his business trips. I spent the days at the hotel or wandering around a bit downtown, but when he was done with his meetings for the night, we'd go out to dinner or to see a show. It was so, so . . . pleasant."

Gwen smiled warmly at her. Although Louisa's memories were tinged with bittersweet edges—like a white carnation with pink-rimmed tips—the unevenness of the color pattern only added an unusual dimension to the flower, giving it more character than it might have had otherwise. And she realized with a start that she was, herself, adding memorable moments to her formerly untouched snowy petals of inexperience. When it came to world travel, speckles of pink now permanently decorated the white. Each dot a place she'd now visited.

How very much she'd seen and done in just this first half of the trip. She would carry these memories with her forever, or until—like Colin—they were lost to the calamities of illness or the blockages of old age. But these were the memories of *her* life. Had she collected enough of them for someone who'd lived three whole decades already?

In the momentary silence between Louisa's comments and Gwen's thoughts, Thoreau's distinctive voice snapped the airwaves and reached their ears. "The hell I will," he said to his brother in a tone so incredulous that Gwen couldn't begin to guess what Emerson had suggested. The latter replied with words far too hissed and low for them to hear, but she gathered they were not complimentary phrases.

Guido had the bus engine running just outside of the building. Just before Aunt Bea hopped onto it, she pulled Gwen aside and whispered, "You got your keycard for the hotel room, right?"

"Yes, of course," Gwen said.

"There's still time to slip it to me," her aunt said, her mischievous eyes darting around the lobby to take in the tour members who remained. "You could pretend you lost it. Or left it in the room by accident. Then those handsome boys will insist on letting you stay with them in their room tonight. You wouldn't want to wake up your dear old auntie too late now, would you? She needs her beauty sleep, you know."

Gwen stared at her. Shook her head.

"Well, c'mon, honey! Quick. Hand it over."

"No, Aunt Bea."

The older woman rolled her eyes and sighed. "You are so stubborn, child," she mumbled just before ambling toward the bus. "Can't say I didn't try to help you."

If this was what passed for *help* these days, Gwen could only imagine the magnitude of disaster that woman could create when trying to be *un*helpful.

"Good night, Aunt Bea," she called after her, unable to keep from chuckling slightly in spite of herself. Forget Cynthia or even Emerson. Her aunt was the *real* piece of work.

Beatrice just shrugged and started muttering something to Hester as they boarded Guido's bus and found their seats. There were only a few other tour members that followed them as most everyone else was already prepared to depart. With the very notable exception of their tour guide.

Hans-Josef was not at all anxious to leave the Vigadó. After having a lively discussion with a couple members of the orchestra, he emerged from the concert hall and strolled toward Gwen and the other two women in the lobby. It was obvious that the happy German melodies were still scampering through his Austrian brain because he walked with a distinct dance in his step, his smile positively luminescent.

He inhaled, deeply and dreamily, drawing the dry lobby air into his lungs as if it were aromatically scented. "This is a night I do not want to see end," he said.

Cynthia, with a gift for taking matters into her own hands, shot an exasperated glance at the Edwards brothers and turned the full force of her grin on Hans-Josef. "Why should you see it end?" she inquired, beaming at him. "I think you should come out with us." She hitched her thumb at Emerson and Thoreau. "Those two are debating restaurants to take us to and, by the time they decide on one, every place in Budapest will be closed. I just want to go to a bar. To grab some pub food and a nice drink or two and talk about the performance. Doesn't that sound like a far superior idea?" she entreated. She glanced first at Louisa then at Gwen before returning her attention to Hans-Josef for confirmation that, yes, her idea was indeed the better plan. And while their reasons for agreeing with Cynthia differed, all three of them were unanimously in favor of it.

"Brilliant!" Cynthia said, only a tad smug. "Do you need to go back to the hotel first with Guido? If so, we can wait for you. If not, perhaps you can help us select a good place to go and we'll follow your lead."

This suggestion was met with a tremendous amount of enthusiasm on their tour guide's part, but Gwen didn't know if it was Cynthia's flirtatiousness, the continuation of an enjoyable evening or the prospect of wrestling the leadership role away from those pesky Englishmen that was the greatest allure.

"I do not have to ride back with the group," Hans-Josef insisted. "Let me just inform Guido of our plans."

And before the Edwards brothers had any notion at all that their control of the situation had been usurped, they found themselves dragged along by Cynthia to a hopping Budapest bar of Hans-Josef's choosing and forced to contend with far less complicated menu items than they had planned.

"My apologies, Gwen," Thoreau murmured, studying the bar menu. "They do seem to have a rather large selection of bratwurst, however."

She laughed. "Don't worry, I'm not that hungry. What could you and Emerson have possibly been arguing about for so long, though?"

He studied her for an endless moment. "I suspect you'd rather not know."

She blinked at him. "Yes, I would."

But he just shook his head and changed the subject, a simple task given their new circumstances.

With Hans-Josef among them, there were now three pairs and three native countries represented. The group dynamic had been considerably altered with just that one additional person, and the setting was markedly different than anything they'd encountered together as a group. To Gwen, it was all a bit surrealistic. The bar was loud, smoky, dark and unmistakably foreign to her eye, not having been one to go clubbing in big cities when in the States. It was also overly hot due to the crowds, necessitating Cynthia's almost immediate removal of her flimsy black shawl, an action that created an instantaneous response around the table.

"It's dreadfully warm in here. Am I the only one in a cover-up?" she demurred, fanning her face and fluttering her eyelashes prettily as she untied the little bow holding the garment around her.

While her dress was already plainly low-cut, the shawl had managed to cover not only Cynthia's bare shoulders but it also fell across both sides of her chest, adding a density to the fabric in that location, which was gone the second she lifted it away. It was clear in an instant that the woman wasn't wearing a bra—a discovery of some interest to the men at the table. It was also impossible for any of them to ignore the two new guests they had joining them: Cynthia's very visible nipples.

Louisa exhaled on a laugh, smiling at her friend's triumphant expression. Gwen, realizing that this was no unintentional wardrobe malfunction, caught herself before she giggled and, instead, watched as the three guys reacted in dramatically different ways to the same visual stimuli:

Hans-Josef's jaw dropped and he actually *turned his chair* to face her, his eyes riveted to her lips while she spoke to him, but very much focused on her chest when she was speaking to anyone else. The tour guide actively tried to engage her in conversation, even going so far as to let it slip that he was a man interested in committed relationships. Cynthia smiled winningly at him and fiddled with her plunging collar just to torment him a little more.

Thoreau pointedly avoided looking anywhere below Cynthia's neck and embarked with Louisa on a spirited discussion of some eighties British TV series called *Lovejoy* about a scruffy antiques expert who managed to get into these scrapes with a variety of unsavory sorts. Gwen was quickly confused by their detailing of certain episodes—was it a comedy, a drama or a mystery?—and she tuned them out after five minutes.

Emerson didn't look at Cynthia at all. He studied Gwen silently and with a tense jaw for several minutes, downed his Pilsner in record time and announced that he was going to the bar for another one. He asked if he could bring her back anything, but she'd already gotten both a drink and a brat and had barely touched either, so of course she said no. He strode off as if being chased by an invisible Vajdahunyad vampire.

Gwen immediately felt that fifth-wheel feeling again. Amazing how that happened no matter which four other people were involved. She couldn't deny that *she* was the person who didn't quite belong, and this was only heightened by the fact that Hans-Josef was all but drooling over Cynthia, Louisa and Thoreau were laughingly reminiscing their way through several seasons of that weird antiques show and Emerson—the person who should have completed her pair at the table—was across the bar, trying desperately to escape from the situation. She knew enough to know there were reasons beside her presence for this, but that didn't keep her from feeling left out. And it didn't keep her from admiring his swift and decisive exit. Perhaps she should do the same.

"If you'll excuse me," she said, rising softly from her chair. "I'll be back in a few minutes."

Hans-Josef nodded pleasantly at her and continued to ogle Cynthia, who was having such an enjoyable time that she waved cheerily at Gwen and ogled Hans-Josef right back.

Thoreau shot her a sharp look. "Ladies' room?" he guessed.

She shook her head. "Outside. I just need some fresh air."

"It *is* smoky in here," Louisa observed.

Thoreau motioned to stand. "We could join you, if you'd like." He glanced at Louisa for agreement and she nodded.

Gwen appreciated the gesture. It was nice that they tried to include her. The fact that she didn't fit in despite their efforts wasn't their fault. "No, don't get up. You two look comfortable where you are, and I won't be gone long." She smiled at them both. "Thank you, though."

Thoreau winked at her. "As you wish. But we're here if you change your mind."

She appreciated that, too, but she had no intention of changing her mind. She'd needed a breather from the group—literally, figuratively—for several hours and had been long looking forward to a moment when she could collect her thoughts.

The swirl of cigarette smoke followed her out of the bar, but the night air helped to dissipate the worst of it. The sky was a cloudless indigo with even a few very faint star patterns detectable above the slowly extinguishing city lights. She located the Big and Little Dippers, marveling that the constellations she could view from home were, likewise, visible these thousands of miles away in Hungary, however dimly. This familiarity was comforting. It was, perhaps, a smaller planet than it had felt to her as of late.

She remembered a night not long ago when she and Richard had been strolling past dark and they had gazed into the evening sky, connecting the starry dots to form those distinctive outlines. Pinpointing the sacred position of the North Star. In space and through time, it remained constant. Her mom and dad had seen it as children. Someday, if she ever had kids of her own, they could gaze upon it, too.

This knowledge was also comforting.

And Richard. The certainty of him—her familiarity and knowledge of him—this was the most comforting of all. Especially given the strangeness of these past few weeks. The many unsettling events. The collection of new and challenging personalities.

She had, perhaps, needed a breather from her life back at home but, having been granted the time away, she'd come to appreciate many things about her real life even more. The constancy of it. The calmness. The competence with which she navigated the ins and outs of her day. Not only did she lack fluency of speech here in

Europe, but her actions lacked the confident smoothness she craved. She worked so hard to be precise and well prepared at her job and in her life. Here, she was ever hesitant, faltering, inarticulate. She wouldn't miss these flaws in herself when the tour ended. Not at all.

She would, however, miss Emerson. And Thoreau. And maybe even Louisa, Hans-Josef and Cynthia. Yes, even *her*—albeit just *a little*. It was hard to believe that in a couple of short weeks their trip would be over and she'd probably never see any of them again. Would it be enough merely knowing they existed somewhere in the world, even if they never spoke or even e-mailed each other? Would knowing her have any lasting impact on their lives in the way she was certain knowing them would have on hers—even if their paths never again crossed?

She inhaled fully and tried to hold the fresh foreign air in her lungs for, perhaps, a few seconds longer than necessary. Long enough to tease out the memory of her breathlessness at being kissed by Emerson. The warm, floaty feeling of it. The peculiarity of it, too. It was a dichotomy she felt increasingly discomfited by the more hours and days that passed since it happened. She had never been one to weigh the kissing techniques of one lover against another (she had also never dated more than one man at a time in her entire life), so this odd opportunity to compare and contrast left her even more unsure of herself and her judgments than her deficiencies in European traveling experiences and her overall lack of sophistication.

She desperately wanted to go back to feeling capable and proficient in some aspect of her life once more.

As she released the last of the air and inhaled again, she became aware of a silky, languorous tune drifting down the block and caressing her with its melody. She could spot the man—a gypsy violinist—playing soulfully for himself and a handful of passersby on the street corner across the way. The song, however, she did not recognize, but she found herself swaying to it nonetheless.

Then, he followed this offering with a more vibrant piece, a toe-tapping dance number that had a few members of the crowd singing along in Hungarian. Gwen smiled and took a few steps closer. He was *good*.

He'd just finished to a round of enthusiastic applause and embarked on an even livelier tune when she felt the air currents whirlpool around her and another harmonic sound intermingle with the melody.

"Gwen," Emerson said simply. She turned to face him and he moved forward, his expression serious. "My brother said you were out here. Are you all right?"

"Yes." She pointed down the block, the gypsy musician in full swing, his body completely at one with his instrument. "String theory in action," she said with a laugh.

He raised one eyebrow and she saw his lips twist into a grin. "So it is."

They listened together through the entirety of the song, and Gwen could see Emerson visibly relaxing. Spending so many hours with his brother that day had clearly set him on edge. She was glad to see some of that tension ebbing away and found herself hesitant to say or do anything that might precipitate its return.

However, as Aunt Bea used to say, "You can't make a cake without breaking some eggs." She was going to have to risk Emerson's good humor for the hope of finding out what had been going on between the brothers, particularly as it related to her.

"Thoreau is a complex person," she ventured.

Immediately, Emerson's expression turned darker. "Yes."

"I was noticing the two of you . . . interacting silently all through the day. Almost as if you were competing against each other in a live board game." She paused. "You two seem to do that a lot, don't you?"

He inhaled as if for fortification and fiddled with a leaf he'd picked up off the ground. "Yes."

"And, maybe I'm wrong on this—" she began. "But it really felt like you guys were *especially* at odds today. I can't help but feel as though there was a reason for that conflict, and that I'm a part of it. Would you say that's true?"

She could see him swallow as he nodded. "Yes. I'm sorry,

Gwen." His eyes were fixed on the musician, but she could tell that wasn't where his attention was. She waited until he was ready to speak. "We did argue about you, and I apologize if that made you uncomfortable. We're ... not always easy to be around, I'm afraid. But, today, you're correct. There was a bigger problem than usual."

The gypsy violinist shifted to a new tune, this one more melancholy than any Gwen had heard thus far. Several people still stopped to listen to him, but others drifted away in the sad footsteps of the haunting melody.

"You didn't seem to want me along on the castle excursion," she said, giving voice to her suspicions from earlier in the day. "You seemed angry at your brother for asking me to come." She bowed her head. "I guess I wanted to know why."

"I *was* angry when Thoreau asked you," he admitted, "but not because I didn't want you to join us." He crumpled up the leaf and tossed it to the sidewalk. "I wanted to be the one to ask you. Not him. I also wanted to make sure you knew what it would entail, who else was going, how long we'd be gone. And I'd been trying to respect your wishes. To give you space ... after Venice." He sent her a significant look. "I didn't like what Thoreau was doing, and I'm still not sure where your feelings are in all of this, so that doesn't help."

"What my feelings are?"

"Precisely," he said, his tone bitter. "Your feelings about my brother." He scored his fingers through his sandy hair, his expression very grave. "I'll acknowledge that many women are attracted to him. He has, I suppose, the tall, dark and handsome effect, and he is very intelligent, annoyingly responsible and moderately witty. When he tries hard," he added with a shrug. "I've seen the two of you talking a fair bit. I realize you have a boyfriend back home and you've set limits between us because of it. I might not like it, but I can accept that. It was a relationship that predated our meeting, and I appreciate that you wish to honor your commitment to him. But with my brother—" He stomped on the leaf a few times with his shoe, grinding it into the pavement. "He can be flirtatious without necessarily being sincere, and I'm sorry to tell you that if . . . if you actually kind of like him. If you were trying to decide whether or not he was, perhaps, the better choice."

She stared at him in astonishment. He thought she liked *his brother?* And he was angry about it? "Emerson—" she began.

"No, look, please don't misunderstand. I love my brother. I want him to be happy. But anything he says or does here on this trip is just a game for him. I told him to stay away from you, but he wouldn't listen to me, Gwen. I told him for my sake as well as yours, but there's someone else involved, too. He's in this messed-up, mixed-up relationship with a woman back in London and he—"

"Amanda."

"Yes, Amanda. And he—wait—" He stopped, his jaw dropping halfway. "He told you about her?"

Gwen nodded. "Before we even got to Florence. This is his tester trip. He's trying to figure out how he feels about her and their relationship. She wanted him to stay in England this summer, but he felt he needed to take a break. He's pretty hung up on her."

He swore under his breath. "He told me he had not mentioned Amanda to you. That the subject never came up. That he had no intention of sharing—"

"He was playing with you. Thoreau likes mind games." She cocked her head and studied him. "But you've always known that. He's your brother. He lives to push your buttons and vice versa. What made you think this time was so different?"

"I, well . . . I'm not certain." He massaged his temples with the pads of his thumbs. "I cannot figure why he'd lie about this. Why he'd go so far out of his way to screw with me and to use you in the process. I'm having a bloody hard time forgiving him for that."

Gwen bit her lip. Thoreau *had* been flirtatious, but he'd let her know almost from Day One not to take him seriously. As for why he'd lie about that to his brother, however, she was almost as clueless as Emerson. She could see Thoreau setting up his real-life chessboard and moving certain human pieces into place. She could tell there was a well-thought-out strategy behind his moves. But she really had no idea what outcome he was hoping to create, and she didn't know why he wanted it either.

The biggest mystery, though, revolved around Emerson's reasons for caring. Why on Earth would it matter to him whether or not she ended up with his brother? *He* wasn't looking for commitment. He wasn't going to be interested in her one way or another after the tour ended. Was it, perhaps, as simple as that Emerson didn't want to lose to his big brother . . . even when the "prize" was of little consequence to him?

The musician had been playing a series of soft, flowing songs but, whether the earlier crowd preferred the more upbeat numbers or if the hour was just getting late, the listeners had dispersed into the night, leaving the man alone with his violin.

In a sudden movement, Emerson thrust his hands into his pockets and took several long strides in the direction of the gypsy. "Follow me," he whispered to her, that feverish, childlike excitement returning to his expression after several hours of absence.

So she followed him, watching as Emerson greeted the man and complimented him in short German sentences. Emerson, still speaking, thrust a number of bills into the man's violin case, making the gypsy musician grin broadly. Gwen didn't understand what was being discussed, but there was much nodding, smiling and glancing in her direction. She expected an introduction to take place as soon as she got to them and she wasn't disappointed.

"Gwen, this is Tibor," Emerson said.

She said hello and shook his hand. "You play beautifully," she added, hoping he would understand English well enough to glean what she meant. Then she took a step back. He would, no doubt, play again now that Emerson had given him such a healthy tip. Probably a song of Emerson's choosing.

But the man didn't play again. He held out the instrument to her.

She squinted at him and then at Emerson. What, exactly, was going on?

"Take the violin, Gwen," Emerson said, amused.

"Wh-why? Did you buy it?"

He laughed. "No. I just borrowed it for us for ten minutes. I've promised Tibor we wouldn't destroy it." He carefully took the instrument from the musician's hands, held it up to his chin and, with the bow drawn across the strings, played a few experimental notes. They sounded *very* screechy. He laughed at his efforts and made her take the violin. "Your turn."

"But I can't play—" she started to say.

"Yes, you can." He sighed. "It's clear I can't play this instrument at all, but even I tried it. You've at least learned a song or two, even if it was years ago. Play us something, Gwen. Anything. It'll be all right. Just think of the last tune you remembered practicing and play whatever parts of it you recall."

"Oh, no. Really, Emerson, no. It's been too long since—"

But Tibor nodded with encouragement and said something in German that Emerson haltingly translated for her. "He's telling you that his violin has a soul . . . no, that's not quite right. It has 'a good spirit.' It will guide you as you play. Help you along."

Gwen doubted this, but to refuse any longer might offend the musician, and she didn't want to do that. He would probably be offended enough when she massacred the notes. But the violin did look . . . for want of a better word . . . *friendly*. Almost welcoming.

She reached for it, feeling the smooth arch of the neck under her thumb, the tautness of the strings, the careful craftsmanship of the polished wood, the inward curl—like a seashell—on the end of the violin itself and the sunken indentations at the bottom of the bow when she grasped it. Her fingers slipped at once into the correct position. Muscle memory at work.

Sliding her chin into the curving resting spot, lifting up the instrument and drawing the bow across the strings near the bridge, she made her first sounds in over a decade.

She didn't attempt to play any song she knew at first; she just tried to reacquaint herself with the notes again. Initially, she sounded as scratchy and screechy as Emerson had, but her hands soon readjusted to the pressure of the bow dancing across the violin, to her fingertips pushing into strings again, to the stretch of her palm as she reached to hit the notes.

She ran through a scale or two and sounded, to her own ear, like a child. One rusty from having not practiced as she should. In some ways—musically, at least—she realized she *was* still a child. After her mom died, she tried to play on and off for a few years more, but her dad had lost heart in teaching her, and in his own music, too. Their lessons became increasingly less frequent and songs filled the air in their house only occasionally until, eventually, they disappeared altogether.

Gwen couldn't deny the embarrassment she felt in being listened to by both Emerson and the musician, but they didn't appear to be cringing (yet) at her playing. She recognized that, while inexpert and uncomplicated, her notes were at least growing stronger, clearer and more freely flowing. She thought back to a song her dad had taught her when she was about nine or ten. Her mother had liked it and, so, Gwen practiced and practiced until she'd memorized the short Shaker tune and could play it for her sometimes.

Even after all of these years, her fingers still recalled their positions, gliding into place without excessive concentration. A childlike performance set in 4/4 time, she knew, but it was error-free and she filled those six fleeting lines of music with as much heart as she could pack into them.

Then she handed the violin back to its owner. "Thank you," she whispered to Tibor.

He murmured something back at her in German or, maybe, it was Hungarian this time. His warm smile told her that his words were kind.

Emerson was quiet, but his eyes shined. He beamed his delight at her. "You didn't play long, Gwen, but you played well. Thank you for trusting me. . . ." He let that thought trail off.

It was true. She *had* trusted him. She had to in order to play. It might have seemed like a small thing to some but—for her—it was a big, heart-pounding leap of faith.

They thanked the man again and wandered back toward the bar, listening to the beautiful gypsy music flowing behind them like a veil. Gwen almost couldn't believe the same instrument could produce such vastly different sounds.

"What was the name of the song you played?" Emerson asked. "The tune sounded familiar to me. A little like 'Lord of the Dance.' I quite liked it."

"You're right to connect them. 'Lord of the Dance' was adapted from it. The song is called 'Simple Gifts.' I learned it as a kid," she said. Then, "And I'm sure you could hear how *very* simple it was." She tried to laugh off the awkwardness she felt. "I know what I played was pretty amateurish, Emerson. You don't have to try to flatter me or humor me. I know I'm not a *good* musician like Tibor. Or like you."

He wrinkled his nose as if in disbelief and shook his head in emphasis. "The point isn't always about being 'good,' which is subjective anyway. Playing music is about expression, interpretation, personal perspective set to a melody. There are lots of people who can play notes *accurately*, even really complex sequences. You know as well as I do that this ability is just a matter of skill, often based on years of practice. That skill isn't a bad one to have, of course, but competence isn't enough to create a transformative experience."

She raised an eyebrow at him. "You said we were hardwired as humans to respond to the music of the spheres, Emerson. I would think playing accurately would do that. The musician would hit all the right harmonics."

He laughed. "True. From a vibrational, string-theory standpoint, certainly. As listeners, we can't help but respond to the beauty of the sounds in relationship with each other. But playing music and listening to it are different things. Complementary, but far from identical. You know that. It's one thing to create a musical impression, another to merely listen to it. Listeners have the right to subjectively qualify a piece as 'good' or 'bad,' based on what they've heard before and how well trained their ears are. But players have to have a different criterion for judgment. They can try to gauge the reaction their performance has on their audience and base their appraisal of quality on that . . . or they can evaluate their performance on how close it comes to meeting their own expectations."

"Which are—what?" she asked.

"Which are, among other things, whether the player expressed the feelings he or she wanted to share. Whether that simultaneous sense of release and connection happened. Whether the act of playing itself was an emotional one for the player. The world may call a man a 'good' musician, even a 'successful' one, but if he hasn't expressed the truth in his heart, how good could the performance really be?"

She thought on this for a moment. "I think it would be easier to express the truth if one hit the correct notes."

"Probably." He paused, seeming to study her. "Your soul shined through when you played, Gwen. It *meant* something to you, and you were honest about expressing it. The violin itself means something to you. I saw a glimpse of the real Gwendolyn Reese just now. I can't judge your performance as a creator, only as a listener, but—to me—it *was* good. You'll have to decide for yourself if you expressed through it what you most wanted to. Either way, it's obvious you have the spirit of a musician. You shouldn't hold yourself back from playing." He reached for her right hand and tenderly rubbed her fingers. "You've got a solid base. Why not take violin lessons again?"

Why not, indeed?

Only, perhaps, because she'd wrapped up her musician's heart and soul in sentimental brown paper and unbreakable string, and tucked the package away with her other dusty daydreams, the memories of her parents and the carefree childhood that had gotten cut short when she was far too young. She did not mention this.

Instead, she shrugged, managed to smile at him and squeezed his hand quickly before letting him go. "Maybe I will," she said before they reentered the smoky bar.

It was interesting, though, that she didn't tell Emerson about her background or explain any part of her sad history to him at a time when it would have been most logical to do so. She'd had many conversations with Richard about the loss of her mom and dad and, in his typically soothing tones, he'd kindly comforted her. However, she'd almost never broached with Richard the subject of her love of music. At most, she might mention her love of *musicals*—but that wasn't exactly the same thing. She'd expected him to infer her passion. Understand it. Yet, it was clear after talking to Emerson that Richard *hadn't* understood. Perhaps that was why she never tried to go deeper into the topic with her boyfriend.

With Emerson, by contrast, she'd delved headfirst, by her standards, into sharing her adoration of music with him, but she hadn't revealed much of her personal history. Was it that she didn't trust him with that knowledge?

No.

She'd trusted him with every element of her being when she'd played for him. She couldn't have exposed herself more if she'd stripped down and pranced around the streets of Budapest in her bra and panties.

It was not a matter of trust. Not exactly.

It was that she didn't want him seeing that other side of her. That lonely, overly structured schoolteacher she'd become thanks to nearly two decades of fear. She knew she could never pull off an air of being sophisticated and worldly—he would've had to have been blind and deaf to ever believe *that*—but at least she felt she wasn't being viewed by him with pity.

Richard, for better or worse, knew this sadder side of her being and, for the most part, wanted to be with her anyway. It was probably not right, just for that reason alone, to yearn for a romantic relationship with Emerson. Perhaps such intimacy was best reserved for Richard—a man who knew some of the deeper, unpleasant truths about her—even though he, too, didn't understand *all* of her. Recognizing her passion for music, after all, couldn't be as important a nugget of personal knowledge as grasping the magnitude of the loss of her parents. Could it?

However, she had begun to get the unsettling sensation that she might also *need* a friendship with someone like Emerson, in addition to her bond with Richard. A different kind of relationship for a different side of herself.

It reminded her of something Aunt Bea had said once when Gwen asked her why her friends were from so many walks of life. Her aunt didn't mingle just with the seniors she met at the community center, or just with her longstanding neighborhood pals, or even just with the S&M club members. Unlike Gwen, Beatrice talked to *everybody*—young or old, male or female, Midwestern or foreign, slim or chunky. She picked up new acquaintances like the Pied Piper picked up street children.

She told Gwen, "No one can be your everything." She said people needed multiple close friends in their lives to share their assorted interests. Even when Uncle Freddy was still alive, Aunt Bea always made time to hang out with the bingo ladies or the classics book club or the kids at the pool. "Makes my life richer," she added. "No *one* person can complete me—that's just nonsense. I'm a complex women. A full mosaic. I want every side of me to shine, not just one or two sides of me."

And *that*, Gwen realized with sudden insight, was the hidden gift her aunt had been trying to give her by offering her this European trip. The chance to polish a few pieces of her personal mosaic. Aunt Bea had left it up to her to choose which sides she wanted to work on, but she'd subtly given Gwen the task of buffing up a handful of muddied, dust-covered fragments of herself. Chipped slivers of multihued ceramic that had been left untouched for years.

Gwen had only to select them and spend the summer making them sparkle.

8

The Bold, the Beautiful and
the Bad-Boy Brothers

I t would come as no surprise to most anyone that Gwen watched very little daytime TV. She caught the news during the evening and the occasional movie of the week, but she did not go out of her way to watch programs such as soap operas—unless coerced.

It would likewise come as no surprise that Aunt Bea was, in Gwen's opinion, freakishly fond of soap operas, and nothing could have equaled her delight when she came across *The Bold and the Beautiful* on Vienna cable the following night, dubbed in German. She had no scruples whatsoever against squealing down the hall, rousing Hester, Connie Sue and Zenia from their near slumber and coercing them (and Gwen) into watching it with her in their hotel room.

Well, in Zenia's case, there really was no coercion involved.

"This might just be the most beauteous thing I've seen since that Moroccan weave scarf I once held in my grandma's house," Zenia pronounced in awe as she watched Ridge, eldest son of the wealthy Forrester clan (although, biologically, he was actually the offspring of billionaire shipping magnate Massimo Marone, who'd had a one-night tryst with Ridge's mother Stephanie prior to her involvement with Forrester patriarch Eric, who married her because she was pregnant with his child—or so he'd thought), explain in perfect *Deutsch* his latest ploy to dominate the world of upscale fashion, outwit the Spencer media moguls and, simultaneously, vacillate between his attraction (which led over the decades to multiple marriages, divorces and remarriages) to the ever-scheming Brooke Logan and the wildly promiscuous Taylor Hamilton Hayes.

Gwen knew all of this, not because she understood a word of the dialogue, but because her aunt talked about these characters as if they were real people and because Austria was, apparently, several months behind in their broadcasting of the soap—having had to take time to dub the episodes and all—so Zenia and Aunt Bea could cheerfully enlighten the rest of them on the characters, their convoluted relationships to the others and, occasionally, on their stated (and unstated) motivations.

"You see," Aunt Bea explained to her captive audience, "Ridge's relationship with his half brother Thorne was already extremely competitive, but their rivalry was complicated further by the family's discovery of Ridge's paternity some years back, which made their mother, Stephanie, even more protective of Ridge. And her husband, Eric, still showed favoritism to him, despite the two not sharing a drop of DNA. Thorne was incredibly jealous. But, even before Thorne found out about the paternity test, he and Ridge had tons of battles over women. One night, Thorne got sick of feeling like the underappreciated younger brother, took a bunch of sleeping pills and tried to shoot Ridge with Stephanie's handgun. . . ."

"I should watch this show to get me some more good ideas for my murder mystery," Hester interjected.

Zenia nodded. "It's the best."

Gwen paid scant attention to the backstory surrounding the soap, but she couldn't help but superimpose what little she knew about Emerson and Thoreau's family history onto the ruthless maneuverings of the Forrester clan. Sure, the Edwards brothers weren't known for attempting to commit acts of homicide (at least she hoped not!), but Gwen had certainly inferred that some of the tension between them stemmed from perceived differences in parental treatment. A common enough complaint, even in non-TV families.

She remembered Thoreau mentioning way back on their bus ride to Florence that Emerson was too used to getting his way with their mother. And he'd let other things slip, too. That Emerson's personality was more like their father's and, as a result, their mother was extrasoft on Emerson after their dad died. That Thoreau always had to be the responsible one. That neither liked to be in second place but that Emerson had "a real complex about it," at least according to his older brother.

But Emerson had given her a few clues, as well. He'd hinted that he wasn't respected as much as Thoreau by their family as a whole. That he was considered a handsome enough kid but not an accomplished one for too many years, in his opinion. That his elder sibling got more of their dad's attention before he died, while he had to be content with "just being more like the man, without getting to know him."

Even Cynthia chimed in once and, in an aside to Gwen, admitted that the brothers were a bit intimidating, even for her. That if Gwen thought Emerson could be a pain to deal with for just a few weeks, imagine what it was like working with him all year. . . .

Gwen couldn't imagine. She realized in the pulse of the moment how quickly this trip was going by. That this Grand European Adventure was a mere blip in time, yet another reminder that she might never see Emerson—or any of the Brits—again after it was over.

She tried to shove that thought to the edges of her mind as they went on sightseeing excursions through Vienna, however.

This latest stop on the tour further awakened in her stirrings of wanting to play the violin again. It would have been impossible to avoid this in a music city like Vienna. Songs and musicians were everywhere—on every street, every corner, every open space large enough to hold a crowd. The pedestrian mall-like walkway in the *Innere Stadt*, the old city center, was littered with practicing music students. And even on the broad boulevard surrounding the historic heart of Vienna, the *Ringstrasse,* the casual listener could often hear the strains of a string quartet rehearsing classical works for the enjoyment of passersby. Aside from Budapest, she had never been in a place that so revered music. It set her spirit aloft.

Hans-Josef was, at last, fully in his element. He was translating everything from the German, speaking with joy in his voice and a spring in his step, reveling in being back amongst his countrymen.

"I hope you enjoyed your visit to Schönbrunn," he said enthusiastically, prattling for a good twenty minutes more about the famous Viennese palace and gardens, which had once been the Hapsburg monarchs' imperial summer residence. Meanwhile, Guido tried to steer the bus out of the packed parking lot and in the direction of their last major site of the day.

Gwen's eyes were blurry. They had already spent *hours* seeing the Hofburg, a palace that now served as the President of Austria's official residence. Taking photos of a famous statue of Johann Strauss II, who wrote both the famous waltz "The Blue Danube" (the actual river looked more like a murky gray to Gwen's eye, but she was careful not to mention this) and the operetta *Die Fledermaus,* which Hans-Josef was quick to remind them they'd heard some selections from while in Budapest. Driving by Beethoven's grave at the Central Cemetery and the well-known St. Stephen's Cathedral. And, finally, visiting Schloss Schönbrunn with its breathtaking gardens, endless and extremely decorative palatial rooms and the *Tiergarten,* the world's oldest existing zoo, founded in 1752. They'd even gotten in on a short, late-afternoon classical concert featuring the music of Wolfgang Amadeus Mozart while at the palace.

A musically inspirational day, yes, but also an exhausting one.

Their final stop was the Prater—Vienna's principal park and home to the *Riesenrad,* the city's legendary Ferris wheel. Guido let them out close to the entrance so they could stroll along the park's main avenue, a street closed to motorists and lined with gorgeous horse chestnut trees. Despite her fatigue, Gwen felt the now-familiar pull back through time that she'd gotten so often in Europe. Save for the clothing of the tourists, she might have believed herself to be back in the eighteenth century.

"Look around. Explore," chirped Hans-Josef with an almost outrageous level of cheerfulness. "Take a ride on the Ferris wheel. Visit the planetarium or museum in the park. Or just stop for refreshments at one of the restaurants or coffee shops. Guido will meet us in one hour and a half to return us to the hotel for the night. Or, if you prefer to stay longer"—he looked at them as if they'd be insane not to want to stay indefinitely—"it is easy to find a taxi there." He pointed toward the road they'd driven up on. "Okay? *Ja?* Off you go now."

And Cynthia, who had been hovering close to their tour guide, and who had been inseparable from him since their bar night in Budapest, nodded enthusiastically.

Hans-Josef winked at Cynthia (that's right, *winked at her*) and offered her his elbow. They linked arms and took off like a single unit in the direction of the Ferris wheel. Looked like they'd both finally found the on-tour romance they were seeking.

Louisa watched them walk away with a smile that was half happy for her friend, half wistful for herself. And Gwen watched her watch them. Sometimes it was obvious to outsiders what made a person happy:

Hans-Josef loved his native language and his home country, people who were prompt and well dressed, activities that were efficiently planned and well organized.

Cynthia lived for being perceived as special, as important enough to be paid attention to and, while she'd accept that heightened interest from a woman, she found it irresistible when it came from a man.

Davis and Ani—though separated by age, race and nationality—were united in their adoration of strategy games and their determination to be the best at them.

Zenia embraced anything artistic and did so with her whole heart.

Back at home, Richard got a bolt of satisfaction from filing

claims with care, getting his deskwork done early, patiently handling concerned customers.

Aunt Bea desired little more than conversation with a wide
range of people—the mere interpersonal interaction was enough
for her.

Thoreau got a charge out of analyzing everyone's actions and, in
the case of his brother, using that deep understanding to play mind
games.

And Emerson—enigma though he was—had let her glimpse
into his soul a time or two, enough so she could see the way he enjoyed merging the mathematical with the musical, the scientific
with the poetic, the historic with the artistic.

But what of Gwen? What did she *love?*

Was it enough that she *appreciated* structure? Was clinging to
that the same as the way she lost herself within the beauty of a
melody? Rhythm and meter *were* structural elements, after all. . . .
Yet, the precision she clung to in her daily life was not, she feared,
related to her ability to keep time in music. That was not what she
had been doing in these past two years since her dad died. In
songs, the underlying beat provided a constancy within the composition that allowed the melody to soar freely. By contrast, in her
real life, her persistent routines were less like tempo and cadence
and more like oppressive steel bars—vertical measures that kept
her spirit trapped by the tedium of her habits.

"Do you wish to go on the *Riesenrad?*" Emerson asked her,
throwing around the German word just because he could.

"Have you been on it before?" she asked him.

He nodded. "It's rather nice. A bit different from the usual carnival ride in that you can walk around in the box, as opposed to
just sitting as it spins but, really, if you've been on one Ferris
wheel . . ."

She smiled, remembering going with her parents to the Iowa
State Fair when she was about six. She and her mom went up in
the Ferris wheel just after sunset, the smell of buttered corn and
roasting hotdogs wafting up toward them. The surprising coolness
of the metal restraints after the heat of the day. The stickiness of

pink cotton candy still on her fingers. And she could recall looking out over the lights of the city when their swinging basket reached the top. Glittery palm-sized globes of light sparkling as night washed over them.

She was little then, but she'd felt even littler. Just thinking about it brought back those same feelings of both awe and insignificance. What did it matter . . . the life of one young American woman? What could she do that was at all special?

She blinked back a sudden and surprising tear, wiping it away— she hoped—before Emerson could see it. "Thanks, but I don't think so. I think I'm going to find a café and try some of this famous Viennese coffee."

He studied her expression for a moment, calmly. "Would you welcome company?"

She studied him back and realized yes. Yes, she would. She wanted nothing more than some quiet "alone" time *with* Emerson.

So, after a quick word to Thoreau and Louisa, who were debating whether to go to the planetarium with honeymooners Peter and Sally or to the museum with Dr. Louie and Matilda, Gwen and Emerson trooped around the park until they came across a small, family-owned coffeehouse, Café Danube. They soon found themselves seated comfortably on the patio outside, an Austrian newspaper on their table.

"Going to read the headlines to me?" Gwen asked, after their waiter served them each a glass of cold tap water and took their beverage orders.

He laughed. "I shall do it, if you really want me to, Gwen. But you should know, I'm more of a romance-language lover. My brother, on the other hand"—he wrinkled his nose—"is the go-to gent for German." He flipped through the newspaper without really reading it. "It was hellacious being related to him when we were schoolboys," Emerson admitted. "He was irritatingly good at everything. And five years ahead of me to boot."

She nodded. This was a persistent theme in the relationship between the brothers. It seemed that even now, even when Emerson should have felt as though he'd proven himself as an incredibly accomplished adult, he wasn't really over the years of competition that had existed between him and Thoreau. Who had fostered this rivalry?

"How old were you when your dad died?" she asked.

"Thirteen."

Just a year older than she had been when she'd lost her mom. "That's—that's very young."

He cleared his throat. "It is."

"So, Thoreau was actually an adult then. Already eighteen," she murmured, recognizing the gulf between the brothers at this gross disparity in experience. She would've given anything—*anything*— to have had her mother in her life through adolescence, through high school. She understood immediately the depth of Emerson's loss.

Her own brothers, of course, really got shortchanged. They'd been so very young—six and four at the time Mom died. Her youngest brother barely remembered their mother. But Emerson's situation was similar to her own. They'd both been young enough to need a guiding parent of the same gender to help them transition through a tough stage of childhood and, yet, old enough to know acutely what they'd be missing by not having this.

"My brother's childhood and mine were quite different," Emerson agreed.

Their coffees came and Gwen knew she could easily change the subject. He had not asked about her parents and, unless someone chatty, like Connie Sue or Hester, had told him, it was a part of her history that she really could keep to herself, just as she'd planned.

Only, suddenly, she didn't want to do that. Suddenly, she wanted him to know he wasn't alone. That she really and truly *understood* what he'd experienced.

"My mother died when I was twelve," she said, blowing gently on her demitasse cup of coffee. It smelled heavenly but looked very much like tar. She wondered briefly how it would taste. If it would be bad for her health. She wondered things like that a lot— too often, perhaps. "A brain aneurysm," she added. " Totally unexpected." She ran her finger down the side of the cup and glanced up at Emerson, letting him see fully into her sadness. "I never . . . ever . . . got over it. Even now. It still doesn't make sense to me."

"Oh, Gwen. I'm very sorry," he said on a sigh, catching her gaze and holding it.

If she'd feared him pitying her, she was wrong. The look he gave her wasn't laced with pity (like that of her teaching colleagues), or sympathy (like Richard's default expression), or even empathy (like her experience with the few girls she'd met in college who'd also lost a beloved relative).

No. Emerson's gaze was instantaneous and comprehensive understanding. It was utter recognition of the hole in her childhood. Of the gap that could never be filled. And, somehow, the simple knowledge that *he* understood *her* softened the very edges of that crater of loss in her heart.

"I'm sorry, too," she said. "For both of us."

He then told her a few tales about Thoreau, as if trying to lighten the conversation. About how his brother "dated demonically" all through his university years, was a serial monogamist and had gotten engaged to his ex-wife long before it would've been advisable.

"He kept trying to replicate Mum and Father's marriage," Emerson said with a (sort-of) laugh. "I always thought that to be unrealistic, but he was more of an optimist in that regard."

Gwen couldn't help but remember their first discussion on this topic, back at Festival del Gelato in Florence. Only she had more information now. More insight into how and why he thought as he did.

"You don't want to commit to a relationship because that would mean being like Thoreau," she blurted. "Having yet another area of competition between you."

The two men, she realized, had sectioned off the universe, as if by subjects, and stamped their names on the pieces in which each claimed superiority. Thoreau had already called "marital commitment" as *his;* therefore, Emerson had to excel at its opposite—"dedicated bachelorhood."

Emerson's lips twisted into a smile. "You think you know me so well," he chided, taking a sip of his coffee. He motioned for her to do the same.

Strong!

She swallowed, blinked a few times and reached for the nearby glass of water.

He chuckled and said, "Drink as much water as you need. The waiter will keep replenishing it, whether you want it or not."

"Why?" She gulped about half a glass more after taking her second sip of Viennese coffee. The stuff must have been brewed in asphalt.

"Tradition," he explained. "They bring additional water unrequested through your visit. It's an unspoken message that you're a welcomed guest, not one who should feel pressured to leave for other patrons."

Gwen could appreciate that and, as if on cue, their waiter headed over to them with fresh waters. Emerson thanked him and requested something from the dessert menu called *Sachertorte*. "You must try this. Trust me."

As they waited for it, a clock in the distance struck seven p.m., and live piano music drifted out to the patio to greet them.

After listening to the café pianist for a few minutes, she said, "You play just as well, you know. Quite possibly better."

"Thanks." He drank more of his coffee. "The music means a lot to me. When I'm not trying to show up Thoreau, when I'm just thinking about the notes, there's no competition. Not against some stranger playing in a coffeehouse. Not even against myself. It's just me, in harmony with the song. You understand what I mean?"

Gwen hadn't played in public enough to have felt the sting of competition (a couple of recitals for her family and a few of her parents' friends when she was ten or eleven hardly counted), but she had experienced acute self-consciousness when playing for Emerson and the gypsy violinist and also, as with the impromptu singing on the trip, whenever she was asked to join a group in song. There were nights, back at home, though, when she was listening to her favorite Andrew Lloyd Webber soundtrack in the car or in the kitchen and she would lose herself in the music so completely—even singing along in full voice—that it would startle her when she realized she'd been harmonizing aloud. Even though no one could hear her, just the thought of an imaginary audience listening in and, possibly, judging her was enough to make her heart race and her palms sweat. Enough, actually, to silence her. But the moment of deep immersion just before that awareness was bliss.

"Yes. Sort of," she told Emerson, remembering, too, what he'd said in Budapest about how the experience of being the creator of the music was different from merely being a listener. That a listener could rate a performance as "good" or "bad" based on the sharpness of his ear and his prior background in music. But that the person playing had a more complex task—whether or not he expressed through the song what he most desired. Whether or not the music touched the heart of the performer himself. Or, in this case, *herself*.

The waiter returned again with a large piece of very chocolaty-looking cake. Two forks.

"*Sachertorte*," Emerson said simply. "Taste it. You'll adore it."

She picked up one of the forks and speared the moist tip of the cake. "Mmm. It *is* good," she said after the first bite. "There's a filling of some sort in it. I can't quite figure—"

"Apricot," he said in that know-it-all tone of his.

He was smirking at her while speaking. So very cosmopolitan, was he. So very worldly and sophisticated and experienced. So very sure of himself. She couldn't help but grimace and, in an effort to make him act marginally less victorious, she scooped up another forkful of cake and stuffed it in his mouth.

He looked surprised but not displeased as he chewed. Then he picked up the second fork, heaped it with more cake and decorated her lower lip and chin with the chocolate glaze until she gave in and opened her mouth for it.

She found herself laughing, her hands half covering her face like a mask. He was so *goofy*. So youthful, even at age thirty-five. So uninhibited that it was starting to rub off on her.

He was laughing, too, of course, and attacking the remaining cake with his fork to try to score the biggest scoop. She battled him with her fork on the plate, as if in a duel.

She had just managed to wedge another forkful between Emerson's lips when, in a move so quick that time must have been fast-forwarded, he leaned across their little table as if to kiss her.

But he stopped. His chocolate-smeared lips hovering close to hers, but not quite touching.

He swallowed his bite of cake, took a breath and pulled back a few inches. "Gwen . . ." he murmured.

She gazed up at him, time instantly having been switched to pause, and tried to express through her eyes her strong *liking* of him. And, yet, that liking was at odds with the life plan she had mapped out for herself. She was thirty, after all. It wasn't prudent to live without direction. But she also couldn't shake the disquieting suspicion that what she thought she'd always wanted might no longer be the case.

Life was full of so many dualities and inconsistencies.

She shook her head and he sat back down. "I'm sorry, Emerson."

He shrugged and set his fork on the plate. She, too, had suddenly lost interest in the cake.

"It's quite all right," he said with a sigh, looking down, his attention focused on something crawling on the ground. "My fault for not remembering what you'd told me." Then, after another beat, "I don't always know what I want either."

"You don't know what you want to order?" said an amused male voice behind her. *Thoreau.* In front of her, Emerson looked up and stiffened. "Might I suggest some tasty *Wienerschnitzel?*" his brother continued, clearly in the mood for mockery.

She turned to fully face Thoreau, spotting Louisa and the honeymooners trailing several paces behind him. "Oh, hey, there," she said. "We, actually, just had some cake," she explained, since Emerson was not quick to offer a reply. She swiped the chocolate smears off her mouth and chin with her napkin. "But we're done now."

"And, also, we were just leaving," Emerson added as he pushed to standing. "Would you like our table?"

"What? No, no. Don't race away," Thoreau said.

Both she and Emerson had risen, but Thoreau spanned his arms between them like an eagle, placed his hands on their shoulders and, literally, pushed them back into their seats. He glanced at their two-thirds-eaten cake and raised a brow. "*Sachertorte*, huh? Not as good as you'd expected?"

"No, it was great," Gwen said loyally. "I guess we just weren't as hungry as we'd thought."

Thoreau smirked. "Troubled by indecision, are we?" he mused, although there was a pointedness about it Gwen couldn't ignore. He gazed speculatively at his younger sibling just as Louisa, Sally and Peter reached them.

Gwen realized she and Emerson hadn't seen the four of them coming, but that the reverse wasn't necessarily true. While the others may have been too far back to observe with any clarity, Thoreau had outstripped the rest of his group and had, most likely, seen that almost-kiss. She suspected Emerson realized this as well and pieced together the not-so-subtle insinuations his brother was leveling at them.

"I'm delighted we decided to go to the planetarium," Louisa said pleasantly. "I haven't studied astronomy or physics since my first year at university." She sent Emerson a sheepish grin. "But the night sky is always so gorgeous, and all that talk of black holes and quarks and such is endlessly fascinating."

Sally was quick to agree, and her husband further observed that it was incredible to think of how much energy was packing into even a small white dwarf and how vast the distances were in our solar system, let alone between galaxies.

"I've been a fan of math puzzles and science wonders for almost six decades," Peter said, "but the idea of a light-year still boggles my mind."

"Oh, indeed. The universe is simply bursting with paradoxical elements," added Thoreau. He nudged his brother. "Wouldn't you agree? Weren't you just spouting off about *contradictions* the other day? Some *boring* Bohr theory, as I recall," he said, laughing at his own joke.

Gwen saw Emerson clench his jaw. "Bohr's principle of complementarity is not what I'd term *boring*, Thoreau," he said, his expression hard. He turned a softer eye on Gwen, Louisa and the honeymooners, however, and explained that they shouldn't let its name fool them. "The complementarity principle is actually about contradiction. Some objects have multiple properties that appear to be contradictory. Basically, it's impossible to view both properties at the same time, despite the way they can coexist simultaneous in nature. You understand the way light can be either a particle or a wave, depending on the situation? Normally, any electron that's both a particle *and* a wave would seem to be impossible because they're mutually exclusive. Not true in this case."

"I would wager *people* are far more contradictory than even light," Thoreau suggested thoughtfully. Gwen narrowed her eyes at him, and Emerson shot him a look that was just shy of scathing. The others did not appear to notice anything amiss.

Peter nodded at Emerson's explanation, and asked a few qualifying questions. Louisa bobbed her head in appreciation. And Sally smiled kindly at Emerson and everyone surrounding him.

While Gwen wasn't necessarily well-versed on the nuances of Bohr's theory after this one lesson, she had to admit Emerson had encapsulated it well, and Louisa gushed, "You're such a brilliant teacher, Emerson. I remember some French writer saying that what makes a person a genius is the ability to reduce the complicated to the simple."

Thoreau seemed to develop a nasty cough at the word *genius*.

Emerson thanked Louisa then abruptly stood up. Gwen sensed there was no way his brother would be able to push him down this time. He flagged their waiter, who immediately came to their table with glasses of water for everyone.

Handing several bills to the man, which amply covered their coffee and cake, Emerson smiled tightly and announced that he and Gwen were going to the park and would be taking a taxi back much later. He politely wished them all a good evening.

This plan was news to Gwen, but she played along.

Thoreau, sharp as ever and unusually ornery, went for the part-

226 *Marilyn Brant*

ing shot. "Have fun, kidlets," he said condescendingly. "But do remember, *'It's not what you look at that matters, it's what you see.'* Henry David Thoreau."

Emerson took several strides away from the group, so she thought Thoreau may have succeeded in getting that last word. She should learn never to underestimate the younger of the Edwards men.

After a few additional paces, in a strike so witty and so intentionally ironic, Emerson turned and called over his shoulder. "Brother, *'I hate quotation. Tell me what you know.'*" He grinned. "Ralph Waldo Emerson."

Gwen caught the barbed glances between them—this latest skirmish cutting yet another notch in the backboard of their combative history.

Their adventures in Salzburg were not exactly off to an auspicious start.

Hans-Josef, who'd long awaited his morning off in his hometown, put Guido in charge of getting them to and from "The Sound of Music" tour. The tour itself (complete with the lake views from the Julie Andrews version of the film, the tree-lined drives, the lush gardens, the wedding church and the famous gazebo) had been lovely—once they got there. Guido, whose laid-back Italian nature jibed well with the streets and driving customs of Italy, southern France and even Hungary, was not entirely well suited to the precision of a German-Austrian border city. Or, more specifically, to their police force. And with their tour guide absent and unable to insist upon strict punctuality, not only were they late in getting to see the hills coming alive, but Guido also procured a rather pricy speeding ticket.

Gwen, however, was amused by the way Guido laughed at it— once the policeman was well out of sight—and banished the thin paper to a half-folded, half-crumpled footnote in the bottom of his beverage holder.

Hans-Josef, when he rejoined them that afternoon, was less amused. Perhaps it was only on account of his free time having ended, but their tour guide wasn't in the best mood to begin with and this ticket didn't help. Looking rather like Liesl's too-serious boyfriend in the much-beloved musical, he reprimanded their bus driver sternly. Even having Cynthia hanging on his arm and trying to tug him away did not restore his humor with any immediacy.

Richard would have acted like that, too, Gwen realized, having just spent the better part of a half hour comparing the two men in her mind again. Had he been in Hans-Josef's position, he would not have dismissed the ticket and moved on with the afternoon portion of the tour. No. He would have scolded and grudged and sucked the fun out of someone's day. Even though she was rarely inclined toward being late herself (and she'd *never* gotten a speeding ticket), she found herself displeased with this trait Richard and Hans-Josef shared. It was almost . . . self-righteous.

Thankfully, the beauty of the Alps served to distract her more than once. The hazy shades of alternating blues, greens and whites in the distance. The stunning peaks that looked more like a Universal Studios backdrop than real life. The crispness of the air at high elevation and the chirp of birds calling to others in the flock as if to say, "What a beautiful day! To be young and free and in the mountains!"

Upon returning from their afternoon drive to see the gorgeous alpine vista that was Eagle's Nest, Gwen found herself nestled between Zenia and Connie Sue on a small café bench in downtown Salzburg, waiting for their tables to be set. It was dinnertime and, while she wasn't normally overly hungry for any meal, the high altitude must have been playing with her appetite because, for once, she was ravenous.

"Hmm. How much longer do you think it'll take before they'll be ready for us?" she asked the older ladies.

"Dunno," Zenia said, unconcerned. She elbowed Gwen and pointed to a distinguished-looking man in his early fifties—salt-and-pepper sideburns, trim and dressed in a navy sport coat. "I could feast on him, though. *Hello-ohhh!* Captain Von Trapp," she beckoned, waving an arm at him.

Gwen ducked her head, both out of embarrassment and to

avoid getting bashed in the skull by Zenia's wild swinging. Thank-fully, the man soon walked deep into the restaurant, either having not heard Zenia's call or not thinking she was talking to him.

Connie Sue giggled. "Why, honey," she said to Zenia, "you gotta be faster than that if you want to hook 'em. If you're not quick enough to call the tile you want, it's dead forever."

Gwen squinted at Connie Sue but didn't bother to ask. If they were talking about "tiles," it must have something to do with mah-jongg and, really, she didn't want to know.

Zenia laughed in response and took on the stagey voice of an ac-tress in a Southern drama. "I don't want me some old tile some-one's already discarded. Don't you know I be picking ahead, Miz Connie Sue?"

Connie Sue burst into a fresh round of giggles, her plump body jiggling in delight next to Gwen. Then, as if sensing her confusion, Connie Sue was moved to explain, "Sweetie, in a mah-jongg game, some players allow each other to 'pick ahead,' to choose the tiles that they want in the next round, instead of waiting. *We* don't play that way." She sent Zenia a pointed look. Zenia was not averse to attempted cheating. "But, for people who do, it's kind of like predicting the future."

Interesting concept, but then the rules of mah-jongg were full of quirks and oddities. She remembered something Aunt Bea had told her about the game once and mentioned it to the other women. "It's mostly a really unpredictable game, though, right? I heard the winning hands are different every year."

Zenia nodded. "Yep, the winning combinations of tiles change from year to year. They're on a special mah-jongg card that you can get online or at a store. So, the 'best' future for a player changes all the time. Between games. And between years."

"As capricious as life," Connie Sue added, and Gwen marveled anew at how well these seniors seemed to handle the fickleness of both the games they'd played and the real world they inhabited. How willing they were not only to take risks but to let the chips of randomness fall where they may. Gwen had never liked the feeling of being in flux, but she figured making peace with it was, somehow, the key to contented longevity.

Hans-Josef appeared before them. "We will eat in four minutes," he stated, tapping his watch and looking as if he might break into "Sixteen Going On Seventeen" at any moment. Clearly, his good humor had finally been reestablished, no small thanks to the restorative properties of the Alps and a lengthy semiprivate conversation with Cynthia.

"Great!" Zenia enthused, bounding unsteadily to her feet, shackling their tour guide's wrist with her firm hand and pulling her toward him. "I got a seating request. There's a man who just walked in. So tall"—she gestured—"with black-'n'-white sideburns and a nice blue jacket—"

"You want to sit at a table near him?" Hans-Josef interjected, having learned by now that Zenia was not shy about introducing herself to any potential objects of her fleeting affection. He tried, unsuccessfully, to get her to release his wrist.

"Why, no." Zenia grinned naughtily. "I wanna sit *at* his table, preferably on his lap." She tugged him in the direction of the door. "And you're gonna help me."

Hans-Josef's smile faded to an expression of alarm, and Connie Sue laughed loudly and whispered in Gwen's ear, "So long, farewell," as Zenia and Hans-Josef disappeared into the restaurant. Then, after a beat, she added, *Auf wiedersehen,* good night."

Gwen shook her head as Connie Sue motioned for her to quickly follow. "Being a tour guide must be a challenging job," Gwen commented to the older lady, just as Cynthia pushed between them, racing to catch up with her now-agitated Austrian boyfriend and the strong-willed woman who had him in her grasp.

"Any job is challenging if you lack a sense of humor, honey," Connie Sue replied pleasantly. "We could all use more of that."

9

Illuminations

Friday–Sunday, July 20–22

Connie Sue's wise words rang true in Gwen's mind. She mulled them over during their drive through the scenic Black Forest of Bavaria and its neighboring German states—complete with a stop at a Munich *biergarten*, a Würzburg *bratwurst haus* and a Heidelberg *apfelstrudel* bakery—as they approached the French border and zoomed toward Paris.

"Someday you'll have to come back to Germany," Emerson told her on the bus as they crossed the Rhine River into the French city of Strasbourg. "To see Mittenwald. It's a small Alpine town in Bavaria, but it has a great tradition of violin making. It's quaint. Not too far from the Austrian border."

"I'd like to come back to Europe someday," Gwen admitted, realizing for the first time just how true this statement was. It was funny to think that, only a few weeks ago, she couldn't imagine the need to see a European city twice. But now . . . She had to laugh at herself. She was beginning to feel almost sentimental about Rome. Wishing she'd dwelled longer in the cool halls of the Vatican or studied the Bernini sculptures more carefully. Hoping—however irrationally, illogically or unscientifically—that the coin she'd pitched into that decorative fountain would, indeed, hasten her return to the Italian capital.

"Well, perhaps this will remind you." He pulled something out of his small backpack. A brown paper package, tied up with string. And it looked like a compact disk—one of her favorite things, of course. She smiled, wondering if he'd done that purposely. Before she could ask, he added, "I found this at a music store in Vienna. But it was recorded live in Budapest."

Gwen thanked him, removed the wrapping and studied the CD inside. Gypsy music. Or "Romani," as Emerson explained. Mostly stringed instruments. Lots of guitar and violin and some kind of dulcimerlike thing called a cimbalom. "I can't wait to listen to it," she said warmly, recognizing only as the words left her mouth that this would be unlikely until she had access to a CD player and that was back at home. The realization tempered her enthusiasm.

Emerson was looking at her curiously as she gripped the disk tighter and read through the song selection a second time. "Sorry, I wasn't able to wrap it in nice paper," he said. "I didn't have any on hand, and I'm actually dreadful at handling it even when I do. It always tears."

She tried to envision him struggling to gift wrap a present, but found it hard to imagine him being bad at anything. His hands were so agile. So capable. A man who could play piano as he did would surely be able to fasten the edges of paper with tape or attach a fancy bow with ease. Not that his gift required any further embellishment—she loved it just the way he gave it to her. Most likely, Emerson was just making an attempt at being modest.

It did occur to her, however, that she would have loved for him to have attached a note of some kind to the CD. She'd never even seen his handwriting. How impractical it was of her to be growing attached to a man, if only in mere "friendship," whose signature she wouldn't recognize! In truth, she knew so little about him . . . almost nothing from his daily life . . . and if that wasn't a reality check for her, she didn't know what else might serve as one.

Their bus pulled up to their Parisian hotel around dusk, the iconic silhouette of the Eiffel Tower rising in the distance. A distinctive birthmark on the face of the classic city.

They checked into their rooms, changed for dinner and, as

night fell and lamps began to flicker on, Hans-Josef and Guido took them on an evening drive through *La Ville-Lumière*—indeed, true to its name, Paris was the City of Light—before they stopped for a delicious group dinner on the famed Champs-Élysées.

Finally, with the delectable scent of *boeuf bourguignon* and *crème brûlée* still clinging to their memories like the fragrance of pleasure, they wove their way back through the sparkling city. Views of a lit-up Eiffel Tower, Notre Dame Cathedral, Sacre Coeur, Louvre and Arc de Triomphe illuminated their night.

When they passed by the Paris Opera House (or *"L'Opéra Garnier"* as Hans-Josef called it, using its proper French name and describing the building's illustrious history), Emerson stole a glance in her direction. This was the setting of *The Phantom of the Opera*. The place where one of the counterweights for the grand chandelier really dropped in 1896, killing someone and igniting the imagination of author Gaston Leroux, who went on to write his classic Gothic novel.

As Gwen stared, mesmerized, at the imposing, impressive edifice, she could almost hear Emerson humming to her from the score of Webber's musical, as he had in that Venetian mask shop, right before he'd kissed her.

Well, no. The humming wasn't only in her imagination. He was doing it again. In the seat just across the aisle from her. Providing a disquieting musical accompaniment to their drive. And, soon, he wasn't alone. Soon half the tour members were humming *Phantom*'s title track along with him, Dr. Louie most enthusiastically of all. Hans-Josef, with a good-natured shrug, gave up trying to give them a detailed commentary and instructed Guido to just circle the opera one more time.

"So, why didn't you guys form some kind of a cappella club instead of a sudoku and mah-jongg group?" Gwen grumbled to her aunt.

Bea just laughed and kept humming.

And Emerson did the same, gazing at her with knowing eyes as he led the group, the vibrations of their collective cacophony making the air currents hip hop around her. His brother even joined in after a time, holding his index finger and his thumb apart, at a pawn's height, and moving them on an invisible board in space-time to the music.

The moment was somehow both menacing and magical. As much a portent of things to come as a prologue to a play. Like the orchestral opening notes accompanying the rising of the curtain, Gwen sensed the appropriate theatrical foreshadowing. She saw the players onstage—most conspicuously, Emerson and Thoreau with their persistent dualities, which they wore as flagrantly as costumes. She remembered other players hidden carefully in the wings—like Richard with his impending arrival and his tacit expectations.

But, despite the real-life play having begun, she did not yet know the dramatic nature of the production. Would it reveal itself to be a tragedy or a comedy? Would the actors sing or merely speak? Would she be relegated to the role of an unnamed extra? A removed audience member? Or, was she an integral part of the cast?

Theater. Chess. Physics. Life. Four disparate yet surprisingly similar games of skill, woven together like one of Zenia's fiber-art masterpieces and presented to her like a multihued scarf. One fit for wearing. Or, perhaps, if Hester had her way, for strangulation.

And in sensing this absurdity, finally . . . finally . . . she laughed. At herself. And at the goofiness surrounding her.

Like Hans-Josef, she shrugged off the oddities of the group, stopped fighting her instinctive desire for order and gave herself permission to slip into the chaotic, entropic silliness of the moment. She might not be a central part of the show yet, but at least—from her place at the fringes—she was fully enjoying the performance for a change.

The next day was their action-packed induction into the Saturday stream of Parisian tourism, starting at nine a.m. when the Eiffel Tower opened to the public.

"As visitors," Hans-Josef said, waving a brightly colored brochure in the air to get their attention, "you have the choice to climb the steps as far as the second floor or to take the elevator up. It is one hundred fifteen meters to reach that second level. Three hundred forty-seven steps to the first platform, three hundred twenty-seven more to the second and—"

"I'm climbin'!" Zenia pronounced fervently. "I've been training for this." She pumped her arms and gave their tour guide a playful slug in the bicep. "You're leading us, right?"

"Er, *ja*," he said slowly. "I will climb if there's anyone who wants—"

"Well, good!" Zenia interrupted again. She nodded at Cynthia and motioned the woman closer. "You wanna get his pulse racing, right? You wanna see those cute legs of his take to the stairs, don't 'cha?"

Cynthia glanced between Hans-Josef's cute legs and Zenia's expectant expression and emitted an embarrassed giggle. She bobbed her head and got as far as, "Um, I . . . uh—"

"I knew you did!" Zenia interjected. "Do we need tickets? When do we start?" She fiddled with the timer on her wristwatch and swiveled around to take in the swarm of tourists headed toward the base of the tower from their respective tour buses. "Oh, quick. Let's get goin' before that Portuguese group gets here." She took a few excited strides in the direction of one of the tower's entrances and jogged a little in place. "How many steps all the way to the top?"

Hans-Josef cleared his throat and waved his brochure rather frantically at Zenia. "One moment, please. To reach the top of the tower, it's another two hundred seventy-six meters or about one thousand more steps. Sixteen hundred sixty-five steps total or three hundred twenty-four meters or one hundred eight stories," he informed them, visibly proud of his ability to recount the numbers with his trademark meticulousness. "But we are not allowed to go all the way up by foot. No matter how we get to the second floor—by climbing or by lift—we must all take the elevator up to the topmost level."

"Well, what *are* we waitin' for?" Zenia said. She nudged Cynthia. "Tell him we need to *go!*"

It was unclear to Gwen whether Cynthia was as enthusiastic as Zenia about climbing *La Tour Eiffel* or if she was just pleased to be seen as the go-to girl in regards to influencing Hans-Josef. Regardless, Cynthia took keenly to the task of hurrying along their tour guide. Soon, with Hans-Josef, Cynthia and Zenia in the lead, about half the group followed them in their zoom up the stairs. The other half balked openly.

"I ain't crazy," Hester murmured to Connie Sue as she made for the elevators. Aunt Bea, strolling leisurely beside Colin, elected to take the lift as well. But the honeymooners—Sally and Peter— were raring to go the climbing route, as were Matilda, Dr. Louie, Kamesh and Ani. Louisa and Thoreau had each been to the top of the tower a few times before, so they informed Gwen and Emerson they were going to spend the next hour having tea at a café nearby.

"You're welcome to join us," Louisa said politely. "But, perhaps, since you've never been up before . . ." She let that thought trail off.

"Yes," Gwen agreed, unwilling to let her lack of travel experience embarrass her this time. "I ought to go up there." And she wanted to. After all, how many of her colleagues from her tiny corner of her home state could say they spent the summer visiting the most famous landmarks of Europe?

"Climb or lift?" Emerson asked her.

Before she could reply, Thoreau cut in. "Doesn't she have the option of you carrying her?" He raised a mocking eyebrow at his brother. "Or are you too much of a *modern man* for that?"

Gwen wasn't at all sure where, when or why the seemingly innocuous phrase had morphed into an insult, but she was certain the sarcastic delivery of those emphasized words referenced *something* from the brothers' past. Emerson's expression told her she was correct.

Emerson's fist told her something more.

Like a comet streaking across the heavens, Emerson's right hook to Thoreau's jaw moved in a flash of grace imbued with fire. The elder of the two men grunted upon impact and cradled his bruised mouth and chin with one hand while warding off his brother with the other. The younger man scowled, unclenched then reclenched his hand and verbalized a phrase one wouldn't say, even in a place where people were unfazed by crude remarks. When he repeated it—in flawless French—it sounded even filthier. Some nearby college kids gasped.

Gwen was not typically one to step into a fight between strong men. In fact, in her entire thirty years, she had never found herself in such a position. But extreme times called for extreme measures, or at least for spontaneous action—which in Gwen's world was, indeed, a radical undertaking.

She grabbed Emerson's nonpunching hand and tugged until he turned to face her. There was something haunting his expression—a phantom personality mingling with his real one. Or, maybe, they were both *real*, just different sides of the same creature, battling it out within one body.

A look of silent agreement passed between her and Louisa, and the British woman moved to prevent Thoreau from physically retaliating against his brother while Gwen kept her hold on Emerson. They succeeded in separating the men only by wrenching them in polar directions—crisscrossing beneath the tower and emerging from its shadow on opposing sides—making the schism between them as literal as it was figurative.

The only thing Gwen understood for sure about the past three minutes was that Emerson's strength far surpassed her own. If he'd been determined to go after his brother, he would have. So, the fact that he let her lead him away meant that he must have *wanted* that fight to end. She suspected the same was true of Thoreau, although, as the initiator of the dispute, she would have liked to have known what had sparked his desire to instigate it. Perhaps Louisa would have some luck in figuring that out. Gwen had her hands full with the still-angry younger sibling.

When they had moved past the Portuguese tourists and even past a conglomeration of Scandinavians, she stopped walking. She took a deep breath and, still holding his hand, she squeezed it until he met her eye. "What. Was. That. About?" she asked slowly.

He clenched his jaw and shook his head.

"Emerson, I'm serious. I want to know."

"I'm serious, too. I do not wish to talk about my family conflicts. But I'm terribly sorry. We can go back to the tower and you can decide if—"

"I don't want to go to the tower right now and I don't want another apology from you. I *want* an explanation," she said stubbornly. "And I don't care if you think it doesn't concern me. It concerns me *enough*. When I get home, I'm going to remember the battles between the two of you just as clearly as I'll remember seeing the *David* or listening to the operetta. Your little 'conflict' was going on then, too, affecting my experience." In an act of frustration, she pulled his fingers toward the base of her throat and placed them against her Mouth of Truth pendant. "You're touching the oracle now. You have to be honest with me."

He fought against the smile that kept trying to rise on his lips and—to Gwen's relief—lost the battle after a few seconds. "What? *Now* you believe in its powers?" he asked. "*Now* you're willing to tell the truth for fear of losing your hand?" To emphasize his point, he cinched her wrist with his fingers and gripped extra tightly, making a chopping sound.

She pulled her hand away and crossed her arms. "I will if you will," she stated boldly. "But *you'd* better be the one to start."

He inhaled, slow and deep, then placed both of his hands on her shoulders, caressing them and her upper arms. "All right. If you *must* know, I'll tell you. Not here, though." He glanced around at the grassy lawn surrounding the base of the Eiffel Tower. "It's open until midnight. Let's come back a little later and take in Notre Dame and the Louvre on our own, not with the group. Are you all right with skipping out on the tour, Gwen? I know the city well enough to show you the highlights."

She nodded. She knew she'd learn just as much—if not more—by seeing Paris through Emerson's eyes than she would on any tour bus. "We should tell someone before we disappear, though."

He pulled out his mobile phone and punched in a number. "Hello, Cynthia?" he began and then relayed their plans to blow off the group for the rest of the day. "You'll tell Hans-Josef for us, right?" He smiled at Cynthia's sultry response to the affirmative. (Gwen could hear her voice through the receiver, too.) And when the British woman informed him that she, Hans-Josef and Zenia already reached the first level and were "just waiting for the others to catch their breath," he said, "Oh, cheers. Well-done. Enjoy yourselves." Then he snapped the phone shut, ran his fingers through his sandy hair and looked intently at Gwen. "We're free. Tell me, do you like boats?"

Although not on their original tour itinerary, Gwen had to agree that a boat ride down the Seine on a warm summer's day was a worthy use of the sunshine. They hopped aboard a privately owned specialty line that ran from the bridge nearest the Eiffel Tower, Pont d'Iena, and worked its way down the river—past Pont des Invalides and Pont de la Concorde, past Quai des Tuileries and Quai du Louvre—all the way to the famous Pont Neuf and beyond.

There they disembarked to check out Notre Dame Cathedral on Île de la Cité, just as Emerson had promised, as well as the street vendors on the Quai de l'Hôtel de Ville. They also crossed over into the Left Bank to visit the curious curlicuelike walkways of the Latin Quarter with its quirky little shops and cafés, so near the Sorbonne University. They passed several pleasant hours this way, but none of these stops held Gwen's interest like their outing to Jardin du Luxembourg, the garden of the French Senate and the largest public park in the Saint Germain district of the city.

Emerson chose a place for them in view of the Fountain of the Observatory, a creation in bronze that was the work of four French sculptors, each who carved or designed a different aspect of the composition.

"My favorite spot in this park," he told her, as they settled into a nearby bench. "It's exceptionally calm here. Quiet."

She'd been patient, knowing Emerson was a man of his word, but she met his gaze when he said this and rubbed her necklace as a nonverbal reminder. Time to talk.

He nodded. "Yes. Right then." He fiddled with the cap of a water bottle he'd gotten for her in the Latin Quarter, twisting it on and off, as if the container held the genii of his family history and he was trying to decide whether or not to release it. "There, uh, was some weight behind my brother's words."

"I gathered that." She paused, and when he didn't immediately speak, she added, "What does being a 'modern man' mean to you?"

He swallowed. Cleared his throat. Twisted the cap off so fast it made a snapping sound. "It—It's not so much what it started out meaning, Gwen, but what it turned into. Thoreau and I, as you've already noticed, take opposing positions on things sometimes."

"Often," Gwen interjected.

He concurred. "Yes, well, our father liked to consider himself a traditionalist, especially in regards to women. He was a true gentleman—old-fashioned in numerous ways, well-mannered, respectful—and my brother, who saw Father as the ideal husband, tried to model himself after him."

Gwen could see where this was going. She remembered what Emerson had said in Vienna about Thoreau's too-quick relationship commitments and serial monogamy—a diametric contrast to his younger brother's bachelor ways. "So, he took on the role of the traditional guy in the family, which left you to be the modern one, right?"

Emerson sighed. "Yes and no." He scored his fingers through his hair, a nervous gesture she had been seeing with more frequency as of late. "Truth was, Thoreau had to work harder at being 'a traditional man,' so to speak, than I did. He tended to overthink the whole thing and come across as a little phony. Not that he wasn't kind or polite. Just that he wanted to be seen that way so much that he overdid it. He *studied* chivalrous behavior like you would a school subject. Me, I don't know . . . Mum always said I was more like Father. Had more of his personality and outlook on life. So maybe that was something that simply proved easier for me."

She ingested this, chewed on the concept as if it were a potential choking hazard. Based on everything Emerson had said about relationships since she'd met him, he hardly took what she'd consider an *old-fashioned* view on dating. He seemed anything but conventional. It confused her on one level, until she remembered how dramatic he tended to be, and how very committed he was to not stepping into his brother's territory. "So, you were secretly like your father, but you were trying to act like anything but him because your brother had taken on his version of your dad's role. Only, you saw the flaws in Thoreau's act because his performance didn't ring as natural to you, right?"

"Right. And with our father gone, Thoreau was the only male role model I had in the family during my dating years. All I knew was that I didn't want to be like him. But it was frustrating because I couldn't be completely myself either. Because I knew how badly he wanted something I always had—not only to be more like Father, but to have more of Mum's attention because of it."

"Okay, but that can't be the whole story. Something else must have happened, didn't it?"

He slid his palm across his forehead and winced. "Yes. The Christmas when I was twenty, Thoreau was twenty-five. He was already married and almost done with his doctorate. He had his life mapped out until he was a hundred and twelve. I was still at university, not really knowing for sure what I was doing beyond that week. I had a girlfriend who was more serious about our relationship than I was because she *did* know what she wanted. But I thought I was managing everything all right."

He paused and Gwen suspected that what was coming next would prove none of them were "all right."

"We all met at Mum's for dinner and Thoreau was in rare form. Acting the father figure, carrying on in a cheeky way to my girlfriend that she would have a tough time getting me to commit and settle down. He was just needling me through her, but I wasn't in the mood for it that night. I kept getting angrier and angrier, but trying not to show it. I was furious before the meal even started." He closed his eyes and sighed. "And when we got to the table, Thoreau made this big production out of holding the chairs out for all the women—our mum, his wife, my girlfriend. He had the nerve to criticize me while he was doing it. Said I was being thoughtless and 'not respectful of the ladies present,' which was a bunch of rubbish. Pulling out a fucking chair for a woman doesn't make a man respectful. Listening to her opinion after she sits down in it does."

Gwen blinked at him. Whoa. Strong feelings on the subject, huh? She elected not to comment. She wanted to hear the full, uninterrupted story and only nodded encouragingly, waiting for him to continue.

Emerson rubbed his forehead again like he was trying to erase a memory. "The cowing bastard wouldn't shut up with the judgments, though. He got into his psychoanalyzer lecturing mode and said I shouldn't be such a self-centered loafer. In that *teasing* voice of his, of course. That if I were *really* like Father the way everyone *said*, I would try to act more considerately." He shrugged. "I just exploded. I'd been constantly compared to our father without having had the benefit of seeing his behavior firsthand for years. I was mightily sick of it. But what was worse was that I was embarrassed. I felt as though Thoreau might possibly be right. I was drifting, not really sure of anything. Or anyone."

Gwen watched him squeeze the mostly empty water bottle until the plastic container resembled a warped hourglass. "Like your girlfriend?"

"Yes. She looked at me differently then, as if she were suddenly seeing in me all the defects my brother had helpfully pointed out. His ex-wife was always a bitch, so I ignored her censuring glares. But Mum's reaction was the worst. I could tell she was distressed and disappointed when I shouted at Thoreau. Because of what I said. That I didn't want to be like him or like Father. That I wanted to be a modern man who was free from them both. And Mum was hurt even more because she knew, at that moment, I really meant it. It wasn't a happy Christmas."

Gwen agreed that it sounded like a perfectly wretched one.

"Anyway, I'm sorry about making such a sodding mess of your

morning. Creating a spectacle. Letting my brother get to me like that. It was a low blow on his part—Thoreau knows best how to push my buttons—but I should know better than to react to it."

She wondered about this. Wondered at the strategy game Thoreau was playing with his (mostly) unwilling brother. She felt Emerson had been truthful with her, but she was just as certain there was much more to the story. One might say an *entirely* different side, which she would have to seek out from its source. Later.

They spent another hour wandering around the grassy park and talking, the sun slowly sliding between some of the taller buildings in the distance and playing a game of hide-and-seek with a handful of cotton-puff clouds. Gwen glanced at her watch.

"When does the Louvre close?" she asked.

Emerson's eyes widened as he caught sight of the time. "Bloody hell," he breathed, grasping her hand and jerking her toward the Rue de Tournon. She followed him as he hunted down a taxi and mumbled something about the Pont des Arts to the driver. *"Très vite, s'il vous plaît,"* he entreated. Then, to Gwen, "It's four-thirty. The museum closes at six on Saturdays, and they start shutting rooms down in an hour." He appraised her silently for a second as the taxi sped across an intersection. "Good thing your aerobic level is so high. We shall need to run some stairs."

He may have been smirking slightly as he said this, but he wasn't at all joking. From the moment they passed through the famous I. M. Pei glass pyramid entrance into the museum, they were *running*. Three different guards warned them to walk. So they slowed down for the duration of a hallway or two but were soon sprinting again.

"Just so you know," he said, panting a little as they raced to get to the Egyptian "Temple" area on the ground floor of the Sully wing, "most people devote an entire day to this museum, not sixty minutes. You'll just have to come back for the other seven hours."

She laughed.

"Not kidding, Gwen. Let me know when you're going to return and I'll Chunnel over from London to meet you for the day. What are you doing over the winter holidays?"

"I, uh, well . . . December's a long ways away and, um . . . " she sputtered, all the while ignoring most of what they were zooming by in the "New Kingdom 19th Dynasty" section. Might she be able to see him again post-tour, after all? Just the thought had her pulse picking up speed, never mind their race walking.

He halted abruptly and pointed at a colossal statue in Egyptian antiquities. *"Ramesses II,"* he informed her. "About 1250 B.C."

She nodded. "Okay."

He nodded back. "Okay," he mimicked. "Must show you a few more things down here, then we need to get up to the paintings and sculptures."

She couldn't help but be amused by the irony. For the first time, she was in a situation where her "guide" was all but ticking off items on a mental checklist—so efficient of him!—and yet, here she was, wishing they could just slow down and soak it all in.

They zipped through the Michelangelo Gallery in the Denon wing and saw his sculpture *The Slave*, which brought her experiences in Florence to mind. They also got a quick peek at *Eros and Psyche*, a sculpture by Canova, who was a new artist to her, before jogging up to the first floor to take a look at Delacroix's well-known painting, *Liberty Leading the People*, and Leonardo da Vinci's legendary *Mona Lisa*. They then went on to tackle the second floor's Richelieu wing with Albrecht Dürer's self-portrait, Vermeer's masterpiece *The Lacemaker* and *La Galerie Médicis* by Rubens, which further recalled for Gwen her time with Emerson in Italy.

Aside from the *Mona Lisa*, though, which shocked her by being smaller than she'd imagined—and was also funnier to look at than she'd thought, but only because Emerson had commented in a matter-of-fact way, "Her full name is Lisa Gherardini. That's what she looks like," as if he'd met her personally—there were two other especially memorable pieces.

One they found in the Egyptian department. "An angle harp, sometimes called a trigon," Emerson said, pointing to the Maritime pine, cedar and colored leather that formed the triangular-shaped antique stringed instrument. Gwen read on the placard that the strings were modern additions but, as Emerson explained, they were probably made originally of gut.

She wrinkled her nose a little at that, yet she couldn't help but admire the beauty of the harp and marvel that, so many thousands of years ago, the ancient Egyptians played songs upon it and were even able to tune it so they could precisely match the intended notes.

Emerson reached out and feigned plucking one of the strings. "String theory," he said, with a smile more smug than even *Mona Lisa*'s. "It can be demonstrated anywhere, anytime."

She stuck her tongue out at him.

The other was in a different part of the Sully wing: the Venus de Milo. The late second-century BC statue still managed to be majestic, despite her lack of arms. Gwen found herself drawn to the strong, lovely woman made of pure white marble from the Greek isle of Paros. At six feet eight inches, Venus was still a bit petite for the seventeen-foot Florentine *David*, but in Gwen's mind, she made them a couple.

She stared at the piece for so long that, when the museum guards started shooing them out of the hallways and rooms, Emerson insisted they make a trip to the gift shop their culminating activity so Gwen could purchase a statuette miniature to take home.

"This one, I think," she told Emerson, selecting a plaster Venus de Milo about half a foot tall and admiring another plaster copy, this one of the famed Winged Victory of Samothrace that featured the Greek goddess Nike. The second statue, also made of Parian marble in the original, was one she'd seen only in passing as they were rushing between floors, but she'd found that one beautiful and stately as well. Poor Victory/Nike was missing not only arms but a head, too. "Hmm," she murmured, picking up the second piece. Contemplating whether this might be something Richard would like. It remained regal, even at its diminutive height, so she bought that one, too.

"You'll have quite a museum in your house," Emerson commented, as they exited the building and began meandering down the sidewalk along the Seine in the direction of the Eiffel Tower.

"Yes," she began, but then opted for honesty. "Although, Winged Victory is a gift." When he raised a brow in question, she added, "It's, um, for Richard."

"Ah," he said, nodding and then looking away. After a half block of silence, he stopped, bit his bottom lip and said, "Hungry?"

Gwen was beginning to realize that no one did meal time like Emerson. If he wasn't entertaining her or introducing her to regional delicacies, he was tantalizing her senses—every single one of them—by feeding her something. He'd made the eating of gelato and linguini a sensual act in Italy and the nibbling on cake in Vienna into a game of foreplay, so she was hardly surprised that he could elevate the consumption of quiche into something akin to a passionate afternoon tryst.

"All right, love, we have the spinach and artichoke," he said, pointing to the first quiche tartlet he'd selected from the café's pastry window. "The mushroom and Gruyère." He indicated the second one resting in the central position on their outdoor tabletop. "And, finally, the baked ham with red bell pepper and onion." He looked at her expectantly, a knife poised for cutting in his right hand. "Which should we explore first?"

Gwen swallowed and pointed blindly toward the table. She couldn't bring herself to glance away from Emerson's golden gaze. He was so *interesting* to watch. The flecks of variant color in his hazel irises glinted in the slanting light, matching—if only for a moment—the warm glazed goldenness atop every pastry in the bakery case.

"The mushroom and Gruyère it is," he exclaimed, slicing the quiche firmly in half and, as had become his habit, lifting the first piece for her to try. Not using a fork this time—simply holding the tartlet in his hand—he brought it smoothly to her lips.

Gwen had never understood her aunt's foodie fascination . . . until this trip.

She took a small bite, and the strong but delectable flavors performed the can-can on her tongue. "Mmm," she murmured.

"Good, is it not?" he said, his smile a tad too angelic. He was, she realized, casting a spell on her, using European cuisine as his cauldron. If he was employing his creativity and the tools available to him—magic enough—in trying to erase life with Richard from her memory, he was succeeding.

"It is," she replied, reaching for his half of the tartlet so she could offer him a taste in return. As he took his first big bite, she imagined him at an Iowan picnic. He could make good old American hotdogs, fries and corn on the cob an amorous dining experience, she was sure. A shiver of desire raced through her. "But, then, everything tastes good here."

He raised a sandy eyebrow, the angelic expression morphing into a slightly wicked one. "You, Gwendolyn Reese, know not how right you are."

There were still plenty of tourists milling around the base of the Eiffel Tower by the time they finished their meal and reached it, but the buses were mostly gone and the crowds had thinned considerably.

With nothing to prove, they eschewed the vigor of the stairs for the speed of the elevator.

Paris at twilight.

The dusky purples and blues had been brushed with rouge streaks, and a blanket of indigo waited at the edge of the horizon to cover the city. In what remained of the rosy pastel light, Emerson helped her locate from high above some of the famous sites they'd seen since their arrival: the Obelisk of Luxor down the Champs-Élysées to the Arc de Triomphe, the Opera House, the church at Les Invalides and, of course, the Louvre. These magnificent buildings in this grand city were reduced to miniatures, just like those statuettes she'd purchased of the marble masterpieces. She felt small again, too. Removed from her life on planet Earth. Even tinier and more powerless than usual.

Emerson, as if sensing her pulling away, placed his arms around her, grounding them both in the same moment. She stiffened in his embrace, afraid to let herself relax into it. Afraid of what that might mean.

"It's quite all right," he murmured. "I'm not making a move on you, Gwen. But I like being here with you. You helped me today.

Helped me put some things in perspective with my family." He snuggled a little closer to her as the coverlet of darkness fell and was, simultaneously, pricked with light. Clusters of illumination appeared in random but increasingly noticeable specks across the city. "Thank you," he added, his words making it clear that—despite the vastness below them, around them, above them—she was visible to him. A pinprick of light in whatever darkness he was facing.

And how wondrous that felt. To matter to someone! To be so very small and, yet, if only for an instant, to make a difference in another's life.

She finally settled into his arms, exhaled a breath she'd been long holding and watched—hopeful and aware—as a new cluster of hazy indigo was transformed by the golden shimmers of dancing electricity.

Their final French adventure came in the form of a nine-and-a-half hour joint tour of Monet's house and gardens plus a visit to the massive Palace of Versailles.

Amidst the beauty of Giverny—Monet's village—and the water lilies floating serenely in the River Seine, the artist in Zenia emerged full force and sparkling.

"That's right!" the older woman exclaimed. "This is what I'm talkin' about." She twirled in place, just off one of Monet's walking paths, swerving a bit too close to the water for Gwen's comfort. Gwen and Davis exchanged a look and moved forward so they could snatch her if she spun too near the sloping riverbank.

"Nothin' like Mother Nature for inspiration," Zenia added enthusiastically, her arms flapping to each side like a brightly colored tropical bird who had just found the way back to her own private Amazon. "Artists need to go out into the world. See things. Let the global wonders sink into their skin and change them." She breathed the country air in deep, smiling at the soft blue sky, the weeping-willow greenery, the tufts of grass and the sprays of flowers dotting the landscape.

Hester crossed over to them from one of the bridges spanning the lily-covered waters, listing a bit from side to side in a manner that had Gwen worried. "These things are a little rickety," she said, slapping the railings with each palm. "Bet it'd be easy to throw someone off here and into the water. Death by drowning."

"Or water-lily suffocation," Davis added helpfully.

"Good idea," Hester declared. "I'll have to remember that one."

Zenia beamed at them. "What a great place. For artists. For writers. For musicians, dancers, actors. Whatever sparks your creativity, nature gives it fire."

"That's very poetic of you, Zenia," Hester said.

Zenia grinned and twirled some more.

Once assured that the elderly persons on the tour were staying clear of the water's edge, however, Gwen could relax long enough to see Zenia in action.

The woman lived as she spoke, reacting to the scenery as a gift of artistic discovery. Every natural object fed her creativity and gave her something new to contribute to her loom projects. Gwen could almost see the synthesis taking place. The splash of red and yellow petals lying against a patchwork of dark greens—how this image before them would someday combine with the threads in Zenia's workshop and, quite literally, become woven into her craft. It was a form of alchemy.

Gwen thought about her own relationship with the creative process. It was, perhaps, a bit different with music since, at most, she read the notes she played from a sheet of paper. She did not compose those notes. However, if she did . . . if she did . . . she, too, would have drawn inspiration from the natural world. Who would not be similarly touched?

But the world within and the world without were, at times, at odds, and this was one of those times. She found it hard to relax and concentrate only on the beauty of the setting when she knew with certainty that two of the players in the scene at large were creating only waves of disharmony, and crashing them into anyone and everyone who happened to be nearby.

Emerson had spoken with her, of course, this morning before

they left the hotel and for part of the bus ride, but when he saw Thoreau approaching, Louisa by his side, Emerson disappeared. Thoreau, for his part, greeted her briefly as well, but he'd quickly sidestepped any attempt she'd made to find out what was going on. Cynthia was attached by invisible glue to Hans-Josef and appeared oblivious to all but her own happiness. Louisa, though, shot Gwen a "be careful" look from across the breakfast room and kept Thoreau safely sequestered in her own company so as to keep him away from his brother. Still, despite the absence of an actual fistfight during the day, this kind of antagonism had to stop. Gwen did not, however, immediately have the means to stop it.

At Versailles, they toured the palace and its grounds and, for a while, she lost herself in the magnificence of it. As the group was herded through the famous Hall of Mirrors, she caught a glimpse of her reflection that, at first, was jarring if only because it took her a moment to recognize herself. For a split second she saw herself as a stranger might see her: medium height, slim, bronzed lightly by the sun. She didn't stand out in the crowd. She didn't look foreign or displaced. She *belonged*. What an odd sensation.

She caught sight of Emerson's reflection, too, amidst a conversation he was having with Ani and his father. The three of them had fallen into step with each other and all, likewise, looked confident and engaged in one another's company. Although, from the lines of tension around Emerson's eyes and lips, he looked far from tranquil.

When, at last, they were released into the expansive gardens, she determined she would use the opportunity to hunt down Thoreau and pull him aside. As luck would have it, Louisa had just scampered away from him to convene with Cynthia over something, now that Hans-Josef was busy thanking their palace tour guide, and Thoreau was momentarily alone. Good.

She strode up behind him and tapped his shoulder. He swiveled around and eyed her warily. "Hello, Gwen."

"Hello," she said. "We need to talk. Right now."

He glanced around, scanning for Emerson, no doubt. "Listen, if you're going to suggest that I owe my brother an apology, I've already offered one. He simply requires a bit of space from me today so, really, there's no need—"

She tugged him toward a garden path out of sight from most of their group. "Let's stroll down this lane, okay?"

He reluctantly strolled.

She took a deep breath. "Back in Budapest, I remember you asked me 'what I did' to your brother. I think it's time you answered the same question."

He half laughed. "Back in Budapest, I remember you hedged rather a lot in your response. I would have no trouble doing the same."

She glared at him.

"Besides," he continued, "it's all a bit complex in our case."

"Seriously?" She halted in place, blinked at him and actually put her hands on her hips like she had when scolding her kid brothers as teens or giving a behavior lecture to a classroom of unruly eighth graders. "Are you implying I wouldn't understand?"

He sighed and nudged her until she started walking again. "Don't get testy about it. It's no reflection on your intelligence, but the family background involved is too lengthy to go into here. To understand the entirety of the issue would simply take too long."

"Fine," Gwen said. "How about a few pointed specifics then, like, why did you tell Emerson that I didn't know about your girlfriend Amanda? What strategy game were you playing when you insulted him at the Eiffel Tower yesterday? And where did you sleep last night, since your brother told me you weren't in the room at all? Hmm?"

Thoreau appeared incapable of disguising his amusement. "In regards to Amanda, I didn't tell him you didn't know about her. Er, not precisely." He paused. "I merely asked a rhetorical question when he brought her up: I said, 'Why would I need to tell Gwen about Amanda?' and let him form his own conclusions. It's hardly *my* fault if he didn't think to ask the proper follow-up questions."

"You're a very mean big brother."

He shrugged, unrepentant. Then, after a beat, "I spent last night with Louisa. That's why I wasn't in the room."

Gwen's jaw dropped. *"R-Really?"*

"Yes," he said simply. "Really."

In spite of her shock, Gwen tried to wrap her mind around this statement. Louisa was not the happiest of wives and she certainly had been flirtatious on the tour, but Gwen had gotten to know her a bit better over the past couple of weeks and it didn't seem fully in character for Louisa to go so far as to cheat on her husband. "Where was Cynthia?"

Thoreau bit back a laugh. "In Hans-Josef's room."

Gwen stared at him, assessing. "So, Cynthia and Hans-Josef were having a, um, *romantic* evening. And you and Louisa were up late in her room . . . what? Talking about them?"

"That's correct."

"And was there more to the evening than that?"

He nodded.

"What happened after you finished talking?"

"Then we slept," he said.

"Separately?"

"That's right, Gwen. And that's also a fine example of asking a series of very specific—if, perhaps, a bit too personal—follow-up questions. Emerson ought to take a few lessons from you." He raised that arrogant eyebrow of his, and she slugged his bicep in response.

He winced and rubbed his arm. "Ow. You're stronger than you look."

She rolled her eyes. "What about the insult yesterday morning? Why were you trying to rile him up, Thoreau?"

He exhaled, clenched his jaw and shook his head.

"Do I need to ask you twenty questions before you tell me anything worthwhile?"

"You could try," he said. "But I could parry you on this one."

"Fine. Play your little games, but don't be shocked if Emerson ends up hating you." She crossed her arms and marched a few paces ahead of him. Behind her, he chuckled softly.

"Gwen, you have the wrong idea. Entirely." He reached out and snagged the bottom of her shirt so she'd slow down. "I *love* my brother. He's a pain in the arse and, yes, I have been needling him on purpose during the tour. But my object has been to help him. You might not necessarily understand the strategy I'm using—it's a sibling version of the Bishop Fork—but make no mistake, everything I'm doing is for Emerson's own good. He's not immortal, so he'd bloody well better get his act together. Soon. I'm just trying to nudge him along."

She gaped at him in pointed disbelief, all the while fighting her reaction to Thoreau's words about his brother: *He's not immortal.* No. Emerson wouldn't live forever. None of them would. But even though she already knew this intellectually, she couldn't help but feel shudders of fear and dread at the thought. She did not share these anxieties with Thoreau, however. "What's a Bishop Fork?" she asked him instead.

"A tactical trick in chess. A rather unusual one, actually. The object is to use a bishop to force two pieces into jeopardy at the same time." He used his hands to create the dimensions of a chessboard in the air between them and then mimed picking up a piece in one corner. "Say you've got a white bishop moving from a8 to capture the black knight on c6. Not only does the bishop take the knight but he can simultaneously fork black's rook on d5 *and* his king on e8. The black side has to respond by moving the king to e7 to avoid checkmate, so he loses his rook to the white bishop. It's beautiful, really."

"Thoreau, why are you always in opposition to the black knight?"

His lips twisted into a grin. "Because he can be dangerous—often without realizing it. Knights move so differently from every other piece. When the knight is the one who initiates a fork and threatens both the king and queen of his opponent, it's called either a royal or a family fork. It's a move that wreaks havoc on the board. So it's better—always better—to take a strong offensive against the knights. We must minimize their potential for damage."

"So, you're trying to remove the knight so he doesn't . . . wreck your family?" Gwen guessed, trying to piece together the meaning behind Thoreau's explanation.

"It's not quite so antagonistic as all that, Gwen." He laughed. "But, I'll admit, I've been working to divide my brother's attention. You see, if he gets angry and has to direct his energy and resources to do battle in one area, he's much more likely to let his guard down in another. That's the point of the fork. Emerson isn't capable of letting in a new relationship—one that might put an end to his incessant moodiness and phony commit to bachelorhood—if he's focusing his every strength on erecting walls thicker than those at Windsor. If I'm the enemy, there's a chance he may open himself up to . . . an ally." He smiled at her. "Someone he might look to for solace and solidarity. In other words—you."

She swallowed. "*Me?*"

Thoreau, only ten years her senior but acting the part of a shrewd old man to a naïve teen, gazed at her with a look that was half warmth, half benign condescension. His eyes twinkled as he took a step closer to her and leaned in. "Well, you *do* love him, don't you?"

Gwen coughed and, seized by spasms, wasn't able to answer.

"That's quite all right," Thoreau said kindly, patting her on the back. "You don't have to admit it aloud. Yet."

10

Games People Play

Gwen felt the first wave of nausea hit just moments after they'd crossed the border into Belgium.

She glanced at her aunt next to her—sleeping—and peered around the bus. There was, she noted, a line beginning to form at the back of the motor coach for the small bathroom. She slid carefully out of her seat so as not to wake Aunt Bea, and worked her way down the aisle to stand behind Davis.

He was very fair skinned to begin with, but he looked ghostly white to Gwen's eye that afternoon. She herself was queasy, but the roads they'd been driving on had been bumpy for a good hour at least and in dire need of repair. The few hills they'd encountered felt much to her like the uncomfortable dip and twist of a roller-coaster ride at an amusement park. Davis, however, looked infinitely worse than Gwen felt.

"Are you okay?" she whispered to him as Hester tottered into the tiny bathroom and Louisa stepped out of it. The British woman waved faintly at Gwen as she passed by them.

"Just getting a bad case of the nerves," Davis admitted. "Tomorrow's the big day, after all."

"That's right. The tournament!" Despite the uneven feeling in the pit of her stomach, Gwen tried to show her enthusiasm. Of the

seniors from Iowa, only Davis and Matilda had qualified for the big
sudoku competition. It wasn't as large or as competitive as the
World Puzzle Federation's annual World Championships, but it
was still a big deal in the puzzle-solving world. On the Surrey side,
Ani and his father were both entered (in different age divisions),
and Gwen also discovered that the Edwards brothers—while potential contenders themselves—had jointly agreed *not* to try for
qualifying times.

As Thoreau explained it, "We discussed it this spring and decided it was wisest not to willingly invite that element of competition into our vacation."

Emerson told the story a different way. "He was scared I'd blast
his game to bits because I've had more sudoku practice. Thoreau
tries to act the big man about it, but he really doesn't like to lose."

Gwen had just rolled her eyes (privately) and was glad she—
along with most of the tour members—would just get to enjoy the
event as a silent spectator.

"Not as young as I used to be," Hester grumbled as she got out
of the bathroom and Davis went in. Gwen smiled at the older
woman but gripped hard the cushioned seatback of the empty
chair next to her.

"Me, either," Gwen muttered to herself as she waited her turn.
Zenia and Colin had joined the line behind her.

Just as Gwen got in, the bus lurched to a halt, which did nothing
to help her stomach.

"We will make a rest stop here," Hans-Josef said in his clipped
voice into the microphone, his tone edging toward urgent. "We
have many people who want a break now, *ja?*"

Gwen heard the chorus of frantic *ja*'s from her fellow passengers, but she didn't return to her seat. She locked the door behind
her and promptly threw up.

They were at the rest stop for a full hour and fifteen minutes.

"Food poisoning!" Matilda cried, indignant, after she'd been
sick twice herself. "What was the culprit? The fois gras? The

vichyssoise soup? The shrimp croquettes? The custard-caramel flambé?" She paused. "It couldn't have been the red wine, could it?"

"Whatever the cause, that's the price of being experimental," Dr. Louie told her weakly. He wiped the sweat off his brow with a white handkerchief and collapsed onto a bench nearby. "We were *too* adventurous, perhaps."

Gwen wasn't able to narrow down the villainous food item. At Emerson's insistence, she'd tried all of the dishes Matilda mentioned at Le Buffet Français—their unfortunate roadside stop a couple of hours before. Emerson shot her an apologetic look as he stumbled into the men's room for the third time.

Only honeymooning Sally, who was a strict vegan, seemed unaffected by the meal. She, unlike the rest of them, had ordered a simple garden salad off the menu rather than select the easy buffet option. Her husband, Peter, however, wasn't faring nearly as well.

"I didn't eat that much," he kept muttering, first to Sally and then to Connie Sue and Alex. "I wasn't that hungry. I mostly had vegetables, too."

"It's all right, dear," Sally said, rubbing his back as she might that of a young child. "It'll pass soon." And Hans-Josef, who'd fought a bout or two of nausea himself, motioned for them all to get back on the bus when they were ready.

However, Sally's doting reassurance to Peter turned to shrill concern as her husband's condition grew worse the closer they got to Brussels.

Dr. Louie, still recovering from his own battle with the tainted meal, knelt beside Peter in the bus aisle and asked him a series of questions about his condition. After listening to his responses, Dr. Louie turned sharply to their tour guide and driver. "Hans-Josef. Guido. We need to get Peter to a hospital *right now!*" He searched the faces of his fellow passengers. "Who here has aspirin on them? I need it."

Matilda's hand shot into her purse and she pulled out a few sealed caplets.

Dr. Louie nodded once at her then asked, "Water?"

Sally fumbled for her water bottle—half empty, half full, twice as big as it needed to be, whatever—no one cared about word-smithing or witticisms now. She relinquished it to the retired vet.

Then Dr. Louie said, "Peter, listen carefully to me. I don't want you to be alarmed, but you need to take these tablets this instant and keep me updated on how you're feeling. We'll be at the hospital in—how long?" He glanced at Guido.

"Ten minutes," the Italian bus driver supplied.

Peter hastily took the aspirin and washed it down with water. "What's happening to me?" he asked, his voice feeble alongside the relative strength of the other man's.

Dr. Louie, who must have had an excellent bedside manner with dogs, cats and random pet iguana patients—and their own-ers—in his days of working his veterinary practice, held Peter's hand and, for once, spoke softly. "You're having a heart attack, Peter. But don't worry. We'll take care of you."

In the hospital waiting room, Gwen worked hard to keep from all-out panicking.

It was ridiculous for her to be this worked up. Peter would be fine. Just fine. He was only sixty. But her dad had been only sixty, too . . . oh, God! Too young. Too, too young.

She might not have been as close to Peter and Sally as she was to the others. And she might have been annoyed by his silly math jokes and puns. But, as she watched his wife of forty years pace around the room with friends from both sides of the Atlantic doing their best to comfort her, Gwen wanted nothing more than for Peter to walk out of that Belgian emergency room and start crack-ing jokes about the Pythagorean theorem.

Emerson and Thoreau, apparently in a period of détente, were taking turns bringing everyone cups of tea or coffee and trying to help Hans-Josef and Dr. Louie get updates from the hospital staff.

Even without strong European coffee coursing through her veins, Gwen's hands began to shake. Life was too short. Too short! Why did people have to die so young? Why did they have to die *at all?* What was the point of living if, just when you began to feel things, just when you started to really see the beauty in life, it all got snatched away? Why was it that when you loved somebody who was central to your existence—loved him or her with your whole heart and soul—they could be taken from you?

Her hands shook more violently and, then, she realized it wasn't only her hands that were trembling. It was all of her. Her whole body, inside and out.

A strong arm snaked around her shoulders and steadied her. Tightening and drawing her in with a firm, soothing grip. Zenia.

"It's gonna be okay, child. Don't you worry your sweet self," she crooned softly.

"But I *am* worried. I can't just stop," Gwen confessed. Her voice was shaking, too. "Everyone around me dies. I hate that. I hate, hate, hate it."

Zenia hugged her closer. "Fear of death is somethin' we all fight. There are only a few ways to deal with it, as far as I can see anyways. Some people bury their fool heads in the sand and ignore it. Some people never do nothin' 'cause they're so afraid of it. And some people—the artists in the world—we channel it like a satellite signal. We take that fear and let it drive us to create something lasting and beautiful. And there are lotsa artists out there. Sometimes their art is medicine and their project is to help save a patient. Sometimes their art is cooking a yummy meal. Me, my art is my weaving." She squeezed tighter still. "What about you, Gwennie-girl? What's *your* art?"

Gwen sniffled and shook her head. "I don't know. Maybe I don't have one."

Zenia made a dismissive sound. "Maybe you *do* and you're just scared to own it." She rubbed the spot on Gwen's skin that she'd been squeezing so hard. "You think about it. You think of what you love. What makes you happy. What makes you forget that time is even passing by. That thing that you want to keep doing and keep making more beautiful. *That* is your art, honey."

A few minutes later, when Gwen's shaking had mostly subsided, Emerson came up to them to offer them each a cup of coffee. It was only then that Zenia removed her solid arm from around Gwen's shoulders. Gwen smiled at the older woman and gratefully took the Styrofoam cup from Emerson.

"Thanks," she said, addressing them both.

"I see a chair open over there," Zenia said, pointing. "I'm gonna sit these old bones down awhile and let you young people talk."

Gwen glanced after her as she strode away on very sturdy, not remotely tired-looking legs. "I just adore that lady," she whispered to Emerson, realizing the full truth of it as she said it aloud. Her aunt's friends were outlandish at times, but they were class acts.

"She's a smart and charming woman," Emerson agreed. "Frightening, too, when she's determined to have her way."

Gwen laughed, thinking of the poor Austrian seaman Zenia had cornered in that Salzburg restaurant. "That she is."

"And how are you?" he asked. "You look a bit shaken."

"I think I'm okay now. Better anyway." She paused. "It was scary there on the bus. It brought back some not-so-great memories. But I'm relieved we were able to get Peter to the hospital this quickly. Imagine if we'd still been out in the countryside somewhere." She shuddered, remembering how long it had taken her and her brothers to get their dad to the hospital when he'd had his attack. They were in the country, visiting friends about thirty miles from Waverly. Maybe if they'd gotten there faster . . . but, no. They couldn't have been any speedier. The paramedics from the medical center met them halfway and were on top of things immediately. And when the cardiologist got there and did his examination, he said this would have been a tough case even if an emergency vehicle had been on the scene from the first minute. Still, Gwen couldn't help but wonder sometimes.

Emerson nodded but said nothing at first. She noticed how his gaze had turned distant. She knew he wasn't looking at the people in the room. That he wasn't in the present time at all.

After several moments, he frowned. "This nearness to that line between life and death never gets easier for me either, Gwen. When my father died, I tried to find answers. Tried to wrap my mind around the *right* way of thinking about it. Rationalizing it.

The inevitability of it frustrated me, and I could only think about it in binary terms for a while. Either you're alive or you're dead. But then . . ." He let this thought trail off and Gwen, who still thought about mortality in binary terms and who couldn't quite envision an alternate perspective, had to know the rest.

"But then *what?*" she asked.

He scrunched up his face as if debating whether telling her would be too odd or, perhaps, too painful. Nevertheless, he exhaled and spoke. "But then I started to consider death as just *one* possibility. One potential outcome out of an infinite range of possibilities in every day. Eventually, we'll all die. That's a certainty. That's one outcome that will definitely happen at some point in time. But I didn't have to look at my days as if they were a slow death march to The End either. Just like there are different possible winning hands in mah-jongg every year and those hands change from year to year . . . and in quantum mechanics the uncertainty principle recognizes our ability to measure in probabilities only, not in exactitudes . . . death, therefore, is just one variation in a person's earthly life. It will be the *final* one, yes, but it's only *one* possible outcome in a twenty-four-hour period, amongst thousands of other possibilities."

He moved in closer and hesitated again. She nodded, encouraging him to continue.

"By accepting that death is there, one possibility alongside many others, I give weight and power to *all* the other choices. Death is present, but so are scores of other potential outcomes. For me, I live my life better when I make peace with that." He tilted his head and studied her expression. "Does that make any sense to you?"

Strangely, thankfully, it did. "Yes," she murmured, as a ribbon of peace flowed deep within her and tied a simple but sturdy bow around her heart. It covered up, if only for a moment, a few of the scars left there by losses in her past.

Dr. Louie's resonant voice cut through the hospital chatter surrounding them. "The doctors just gave us some good news," he announced. He patted a watery-eyed Sally as he spoke. "Peter is going to need to stay here for a few days of observation, but he's going to be just fine."

A cheer went up.

"Thanks to Louie and Guido and Hans-Josef and—and all of you," Sally said with a happy sob. "Bless you all for helping to take care of both of us and for getting Peter here in time to save him."

Gwen glanced around the waiting room—there weren't any dry eyes. Fatigue and relief had made claims on them all. But, while tears glistened in Matilda's eyes as well, as she gazed at Dr. Louie with her usual admiration, Gwen detected another emotion on the older woman's face and recognized it for what it was: pride in her man.

While Peter, Sally and Hans-Josef remained at the Belgian hospital through the night and into the next day, Guido was put in charge of getting the rest of them to the hotel to sleep. Then, bright and early the next morning, he drove them through the city for a quick tour to see a few highlights, like the Manneken Pis, a famous bronze fountain statue near the Grand Place of a little naked boy urinating ("How *unique!*" Connie Sue enthused. "And, oh, what cute little outfits they have for him . . ."), and the Atomium monument, which was built for the 1958 Brussels World's Fair and depicted "a giant atom."

"Technically," Emerson told her, "it's nine steel spheres connected so that the whole structure forms the unit-cell shape of an iron crystal, magnified about one hundred sixty-five billion times."

"That's a lot," Gwen commented.

He grinned and snapped a picture of it. "It is."

Finally, Guido delivered them to the International Sudoku Championships, which were being held at a huge convention center in downtown Brussels in the lively Mont des Arts cultural quarter of the city.

The first hour was registration for the competitors. They were given numbers to wear, as if runners in a marathon, as well as sharpened pencils, notepads, schedules detailing when and where they needed to go for the preliminary rounds and special lapel pins, which were a mark of respect among the competitors and envy among the spectators.

"How does this work?" Gwen asked Aunt Bea, who had just returned from fussing over Matilda and helping her fasten her pin and number.

"At this tournament, the players get divided up into three age divisions—young adult, adult, and seniors—and two skill levels—intermediate and advanced," her aunt explained. "Then they compete in heats to see who'll progress to the finals. The intermediate players have to solve two puzzles during their heat. The advanced players have to solve three. Their finishing times are added up and the player who ends with the fastest overall time is a finalist in the spectator round that we can all watch."

"We can't watch the heats?" Gwen asked, not sure how interesting that would be but it had to be an improvement over standing around in the hallway for five hours.

Bea shook her head. "That's done silently in thirty-minute blocks of time. The contestants use pencil and paper to figure out the puzzles. They work at a desk, just like taking a school test. It's only on the last round when the finalists solve their puzzles on dry-erase boards onstage, so everyone can see. It's real exciting."

Back in high school, Gwen had spent a couple of years on the math team. She had solved timed algebraic equations in a room full of like-minded teens and, while she'd experienced the geeky rush of completing a tricky multiple-step, high-level math problem with the clock ticking for added urgency, she found herself doubting she'd feel an equal degree of excitement watching someone else try to do something similar on a public platform. It was, perhaps, a degree or two more fascinating than monitoring her eighth graders as they took a chapter test on integers and variables.

"Hmm. Fun," Gwen managed.

Her aunt grinned at her. "Give it a chance, Gwennie. You've seen how much you've enjoyed the new things you've tried on this trip. Consider the possibility that, yes, it *will* be fun."

Bea was right, of course. Gwen had opened herself up to experience in Europe and had certainly come away with a lot of it. New memories, new sensory delights, new friends. Friends who'd raised the bar on what constituted excitement. Her willingness to allow herself the possibility of being changed had been the first step, and this latest event was just the most recent in her summer transformation from being a zero-sophisticate to . . . well, a slightly less naïve citizen of the world.

"I'll give it a chance," Gwen agreed. And, of course, the funny thing was, as soon as she gave herself permission to have fun, a simmering excitement within her came alive, feeding off the high energy and spirits of the others and quickly becoming all her own.

The first of five preliminary rounds began and, as the competitors required silence behind closed doors, the spectators and moral supporters milled around in the open hallways and public gathering spaces to chat with each other, purchase food from an array of vendors (although the tour-group members were especially careful with their diets that day, and most stuck primarily to breads and bland items) and learn a few algorithm tricks and puzzle-solving strategies from some expert sudoku players who'd been hired by the organizers to give demonstrations.

Cynthia, on her own without Hans-Josef for the day, meandered over to where Gwen, Emerson, Louisa and Thoreau were standing, which was in front of a sudoku exhibit table featuring n^2 Triples in Latin Squares, during the fifth and final heat for the young-adult division.

"Any word yet on how Ani did?" she asked. "I thought he was competing in the fourth round."

Thoreau nodded. "Kamesh passed by me in the hall about ten minutes ago. Both he and Ani scored in the top five of their age divisions in the intermediate level. Neither were in the number one spot, so they won't move on to the final round, but Kamesh was still very pleased. They'll each get a signed certificate, a personal invitation to next year's championship at a discount off the regular admissions fee and an honorable mention in their *SUDOKU-4-U* bimonthly newsletter." He glanced at his brother and raised an amused eyebrow. "You subscribe to that, don't you?"

Emerson, who'd been on his best behavior since the hospital

yesterday, only raised an eyebrow in return and calmly replied, "Why, yes. I do. I'm sure it's not as riveting to read as your weekly *Rook & Crown Chess Masters Digest*, but not all of us expect the same degree of entertainment from our games as you do."

Thoreau chuckled. "Touché," he said and, in a gentlemanly act, kindly let Louisa change the subject.

Louisa turned to Cynthia and said, "Davis made it into the top five of his advanced trial, too, and he was so tickled, I saw him jumping around afterward."

"I believe he volunteered to help set up for the final senior rounds," Thoreau added.

"What about Matilda?" Emerson asked. He glanced at Gwen. "Have you seen her?"

She shook her head. "Matilda's in this trial right now, for the intermediate level." She glanced at her watch. "Aunt Bea was going to stay near the door of the room, so she'd be the first to know the result. She promised to let me know right away."

This proved unnecessary, however, since all of them could hear Zenia's distinctive whoop and holler. "Glory be and praise to the Lord!"

And moments later Aunt Bea came running up to them, breathless. "Matilda's number one! She's going to the finals!"

So, after the two youth and two adult competitions, for intermediate and advanced players, Matilda's group was up. Five sudoku players—the winners from each heat—stood onstage with privacy dividers between them. Matilda was the one standing all the way to the left. At age eighty-three, she was the eldest of the intermediate seniors and the only woman in this final round.

Dr. Louie, Zenia and Aunt Bea wedged their way into the front row, left side, so they could be closest to her. Gwen and Emerson found a pair of seats right behind them, while Cynthia, Louisa and Thoreau were in the same row but a little farther down. Scattered throughout the auditorium were Connie Sue, Alex, Colin, Hester and a still jubilant Kamesh and Ani. Davis, however, was onstage, radiating good-luck vibes at Matilda as he helped set up the dry-erase boards for each contestant (with the final puzzle still covered with black paper, of course) and passed out markers, erasers and water bottles to all five players.

When it was time to start the clock, each competitor uncapped his or her marker, removed the black paper and began to solve the puzzle on the 9x9 square grid underneath. Box by box, the empty squares were filled with numbers, all ranging from one to nine. Because the word "sudoku" meant "single number," the same single integer was not allowed to appear twice in the 9x9 row or in the 9x9 column or in any of the nine 3x3 sub-blocks of the larger 9x9 grid. A smattering of clues were given, of course—individual numbers tossed like a handful of breadcrumbs across the grid—but the players needed to use advanced mathematical algorithms to make use of them so they had a chance at solving the puzzle quickly.

Gwen and her tour mates watched in utter silence as the competitors filled up their grids. To Gwen's eye, Matilda looked exhausted but determined. With her fluid handwriting and mental precision, she put a digit in every empty box. Three of the men finished before her—their finishing times written by the timekeeper on their boards—and the last man finished just after her. Each turned to face the crowd and cap their marker when they were done. No matter what her placement, Matilda was smiling, obviously gratified to have achieved what she did.

Everyone in the audience waited patiently for the organizers to carefully check the accuracy of all five puzzles before declaring the winning order. There were whispers when, after examining the dry-erase board of the number two finisher from Germany, it was revealed that he'd made a few errors due to a numeric reversal. He was moved to fifth place, which put Matilda at third! It was decided that the man from Denmark, who finished in the fastest time, was winner. The new second-place finisher from Thailand was next, then Matilda, then a man from the Czech Republic and, finally, the German. At last the crowd could show their support with enthusiastic—even downright boisterous—cheers.

Zenia had been forced to contain her zeal for far longer than was natural. She was squealing, shrieking, clapping and bouncing up and down in her seat. "You're amazing, girl! So proud a' you. Whoo-hoo, lady!"

Aunt Bea was half cheering, half consumed by laughter over Zenia's reaction. And Dr. Louie whistled and pumped his fists a few times in between claps. Matilda was grinning at him.

He turned around to high-five Emerson and Gwen. "She's something, isn't she?" he said.

"Something wonderful," Gwen replied, willing him to really *look* at Matilda and see the love streaming from her toward him.

Emerson readily agreed. As soon as Dr. Louie turned around, though, and the contestants had a chance to shake each others' hands and congratulate their fellow finalists, Emerson leaned forward, just inches behind Dr. Louie's right ear, and said loudly. "You know, Gwen, Matilda is a most *amazing* lady. Look at how those younger, international men are hovering about her. She might be an octogenarian, but she's still quite a catch."

"I know. She's beautiful," Gwen said, slanting a look at him. What was he up to?

Emerson smothered a grin. "I'd wager one of those other contestants is going to ask her out for tea tonight unless she has other plans. How long has she been a widow?"

Before Gwen could answer, Aunt Bea swiveled toward Emerson and, with a devilish glint in her eye, said, "Over twenty years. High time that woman had a hot date." Then she winked at Emerson and turned back.

Dr. Louie had finally stopped clapping and was staring at Matilda, who was laughing onstage with the rather attractive seventy-something Danish winner. Gwen could hear Dr. Louie say to her aunt, "Has it really been *that* long?"

Emerson grabbed Gwen's hand and pulled her out of the row. "We can congratulate Matilda later," he whispered. "I suspect she'll be kept rather busy this evening."

When they were safely out in the hall, she laughed aloud. "Who knew," she told him, "that you'd be playing Cupid? I never would've guessed that!"

He caught her gaze and held it for a moment as tenderly as he held her fingers in his. Then he stepped back, let go of her hand and glanced down. "You haven't uncovered *all* of my secrets yet, you know. I still have a few left."

They made quick work of leaving Brussels the next morning. After a brief stop at the hospital to say goodbye to Sally and Peter, who were going to stay put just a few days longer before returning to the U.K., Guido drove the rest of them up to Ostend, a Belgian city on the coast. There they bid farewell to their wonderful Italian bus driver, too (Gwen had to brush away a few tears when she hugged him), and Hans-Josef ushered them onto a hovercraft for the two-hour ride across the English Channel to Dover.

Then, voilà, they were in England.

"Normally, we would travel to London directly," Hans-Josef said on the short bus ride they took from Dover to the city of Guildford in the heart of Surrey—home to an impressive twelfth-century castle, a modern university and a legendary cricket club—located about twenty-seven miles southwest of London. "But, as county Surrey is the residence for half of the members of this tour, we arranged to make a one-night stop here so our English friends"—he looked directly at Cynthia and smiled—"can show us the beauties of the region."

With a population of nearly 70,000, this "little suburb" of London, which was what Emerson and Thoreau kept calling it, had over 10,000 more people than Dubuque, which Gwen had always considered to be the big city. If nothing else, this trip had certainly given her a few lessons in perspective.

"Some of our English travelers may wish to end the tour here. To go home, rather than stay at the hotel," Hans-Josef added, as they pulled up to a lovely bed-and-breakfast, large enough to accommodate all of them. "If that is the case, please see me about final arrangements or let me know which London excursions you still wish to participate in. We have a big group signed up for the theater outing on Friday night, but we do have a few extra seats available, if needed. And there are also reservations required for our final tour dinner on Tuesday."

They stepped off the bus and collected their luggage.

"Right," Emerson said, glancing from side to side and taking in the current state of his hometown. Overall, he looked pleased. He inhaled deeply, turned to his brother and said, "How long do you think we can be in the area before Mum rings us?"

Thoreau consulted his watch. "You gave her a copy of the itinerary before we left?"

"Of course."

"Hmm. An hour, then. Possibly two." Thoreau scrunched up his forehead. "There's something I ought to, er, take care of before she demands our appearance tonight. If she reaches you first, will you tell her I'll see her later?"

"Will do," Emerson said, then added, "but do try to avoid proposing to anyone for at least forty-eight hours, all right?"

His brother flashed him a rude hand gesture but then smiled, waved and walked away with his bags.

"Something to do with Amanda?" Gwen guessed, when Thoreau was out of earshot.

Emerson nodded. "It was a bloody miracle he didn't call her from the White Cliffs this morning, just as soon as we set foot on British soil again." His tone was snarky but Gwen couldn't mistake the notes of affection that had slid into his voice again. Not that all was forgiven or forgotten—on either side—only that they both seemed to have remembered, after Peter's heart attack, that there was something deeper between them than competition and old grudges.

"Here, let's take your bags to your room. Then I have an idea."

Emerson's idea involved going on an excursion of his creation through Guildford, Woking, Farnham, Ashford, Egham and the surrounding cities to give her a decent sense of county Surrey. Gwen told him this sounded like fun and asked if there was a bus that drove in a circuit to all of these sites.

He looked at her as if she were speaking in a foreign tongue. "Gwen," he said slowly. "Guildford is my hometown. I *live* here."

He paused and enunciated extra carefully to make sure she understood. "I have a flat two miles down the road. And a motorcar." He slung his bag over his shoulder. "Come. We can walk there."

Emerson's flat was about the size of Gwen's condo in Dubuque, but more cluttered. He had a framed poster of some star cluster or galaxy or something on his wall—"Andromeda," he informed her when he caught her staring at it—floor-to-ceiling bookshelves that were overflowing with novels and various textbooks, a maple desk half covered with paper on one side and, on the other, a computer with Post-it notes stuck to the edge of the screen.

A spinning four-sided shelf sat within arm's reach of the desk, stuffed with CDs and DVDs. She went over to take a look at the music: classical, jazz, theatrical soundtracks, R&B, hip hop. She turned it to find more: world music, Top 40, rap, opera, country western, even some stuff in Spanish, German, Japanese.

"What, no Gregorian chanting?" she teased. "No Celtic dance tunes?"

"It was a busy term. I haven't added to my collection in a few months, but I'm pretty certain I've got some Celtic music somewhere." He paused. "Not sure about the Gregorian chanting, though."

She laughed. "Why don't you live in London, Emerson? Nearer to your university? Or why not teach here instead?"

"It's too expensive to live in London and, besides, my mum lives here. Easier to be nearer to her. And to my brother." He shrugged. "Getting to the uni is very easy—it's just up the A3—but I rarely drive in. Not when we have such reliable trains. If I need to stay late in the city, I have friends I can bunk with for an evening. As for teaching here, I might do that someday. Now, though, I like the variety of being part of both places. I like that you don't have to get too far out of London to find some nice rolling countryside." He motioned for her to follow him outside. "May I take you to a few of my favorite spots?"

She agreed, of course, so, they hopped in his car—a dark red Vauxhall Corsa.

"It's so cute and tiny!" she said, not realizing until she saw his reaction that he might take offense at her description.

"Energy efficient," he countered stiffly, as he zoomed like a racecar driver on the wrong side of the road. Gwen held her breath and hung on to the armrests.

They made several stops at a number of historically significant places, like Runnymede, near the city of Egham, where the Magna Carta was signed; scenic views overlooking the Wey River; a picturesque drive that included Guildford Castle in the panorama; pretty Box Hill, a place she remembered reading about in some Austen novel, in the area just north of Dorking; and the city of Farnham, which had some ruins of an abbey that Emerson wanted her to see.

"How old is it?" she asked, noting the crumbling stones and marveling at how a structure could survive so many centuries. "The fifteenth century? The fourteenth, perhaps?"

"Waverley was founded by the Bishop of Winchester in 1128, so a bit older than that," he explained.

All the summers these rocks had seen. All the winters. All the people that had wandered through the abbey's hallways. "Interesting. Wait—what was it called?"

"Waverley Abbey," he said, looking surprised when she suddenly laughed. "What's so humorous about that?"

"Just that Waverly is the name of *my* hometown." She asked him the spelling. "The very same except for that second 'e'," she added.

He smiled. "So, it feels like coming home to you, as well, yes?"

She glanced around some more and nodded. The abbey and surrounding grassy lot didn't resemble the Iowa landscape overly much, but she did feel strangely at home in this English place. Maybe that was on account of the peacefulness of the area. Maybe that was due only to her standing next to Emerson. He was so familiar to her by now. It felt as though they'd been friends for years, not weeks.

His cell phone rang. "That would be Mum," he said before he even looked at it.

His side of the conversation proved comical:

"Yes." Pause. "Yes, of course." Pause. "I'd be happy to, Mum." Rubbing eyes and grimacing. "Absolutely. I'll be there." Pause. "Oh, yes. *Yes*. He'll be there, too." Pause. "How about seven?" Pause. "You'd prefer *six?* Right. That's fine . . . oh, he will? He said *what?*" Exhaling heavily and biting his lip. "Yes. Yes. Naturally, I'll tell her." Pause. "I will not 'manufacture' an excuse . . . I'm quite certain." He hung up and regarded her apprehensively. "Er, seems while we were on the continent, Thoreau had already given Mum a detailed, uh, report on you. She is anxious to meet you."

Gwen raised her eyebrows. Their mother wanted to meet *her?* Why? Before she could ask, however, Emerson answered her question.

"She's very curious about you. She has a way of seeking out people she finds interesting and, really, it's futile to try to thwart her or she might just contact you in the States." He sighed. "Thoreau and I need to be there tonight at six. You, however, have tonight off on account of 'possible travel fatigue,' according to Mum. But there will be no such excuses tomorrow. She's a bit like the Queen in that regard—what she demands, she gets. And, Gwen, she's demanded to see you." He ran his fingers through his sandy hair. "Hope you don't mind coming to tea."

The next morning, while Aunt Bea was off with Colin doing something in town, Emerson picked Gwen up in his red mini car and drove her to his mother's house. He looked a bit on edge.

"How did last night go?" she asked him. "Everything okay?"

"Erm, well . . ." he began.

"Well, what?" Gwen's stomach flipped, wondering what Thoreau had said, exactly, to his mother about her while they were still traveling, and what Emerson might have mentioned to the woman the night before. She felt a definitive zing of nervousness at the prospect of arriving at the Edwards house. It was really only intended to be a two-hour visit, but two hours of sheer awkwardness could be a *really* long time.

Emerson cleared his throat. "Mum is not what one might call . . .

subtle. She's rather dramatic, actually. She may ask some very bold, very direct questions of you."

In spite of her anxiety, Gwen laughed. "In other words, she's just like her sons."

He grinned. "I suppose that's, indeed, the case. Or, rather, her sons are like *her.*"

Gwen first spotted Mrs. Edwards in the back garden. Emerson had brought her some bakery scones and Gwen had picked up a couple of jams to bring as a gift, but they'd barely had a chance to set down their offerings on the wrought-iron patio table before she glided over to Gwen and enveloped her in an overpowering hug.

Hardly a negative opening move, Gwen thought hopefully, as she struggled to get a lungful of air.

"Hello, darlings!" the woman said, her voice like a wind chime. She released Gwen and stepped back to survey her. "I've heard such lovely things about you."

"Likewise," Gwen said.

At sixty-five, Lucia Edwards was strong—Gwen was still a bit short on oxygen after that hug—but Lucia was also very gazelle-like in her movements. She resembled what Gwen always imagined a British flower child might look like, with her shoulder-length pure white hair, bright fuchsia sleeveless camisole and long, flowing, rose-print skirt. She wore bifocals on a sterling chain around her neck, leather sandals on her feet and an expression on her face that Gwen would describe as impish.

Turning to her son, Lucia stood on tiptoe and planted a kiss on his cheek. "Orange and cranberry?" she asked, pointing to the box of still-warm scones.

"Your favorite," he said.

She chuckled. "I love how you're trying to bribe me. Smart, smart boy," she said, her tone proud. After thanking Gwen for the jams, she studied her youngest son with very shrewd dark blue eyes. "Emerson, your brother is hiding out in the parlor, trying to avoid you for a few extra minutes. Go inside and talk to him until Amanda gets here."

He blinked several times. "Amanda's coming? Really? Does he know that?"

"He will—in ten minutes. Now's your chance to either warn him or wait it out and watch him squirm. Your choice." She shooed him toward the back door, over his objections and despite the worried looks he kept shooting at Gwen. "Oh, for heaven's sake, Emerson. Stop looking so terrified. I'm not going to eat her. Not when I have a nice sausage-and-egg scramble for our tea." Her eyes glittered with a look Gwen recognized from having been around her sons: speculation and strategy, mixed with a dash of mischievousness. "Leave us alone for a moment."

Reluctantly, Emerson walked inside and Gwen could tell that, despite the kindness in her expression, his mother was not a woman whose word one disobeyed.

Lucia sighed happily. "Oh, this is delightful. Now that we're finally alone, I have an important question or two to ask you."

Gwen nodded, steeling herself for an onslaught of intensely personal and most likely embarrassing queries. She couldn't have guessed more wrongly.

"I'm planting pink hydrangeas and white baby carnations on either side of the patio door," Emerson's mother informed her, pointing at the two sides. "The two planters on the left are turquoise-glazed pottery, rectangular, with the dimensions of one foot by two feet each. The three flowerpots on the right are brick-red ceramic tile, circular, with a diameter of eighteen inches each. Now, if I have more carnation plants than hydrangeas, on which side should I plant them?"

Gwen calculated. "The baby carnations should be on the right," she answered, almost immediately.

"Why?" Lucia asked.

"Two reasons," Gwen said, shifting into logic mode. "I know you're an artist. From a color standpoint, you wouldn't pair pink with brick red. Pink would go with the turquoise and white with the brick red. But, also, from a mathematical standpoint, the total area of the round pots is larger than the area of the planters. So it would make sense to put the carnations on the right side, where the colors would be a better match and they would have more space to grow."

Lucia, giddy with some internal source of mirth, licked her bottom lip like a cat and grinned broadly. "I like you, Gwendolyn Reese. Not only is your assessment of the colors correct, but your math is impeccable as well." Then, as if to prove she was very much Thoreau and Emerson's mother—not only in math and strategy, but in high drama, too—she added, "In the game of life, I think people are a lot like plants. Figuring out what type of flower someone is helps determine where they'd be happiest. Where they'd grow best. What nutrients they'd need. Which pot would be the most appropriate fit, so to speak."

Gwen smiled noncommittally. Was Emerson's mom going to tell her that she thought Gwen was like some kind of weird plant? A milk thistle, perhaps? A snapdragon?

"And Thoreau had no idea how very right he was," Lucia mused, leading Gwen in a circuitous path around the yard that, eventually, brought them to a garden wall near the side of the house, which featured an artistically designed tile mosaic the brothers must have done when they were boys.

Gwen saw Emerson's handprint when he was, maybe, about six years old. Involuntarily, she reached out to touch it, smiling at those little fingers and tracing a few of them with her own. "Thoreau was right about what?" she asked.

"That you belong with my son," Lucia stated.

Gwen swallowed and gently shook her head. "Oh, look, um, Emerson and I are just friends and—"

Emerson's mom laughed gaily, like she was in on some hilarious joke that, clearly, Gwen had missed. "I wasn't speaking of Emerson, darling," Lucia said. "But I do think you may be utterly perfect for Thoreau."

This Gwen could say with certainty: The Forrester family's machinations on *The Bold and the Beautiful* had nothing on morning tea with the Edwards clan.

Still reeling from Lucia's comment, Gwen trailed after her as she spun once on her toes and headed inside. "No, I don't think—" Gwen began, but Lucia cut her off.

"Do me one small favor, dearie—and do yourself one, too—watch Thoreau. Take a good long look at him. Consider him as an option. Carefully. Don't dismiss the idea too quickly."

What was Gwen supposed to say to that? *No, I don't want to consider your eldest son . . . ?* It was bad enough sorting through her conflicting feelings about Emerson and Richard; she didn't want to toss Thoreau in there anywhere. Not when she'd already kissed his brother. Not when she had an almost-fiancé back home. But, again, Lucia Edwards was not a woman one openly disobeyed, so Gwen clamped her mouth shut and followed her into the living room.

A pretty, dark-haired woman was there, standing awkwardly between the two men. Amanda, Gwen guessed. And the tableaux the three of them made looked very much like one of those soap-opera cutaway moments when the actress the viewers had been following walked into a room, only to find herself in the midst of a heated drama being played out before her.

Lucia brushed past Gwen and hugged the woman. "Amanda, darling. So glad you could join us." She beamed a bright smile at her boys. "I'll leave you two to the introductions so I might finish up in the kitchen. I'm feeling rather peckish now. Tea will be served in ten minutes." She glided away.

"Hi," Gwen said politely.

"Hello," Amanda replied, adding a small wave.

Emerson, who'd looked plenty concerned on the car ride over and in the backyard, was even less relaxed now. The crease between his brows deepened when he spotted Gwen behind his mother, while Thoreau, whose complexion was already heightened by some unspecified emotion, could only nod distractedly at her as his brother belatedly introduced the women.

She and Amanda shared a glance and, in that one instant of eye contact, Gwen deduced something important: Amanda was at least as nervous as Gwen was, and she was also *nice*. She might not be perfect. Thoreau might have relationships issues with her. But she was a good person. She wasn't here to play games. Like Gwen, she was here because Lucia had demanded it and because—also like Gwen—she had a sense of loyalty toward one of the Edwards brothers. Thoreau, of course, in Amanda's case. Gwen turned an interested eye on him. He caught her gaze and returned it, looking perplexed.

When they were called in for the light meal, she did as his mother had asked and studied him. Carefully, just as Lucia had requested. She saw Emerson watching her, even more bemused than his brother, but other than a hastily whispered, "What did my mother say to you outside?"—to which she'd shrugged and murmured, "Nothing very serious"—the conversation that swirled around them at the table was deceptively ordinary and civil:

"Would you like more tea? Cream, milk or sugar?"

"And how did you find Vienna? Beautiful this time of year . . ."

"Shall I pass you the scones? Some apricot jam, perhaps?"

Thoreau caught Gwen looking at him at the table, too, but his gaze immediately shifted over to Amanda, who was doing her best to navigate the disquieting normalcy of the meal with a smile and a resolute attitude. Gwen wondered at that. Wondered at their relationship and how it had weathered the weeks apart. There was something between the two of them—that much was obvious. But it wasn't until Lucia asked Amanda a question about her summer that Gwen saw the first real flash of truth. The dark-haired woman responded with an almost imperceptible grimace before explaining, in a strikingly cheery tone, that she'd spent a fun holiday week with her sister and young nieces. Gwen's gaze shot back to Thoreau and saw a bolt of pain in his expression that he quickly masked by reaching for another serving of egg-and-sausage scramble.

Ah. Real emotion. Right there.

Lucia might be the mother of both of these men, but Gwen was sure she was dead wrong about her eldest son. No matter what Thoreau himself might have said, his heart was tangled up with Amanda's. There was nothing between him and Gwen. Nothing she would have wanted there to be, either. Even if Emerson in no way factored into the equation, she still wouldn't have chosen his brother. Didn't Lucia know that? What game was their mother playing?

"Would you like to try a new tea? The chamomile now?" Lucia asked Gwen, pointing to the teapot a few inches from Thoreau's place setting. "Or do you prefer the original English breakfast blend?" She indicated the teapot nearest Emerson.

Gwen met her gaze. "The *original*, please."

A corner of Lucia's mouth lifted in a grin. "Are you quite sure?"

"Yes," Gwen said decidedly.

Lucia's eyes twinkled as she asked Emerson to refresh Gwen's teacup.

Emerson glanced between the two women and chewed some more on his bottom lip. "We ought to get going," he said at the earliest possible moment. "Thoreau and I don't need to join in the London sightseeing today, but I do need to make sure Gwen is back in time for the tour."

Amanda piped up with a pressing commitment for the afternoon, too. Thoreau immediately offered to see her out and, soon, the quintet was disbanded. Before Gwen could escape the Edwards house, however, Lucia cornered her alone one more time.

"Thank you for taking my request seriously," Lucia murmured, "even though you seemed to come to a decision rather swiftly."

Gwen nodded and took a step back. "Thoreau and Amanda belong together. I don't know what he might have said to make you think otherwise, but they're clearly committed to each other."

"Yes, and you helped that along nicely."

"How do you mean?" Gwen asked.

Lucia leaned closer and lowered her voice even more. "Over the past month, Thoreau told me about how he tried a few times to worry his brother into thinking there might be something between the two of you. Thoreau is not used to having the tables turned on him, however. He's too often the manipulator in social stratagems. Even Emerson doesn't go to Thoreau's extremes in playing out his chess moves with real people. Thoreau needed to feel the sting of his meddling, if only to make it clear what he'd be losing if he didn't play things straight with his lady friend."

Gwen processed this. The morning had clearly been some sort of ploy on Lucia's part to . . . what? Be a matchmaker? Teach Thoreau a lesson? Kind of an ironic way to go about it. "So, you were just trying to make Thoreau uncomfortable?"

Lucia smiled peacefully and nodded. "People don't change unless they're made uncomfortable, Gwen. It was a useful tutorial for Thoreau. And, of course, I needed to shake up Emerson a bit while I was at it. Sorry not to explain this all in advance, but you would not have reacted so perfectly and naturally if I'd clued you in."

Gwen crossed her arms and stared at the woman. This was one bizarrely dysfunctional family. Was every freaking thing they did part of a big strategy game?

"Emerson has been very kind to me," she said coolly, the irritation she felt making her valiant. "And I can't say I like the way you and Thoreau have been trying to control him." She exhaled. "He and I are *friends*. And, as a friend, I don't want to see him hurt. Please don't use me as a pawn in a game like that again."

Lucia laughed and wind chimes danced in the air. "You're no pawn, Gwen. Not really. But I truly apologize for my interference." She observed her with those shrewd eyes. "Of course, if that's how you feel, I'm relieved. You deserve him, then."

Gwen opened her mouth to contradict but Lucia waved her off.

"No, I'm quite sincere. I'll be interested to learn how it all works out. It will, of course, be up to you to decide if he deserves *you*." Lucia let that thought hang in the air between them for a few moments before seeing Gwen to the door, where Emerson was waiting with palpable impatience. He'd somehow managed to keep it under control, but his intensity all but made the light waves vibrate. "Just fascinating!" his mother said, under her breath. "Pity you don't live in England, Gwen. We could do this more often."

Gwen couldn't quite bring herself to agree, but when she saw the fierce concern in Lucia's eyes as she said good-bye to both of her sons, Gwen would have been blind not to recognize how much their mother loved them. She was manipulative and meddle-some—a dangerous combination—but she was also trying to make sure, in her own way, that her boys were happy. Gwen sensed Lucia would do whatever it took to achieve that.

While she doubted her own mother would have gone quite as far as Emerson's, her mom *might* have—had she been given the chance. Aunt Bea, in trying to parent a motherless child, had pulled her own strings, hadn't she? Played her own kinds of games . . . And Gwen realized how grateful she was to her aunt for that. For loving her enough to be intrusive, even at the risk of irritating her. For caring so much that no small thing—like Gwen's fragile heart—could be overlooked.

Emerson drove the short distance to the bed-and-breakfast and dropped her off before noon—time enough to collect her belongings and take the final bus trip of the tour.

"I apologize for my mum, although I did warn you," he said, pulling into the parking lot, but letting his car idle. "Er, what was with all of those looks between you and my brother?"

She shook her head. "Nothing, really. Just watching to see how often he kept tabs on Amanda. He likes her a lot. Loves her, maybe."

Emerson relaxed, marginally. "That he does. It's been odd to see him work so hard to change. For him, you realize, it's a big risk *not* to commit quickly. I can respect him for that, even though I don't entirely understand the drive to do it."

She pressed her lips together and tried to smile. "I think I *do* understand. Entirely," she admitted. "I think he hopes that by committing—by getting the most significant pieces of his life in order as soon as possible—he'll be able to control something that really can't be controlled." She sighed. "It's a kind of insurance. A security thing. A way to ward off the sense of chaos that's just at the end of our fingertips. Life is uncertain. Choosing a mate quickly makes it seem less so somehow. You've got an ally with you then."

He listened and seemed to be studying the contours of her face as she spoke. "That makes sense, I suppose. I always thought it was rather the opposite, though. Kind of a selfish thing. That bringing a mate into the chaos would make both people more unstable, rather than be a means of steadying each of them. I'll have to think on that some more." He cocked his head to one side. "I know you're not free to date other men, but you should know something. Knowing you has been . . . a good influence on me." He rubbed the bridge of his nose. "Thanks."

"Thanks to you, too," she murmured, surprised and touched that he'd say that. Knowing him had certainly changed her. It stunned and gratified her to imagine she might have impressed him in any substantial way.

The car idling settled into a low hum as the two of them sat there, looking at each other, for a few long moments.

"I'm going to pass on the London sites for today," Emerson said finally. "But I may join in on a few excursions this weekend, and I'll see you most definitely tomorrow night for the play."

She might have to wait twenty-four whole hours to see him? She tried to wrap her mind around that—around her attachment to him—as she hugged him good-bye. She was beginning to miss him already. It was ridiculous, of course. It wasn't as though they could have a relationship anyway—even if she were free to have one; they lived on separate continents.

He hugged her back, perhaps a bit more forcefully than she'd expected, and drove off in his speedy little red car.

Gwen rejoined her group in the lobby and soon found herself spending an enjoyable afternoon in London. They took a double-decker bus on a sightseeing extravaganza through the city: London Bridge, Tower Bridge, the Tower of London, Big Ben, the Houses of Parliament, Kensington Gardens, Buckingham Palace, St. James's Park, Harrods, Royal Albert Hall and more.

"This is just to acquaint you with the city," Hans-Josef explained. "You will have time to visit all of these places in the next few days, if you wish." He smiled at Cynthia—one of only two Brits who'd elected to go on this orientation tour.

Cynthia smiled back, dazzling and heartfelt.

Dr. Louie and Matilda sat side by side. Gwen thought she spied them holding hands.

And Ani, seated a few rows behind the rest of the group, was paying no attention to the sights that were whizzing by. He knew them all already, anyway. His attention was focused on a pretty Finnish teen who was visiting London with her parents.

"Saija," Kamesh had whispered to Gwen and Aunt Bea before dropping his son off for the tour. "They met on the Sudoku Gurus online loop and have been e-mailing and texting all summer. Non-stop this week." He glanced heavenward and shrugged.

The group's lodging accommodation in London was a seven-story hotel near Victoria Station and nearer still to a pub called The Twist & Shout—a newish place known for their ales, their classic sixties rock and their well-cooked bangers-n-mash. After the city tour, Aunt Bea, Zenia and Hester insisted on stopping there for dinner, and Gwen couldn't bring herself to turn them down.

Even without Dr. Louie in attendance, Gwen found herself being dragged into public singing. It wasn't quite intended to be karaoke, but Zenia belting out a musical command to shake it up, baby, ("Now!") was infectious, and soon pub patrons at other tables were jumping in.

Gwen, a mass of intellectual puzzlement and emotional confusion after her morning with the Edwards family and her afternoon foray into London Town, found a special solace in the freedom and fun of the music. It seemed pure stubbornness not to join in, too.

They were still singing and laughing when they got back to their hotel. Gwen had never let herself be so open and carefree. It was *exciting!* And, besides, she was a tourist here in England. No one outside of her intimate little travel group even knew her. She took a deep breath and sang Zenia's favorite line—solo this time. Zenia clapped. Hester giggled like a schoolgirl. Aunt Bea grinned at her and said, "Brava, Gwennie!"

And, just as she was punching in the up button on the elevator, another person cleared his throat and chimed in. "Hello, Gwendolyn," the recognizable male voice said.

She swiveled around and looked for the sound. It took her a second to place it. "Richard?"

Her eyes focused and she saw him, standing at the edge of the lobby. They must have walked right past him. He smiled but he was looking at her oddly—as if she were someone he didn't quite recognize.

He held out his arms for a welcome hug. "I'm here."

11

Beware of What You Wish

Friday–Sunday, July 27–29

"How was your flight?" Gwen stammered, stepping out of Richard's embrace.

He scrunched up his forehead. "Way too long, but the plane landed on time, and I got here and checked in. I was kinda surprised not to see you for a few hours." A flash of hurt crossed his face but he looked down quickly, perhaps to mask it. "Didn't you get my e-mail?"

"Your e-mail? A recent one?" she asked, realizing as she said it that she hadn't checked her messages since before Brussels. "No. I'm sorry."

He smiled understandingly and hugged her again. She was flooded with that familiarity she loved. And his warmth. And his kindness. She *knew* Richard. Unlike Emerson, Richard wasn't some kind of enigma. She'd met Richard's family, too, and, while his mom didn't possess the effervescence so natural to Lucia Edwards, she also wasn't a master manipulator of her children. A woman thinking of marrying somebody had to consider these things. After all, you never just married the man; Gwen knew you also married everyone he was close to and cared about. Could she, for instance, handle not only Emerson but his brother and his mother, too?

Suddenly, her recollection of the Edwards event that morning bordered on surrealistic and foreign. She didn't have to be challenged by *anything* with Richard and his family. It was all so understandable with them. So clear-cut.

She'd forgotten Aunt Bea, Zenia and Hester were still standing there until her aunt broke into her thoughts. "Glad you got here safely, Richard. Hope you'll have fun in England." She paused. "Um, Gwennie, we're headed up to bed. You got your room key, right?"

Gwen smiled involuntarily. Funny how her aunt had been so keen to have her "lose" her key when Emerson was the man in question. But, Richard looked tired tonight. They wouldn't be having a wildly romantic evening anyway. "Yes, Aunt Bea, I've got my key. We're just going to talk for a few minutes. Maybe in the hotel restaurant?" She glanced at Richard for confirmation, and he nodded. "I'll be upstairs soon," she told her aunt.

The three older women said good night and, as the elevator doors closed in front of them, Gwen could hear Zenia shouting, "Shake it, shake it, shake it, yeah!"

She laughed and turned back to Richard, who relaxed visibly after Aunt Bea and her friends were gone. The two of them meandered to a relatively quiet spot in the restaurant, ordering a pot of hot decaf between them. Then they held hands across the table and smiled at each other. It was lovely and so, so familiar.

"How was the picnic?" Gwen asked eventually.

He frowned. "Not as nice as it would have been with you there." He cleared his throat a time or two. "I take for granted how much I've gotten used to spending time with you, Gwen. I got to talk with my colleagues and their families, but I'd wished you'd been with me," he added wistfully. "Oh! I didn't have anything to do a few weekends ago, so I watched parts of a few old movies. One of them was this musical, *The Sound of Music*. There was a nun, I think, and a whole bunch of children. They were dancing and singing in the mountains somewhere—"

"Austria," Gwen interjected. "Mostly Salzburg."

He nodded. "Right. I figured you'd know the one. I probably

watched a good fifteen or twenty minutes of it." He yawned. "It was kinda long, but the scenery was nice." He yawned. "Sorry. I didn't get much sleep on the plane."

"It's okay. I know jet lag is tough." She remembered how she'd felt after landing in Rome. And, oh, she was pleased he'd watched any part of the musical on his own. That was progress! "I'm glad you saw some of *The Sound of Music,* and you reminded me of something, too. Tomorrow night we're scheduled to go on an excursion to see *The Phantom of the Opera.* You don't have to go if you don't want to, but I can get a ticket for you from our tour guide if you do."

He yawned again. "Sorry. Well . . . to get to spend a little more time with you, I'd be willing to give it a shot. How long is it?"

"About two hours and twenty minutes."

He rubbed his forehead, sighed and then smiled at her. "Sure. And, um, maybe in a day or two—once I get used to the new time zone—you can join me in my room . . ." He let that thought trail off but raised his eyebrows, indicating that he'd missed their *hanging out* time. "Would you like that?"

She smiled back at him. "Sure."

The whole of Friday was spent sightseeing in London.

Richard was still not quite acclimated the next morning, but he was clearly trying to be a good sport. He joined her for visits to Trafalgar Square, Westminster Abbey, Piccadilly Circus and the Globe Theater—rebuilt to honor William Shakespeare.

Neither of the Edwards brothers were in attendance on these excursions, but Davis picked up the quoting torch they'd left behind. After a significant look at Matilda and Dr. Louie walking side by side near the Globe's stage, then a glance at Hans-Josef and Cynthia talking privately by some theater seats in the corner, he turned to Gwen and Richard and said, " *'Can I go forward when my heart is here?'* " He patted his chest. *"Romeo and Juliet."*

Richard looked at him with a baffled expression, but Gwen smiled. It was funny how quickly she'd grown accustomed to these quirks. How rapidly she felt herself to be a little less naïve, a little more knowledgeable . . . and after just these few weeks in Europe. Nothing like Emerson or Thoreau, of course, but she sensed the differences between her and Richard in that regard immediately. He'd always been the more worldly of the two of them when they were back in Iowa, so this burgeoning feeling proved an interesting reversal.

That evening, the two of them went to a neighborhood pub for an early dinner alone before getting ready to go to the play. Richard had yet to try traditional English fare, so Gwen wanted to introduce him to fish-'n'-chips and shepherd's pie. In spite of a few protests, he let her order these for them.

"You can have most of the shepherd's pie, if you like that best," Gwen said, unable to keep from thinking that such a meat-and-mashed-potatoes dish could hardly be distasteful to him. "I think you'll love them both, though." She'd tried it for dinner in Surrey, the night before she met Emerson's mom, and she'd really enjoyed the flavors. Thoreau, however, claimed their mother made the best version ever. Gwen doubted she'd ever get to try that one.

Richard yawned. He was beginning to drag again after such an active day. "I'll taste it," he said, which was very adventurous indeed for him. It was not his usual baked chicken after all. "I'm getting a bit tired, though. Did you say the play is going to last for over two hours?"

She nodded, getting that sinking feeling. "Look, if you don't want to go tonight, Richard, I'd understand—"

He yawned again. "Oh, I do. I do," he insisted, but he didn't come across quite as convincingly as he had the night before.

When their meal arrived, Gwen picked up one of the large "chips," which looked like what Americans called steak fries, and held it up to Richard's mouth.

He backed away. "Um, what are you doing?" he asked.

She grinned at him. "Take a bite." She brought it closer to his lips again. "It's good. Sometimes my British friends will dip their fries in vinegar, which is different but, also, kind of interesting. Very tangy."

He shuddered and backed away again, leaving her holding the

large fry in the air between them. "Just put it on my bread and butter dish, Gwen. I'll try it in a sec."

She swallowed and slowly put it down on the small white plate.

He smiled tightly. "Thanks." He then fished something out of his pocket. Hand sanitizer. "Can't be too careful these days. Lots of, you know, foreign germs," he explained.

She didn't say anything, but she watched him clean his hands. He offered a dab to her, too, which she took reflexively. It smelled of citrus and antiseptic. As she slowly rubbed the sanitizer between her fingers, she watched as he picked up the fry and took a tentative bite from the side she hadn't touched.

"Not bad," he said pleasantly.

"Would you like some fish?" she asked, motioning with her fork at the platter nearby. "Could I hunk off a piece for you and give you a bite? I haven't touched my fork yet," she added hopefully.

"Oh, I can do it myself," he said, using his knife to cut off a section and his own fork to stab into it. Then he took his clean spoon and put a few scoops of shepherd's pie onto his little bread plate. "This is good," he said, after tasting it.

"I'm glad you like it," Gwen murmured, but she realized there would be no feeding of English pub food to each other that night. She couldn't help but feel that this left something lacking in the meal. It was just *eating* together. It wasn't a romantic dining experience.

A couple hours later, they disembarked from the bus hired to take them to and from the Haymarket section of the city's West End. Richard, always impeccable with his clothing, earned a rare nod of approval from Hans-Josef as the tour guide handed them their theater tickets and ushered them all inside. He nodded at Gwen, too, and added a smile.

"We will be sitting all together in a block on the first level," Hans-Josef informed them. "Several of the British members of the tour will be joining us for this performance and may already be seated. For anyone going back to the hotel afterward, we will meet in the lobby following the show. So, if you want to buy some souvenirs then, you will have a chance."

Next to them, Hester was growing impatient with excitement. Her eyes grew wide as they entered Her Majesty's Theatre, where Andrew Lloyd Webber's *The Phantom of the Opera* had been running since October 1986. Four levels. More than 1,200 seats. Rich and ornate in every detail. "Ohhh, this place is better than a haunted house for a misadventure," Hester said in awe. "Just look at all those heavy railings up there." She pointed. "Could bash someone's head in real easy on those."

"What?" Richard asked, overhearing this comment.

Hester turned to study him for a second. "You clean up awfully nice, young man." She winked at him then flashed a grin at Gwen. "Bet'cha he'd make a great murder suspect." She poked her bony index finger into the middle of Richard's chest. "Do you know how to use fencing foils by chance? Ever fight in a duel?"

Mutely, Richard shook his head and stared at Hester in alarm.

"Too bad," the ninety-year-old woman said, ambling down the theater aisle several steps ahead of them.

"What was *that* all ab—" Richard began, but Gwen stopped him.

"Just step over here and look at this theater for a second," she urged him. "It's so, so beautiful."

Aunt Bea, who'd come in a few people behind them, squeezed Gwen's arm and smiled joyfully at her. "I know you've been waiting for this, Gwennie. Enjoy it."

"Thanks, Aunt Bea!" She couldn't get the shimmy of excitement out of her voice, and she didn't care. Oh, this was going to be *incredible!*

Richard peered around at the cavernous theater, seemingly impressed by their Victorian surroundings. Certainly, he would know enough not to sneer at the classic beauty of the interior, but Gwen sensed he wasn't as mesmerized by every luxurious detail as she was. The gold filigree. The thick, velvety red of the curtain. The enormity of the hall itself. The set displaying the show's famous chandelier, sitting like a limp collection of crystals onstage, awaiting the start of the production when it would be put to use. And no one could be more anxious than she was for it to begin.

They reached their row and found their seats. Richard was to Gwen's left and there were a number of empty spots to her right. A few minutes later, Gwen heard a few recognizable voices and caught sight of Kamesh, Ani and a lovely woman in her late forties who looked to be Ani's mother. They waved hello to Gwen and to several members of the tour in the rows ahead and behind, checked their tickets and sat down, leaving just one seat available next to Gwen.

She glanced around the theater again, taking in its magnificence and, also, if she were fully honest (she touched her Mouth of Truth pendant as a reminder of that), looking to see where Emerson was seated. She caught sight of Thoreau and Amanda. He'd brought her—good! They were a few rows ahead, but there was no sign of the younger brother.

Just as the house lights dimmed, though, she heard some shuffling at the end of the row, and there he was. Emerson. Coming to sit beside her. Her heart paused for a second, like a 4/4 rest in the middle of a song, and then pounded suddenly—in a crescendo—at simply the sight of him.

"Hello," he whispered, scooching around Ani and his parents and settling into his seat. His face broke into a devastating smile as he looked at her.

"Hi," she whispered back, almost breathless from her racing heart.

"It was a long twenty-four hours," he murmured.

"It was," she agreed.

Richard cleared his throat and leaned forward, peeking around her to glance down the aisle at the new arrivals. He looked at her questioningly. "These are your tour mates, too?" he asked, surprised.

"Oh, yes," she said, realizing she hadn't told him much about the British contingent of the tour group yet. It hadn't really come up via e-mail and, anyway, she and Richard had only been in correspondence a handful of times over the past month.

Emerson leaned forward, too, his smile fading as his eyebrows rose. He glanced a time or two between Gwen and Richard before politely extending his right hand to the man on Gwen's left. "Emerson Edwards," he said. "And you might be?"

Richard shook his hand firmly. "Richard Banks. Gwen's boyfriend."

Emerson nodded slowly and Gwen saw him swallow a time or two before speaking. "I've heard rather a lot about you," he said with a civil, if somewhat tight, smile.

There was something in his tone that—while pleasant enough—set off a few warning bells in Gwen's ear. She glanced sharply at Emerson, then at Richard, who'd tilted his head to one side and wore an expression of caution.

"Good things, I hope," Richard said, pulling his hand away and sitting a little taller.

Emerson bit down on his bottom lip and, again, forced his mouth into forming an awkward smile. "Naturally. And Gwen wouldn't lie, would she?"

While Richard processed this, Emerson smiled rather dangerously at Gwen and shot a pointed glance at her necklace. She felt her cheeks heat up.

He turned his gaze to Richard again. "How fortunate that you're able to join us. That's a pleasure I did not expect." Then, to Gwen, "I don't recall your having mentioned *that* possibility."

Which, of course, she had not. In her defense—not that she could say this aloud—it hadn't occurred to her to bring up the subject with Emerson, although she did remember, somewhat guiltily, having mentioned it once in Budapest to Thoreau. In many ways, however, she'd put all thought of Richard's visit out of her head until he actually showed up. She'd half expected him to change his mind, and she'd been as startled as anyone when she'd first heard his voice in the hotel lobby.

Richard regarded her strangely, Emerson mockingly.

"I, um . . ." was all she managed by way of trifling apology to them both before the lights dimmed the rest of the way and she was saved from having to offer an explanation. As the orchestra struck the first few powerful notes, Gwen and the men on either side of her sat back in their seats and faced forward. She had never appreciated Andrew Lloyd Webber more.

From the magnificent opening notes of the overture and the rising of the chandelier to the trademark songs that made this musical legendary for a quarter of a century, Gwen was riveted. She knew every note and every verse of "Music of the Night," yet, it was so much fuller, so much more spine tingling to hear it performed live. The Phantom invited her—almost personally, it seemed—into his dark and private world. It was an intimate seduction, luring her deep into a hazy dream. Only she began to wonder which was the dream state . . . and which was reality. They blurred together—the fantasy before her so tangible that it felt as if it were the only truth.

She suddenly understood the euphoria Hans-Josef had experienced when he'd heard the operetta in German. These were Gwen's songs. They *spoke* to her—not just because they were performed in her native tongue, but because the music itself was the language of her soul.

When Raoul and Christine sang "All I Ask of You" as a duet, followed by the Phantom's hurt and angry reprisal, Gwen couldn't keep her eyes from watering. Tears streamed down her face and splashed carelessly onto her blouse. She wasn't even aware of it at first, not until Emerson pressed a clean tissue into her hand.

She pulled her gaze away from the stage for an instant and met his eye. Even in the relative darkness of the theater, she could see the golden glow of his hazel irises and the way his expression softened the longer they looked at each other.

Richard stirred beside her. "You okay?" he whispered, seeing the tissue, then the tears.

"I am," she whispered back, dabbing her eyes and mouthing a soundless "thank you" to Emerson.

He rested far back into his chair and, out of Richard's view, he gently rubbed her right shoulder for the last few minutes until intermission. She understood the gesture for what it was: a shared communion with the music.

"Remarkable, isn't it?" Emerson said during the twenty-minute break. "Was it what you'd expected?"

She shook her head. "Oh, no. It was much, much better. It was incredible, amazing and so unbelievably beautiful." She glanced over at her boyfriend. "Right, Richard?"

He blinked a few times and tried to stifle a fresh yawn. "Oh, yes," he agreed readily, if not completely sincerely. Gwen had caught him yawning or stretching or in some small way distracting her every five minutes of Act One. She kept hoping his fidgetiness and difficulty concentrating was on account of the jet lag.

Act Two was just as good, although seventeen minutes shorter, than the first. When it was over and the curtain calls had been made (Gwen clapped until her palms were chapped), their group milled around the lobby for a while, chitchatting with one another and buying T-shirts, CDs, program booklets and other promotional items.

Thoreau and Amanda walked up to where Gwen, Richard and Emerson were standing. Upon being introduced to Richard, Amanda was exceedingly polite, but she glanced at Gwen curiously, and Thoreau, though he managed to keep his voice level, responded by narrowing his eyes speculatively and then embarking on a match of Twenty Questions with her American boyfriend. No doubt, this was the preliminary round in one of his psychological games.

Emerson dealt with the tension by pacing back and forth between where Thoreau was grilling Richard and where the vendor, who was selling soundtracks from the musical and a few piano songbooks, stood.

"So, what do you do in America, *precisely?*" Thoreau asked, generously allowing Richard to answer. "And your family comes from *where* in Iowa?" He listened. "Hmm. So near our Gwen," he said dryly. "How delightful." He collected some more information and sniffed. "Tell us, Richard, what are your first impressions of London society?"

At this, Amanda rolled her eyes at Gwen and excused herself to go to the ladies' room.

Gwen could take little more of the inquisition either, but Richard seemed to be really enjoying himself for the first time that night. She hesitated pulling him away and, instead, slid over to talk with Aunt Bea and Connie Sue for a few moments.

However, once she was out of Richard's view (he had his back to her) and it was just the three guys standing there, Thoreau's devilishness escalated a notch. He winked at Gwen on the sly and asked Richard conspiratorially, "So, what did you *really* think of the performance? You can tell me."

Gwen heard Richard laugh. "Not as bad as I'd expected, I guess. It was long. All of these musicals are so long. But"—he shrugged—"we gotta keep the womenfolk happy, right?"

Emerson sent Gwen an inscrutable look and stepped away to examine the vendor's display again. Thoreau pursed his lips together in triumph and Richard, sadly unaware that another Edwardian game was in progress, added, "I would've rather been watching a baseball doubleheader, wouldn't you?"

Gwen decided that, perhaps, she wouldn't rush in to rescue Richard from Thoreau's psychological examination.

"Mmm," Thoreau said. "I say, I'm more inclined toward cricket myself, but my brother is a hearty fan of American things—aren't you, Emerson?" He glanced around for him, pretending innocence.

And Emerson, several paces away but still within hearing distance, shot a dagger-look at his brother, then waved good night to Gwen as he disappeared into the crowd and was gone for the evening.

It had been after midnight when Gwen and Richard stumbled back into the hotel lobby, so they just went to their respective rooms and slept. Late.

By contrast, Aunt Bea was up with the larks of London—off on some Saturday-morning excursion with Colin. Gwen saw the note her aunt had left when, finally, she crawled out of bed. She decided to use the down time to pack anything she wouldn't need between now and Wednesday noon, when her flight left Heathrow for home.

Home.

It would be good to get back. To be in a routine again. To do her daily exercises, eat her healthy meals, plan her regular school-year schedules. It would. Really.

She made the bed, taking care to do it neatly (she was so out of practice), and spread out everything she needed to repack onto the thin comforter. Some things were easy to put away, like the dirty laundry she'd collected since Paris (she and Aunt Bea had done a quick load of wash there, so she still had plenty of clean clothes) and her *Viva, Roma!* guidebook. She folded the still-clean items and put them in one hotel drawer—just enough remaining outfits to finish the trip—and made sure her toiletries were contained to her one small cosmetic bag. She might need to grab that quickly if she spent the night in Richard's room soon. . . .

As for the rest, it was mostly souvenirs, but each item held so many memories. She laid them all out on the bed and studied them. Against the navy-blue coverlet they dotted the mattress like a constellation in the night sky. Like seeing the Dippers and Polaris in Budapest. There was the gypsy music CD Emerson had given her. The Venetian celestial mask she'd gotten on that one memorable day in Italy. The statuettes of Venus de Milo and Winged Victory from the Louvre. Her *The Phantom of the Opera* ticket stub and program from the show last night. And, on her nightstand, reminding her of both Florence and Rome, the golden Mouth of Truth pendant, which was like the North Star these other souvenirs were pointing to. She recalled Emerson touching it once, and, quoting his namesake, he'd said, '*The greatest homage we can pay to truth is to use it.*' "

There was a knock on her door. Richard.

"Good morning," he said, rubbing his eyes.

"Good morning. Feeling a little less groggy today?" she asked.

He nodded. "Yeah, a bit." He took a few steps into the room and spotted the things she had out on the bed. "What are you doing?"

"Just packing."

He looked surprised. "Are you thinking of leaving early? Your flight is not for four days."

"Oh, no. I just didn't want to wait until the last minute. You know what I mean, right?"

He nodded. "Of course. That sounds totally reasonable." And he just accepted her explanation at that, which—oddly—had a strange effect on her. She should have been pleased that he understood her need to create order and organization, but she'd felt so different in the presence of her aunt, the S&M friends and, especially, Emerson. *None* of them would have let her get away with packing up early like this. They would have chided her. Poked fun at her until she'd loosened up a little and had gone out to enjoy the day sooner. Forced her into eating an unhealthy meal or to visiting a karaoke club or some such thing. It should have been a complete relief that Richard didn't make her do any of these.

Why, then, did she get the sense that it wasn't out of acceptance that he ignored her old control-freakish ways? That it was, instead, because of a rigidity of his own or, perhaps, mere inattention?

She began to wrap up some of the treasures she'd gotten on her adventure.

"What do you think of this mask?" she asked, showing him her prize from Venice.

"Nice," he said with a pleasant tone but little real enthusiasm. "Glittery, isn't it?" He picked up the two statuettes before she had a chance to wrap them. "Oh, honey. These are broken." He glanced in the direction of her suitcase. "If you kept the pieces, maybe we could superglue them back on when we get home."

She chuckled and explained that, no, they weren't broken. They were replicas of the real statues and were supposed to look like that.

Richard did not appear taken with the sculptures. Though he didn't say anything more than, "It doesn't look a lot like art to me," it was clear by his quick dismissal of them that he wouldn't have wanted the miniature Winged Victory she'd gotten him. That he wouldn't display it himself. That if they ever shared a house together, he would very likely be against placing it and her Venus de Milo on the mantel or anywhere publicly visible.

This realization distressed her. Even though Richard was here, he couldn't really share in the earlier part of the trip with her. He'd be polite, of course, but the things that had surprised and touched her in Europe wouldn't be beloved by him. Not the breathtaking scenery, the classical artwork or the beautiful music. It had taken her a while to get into the spirit of being an overseas traveler, she had to admit. It had taken her aunt to begin her introduction to European wonders, someone as charismatic as Emerson to open her eyes even further and "a village" of fellow adventurers to assist them both in their mission. Gwen knew she'd had the benefit of expert help, something Richard couldn't claim. But, he also didn't seem eager to learn. He was merely tolerating his traveling experiences, and she didn't know what she could offer to him that would pierce through his reserve.

They spent much of the day lazily strolling around through downtown London—taking the Tube for a few stops in either direction of Victoria Station, laughing when they heard the distinctly British phrase "Mind the gap" and buying Cadbury bars from the underground vending machines so near the main tracks.

Away from her aunt, the Edwards brothers and the hotel, conversation between Gwen and Richard was less restrained. Still, a budding element of discontent and unease made it past Gwen's filters when she tried to merge her relationship with Richard with the world of the tour group.

It won't be a problem, she thought, *once we're back home again*.

The parallel universe of her travel adventure would fade from her mind upon her return to Iowa; she was sure of it. And, while that saddened her, the lure of normalcy and the seductive dream of the life she'd always expected waited in the wings for her return.

"So, will your aunt miss you if you spend the next few nights with me instead?" Richard asked as they rode the hotel elevator up to Gwen's floor.

Gwen knew for a fact that Aunt Bea was out pub hopping with

Zenia, Matilda, Dr. Louie and Davis. If Bea got in before two a.m. and even noticed Gwen's absence, she'd be surprised.

"I don't think so," she said.

Richard smiled—one that effused his entire face with joy. He looked enthusiastic at the prospect of spending the night ahead with her. And Gwen, though tired, had been without physical companionship for over a month . . . if she didn't count Emerson's one kiss in Venice and the few times they'd held hands.

She knew she should have felt guilty about those moments, but she just couldn't bring herself to regret them. Wasn't telling Emerson they couldn't be together proof enough of her commitment to Richard? Certainly there would be no point in confessing these tiny indiscretions to Richard—not if it would serve no other purpose than to hurt his feelings. She'd made her decision long ago, and Richard was her man. Emerson had initiated that one kiss, but she'd told him to stop. End of story. And as for the way they'd held hands . . . well, that was almost like friends. Wasn't it?

She nodded at Richard, very decisively.

"Good," he said. "Let's get your stuff then."

Sleeping together did not go well.

Richard, with only one eye partially open, grinned at her from the next pillow over. "You're up," he murmured.

"Yes." She'd been up for five hours.

"How'd you sleep?"

"All right," she lied. "You?"

"Oh, great! It's so nice to be with you again." He reached out and stroked her cheek.

"Nice?" she asked, then chuckled softly. She couldn't help it. She remembered Emerson questioning her at the Accademia when she called Michelangelo's work "nice." It wasn't a *bad* word. It just wasn't the *right* word to describe the masterpieces of a genius Renaissance sculptor. She sure didn't want her lovemaking "until death do us part" to be *nice*.

Of course, Richard's overenthusiasm at being together after so long a time had made things go really quickly. Too quickly. And jet lag had claimed him right afterward. And there was the little matter of her comparing Richard's kisses to Emerson's—something that both surprised and disturbed her.

He laughed. "Sorry, Gwen. I meant *very* nice."

"Hmm. Thanks, Richard." She sighed, flipped to the side facing away from him and his one open eye and pretended to fall back asleep until she was sure she could hear his soft snores beside her again.

However, things improved somewhat after they both, finally, rose for the day. They spent the next several hours sightseeing and strolling again. They visited Kensington Gardens and St. James's Park, which Gwen had only seen from the double-decker bus that first day. They ogled Buckingham Palace, along with a hundred other tourists. And they stopped for tea and biscuits at a little sidewalk café and visited a new pub for dinner.

"I'm really not in the mood to be experimental tonight," Richard confessed. "I've had some unusual meals a few times now. I'm gonna go for something a little more normal," he said, ordering the baked chicken and mashed potatoes dinner. "Mmm," he said, complimenting their waitress after his meal came. "Tastes just like home."

Gwen ordered the cottage pie, but she didn't bother trying to feed Richard any of it.

That night when they returned to Richard's hotel room, Gwen—who was exhausted from lack of sleep the night before and drained for reasons that were just beginning to simmer on the edges of her consciousness—suggested that, maybe, she should check in on Aunt Bea that night.

"You and I are both really tired anyway," she said, smothering a yawn. "We could probably both use a good night's sleep." She didn't add that they weren't a couple that had sex on consecutive nights anyway. At least they never did when they were at home. They were more of a twice-per-week couple.

"I understand what you're doing, Gwen," Richard said kindly, "but you really don't have to worry. I'm not ever going to take you for granted again."

This was encouraging to hear, but she didn't understand his thought process. "What?" she asked.

"I'll admit, I was kind of stalling on your birthday. Not getting you a ring right then and all, even though we'd been together two years." He shrugged as if brushing off that little mistake. "But then you were gone from home for so long. It was really frustrating not to get to spend the summer with you. I hadn't realized how much I missed you until after you left. But I've learned my lesson, okay? You don't have to leave tonight to prove a point. I know what'll make you happy."

She squinted at him. "What, exactly, will make me . . . happy?" Gwen herself wasn't entirely clear on this—although, after Zenia's suggestion to try to "find her art," Gwen had given it some thought. Not enough, however. But, perhaps, Richard had a more astute insight into her personality than she had into her own.

He laughed. "A marriage proposal, of course. Don't worry, Gwen. I've got it all planned out perfectly. And I'm not going to wait until October or November, so you don't have to stay with your old eccentric aunt tonight just to make sure I'll miss you." He laughed some more, apparently having attributed her hesitation to sleep in the same room with him as part of some coquettish game she'd masterminded to keep him interested in marrying her. Hmm.

"Aunt Bea isn't really eccentric—" she began, feeling her defensiveness rising.

"She is. And her friends are just bizarre. You know you've always thought so." He shot a smile at her so confident, warm and secure she felt almost embraced by it. Embraced . . . or was it restrained? "Seriously, honey. Just relax," Richard continued. "I know you don't like surprises, so that's why I'm telling you now, okay? There'll be no more wondering about it after tomorrow, I promise. By midnight tomorrow night, you'll be able to tell your aunt and all of her, uh, *unusual* friends that we're engaged."

12

A View with a Room

She'd wanted to be the wife of Mr. Richard Sidney Banks for one year and three months. At the British Museum, standing in front of the Rosetta Stone late Monday morning, Gwen remembered precisely when this had become a conscious desire.

It had been near the end of her first year teaching in Dubuque, and she'd given her math students number codes to decipher, just for fun. When solved, they spelled out phrases for various summer activities, like "Sleep late!" and "Go swimming!" She and Richard had been dating casually for the duration of the school year, but a long, lonely summer stretched out before her. Richard, having seen her cryptography assignment for her class in advance, picked her up from school at the end of that second-to-last week with a pretty pink carnation and a note he'd laboriously written in the same number code she'd given the kids. She solved it and it read: "Only one week until your vacation. Let's have fun this summer!" And she'd been so grateful to him.

Grateful someone wanted to spend time with her.

Grateful he'd worked to communicate with her in the precise language of numbers.

Grateful not to be so very alone.

She felt she'd had a partner against the slings and arrows of the world and, in that moment, had decided Richard was the man she should marry.

But she wondered now: Was gratitude, though a very important quality, *enough* of a reason to marry someone? A strong enough reason to last a lifetime?

"You done looking at that yet?" Richard asked her, motioning for her to join him in moving to a less crowded room.

"I suppose so," she said, stepping away from the famous stone and wishing she had its decoding ability.

Richard, not surprisingly, wasn't interested in staying at the museum for long after that. At first she thought it was because he was anxious to declare himself, as he'd promised. But, as they zipped past exhibit after exhibit, Gwen realized that, no—he just wanted to get through it faster. To say he'd seen it. To check it off his list.

"So, what else is left to do in London?" he asked, glancing at his watch as he pushed open the museum doors to exit.

She tamped down her irritation and recognized at once the irony. She must have driven Aunt Bea insane in Rome.

She touched his arm gently, trying to get him to pause long enough to really look at her. "We could spend months in London. Months in just the British Museum, I think, and still not see everything." She smiled. "Let's slow down and really take in the few things we *can* see today, okay?"

He shrugged. "Fine. But I'm not looking at any more paintings or art stuff. I just don't really . . . relate to it."

In a flash of clear-eyed vision, the kind that only came from experience, Gwen saw something important: She and Richard were a lot alike. One might argue *too much* alike. Richard needed done for him what had taken tremendous effort and teamwork to do for her—a kind of *adventure intervention* along the lines of what Aunt Bea, the S&M friends, Hans-Josef and, of course, Emerson and Thoreau had contributed to her life's education.

Of course, there was one other part to that: her desire to connect. She'd taken steps—literally and figuratively—when she raced down those stairs in Capri and melded with the island's natural beauty, walked through endless miles of Italian museums and saw masterpieces like the *David,* ate gelato at eight a.m. in Italy, hiked up to touch a Swiss glacier, raced through the Louvre in Paris and went to see *Phantom* in London. These experiences, both large and small, had changed her. The difference between her and Richard was that, though she'd been scared of most of it, she *wanted* to be changed. She didn't know if she'd be touched by Europe, but she *hoped* she would be. She was afraid of everything, but she'd actually *wished* on coins she'd thrown in the Trevi Fountain that she'd stop being afraid of life, know for sure if she was in love and someday return to the Eternal City—even though she'd been so sure that day that she'd already "seen" Rome.

Gwen tried to hunt down evidence on Richard's face that he felt similarly. That he actually desired personal change and growth. But she couldn't spot it. And, without that, there was no way she could ever give to him that gift of European discovery that her aunt and Emerson had given to her. Though maybe someone else could . . .

"What's your art, Richard?" she asked him suddenly.

"What's my what?"

"Your art. The thing you love to do most. The activity that, while you're doing it, it feels like time is flying. Or, maybe, you don't feel time at all. Everything else is on pause." She nodded at him, encouragingly. "You know, for some people it's a hobby, like scrapbooking or playing a certain sport or some specific thing they love about their job."

"Oh, sure, I get what you mean now," he said. "Spreadsheets. I love creating spreadsheets. They're just so organized and logical and easy to read. When I'm building one at work, an hour can disappear like nothing."

Gwen blinked at him. "I see." And she did. It wasn't that she didn't understand this fixation of his. It was—again—because she understood it *too well*. So well that she had to take an immediate step back to try to see life from Richard's perspective. Particularly, her place in it. She, too, had been organized, logical and easy to read. She, too, had valued these qualities—not just in herself but in others.

This summer, however, had challenged and changed her and, in the end, made her strive to be a little more like another self. One she sometimes caught glimmers of when she wasn't thinking so hard. Perhaps it was the Gwendolyn Reese she *might have been*, if her youth hadn't been marred by tragedy. If she hadn't had to shift so early from the one being taken care of to the one in the care-taker role—at least with her dad and her brothers. Maybe, in order to be a happy and fulfilled *woman*, she needed to shift back and first become a happy and fulfilled *girl*.

She swallowed and looked at Richard with all the kindness and compassion in her heart. She wanted so much to reach out and hug him because he wasn't at all a *bad* man. He just wasn't the *right* man. Not for her now. How grateful to him she was for that . . . even though it made the situation more difficult. More painful. Tears pricked her eyes. She cared about him enough to prevent as much hurt as humanly possible. Somehow, she had to keep him from proposing to her.

He didn't seem to notice her struggle, though. "Let's go," he said.

As they walked away from the museum, Gwen saw a street mu-sician playing guitar. His voice was raspy, but in a good way. It scratched at her apathy and lifted her spirits.

Contrary to what Richard thought—to what she herself had thought before this trip—a marriage proposal was *not* going to make her happy. But she knew now that she did have strong pas-sions. She was moved by good music, by the beauty of nature, by the remarkable interconnectivity of life. She was grateful to Emer-son, too (not that this meant she needed to marry *him* just because she was thankful), for opening her eyes to the latter and to Aunt Bea and Zenia in particular for reminding her that passions have to be expressed in order to live life fully. That this helped to keep the fear and dysfunction at bay. To expand her window's view on the world and broaden her scope.

"Ready for lunch?" Richard asked, whipping out a slip of paper that had a restaurant name on it. "We're a little early still, but I found a place online that serves more American food. I don't think it's got a menu selection as large as The Surfing Cow's, but it was the closest to it that I could find in London. Somewhere near a place called Leicester Square." He nodded at her like this was a done deal, patted his breast pocket (which bulged out slightly) and grinned at her. "They open in"—he consulted his watch—"eighteen minutes. So, by the time we get there—"

"Um, Richard?"

"Yeah?"

She shook her head slightly, trying to come up with a way to say what she needed to say. Her tears grew from prickles of mist to full raindrops as she said, "I, uh, don't think that's a good idea for today. I don't think—"

He shot her a puzzled look. "Really? You're not in the mood for steak?" He scanned his sheet again. "That's okay, Gwen. You don't have to get all upset about it. We could find a pizza place or, maybe, somewhere with burgers and chicken sandwiches. I was just trying to find us someplace nice."

She sniffled. "I know you were." She stopped and faced him. "I love the gesture. I really do, Richard. And I can't thank you enough—truly—for being my boyfriend, for being my *friend*, especially, and for caring about me over these past two years. I appreciate how you tried to understand me and how you flew all the way over here, even though I know traveling isn't something you enjoy." She paused. "I didn't know I'd enjoy it. And—and it's made me wonder what else about myself I didn't know. There seems to be a lot of things, actually . . ." She sniffled again and took a deep breath. "For one, I'm not ready to get engaged."

He squinted at her, unable to hide his surprise. "So, you want me to wait until the fall to propose after all?"

She shook her head. "I don't want you to have to wait for me, Richard."

"I'm confused, Gwendolyn. I mean, I bought the ring. I came here. I—"

"I know you did. I know. But I also know that I'm not ready to get married yet. I don't know when I will be ready." She hesitated and then finally said the hardest part. "And I don't know who I'll want to marry when I *am* ready." She bit her lip and forced herself to meet his eye. "I'm so sorry, Richard."

He stared at her, the color seeping from his face and then returning full force. She saw him open and then close his mouth several times, but she heard no sounds coming out of it. Then he swallowed hard, blinked and rubbed his eyes before saying, "I— I'll admit I don't know what to say, Gwen. This is a shock. It's not at all what I'd expected."

"For me, too," she whispered. "Life is full of surprises after all, I guess. Even when you work hard to prevent that from happening." She bowed her head and tried to steady her breathing. "I can't tell you how sorry I am."

He studied her expression for a long while and, then, said coolly, "You do realize I'm going to leave here, right? I'm going to fly back home, return this ring and . . . and move on. That's what you're saying you want me to do, isn't it?" He crossed his arms and tried to smother the hurt mixed in with the anger, but it was apparent on his face. She so very much wanted to tell him it was all a huge mistake on her part. To hug him and have him propose in his perfectly predictable way (over steak) after all.

But Gwen didn't want to lead him on when she knew she could no longer be in this relationship without fantasizing about something more. She didn't play games with people's hearts. Not when she knew she could avoid it.

"Yes," she said. "That's what I'm saying."

She reached out to touch his folded arm, but he jerked it away. She accepted that. It was really and truly over between then now. Part of her had already begun missing him and mourning the loss. She struggled to find something to say—anything, really—that might ease his pain.

"In time, I think, this'll be the best thing for both of us," she began. "I think you might want someone who's a little more conventional, a little less changeable than me. Someone—"

"Don't tell me what I want, Gwen. That's ridiculous." He

turned on his heel but, before he marched away, he added, "You don't know what *you* want, and you sure as hell don't know what *I* want. Good-bye."

She watched him stride down the block and, even though he couldn't hear her, she made herself say the words aloud. "You're right, Richard," she whispered. "My point exactly."

Gwen wandered around central London by herself for more hours than she'd bothered to count. When she finally returned to the hotel, she collapsed into a heap on her bed in Aunt Bea's room and fell asleep—dried tears still on her face, heaviness clenching her heart, but a rare sense of peace blanketing her mind. She awoke the next morning to Aunt Bea's gaze trained on her.

"Oh, good morning," she managed.

Her aunt's face looked puffy and a bit sad. "Is it still good, Gwennie?" She held up a clear hotel bag, the kind used for laundry, which had some of Gwen's belongings in it. Specifically, the few items she'd left up in Richard's room. Ah. "He left these at the front desk for you when he checked out yesterday. I'm worried about you. What happened, sweetie?"

Gwen, though she crumbled a bit at first, eventually got out the pertinent parts of the story to her aunt.

Beatrice, to her credit, didn't criticize Richard, tell Gwen "I told you so" or even suggest that Gwen would be happier with some other man sometime soon. Her aunt was a wiser woman than she was; Gwen fully understood that now. Instead, Bea just hugged her, made them both a pot of hot chocolate from the Cadbury mix the hotel kept stocked in the room and told Gwen about her own change of plans.

"I'm extending my stay. Just for two weeks," Aunt Bea said. "There are people here I want to spend more time with and, for us older folks, it's not always easy to make big transatlantic flights. Sally could use a little help with Peter now that they're back home, and I'm involved in a few creative projects with Colin, too. It's fun and, well, I like to feel needed again."

"I need you, Aunt Bea," Gwen admitted. "I always did."

"I know, honey. You know you're welcome to stay on for a couple of additional weeks, too, if you'd like. Maybe there's a, um, reason now to do that?" she asked hopefully.

It wasn't as if this possibility hadn't occurred to Gwen, but a stronger thread of judgment—one braided with intuition and self-care—kept her heading on the path she felt was best. Another week or two in Europe, however pleasurable, wasn't going to tell her what she really needed to know. That, she'd have to find out by herself.

She tried to explain this to Aunt Bea. "And besides," she added. "I've got to get ready for the new school year. We have our first Teacher Institute Day on the seventeenth."

"All right. Just wanted you to know you had options," her aunt said.

"Thanks." Gwen smiled at her. "I know I do."

The farewell dinner started at five o'clock with appetizers and cocktails in one of the hotel party rooms.

"Looky there," Hester said, pointing at a large video screen Colin had brought in, along with a laptop that projected some of his digital pictures from their tour onto it. "Remember that day in Capri? Seems so long ago."

Gwen studied the picture. Colin had taken a shot of Hester and Zenia going through the Blue Grotto in a boat. Then it flashed to a new shot of the restaurant in Sorrento: Emerson and Thoreau were standing up with their wineglasses in hand—eyes closed, mouths open—arguing about Bacchus. She smiled, remembering that night.

She heard a snicker coming from the back of the room and the distinctive sound of Thoreau's voice saying, "Smashingly photogenic, aren't we?"

Then Emerson laughing and adding, "Bloody hell, Colin. You couldn't have waited until we were looking at the camera."

"Th-That's the point of a c-candid shot, boys," Colin replied with good humor.

Gwen glanced over her shoulder and saw the brothers and a

bunch of the Brits clustered behind her, near the entrance. Cynthia and Louisa had traversed the room with glasses of white wine for the new arrivals and, just as Louisa handed Emerson his drink, he lifted his gaze and caught sight of Gwen. He raised his hand in a wave but didn't step forward. Gwen waved back and turned her eyes to the screen again.

The latest image was a photo of Peter, Sally, Connie Sue and Alex having their picnic in the shadow of the Leaning Tower of Pisa, followed by a snapshot of Gwen standing in front of the famous building. Then a shot of Aunt Bea, Colin and Davis posing by a giant flower clock in Switzerland; Louisa and Cynthia armed with packages after their visit to a Murano glass shop; Guido and Hans-Josef leaning against the bus after the operetta in Budapest; Matilda and Dr. Louis on the big Ferris wheel in Vienna; and then Kamesh and Ani poring over a sudoku workbook in Paris.

And then there was a picture of Gwen and Emerson together. In Brussels. Gwen hadn't even been aware of Colin taking the photo, and she doubted Emerson knew about it either until that moment. It was in the hallway, right before Matilda was going to compete in her final round of the sudoku competition. They were talking, just the two of them. Facing each other. Each with one shoulder touching the wall. Nothing more than that. No holding hands or sharing food or overt flirtations of any kind.

And yet . . . yet . . . there was an energy actually visible between them. It'd been captured by the rogue snapshot and fixed in time for all to see. The chattering in the room dwindled to almost nothing, and Gwen felt the stares of the others pricking the back of her neck. She squirmed under the silence and the scrutiny.

Aunt Bea tapped Gwen's arm and handed her something that smelled strongly of rum. "You look like you need a drink, Gwennie."

She nodded and accepted her aunt's offering, grateful for Bea's thoughtfulness and, also, for the change of photo onscreen to one of Cynthia and Hans-Josef together. Kissing behind the bed-and-breakfast in Surrey. That roused the crowd to keyed-up speech again. Across the room, she heard Hester hooting.

And as Gwen glanced in all directions, she realized there were love stories all around her:

Some were tales of heartbreak and loss—like Louisa and her inattentive husband, Zenia and her failed marriage, Hester and the unrequited love (about which she almost never spoke) that kept her single for nearly a century.

Some were stories of old loves remembered—like Davis, Colin and Aunt Bea—all of whom had beloved spouses that had long since passed away.

Some were relationships that were currently strong and steady, or recently rekindled with fresh awareness—like Peter and Sally (who'd delighted everyone by coming to the party for a short while), Connie Sue and Alex, Kamesh and his wife, Thoreau and Amanda.

And some were new loves—bright and hopeful at any age—like Ani and Saija, Hans-Josef and Cynthia, Matilda and Dr. Louie . . .

Every couple had a story. Gwen's tale was merely *one* of them.

Knowing this made it easier to handle this last day of farewells and cheerios. To deal with the demise of her relationship with Richard, say good-bye to Emerson and their tour friends and take a step into her future without planning every possible move in advance.

At dinner, seated all together on a long table, Emerson and Thoreau reprised the dramatic roles they'd held during the first meal they'd shared this way in Sorrento. Emerson was the first to stand.

"Good people of Surrey and Dubuque," he said, "on this night we bid adieu to our European adventure. We raise our glasses and toast the finale of this memorable tour." He glanced at Gwen, seated several spots away from him, for a long moment before continuing. "We thank our friends—one and all, old and new—for their many kindnesses while on our journey. I believe we've all been altered by the experience. It is, I find, hard to say good-bye."

At this, Thoreau stood up. "As Henry David Thoreau once said, *'Things do not change; we change.'* I know that's been true for me." He shot a warm look at Amanda, whom he'd brought along for the festivities. "Time away from the usual world gives many gifts, not the least of which is space for reflection and a chance to appreciate further what we hold most dear."

"Hear, hear!" Dr. Louie interjected.

"Cheers!" contributed Cynthia.

Thoreau raised his glass, too. "We have been witness to many artistic wonders on our tour but, as my namesake also said, *'To affect the quality of the day, that is the highest of the arts.'* Thank you all for the opportunity to get to know you and for the many ways you made each day of the trip more enjoyable."

Emerson, not to be outdone in the quoting department, took center stage back. "As Ralph Waldo Emerson stated, *'What lies behind us and what lies before us are tiny matters compared to what lies within us.'* We have shared much on this five-week expedition, and I've learned to appreciate the beauty and scope of certain qualities found within. Much like my brother's experience, these insights changed me, too." Then, raising a brow at Thoreau, he added, "As *my* namesake also said, *'He has not learned the lesson of life who does not every day surmount a fear.'*" He looked right at Gwen again. "Someone helped me recognize one of mine on this trip and, while I'll have to be ever attentive and try to surmount it every day, I'm grateful for the awareness and the courage this knowledge has given me."

At this, everyone toasted to the changed lives they now had as a result of having traveled together and broadened each other's minds.

Gwen toasted, too. While she didn't yet understand Emerson or how his mind worked, she knew he was both the enigma of the trip for her . . . and the soul of it. She had yet to say her private good-bye to him.

She was working up the courage to do that as the after-dinner tea was served. Caught up in all the post-meal hugs and conversation, she looked away for a few minutes and lost sight of Emerson altogether. She scanned the table, all the way down, but some people were standing up and others were walking away. She glanced anxiously around the room. Where had he gone?

"Pardon me, Gwen?" a male voice behind her asked. Thoreau.

She swiveled around to face him, stood up and walked with him a few steps away from the table. There was not much privacy to be had in a room this size and Aunt's Bea's eyes and ears were awfully sharp. "Hi, Thoreau," she said, scanning the room again. She kept expecting Emerson to materialize at any moment. He didn't.

Thoreau cleared his throat. "I did not see your, erm, Richard here. Was he indisposed for the evening?"

"In a sense," she replied, incapable of smothering her sigh. "We broke up. He flew home." Thoreau's dark eyebrows shot up in surprise. He was so unable to mask his delight at this revelation that Gwen glared at him and said, "Stop looking so happy. He's hurt."

The elder Edwards brother shook his head. "It is not Richard's wounded feelings that please me, Gwen. But I am happy you've taken this step. I realize this must be very painful for you now—" He shifted uncomfortably in front of her. "And I'd made a promise to both my mum and my brother that I would no longer attempt to interfere in anyone else's relationships." His gaze strayed to where Amanda was sitting, still talking to Connie Sue and Sally about something. "I shall try to avoid that. But . . ."

"But what?"

"But, please know, while I'm sorry to have been manipulative in regards to you and Emerson, I do not regret the intention behind it. You've been a good influence on him. He would benefit by spending more time with you."

She bit her lip and shrugged. "What good would that do? I have to leave tomorrow." She glanced around the room one more time. "Where is he, anyway? I haven't had a chance to say good-bye." The last word stuck strangely in her throat.

"Hmm. I cannot tell you. I promised I wouldn't give away his location to anyone. I could give you hints and let you guess, but then I might be accused of game playing." He smiled.

"Oh, c'mon. That's just—"

"Wicked? Yes, I know." He waved his fingers in front of him, like a dark sorcerer might. "It would be so easy to orchestrate these next moves, but I'm pledged to resist." He exhaled heavily and opened his palms. "You're the master of your own game, Gwen. Play it or not. It's in *your* hands now, not mine."

"What?" She put her fists on her hips and shot him her most murderous look. "But how can I even take a step onto the board if I don't know where the other player is?"

"I'm certain you can track him down. Just keep your eyes and, um, ears open." He tapped his right ear, gave her shoulder a quick squeeze and backed away. "Safe travels, Gwen."

"Thoreau—"

He blew her a chaste kiss and returned to the safety of his girlfriend.

She wandered out into the hall, just a few steps from the door. She didn't see Emerson in the hallway or in any directional offshoot of it, so she tried walking several yards to her right until she got to a little open lobby area. No sign of him. She returned to where the party room was and headed down the hall the other way. Still, nothing.

Then she closed her eyes, listening to the chatter of her tour mates as their voices leaked into the hall. That was when she heard it. A sound like the falling of summer rain.

A piano.

The notes called to her as if in prelude, not only an overture of the song to come, but of the melody attached to a long-awaited conversation, meant for two voices in duet. She smiled to herself when, as she drew closer, she recognized with certainty the tune. It was, naturally, from *The Phantom of the Opera*. "All I Ask of You."

He sat at the piano bench, his back to the door, playing those opening measures. More than once he stopped suddenly and started again from the beginning. He was, she realized, just learning the song. The music from the play was open in front of him. He flipped to a new page, paused to tinker with the notes, then returned to the beginning once more, playing the opening so well this time it brought tears to her eyes.

She sniffed once, not loudly, but it was enough. Emerson had good hearing.

He swiveled around and stared at her with those golden eyes of his. "Hello, Gwen. I hadn't heard you walk up."

"I didn't want to interrupt." She took a few steps closer. "Were you trying to avoid me?"

He sighed. "I was not anxious to say good-bye to you tonight, if that was what you meant," he said, letting that thought rest in the air between them.

"I wasn't anxious to say good-bye either." She paused. "I wish you'd keep playing, though. It was beautiful."

He shrugged. "Glad you liked it. I'll admit—" He chuckled softly. "I'll admit, I was thinking of you."

She smiled slightly, catching his joke. "Did you play that one, too? 'Think of Me'?"

Emerson lifted the songbook off the piano ledge and flipped back several pages. He held it up for her to see the title. "Yes. I've been going through it song by song. Some are trickier than others."

"Will you play 'All I Ask of You' again?" She pointed to the music. "I don't care if you hit a few wrong notes. I doubt I'd notice with the way you play." He kept looking at her, though, not at the songbook or at the instrument. "Please, Emerson," she added.

He swallowed, nodded and turned back to the piano. This time when he brought his fingers to the keys, the notes that flowed out were imbued with a passion that extended beyond the powerful tones of the music. They seemed to come from deep within him.

Gwen thought about the words to the song. About two lovers pledging themselves to each other, promising they'd always be loving, sharing, truthful. This was what she'd hoped for in a relationship. This was her dreamed-for ideal. And whether or not Emerson was looking for the same things, she knew herself—and the inner workings of her own mind—a bit better now. If nothing else, she knew a few things she *didn't* want.

She didn't want to be able to predict every experience of her life between now and age eighty.

She didn't want to always be in control, or to be organized, efficient, regimented.

She didn't want to keep an important part of her secret self locked away forever, for fear of it being ridiculed or misunderstood.

Emerson may or may not understand everything there was to know about her, but he grasped one very essential core truth. He connected with her musical passion. And, more than that, he shared it.

At first, Gwen just hummed a few bars of the song, and Emerson—surprised by her musical initiative—smiled at her as he kept playing. But the feelings the notes inspired within her welled up deep inside until she couldn't contain the longing she felt at their harmonies. The Gwen of some other place or time—that less anxious, less closeted version of herself—was determined to make its presence known.

Without consciously realizing what she was doing, until she was actually in the midst of doing it, she opened her mouth at the start of a new verse . . . and began to sing. It was at the part of the song when leading lady Christine was imploring her boyfriend Raoul to say he loved her. As she sang the words aloud, Emerson gazed at her in mild shock, and then joined in. Joined at the moment where Raoul responds to his beloved Christine, saying to her that she *knew* he loved her. Then they finished the verse together, and Gwen stopped singing. Not because she was embarrassed about expressing herself. Not because she felt vulnerable. Simply because it was time for the piano to reign the sound waves alone. To vibrate around them as purposefully as oxygen. And, at that moment, Gwen wanted only to listen to Emerson play those ending notes.

When he pulled his fingers off the keyboard, he didn't get up. He just sat on the bench, his hands in his lap, and looked at her with an expression of gentleness, compassion and wanting. That look was her only signal, but the Gwen-of-the-less-inhibited-self took it as reason enough for genuine action. She may have traveled thousands of miles from home and walked for hours through ancient cities and modern European metropolises, she may have skipped down stone staircases and climbed up mountains to admire stunning natural vistas, but it wasn't until she sat down on the piano bench next to Emerson and put her arms around him that Gwendolyn Reese took her first real step of the trip.

She kissed him.

Gently, compassionately, wantingly.

He kissed her, too, for what felt like a mere instant. Then he pulled back and cleared his throat. "Uh, Gwen? What—er, what about Richard?"

"You know how, in the middle of a song, if you were to alter the tempo and the key, the melody would sound like something else altogether?"

He nodded.

"And midway through a chess match, you could, if you wanted, select a few moves you've never tried before and the outcome of the game could be entirely changed?"

He nodded again.

"And in physics, theoretically, at least, there's this possibility for multiple universes and each of them—"

"What are you getting at, Gwen?"

She took a deep breath. "I chose differently. I chose . . . a different song, a different move, a different universe. Richard isn't a part of any of them."

He blinked at her. "I see." There was an unnaturally long pause. "You are all right?"

"Yes." She smiled at him. "A little shaken, perhaps, at the strength of my own decision. But, yes."

"Well, then." He leaned in and touched the tip of his nose to hers. "Please continue. I'm rather liking this song . . . this move . . . this universe."

And they kissed again. For much longer. So long, in fact, that an epoch might have passed and neither would likely have realized it. Such was the way of *finding one's art*, Gwen thought, when she managed to think for a moment in words. The very fabric of time had little meaning when one was in the presence of one's passions. It expanded and contracted like a magical cloth, and Gwen could feel herself wrapped in its silkiness.

*   *   *

Sometime later, Emerson and Gwen wandered out into the hallway, holding hands and more than a little light-headed and disoriented.

They'd barely walked five yards when they were accosted by Aunt Bea and most of the S&M members, both British and American, who had formed a conga line and were traipsing through the hotel hallways chanting, "Who let the math geeks out? Who? Who?" Aunt Bea had somehow, somewhere acquired an orange feather boa in Gwen and Emerson's absence and, being that she'd taken on the role of line leader, was twirling her boa and bobbing her head in time with the rhythm.

Zenia had, naturally, gotten into the spirit of things, adding a fist pump or two when it was least expected.

Possibly, most comical of all was Hans-Josef, whose hands were firmly fixed on Cynthia's hips in front of him but who, also, had on a dark green alpine hat—like the kind German dancers wore at an Oktoberfest parade—along with lederhosen and suspenders.

"You will join us, *ja?*" their tour guide asked.

Dr. Louie said, "C'mon! What's stoppin' you, kids?"

Kamesh's wife smiled at them and added a cheerful *"Olé!"*

Emerson shot Gwen an amused look. "How about we take a walk instead?" he asked her.

"Yes, please," she said quickly.

Bea piped up, "Well, we'll escort you to the door then. Jump on the back and hold on!"

So, Gwen laughed and took hold of Connie Sue, and Emerson grabbed onto Gwen, and the whole line made its way through the mazelike hallways in the direction of the lobby.

It was funny. Gwen couldn't help but think how very like Aunt Bea this was, leading her on yet another labyrinthine journey. But then, her aunt had taught her a little something about that on this trip. That humans—no matter what age they were or when they lived—were all on a similar quest. They moved into the maze of their life, picking up important skills and understandings along the way, getting into the very heart of the labyrinth. . . . But then, when they felt they'd learned the things most central to their own minds and spirits, they could begin moving outward. Sharing what they'd discovered with the newcomers wandering in. It was a form of generosity Gwen had only just begun to appreciate, but it moved her nearly to tears—even while she was laughing.

Aunt Bea and the rest of the line paused by the front door long enough for Gwen and Emerson to disembark.

Gwen hugged her aunt and whispered to her, "I love you. Thanks for everything."

"I love you back, Gwennie," Bea said, squeezing her tightly. "And you're welcome. Have fun tonight and stay out *late* for a change, okay?"

"Okay," she said.

Then Bea turned to Emerson and hugged him, too, whispering something in his ear that made him laugh aloud.

"I don't know if she'll go for that," he called after Gwen's aunt, as Bea flipped the boa over her shoulder and pranced onward, taking the rest of the conga-ers with her.

"What did she say to you?" Gwen asked, as they waved farewell to the grooving S&M members.

Emerson grinned and shook his head. He motioned for her to follow him outside and Gwen let him lead her around London, just as she'd let him lead her through Florence, Venice, Budapest, Vienna, Paris. . . .

"One of these days, you'll be in my corner of the world, and I can return the favor," Gwen said. "I can show you Dubuque and Des Moines and *my* Waverly." It was, however, an odd, displacing feeling, trying to imagine Emerson in her hometown.

"Hmm. Dubuque. It's along the water, yes?" Emerson asked.

"Yes," Gwen agreed. "The Mississippi River."

"So, it's a little like . . . what? Miami, then?"

"*Miami,*" Gwen cried before realizing he was just teasing her. "Fine, laugh at me. But don't tell me you've been there, too. I know you haven't."

He smiled. "I've been close. Chicago. Milwaukee. This American Midwest of yours. But, indeed, you are correct. I have never set foot in Dubuque proper. I ought to now. Now that I have reason." He shot her a significant look. "Right?"

She nodded first then grew braver. "Right."

He took a deep breath and glanced pensively at the underground station they were approaching. Victoria. "Any interest in seeing Scotland?"

"Well, sure. Someday. I'm curious about the bagpipes and the kilts and—"

"Tonight?"

"WHAT?!"

"That was what your aunt suggested, you see. That I take you by train up to Scotland tonight. To elope." He cleared his throat. "She pointed out that we're far more conveniently located here in London for such a jaunt than we would be, say, in Iowa."

Gwen laughed. "You're kidding me? I finally get over the idea of needing to get engaged *this year* and she's pushing for an elopement *tonight?* Sorry, Emerson! I'm not marrying anyone." She glanced at him and noticed an odd expression skitter across his face. "Well, not yet, anyway."

He squinted at her. Speculatively.

"What's that look mean?" she asked him. "Don't tell me you're changing your mind. Not *you*. Not Mr. 'No Commitment Ever' Emerson. Are you?"

He rubbed his forehead with his free hand. "I'm finding myself, strangely, not *completely* opposed to the idea. At least theoretically. In one potential alternate universe. The part of me who inhabits that particular membrane considers it *one* possible outcome now."

She couldn't help but chuckle at that, recognizing their reversal of opinions. "Please tell me this isn't part of some carefully crafted strategy to win me over on my very last night," she said lightly, even though she didn't really believe he'd be playing games now. "Ever since Florence you've had me wondering if, in fact, you could ever really commit to someone. Believe that you could find The One."

"Gwen," he said seriously. "There's no game tonight." He motioned swiping a chessboard clean of its pieces with the back of his hand. "Amidst all of this traveling, something changed for me. That's all. I stopped playing—oh, God—somewhere back in Austria." He tugged her closer to him so they were facing each other and less than a foot apart. "Do I want to have a romantic last night with you? Of course. But we don't have to do *anything* more than this tonight." He squeezed her hand and gave her a tiny hug. "The tour might be over but, honestly, I don't think our journey is. So, I can wait. Be patient. See what happens on the next trip. The one where I come to visit the States in a few months to see you." He paused and cleared his throat. "So, when do you go on holiday next?"

She thought about this. There was Labor Day weekend and Columbus Day, but these gave them only three days off. Thanksgiving break would only give them four full days together. There was two weeks at the end of December, but it was months away. She told him about all the possibilities. "Don't you need to spend Christmas with your family, though?" she asked.

"Don't you?" he shot back.

"Well, Aunt Bea would understand, although—if you were there with us—she'd want to celebrate with you. And I know my brothers would want to meet you, so . . ."

"So, we'll get it sorted, then," he said, his voice confident. "No worries."

"No worries," she mimicked in a fake British accent, but she had to admit there was a relief in this plan, however vaguely arranged at present. A delight in simply knowing there would be a part two. That no decisions had to be made right at that very second. That there was no rush. That they could spend the night walking, talking and doing whatever they wanted, and that would be enough. Just that. That this was as far into the future as she had to see tonight.

"Okay," she said.

"Okay," he mimicked in a fake American accent, and they both laughed. "Listen, I know we ate not that long ago, but London's known for their excellent curries. You shouldn't fly home without trying some. There's a Tandoori place in Covent Garden, near my mate's flat. He's gone on business to Morocco, so I need to pop over there, pick up his mail and check on the place. I figured we could nab some takeaway while we were in the area and then decide what to do next. Interested?"

"Definitely," she said.

"Right. Follow me then."

She and Emerson meandered through the bustling streets of London and, when they got to the little restaurant, Na'an For You, he ordered about five different kinds of Indian dishes.

"I am not going to be able to eat half of that," she exclaimed.

"You don't have to. Anything left over will be my breakfast. There's nothing like spicy Tandoori to rouse your senses in the morning."

"I usually just have cold cereal."

"Then you don't know what you're missing, do you?" And with that, he guided her through the twists and turns of Covent Garden to the flat, which was up some metal stairs and above a bookstore on a fairly quiet street.

"Liam just left three days ago," Emerson said when they entered, stashing the food in the fridge. "He rang me when we were in Brussels and asked if I could take care of things for the week. He'll be back next Monday. I was actually planning to stay here tonight, after the farewell dinner, so I could do some things in the city tomorrow."

Gwen raised an amused eyebrow at him. "And this is not strategy? Luring me here?"

"No, no! I fully intend to take you back at whatever time you would like, love." He motioned at the living room. "Have a look around. Liam has collected some unusual items."

She noticed the interesting art on the walls right away and took a few steps closer to get a better look. It was all very . . . *Casablanca*. There was a Middle Eastern drum on one table, a brass demitasse coffee set on the kitchen counter, a decorative Moroccan water pipe on the carpet in the corner of the living room. This hint of a foreign world, even more removed and exotic from the foreign ones she'd been visiting, reminded her yet again what a vast place this planet was . . . with so much left to explore. She'd only just scratched the surface, hadn't she?

Emerson came to where she was standing by the window— looking out at the River Thames, which snaked through the city of London and just happened to pass by them. How different was this sight, really, from her view of the mighty Mississippi back home? Their towns were different sizes, sure, and the histories of the cities they became were far from similar. But the *people* weren't so different. They all needed to interact with their environment and each other. They all needed to find meaningful work. They all needed to deal with challenging relatives (even well-meaning ones). And they all needed to learn the skill of knowing themselves well enough to make their own best choices.

"Do you like the view?" he asked.

"It's pretty," she said. "But we've seen a lot of lovely views. They're all beginning to run together for me now. My memories of our adventure. I'm not so sure anymore what will stay a real solid memory and what's just a blurry snapshot that I never looked at closely enough. Half the trip could have been an illusion of things I *thought* I saw." *Or of emotions I thought I felt,* she added to herself.

Emerson put his arms around her, warming her shoulders. "Look outside. It's hard to see the stars here with all the lights of the city, but nature has a way of finding us, even here." He pointed at some indistinct portion of the night sky. "I know the stars are there and the galaxies exist, even when I can't see them. My senses don't have to keep proving to me that they're real." He let go of her and pulled out his cell phone. "I keep this certain quote on my mobile. Just a moment, and I'll find it."

"What? You don't have it memorized?" she said, unable to hide the tinge of snarkiness.

He stuck his tongue out at her like a four-year-old. "It's too long. But it's from my namesake, and it addresses your question. Because, really, what difference would it make? Do you need to count everything, see everything, substantiate everything in order to believe it all exists? Isn't the perception of its existence enough for it to matter?"

Gwen thought about this. Was it *enough* to have had the illusion of being on an amazing, wonderful trip where she was kind of falling in love with someone—even if the relationship didn't hold up to the reality of everyday normal life when she got back home?

She'd never had the experience before, so she couldn't be sure. Emerson, however, quoted from the original Emerson and, apparently, shared his outlook. "Listen to this, Gwen. *'What difference does it make, whether Orion is up there in heaven, or some god paints the image in the firmament of the soul? . . . what is the difference, whether land and sea interact, and worlds revolve and intermingle without number or end . . . or, whether, without relations of time and space, the same appearances are inscribed in the constant faith of man? Whether nature enjoy a substantial existence without, or is only in the apocalypse of the mind, it is alike useful and alike venerable to me.'* See? It's irrelevant. Ralph Waldo says so," he said, a tad too cocky, in her opinion.

"Okay," she said. "That's fine and good for 'nature,' but what about people? What about relationships?"

He grinned. "Why is it that you always think nature and people don't operate under the same principles? It's connected. *We're* connected. To the air molecules that vibrate around us. To the tiny particles we exchange without even touching. To our bodies in gravitational relation to our spinning, pulsating planet. Gwen, what's true for nature is, likewise, true for humankind."

"As it is in physics—" she began.

"Yes!" he said.

"—it is in life," she finished.

"Yes, it *is*." He shot her a triumphant look. "Now that we've *finally* got that settled, shall we walk some more?" He motioned toward the door. "We can stroll though Covent Garden. I can show you a few spots. If you're hungry, we can have a bite first and then go out. Or stay in and watch a few naughty British comedies." He grinned. "If you're tired—I know you have a long flight tomorrow afternoon—we could take a taxi back to your hotel and I could brave your aunt's displeasure at not keeping you out all night."

"Yes, you've neglected to take me to Scotland."

"She is going to be *very* discontented at the news," he said with mock seriousness. "But I believe we're strong enough to weather her wrath."

Gwen laughed. And because she had a choice, because she really understood the many possible choices available to her in that moment, she weighed each option and—independently—selected the one she most wanted.

"I wouldn't mind walking around and seeing more of this part of London," she told him. "But I could save that for my next trip to Europe. I can be patient, too. I'm not done sightseeing here. Not by a long shot." She ran her tongue over her lips, which were inexplicably parched. "We have curries to feed each other. Some British TV to watch. Other things I think we could do . . ." she said, her pause laden with meaning. "So, if you don't have any objection, Emerson, I'd rather stay here. With you. Tonight."

Emerson wet his lips, too, and said, "Oh, love, I have no objection whatsoever."

As they embraced each other and their no-longer-dry lips met, Gwen's heart soared as if in midair. She decided that she didn't know or care whether this was reality or perception. *All* of her senses were engaged. She saw the swirl of the Milky Way around them. Tasted the delectable sweetness of creamy gelato. Smelled the fragrant zest of sauce-drenched linguini. Felt the supple smoothness of a silk scarf. And heard the music to her favorite songs—one in particular.

Love *did* change everything . . . and nothing in her world would ever be the same.

13

Got the World on a String

Wednesday, August 1

Sometime in that netherworld between sleep and awareness—sometime before her flight back home and after she and Emerson made love for the first time—Gwen awoke in London to a new day, a new month, a new chapter in her life.

She glanced at Emerson's face, still sleeping next to her on this August 1 morning, and she saw the man he was right now.

But time was fluid.

She could imagine the boy he had been just as easily. Imagine the years melting away until his sleeping face matched those six-year-old handprints she'd seen at his mother's house in Surrey. Time had been slipping around on her, more so in Europe than it ever had at home, tricking her into disturbingly vivid visualizations. She had no sooner blinked away the mental imprint of Emerson as a child, when his features rearranged themselves into that of an elderly man. It was as if she could view the full spectrum of his life floating across his face, from childhood to old age, just by watching him in slumber.

She slid out of bed, tiptoed over to the window and peered out at a city where people had lived and dreamed and perished for centuries. *And also loved.* She fingered her mother's earrings then glanced back at Emerson.

Humans were temporal. They aged and, eventually, died. And while she could have dwelled on her tendency to morbidly fixate on this quality, she chose instead, in that moment, to let it go . . . To let it rise like the sun. A dancing veil of light being lifted off the water.

Lifted, so as to see all the world more clearly.

And with the film gone from her eyes, she could better appreciate the hazy delights of the night that came before.

Her day of departure would surely be filled with endless possibilities, alternatives and opportunities to make decisions. So, with the glow of the London sunrise behind her, she looked to the West and made her first choice of the day. Gwendolyn Reese, with a song on her lips, tiptoed back into bed with Emerson. Who was now awake—and waiting for her.

A SUMMER IN EUROPE

Marilyn Brant

ABOUT THIS GUIDE

The suggested questions are included to
enhance your group's reading of Marilyn Brant's
A Summer in Europe.

DISCUSSION QUESTIONS

1. Who is Gwendolyn Reese? What is her personality like and how has it been shaped by her early experiences?

2. Who are the people inhabiting Gwen's world at home? What are their roles in her life? When she travels to Europe, she enters a new world filled with new people and situations. How does she handle the change? How would you handle it if you were in her position?

3. The first line of the book says, "The thing no one understood about Gwendolyn Reese was that she was three ages at once: thirty chronologically, forty-five intellectually and fifteen experientially." Do you believe a person can be at one age chronologically but also have different intellectual, emotional, social, etc. ages? What about you? Are you one age . . . or multiple ages?

4. A number of strategy games are referenced in the novel— which games do you most like to play, and have you ever applied the rules of your favorite one(s) to a social situation?

5. In 1908, E. M. Forster wrote the novel *A Room with a View*. Are you familiar with it? If so, do you notice any parallels between Forster's novel and *A Summer in Europe*?

6. The author has created a musical soundtrack for this novel by mentioning several songs throughout and focusing largely on stage musicals, particularly those of Andrew Lloyd Webber. Are you a fan of musical theater? Are you familiar with the songs referenced in the story?

7. In *A Room with a View*, E. M. Forster wrote, "The kingdom of music is not the kingdom of this world; it will accept those whom breeding and intellect and culture have alike rejected." What does this quote mean to you?

8. Have you traveled to countries other than the one you grew up in? What have your experiences been? Have you visited any of the sites and cities mentioned in the novel? If so, what were your impressions of them?

9. Are you familiar with Albert Einstein's attempts at finding a "theory of everything" or the physics doctrines mentioned in the book, like string theory or Heisenberg's uncertainty principle?

10. What is the relationship like between the Edwards brothers, Emerson and Thoreau? How has their mother's behavior influenced them? Do your family dynamics ever resemble that of a soap-opera clan?

11. What did Gwen need to learn about herself in order to understand the people on the tour better—particularly Cynthia, Louisa, Hans-Josef, the Edwards brothers and Aunt Bea? Her personal reawakening begins in Florence, the birthplace of the Renaissance. Coincidental or not? Discuss.

12. What are your thoughts about the love triangle at play between Gwen, Richard and Emerson? Is there a love triangle (from the literary, music or film world) that calls to you? Have you ever been a part of a romantic love triangle? If so, who did you choose?

13. Zenia asks Gwen and then Gwen, in turn, asks Richard, "What is your art?" As an individual, how would you answer this question?

Please turn the page
for an extra feature
from author Marilyn Brant. . . .

Learning to Play Mah-jongg at the Steak-n-Shake

Author Marilyn Brant and friends get their first lesson in the game.

A couple of years back, I got this idea for a story that had a Su-doku and Mah-jongg Club in it. But, while I had a working knowl-edge of the former game—and several half-completed workbooks at home—I didn't know the first thing about the latter. So, I did what most writers do when they're stumped: I turned on my com-puter and started surfing.

I found pictures of the mah-jongg tiles online (so pretty!) and hoped I'd soon come to understand how they were used. But, no matter how many websites I looked at, I seemed to come across only convoluted explanations of the rules, which had me squinting at the screen, perplexed. And I couldn't determine the correct usage for the odd accessory items necessary for the game (annual cards?), which looked a whole lot like objects I'd find in an ad-vanced calculus class—interesting but incomprehensible.

I spent the majority of a workday puzzling over this and, honestly, I hadn't been so confused by a set of instructions since the one time I tried to write an undercover spy novel with a drug-dealing antago-nist. I spent several days attempting to make sense of the step-by-step directions on "expert joint rolling" and "growing weed in the basement" (seriously, the Internet has *everything*), but I found the pages so unintelligible that I just gave up working on the project. I wasn't about to give up working on this new book, though.

So, I did the next thing writers do when they're stumped: I whined to my friends via e-mail.

"Do any of you have ANY idea how to play mah-jongg?" I typed. "I don't get it *at all*."

My good friend Simone Elkeles, a *New York Times* bestselling author of young adult fiction, called with an immediate reply to my plea. "Don't worry, Marilyn," she said in a deceptively calm tone, which was why I believed her. "I was in a mah-jongg league for years. I'll show you how it works."

And that was how it came to pass that, after one of our Chicago-North RWA meetings in 2010, Simone and I were sitting around a table at the local Steak-n-Shake, at 10:30 p.m., setting up the game with our fellow writing friends Karen Dale Harris, Erika Danou and Pamala Knight.

The waitress looked at us suspiciously. "Um, do you ladies want anything to eat?"

"We're learning to play mah-jongg tonight," I piped up enthusiastically.

The waitress gave me a tight-lipped smile and crossed her arms.

"And, uh, yeah . . ." I scanned the menu. "I'll have a burger. With cheese fries."

Karen opted for a patty melt. Erika and Pamala went the burger route. Simone, who'd been fighting a bad cold and found out later she was also running a fever, wanted only something cool to drink. "And napkins," she added, sniffling. "I'm out of Kleenex."

Simone asked me if I'd learned anything more about the game in the week since we'd spoken on the phone.

"Just the stuff my husband told me," I said. "But, you know, he's a world history teacher, so his focus is kind of different. . . ."

I didn't need to explain to a table full of writers how this might be a problem. While my husband's fondness for Asian art and Chinese history was apparent by his eager responses to my questions, his resulting lecture on the pieces and the background of mah-jongg wasn't the particular angle I was looking to find. I needed to learn how to play mah-jongg *as an author*. I didn't need to be an expert. (And I suspected from the beginning it would be futile for me to attempt it, anyway.) I didn't have to be able to recite anything about the history of the game or even know the rules beyond the most rudimentary. No. But I was in desperate search of something very particular: metaphors.

"Basically, what I need most is to know what things mean in the universe of the game," I told my friends, "and how they can be applied to the wider world. So I can connect mah-jongg to life."

"No problem," Simone assured me. "It's easy to play."

Well, after two hours at the Steak-n-Shake, with 144 tiles, mah-jongg cards with tiny print and these little colored disks (for betting?) that I didn't even know existed beforehand, I'm here to tell you it is *not* easy.

Simone passed out a rack to each of us first. In her boxed set, they were long, plastic thingies that reminded me of the ones used in Scrabble to hold those tiles. The sheer familiarity of them lulled me into a false feeling of recognition. So far, so good, I thought.

But then she started pulling out the tiles themselves. And she began grouping them. And naming them. And did I mention there were 144 of them? Yeah. That's right. A lot. There were winds, bams and cracks. There were dots, flowers, jokers, cardinal directions . . . and dragons.

"Are there lions, tigers and bears, too?" I murmured, my head swimming with names I was trying to assimilate.

Simone ignored my remark.

Karen and I exchanged baffled glances, and I ate a few cheese fries in hopes that this would help my memory. It didn't.

"Maybe it's kind of like dominoes," Pamala suggested hopefully.

I liked that idea, but, with the little I'd gleaned about the game online, I didn't think it was remotely that straightforward.

"Okay," Simone told us, after running through the names of the various suits again. "Now that you know what all the tiles are, I'm going to test you."

"Test us?" Erika said, appearing inexplicably delighted. "Oh, good."

Oh, *good?*

I stared at her as Pamala and Karen laughed.

"It's okay, Marilyn," Pamala whispered. "We can work on it to-gether."

I nodded, grateful, but shot a panicked look around the table when Simone got up for a moment to throw away some crumpled napkins. "Do you guys remember any of these?" I hissed, pointing to the tiles.

Erika smiled modestly. I wanted to fling a cheese fry at her.

Pamala looked pensive—less certain than Erika, perhaps, but far more confident than me.

Karen shrugged. "Not all of them," she admitted. "But I think once we see them in action, they'll be easier to remember." I had my fingers crossed that she was right.

"I hope you've been paying attention," Simone said upon her return, "because we're going to play a game. First thing we need to do is to smoosh the tiles."

"Do you mean smush?" I asked.

"No. *Smoosh*," Simone said.

This step was surprisingly easy and just involved flipping over the tiles so we could no longer see any of the suits, and then mix-ing them all up with big, swirly motions in the middle of our table. This made a lot of noise, however, and earned us a rather alarmed look from our waitress.

"Next, we each need to build a wall," Simone instructed us, walking us through the stacking of the now-shuffled tiles into a big square, each of us responsible for building one side of it. With our open racks facing us, we placed the tiles behind them and into two rows of eighteen—one row of tiles atop the other—for a total of thirty-six tiles per player.

With all the tiles now gone from the middle of the table and stacked nicely into four distinct walls, everything looked so orga-nized, well-structured, tidy. I felt a twinge of confidence. That wasn't so hard. We did well. Yay, us!

"So, what do we do now?" Erika asked eagerly.

"The next step is the rouching," Simone said. "It's the trading of the tiles."

"*Rouching?*" I asked. "I've never heard that word. How do you spell it?"

Simone shrugged. "No idea. I don't know if everyone who plays calls it that, but I always have."

"Might be able to find it with an online dictionary," Erika said, reaching for her smart phone.

"Who taught you?" Karen asked Simone, an edge of suspicion in her voice. "Are those the *real* rules?"

"Hey, do you guys want to learn this game or not?" Simone said, exasperated. "My grandmother taught my mother to play, my mother taught me and I taught my daughter, who's a lot younger than all of you and *she* can handle it. These are the rules my family plays by, so just stop worrying about all the words and pay attention."

I didn't actually stop worrying about all the unusual vocabulary, but I did stop *asking* about it. Unfortunately, a spelling lesson wouldn't have helped with the next step anyway.

"So, the next thing we do is exchange the tiles, but it's done in a very systematic way," Simone said. "Everyone gives three tiles to the player on her right, and gets three tiles from the player on her left. Then you trade three tiles with the player across from you. Then you give three tiles to the left and get three from the right. Then you repeat that last step, because you're reversing directions, so you give to the left and get from the right again. And then you go back to exchanging with the player across from you and, finally, you go back to the right. But there's also one last chance to trade with whoever is across from you—as a 'courtesy'—if you both want to. It has to be a mutual decision, but you can exchange either one, two or three tiles then." Simone smiled at us and nodded. "Okay?"

All four of us stared at her in stunned silence.

"What, um, are we supposed to do again?" Erika managed to ask.

"Maybe one more time with that," Pamala suggested.

The waitress suddenly appeared. "Anything else I can get you, ladies?"

I rubbed my forehead. "Do you serve margaritas at the Steak-n-Shake? Jumbo strawberry margaritas, maybe?"

The waitress narrowed her eyes at me.

"I think that's a no, Marilyn," Karen murmured.

I nodded. Then, to the waitress, I said, "Nothing for me, then. Thanks."

No one else seemed to need anything else either, save for a step-by-step handbook for completing the *rouching* . . . or, you know, whatever it was called.

Simone sighed and started taking us through it, and, somehow, we managed to muddle through the trading of the tiles. Pamala and I worked together, but even so, I was incredibly confused. If there was a pattern for doing it, I couldn't catch it, so I amused myself during this latest stage of the setup—we hadn't even begun *playing* yet!—by coming up with synonyms for how I felt: befuddled, perplexed, confounded, puzzled, mystified, bewildered.

Then, finally, the actual game began. The object, it turned out, was to take turns trading more tiles and attempt to make one of the hands listed on the mah-jongg cards she'd passed out to us, which Simone told us were new every year.

There were a million possible combinations on the cards. I squinted at them. One of the winning hands listed in the "Winds-Dragons" category was N EE WNW SSSS DDDD (all in black ink) and another winner, in some other category, was listed as 111 (in red ink) 555 (in green) 999 (in blue) NNN DD (in black).

"So, you're saying any one of these hands will win the game?" Karen asked, pointing to a particularly tricky, multicolored combination.

"Yes," Simone answered, looking triumphant, as if she were actually convinced that we understood now.

"Still think this is like dominoes?" I whispered to Pamala.

She shook her head. "More like really complicated math."

Erika was getting into it, though. "This seems sort of like something I've played before."

Karen, too, was reminded of old card games. It seemed to have struck some kind of poker nerve for her. "The winning hands have ranks, and there are different ways you can win."

Since I didn't play any card games besides "Go Fish," this comparison was lost on me.

"You know," Pamala said, "when we had our chapter's writing conference in the spring, I saw a group of women playing this at the hotel. I didn't know what it was at first, not until I asked one of the hotel people. I just kept hearing this really fast clicking sound. Like stiletto heels on a tile floor. They were picking up and discarding the tiles *that* quickly. It was like combat mah-jongg."

I tried to imagine that. "They must have really known what they were doing."

"Maybe if you grow up with it as a child and have had the exposure to it really early, the randomness and complication of it would seem logical and reasonable," Pamala said.

I stared at the row of tiles we had on our rack and, alternately, the little card filled with possible winning-hand combinations. "Hmm. Maybe."

"I think I'm understanding it. Sort of," Erika said. "But I'm not sure I'll remember any of it later."

"Like a one-night stand," Karen said. "Seems to makes sense while it's happening, but the next morning . . ."

We all laughed.

It was clear to me that Pamala and Erika were getting it, and Karen was quickly catching on, too. I was impressed with all three of them. I could see the lightning of illumination—like the flash of a comet across the night sky—in Karen's expression as she put the pieces together. She said that she thought if she played for long enough that evening, it would probably stick.

For me, however, it would not stick.

Exasperated, I finally turned to Simone and said, "On what planet is this game EASY?" I waved the mah-jongg card at her. "I *like* math. I play sudoku. I regularly use algebra in my daily life, and I solve lots of kinds of puzzles. You know those logic problems where there are seven people who live in seven houses with seven different kinds of cars and a bunch of other variable things, and you're given only a handful of clues to match the right ones up?"

Simone nodded slowly. She looked a bit feverish.

"I *love* those!" I insisted. "I do those for *fun*. But I do NOT get this game. . . ."

My friend blew her nose and calmly told me to chill out and just keep playing.

With the help of Karen, Erika and Pamala, I continued slogging along, understanding intellectually that there was both a reason and a rhythm to the game, even if I couldn't quite catch onto either of them myself. At one point, though, I reached over to grab a tile, and Simone—watching our play with hawk eyes—stopped me.

"You can't do that," she informed me. "You've chosen a tile too soon. You're picking your future."

Of course I was annoyed. Here was yet another example of the complicated and seemingly endless rules of this game. But then it hit me. What she'd just said was such a fascinating phrase. *Picking your future?* What did that mean?

I asked Simone to explain, and she said, "Picking your future tile early means you've called a tile in advance of your turn. You're skipping ahead and laying claim to something you may have to give to somebody else in trade. Since there's a lot of exchanging of tiles in the game, if you have to adjust the hand you're playing, you may have to give away what you thought your future tile would be. This can make players really dissatisfied. So, everyone should just take their turn and have their future revealed to them at the right time. Don't try to jump ahead, because things change and the best future for you might be different from what you thought."

Bingo!

Whether or not I could play mah-jongg with any skill whatsoever was irrelevant. I'd finally found one of the metaphors I'd been searching for all evening. "Please, tell me more," I urged her, having learned at last to ask the right questions about the game. "This is *really* cool."

So she told me a little more and explained how, if a group of players was going to allow picking futures, they'd have to make that decision at the start of play. Many people wouldn't agree to it because they considered it a form of cheating.

Interesting, I thought.

"And what is it with these annual cards?" I asked. "Why are there so many winning hands? Why do you have to get new cards every year?"

"It's all because players need to learn to be flexible," Simone said reasonably. "And not get attached to any one way of winning. If someone else has the tile you need to complete the winning hand you've been trying to get or, worse, if they've already discarded an important tile so it's dead and can no longer be played, you need to choose a different possible winning combination. It's like in traffic, when there's a roadblock on the street you're driving on, you have to change directions. Find a different route to take. You don't know what lies ahead, so you have to be flexible enough to explore multiple options. It makes the journey more interesting."

"Yes . . . yes, it does!" I cried in an authorial moment, akin to finally seeing the promised comet streaking across the night sky. That big connection was there after all! I could *do* something with these intriguing concepts and knew, at last, how I might be able to use them alongside some of the themes in the book. I grasped the annual card and brought it tight against my chest, hugging it. I *loved* mah-jongg!

Simone looked relieved. "Did that help, Marilyn?"

"Oh, a lot," I told her. "I think I can get the game to make sense in the story now."

"Good," Simone said. "That's what friends are for."

"Aw, thank you." I grinned at her, finally giving her back the annual card I'd been clinging to with both hands. "Thanks so much for teaching us."

"This was really fun," Erika added.

Pamala nodded. "Yeah, I liked it."

"And I hope you feel better soon," I told Simone as we helped her pack up the game. "Maybe we can play again when you're recovered and well rested."

Pamala, Karen and Erika all agreed.

"We should!" Simone said with enthusiasm, and we clinked our water glasses and made plans to meet sometime soon for Mahjongg, Round Two.

As we left Steak-n-Shake for the evening, waving good-bye to our waitress and the staff, Karen shot me a sideways glance. "Why do you look so worried?" she asked. "I thought you got all the info you needed."

"Oh, I did," I said. "This was *great,* and I feel I've finally made my peace with mah-jongg. But"—I exhaled—"there's also this sciency thing that's kind of a big part of the story. . . ."

Karen nodded. "Somebody can probably help you figure it out. How sciency is it?"

"Hmm, very." I laughed. "Know any theoretical physicists?"